PENGUIN CLASSICS 🐧 DELUXE EDITION

ROSTAM

ABOLQASEM FERDOWSI was born in Khorasan in a village near Tus, in 940 CE. His great epic the *Shahnameh*, to which he devoted most of his adult life, was originally composed for the Samanid princes of Khorasan, who were the chief instigators of the revival of Persian cultural traditions after the Arab conquest. During Ferdowsi's lifetime, the Samanid dynasty was conquered by the Ghaznavid Turks. Various stories in medieval texts describe the lack of interest shown by the new ruler of Khorasan, Mahmud of Ghazni, in Ferdowsi and his lifework. Ferdowsi is said to have died around 1020 in poverty and embittered by royal neglect, though confident of his and his poem's ultimate fame.

A fellow of the Royal Society of Literature, DICK DAVIS is currently professor of Persian at Ohio State University. His other translations from Persian include *Shahnameh: The Persian Book of Kings*; *Vis and Ramin*; *Borrowed Ware: Medieval Persian Epigrams*; *My Uncle Napoleon*; *The Legend of Seyavash*; and, with Afkham Darbandi, *The Conference of the Birds*.

ABOLQASEM
FERDOWSI

ROSTAM
Tales of Love & War
from the Shahnameh

Translated and Introduced by
DICK DAVIS

PENGUIN BOOKS

PENGUIN BOOKS

Published by the Penguin Group
Penguin Group (USA) Inc., 375 Hudson Street, New York, New York 10014, U.S.A.
Penguin Group (Canada), 90 Eglinton Avenue East, Suite 700,
Toronto, Ontario, Canada M4P 2Y3 (a division of Pearson Penguin Canada Inc.)
Penguin Books Ltd, 80 Strand, London WC2R 0RL, England
Penguin Ireland, 25 St Stephen's Green, Dublin 2, Ireland (a division of Penguin Books Ltd)
Penguin Group (Australia), 250 Camberwell Road, Camberwell,
Victoria 3124, Australia (a division of Pearson Australia Group Pty Ltd)
Penguin Books India Pvt Ltd, 11 Community Centre,
Panchsheel Park, New Delhi – 110 017, India
Penguin Group (NZ), 67 Apollo Drive, Rosedale, North Shore 0632,
New Zealand (a division of Pearson New Zealand Ltd)
Penguin Books (South Africa) (Pty) Ltd, 24 Sturdee Avenue,
Rosebank, Johannesburg 2196, South Africa

Penguin Books Ltd, Registered Offices:
80 Strand, London WC2R 0RL, England

First published in the United States of America by Mage Publishers 2007
Published in Penguin Books 2009

Illustration credits on page 292

THE LIBRARY OF CONGRESS HAS CATALOGED THE HARDCOVER EDITION AS FOLLOWS:
Firdawsi.
[Shahnamah. English Selections.]
Rostam : Tales of Love and War from Persia's Book of Kings / by Abolqasem
Ferdowsi ; translated and introduced by Dick Davis.—1st hardcover ed.
p.   cm.
Translated from Persian.
ISBN 1-933823-11-9 (hc.)
ISBN 978-0-14-310589-3 (pbk.)
I. Davis, Dick, 1945–   II. Title.
PK6456.A12R82 2007
891'.5511—dc22   2006025566

CONTENTS

INTRODUCTION

Rostam is the greatest hero of pre-Islamic Persian legend, and he and his exploits dominate the first half of our principal source for such material, the *Shahnameh*, the magnificent compendium of verse narratives concerned with pre-Islamic Iran that was written down by the poet Ferdowsi at the end of the tenth and the beginning of the eleventh centuries C.E.

As befits an ancient hero he is a larger-than-life figure: he lives for over five hundred years, he undergoes seven trials of strength, cunning, and endurance that put him in the same company as Hercules and his labors, he defeats and kills not only innumerable human enemies but also dragons and demons, he serves as the pre-eminent champion of no less than five Persian monarchs and lives through much of the reigns of two more. After his death, he is constantly evoked by those who come after him as the epitome of magnanimity, manliness, heroism, and loyalty to

the Persian throne. The stories in which he figures are the best-known and most loved narratives of the *Shahnameh*, and are among the most famous in Persian culture.

But Rostam is not simply a paragon of heroic loyalty to the Persian throne mythologized and writ large. Something that runs throughout all the narratives in which he is involved is his insistence that he is his own man, that his service is given voluntarily and cannot be constrained, and that he is at no one's beck and call, not even his king's. If he is loyal it is because he chooses to be, and sometimes he chooses not to be. There is something anarchic about him, a contempt for boundaries and borders (both literal and metaphorical ones), a stubbornness and eagerness to excel, which can remind a Western reader of Shakespearian heroes like Coriolanus or Warwick (called, as Rostam is too, "the kingmaker"), an overreaching that like theirs can lead directly to tragedy. Much of the glamour of Rostam's legend lies in the tension between this fierce independence, which places him outside of authority, and his seemingly inexhaustible (until it is in fact exhausted) service to the Persian monarchy and the country it controls. If the *Shahnameh* is primarily, as its name (the "book of kings") implies, about monarchy, and so about a center of absolute or would-be absolute power, Rostam is a figure from outside of that center of power; he is one who lives, in all senses, at the edge.

We can see this "at the edge" quality clearly in his origins, which indicate his tangential relationship both to the land of Iran and to humanity in general. His parents are the Persian hero Zal and the Kaboli princess Rudabeh. When Zal is born, his father exposes him on a mountainside to die because of his white hair and mottled skin, and he is brought up by a fabulous magical bird, the Simorgh. The implication is that there is something demonic about Zal's appearance, and

indeed there is only one other figure in the *Shahnameh* who is described as having white hair and a mottled skin, the White Demon of Mazanderan, whom Rostam kills in single combat, and who almost kills him. Once one has registered the similarity in the descriptions of the demon's appearance and that of Rostam's father, it is hard not to see this struggle as an Oedipal reversal of a common motif in the *Shahnameh*, the death of sons through the actions of their fathers.

When Zal has returned to the human world the Simorgh remains his protector, and she is later on (through Zal as an intermediary) the protector of his son Rostam; in their ability to call on her magical aid in moments of extreme peril they are given access to magical powers. The supernatural as part of Rostam's inheritance, again in somewhat demonic guise, is even more evident on his mother's side: Rudabeh's father is Mehrab, the king of Kabol, who is descended from the demon king Zahhak, from whose clutches Iran was freed by the noble king Feraydun. Zal's king, Manuchehr, at first opposes Zal's marriage to Rudabeh because this will mingle the demonic bloodline of Zahhak with that of the Persian heroes (and Rostam is the result of just such a mingling). In human terms then, Rostam is certainly "at the edge": he can call on magic, he is descended from a demon on his mother's side, and his father's strange upbringing and appearance also bring with them an aura of the supernatural and perhaps the demonic. Rostam is a great subduer of demons, but as with another Persian hero (and king this time) Jamshid, whose authority over demons seems at times to come as much from his participation in their world as his defeat of it, there is a suggestion of "set a thief to catch a thief" about his prowess.

Geographically Rostam belongs in Sistan, his family's appanage, granted in perpetuity by the Persian kings for their

loyalty to the throne. The area may have been granted by the kings, but when Rostam is uneasy with the political goings-on at the Persian court, it is to this area that he retreats, where he is beyond the reach of the king unless he wishes to present himself of his own free will. Like Achilles, Rostam is often contumacious and moody, and Sistan is his equivalent of Achilles's tent: it's the place he goes to sulk, to indicate that he has washed his hands of his people's problems.

The modern Sistan, the southeastern province of Iran, does not correspond with Zal's and Rostam's kingdom, which lies largely to the east of this area, in what is now the province of Helmand in Afghanistan. The river Helmand (called, in Ferdowsi's time, the Hirmand) marks the northern border of their territory. Rostam's land is therefore on the eastern edge of the Iranian world. His mother is from Kabol, and Rostam dies in Kabol, placing his origin and death even further to the east; indeed, in the terms of the *Shahnameh* placing them in India, as Kabol is seen as a part of India throughout the *Shahnameh*. There are other indications of a strong Indian presence in Rostam's identity: the talismanic tiger skin he wears instead of armor, the *babr-e bayan* as it is called in Persian, has been traced to an Indian origin by the scholar Djalal Khaleghi-Motlagh, and another eminent scholar of the *Shahnameh*, Mehrdad Bahar, has pointed out that some aspects of Rostam's legend parallel and may derive from those of the Hindu god Krishna. Sistan, Kabol, India—certainly, if we take Iran as the center, Rostam hails geographically from the edge, and, significantly enough, from the eastern edge. Significantly because the lands immediately to the east of Iran are seen as the origin of magic in the *Shahnameh*, and this eastern aspect of his identity further ties Rostam to that supernatural and chthonic world his parentage implies.

Often Rostam's heroism too has an "edgy," unstraight-forward quality to it. The supernatural Simorgh, on whose help he can rely, as well as the tiger skin he wears both suggest characteristics of the Trickster Hero, as he is found in many cultures. Tricksters are often associated with magic, and they have something of the shaman about them, one who is in touch with other worlds, often through an animal intermediary, and is able to call the denizens of these worlds to his and his people's aid. Many tricksters are associated with specific animals whose skins or feathers they wear in order to draw on the animal's characteristics for their own purposes. The animals so used are usually known for their slyness, or they are birds. Rostam is protected by the feathers of a fabulous bird, and he wears a tiger skin, and slyness is exactly the quality associated with tigers in Indian lore (e.g., in Buddhist Jataka tales: there is a distant echo of this in Kipling's Shere Khan in *The Jungle Book*).

But of course the pre-eminent characteristic of the Trickster Hero is that he plays tricks in order to win his victories. Rostam wins many of his victories by simple der-ring-do, by his martial valor and manly strength alone; but in a number of his encounters with enemies, and almost always when he is in real danger, he resorts to trickery. In his encounter with a monstrous demon, the Akvan Div, "Rostam realized...that it would be cunning he would have to call on, not strength"; when he enters enemy territory to rescue the imprisoned hero Bizhan he says, "the key to these chains is deceit," and he proceeds by subterfuge; in his most famous combat of all, that with his son Sohrab, he tricks the young man into letting him go when he is at his mercy. He wins his last victory, against Esfandyar, by the ultimate trickery of utilizing supernatural forces against his enemy. He is most deeply identified with the role of

trickster at his death. Tricksters attract tricks as well as per-
petrating them, and Rostam is killed by two related tricks:
he is lured under false pretences to Kabol, and he falls into
a disguised pit where he and his horse, Rakhsh, are pierced
by the stakes that await them. And Rostam then tricks the
man who has betrayed him in such a way that as he dies,
so too does his betrayer. Rostam dies enmeshed in trickery, both tricked and in the act of tricking the man whose
dupe he has become. There is also the curious nature of his
name to be taken into account. He is often referred to as
"Rostam-e Dastan," which can have two different mean-
ings. One, "Rostam the son of Dastan," is the meaning the
poem foregrounds, and his father, Zal, is seen as having
somewhere along the line acquired a second name, Dastan.
But the phrase can also mean "Rostam who possesses the
quality of dastan", and the word "dastan" means "trickery." This, I believe, was the original meaning of the phrase
"Rostam-e Dastan" (probably long before the *Shahnameh*
was written, while the stories of Rostam still had a solely
oral existence), i.e. "Rostam the trickster", the equivalent
of Homer's "Odysseus of many wiles", and only later did
the word dastan come to be identified as the name of his
father (after all, his father already had a name, Zal).

But Rostam's trickery is only intermittently before our
eyes (usually at moments of crisis); when his contempo-
raries speak of him in the poem it is his martial prowess,
loyalty, and chivalry that are emphasized, and this is how his
legend is usually invoked later in the poem, after his death.
If Rostam is in some sense a Trickster Hero, why is it that
we lose sight of this fact for long stretches of the poem?

Karl Kerenyi remarks of the trickster that as he moves from
the world of oral folklore to that of literary culture his image
is sanitized somewhat. In oral culture the trickster embodies,

"the spirit of disorder, he is the enemy of boundaries…[he] operates outside the fixed bounds of custom and law…[his] field of operations is no-man's land." However, as he enters the serious world of literary epic the trickster's rough edges are smoothed away; as Kerenyi puts it, "There were several ways of disposing of him, the first was to reduce his original function to harmless entertainment by stressing his ridiculous traits. A second was to assimilate him to culture heroes…The third was his transformation into a devil." The *Shahnameh* largely ignores the first option, but the other two transformations are apparent in the treatment of Rostam; he becomes a great culture hero, and one whose genealogy is shadowed by the demonic. Despite this transformation, Rostam's ethic is often at odds with that of the court he serves; that is, we can still glimpse the anarchic trickster beneath his assimilation to the values of the stabilizing center. He remains an altogether more volatile, larger-than-life figure than the other courtiers around him; he is a great trencherman, he swills prodigious quantities of wine, he is impatient of control or authority, he ignores borders when it suits him to do so, he very often acts alone (this is true of almost none of the other legendary heroes in the *Shahnameh*), he wins crucial encounters by subterfuge rather than valor.

It's clear that Rostam's legend is not a simple one, and it is almost certainly a composite drawing on a number of sources. We have already noted that part of his legend has strong Indian connections, the surprisingly few pre-Islamic texts that mention him seem to indicate that much of his legend relates to a Parthian hero (early Islamic texts also identify him as Parthian), the demonic aspects of his background may even indicate an indigenous origin for some of the narratives associated with his name. Zabiholla Safa has plausibly suggested that the demonic enemies in

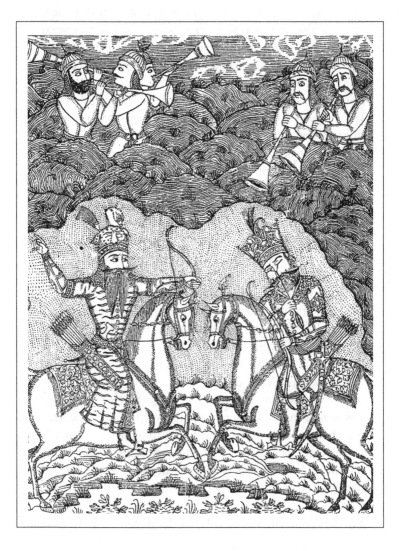

the *Shahnameh* represent the indigenous peoples whom the Iranians conquered when they entered the Iranian plateau. These demonic creatures are presented as uncivilized, given to practicing magic, and dressed in animal skins. Both these last points are of interest when we consider Rostam. Once we move beyond the first two or three generations described in the poem, there is only one "Iranian" in the whole *Shahnameh* who is habitually described as dressed in an animal skin: Rostam. And as we have seen Rostam and his family are associated with magic. Concerning magic and its practitioners, Safa goes on to say, "The Iranian religion was opposed to magic, and for this reason we see that in the Iranian national epic magic and the black arts are rarely ascribed to Iranians, whereas we everywhere see non-Iranian peoples, and those who did not believe in the Mazdean faith, described as practicing magic."[1] This is the case in the early stories of the *Shahnameh*, which in general ascribe magic to those fighting against the Iranians, with the exception of Rostam who, through his father Zal's ties to the Simorgh, has access to magical powers. Indigenous heroes are sometimes refashioned as heroes of a conquering culture, and it may be that parts of Rostam's legend predate the coming of the Iranians to the Iranian plateau, at some time during the second millennium B.C.E. There is the curious fact that Rostam's climactic battle is against an Iranian crown prince and that both his sons (Sohrab and

---

1. There is real irony in the fact that in the West, throughout the Classical period, Iran was seen as the home of magic, despite the Zoroastrian condemnation of it, and the very word "magic" comes from a word for a Zoroastrian priest. As with the ability to predict the future (fortune tellers are nearly always "foreigners" within the culture in which they operate) magic seems to have been something whose origins and expertise are always placed elsewhere. As the Greeks and Romans looked to Persia for its origins, so the Persians looked to India.

Faramarz) are to be found fighting against, rather than for, an Iranian monarch; this does suggest that at least part of Rostam's legend incorporates elements from stories associated with someone who fought against, rather than on behalf of, the Iranian polity.

Further evidence of Rostam's at best oblique relationship with the values of the Persian court would also seem to come from his ambiguous relationship with Zoroastrianism. Although Ferdowsi in his *Shahnameh* plays down any such suggestions, a number of other texts that preceded the *Shahnameh* or are contemporary with it state that Rostam emphatically rejected the "new" religion of Zoroastrianism, and this was the reason for his break with Goshtasp's court. This would seem to be borne out by the fact that Rostam's last great battle is with Esfandyar, the proselytizer for Zoroastrianism *par excellence*, and that previous to their combat Esfandyar emphasizes his own religious credentials while insulting Rostam for his demonic lineage. Further, Esfandyar has killed a Simorgh, who is the supernatural being to whom Rostam turns when most in need, and Rostam calls on his own Simorgh's aid to defeat Esfandyar. Beneath the bluster of Esfandyar's father, Goshtasp, and beneath the rhetoric about honor and loyalty, the heroes' clash seems to be as much one of world views and religious values as it is a political or personal confrontation, and though it ends in the death of a representative of the new order, the consequences of that death involve the destruction of Rostam's family, and of the cultural world they inhabited. In the deepest layers of the Rostam legend, as it appears in the *Shahnameh*, we glimpse a last shadowy representative of a magical and animist pre-Zoroastrian world, one which disappears forever with this great hero's death.

THE TALE OF SAM AND THE SIMORGH

Now I shall tell an astonishing tale, taken from the stories our ancestors told. See what strange events Fate unfolded for Sam: listen well, my son.

Sam had no child, and his heart grieved at this. There was a beautiful woman living in his private quarters; her cheeks were like rose petals, her hair like musk. Her face was as splendid as the sun, and Sam had hopes that she would bear him a child. And this happened; after some time she gave birth to a beautiful boy, whose radiance lit the world, but although his face was as bright as the sun, his hair was completely white. Given how the child looked, Sam was not told of his birth for a week; all the women of his household wept over the boy, and no one dared tell Sam that this beautiful woman had given birth to a son who was an old man. Then a courageous wet nurse, who had a lion's spirit, came bravely before Sam and said, "May Sam's days be prosperous, and the hearts of those who wish him ill be torn out. In your women's quarters, a fine boy has been born from your beloved. His body is like pure silver, his face like paradise, and you will find no ugly spot on him. His one fault is that his hair is white; such is your fate, my lord."

Sam descended from his throne and went into the women's quarters. When he saw his son's white hair he despaired of the world, and lifting his face to the heavens, he complained bitterly. "O God, who is above all failings and faults, whatever you command is good. If I have committed a grave sin, if I have followed the ways of Ahriman, I repent and pray that God will grant me forgiveness. My grieving soul writhes with shame, and the hot blood boils in my heart. What shall I say about this ill-omened child when men ask about his black body, and his hair as white as jasmine? Shall I say he is a demon's child? He is like a leopard, whose skin is of two colors. No longer shall I call down blessings on Persia; I shall quit this land for shame."

He gave orders that the child be taken far away, to the place where the Simorgh has her home. They took the boy and laid him down in the mountains, then returned to the court. The day ended, and the champion's innocent son had no knowledge of white or black; his father had cast all kindness from his heart and acted evilly toward his unweaned child.

When the Simorgh's chicks grew hungry, she flew up from her nest; she saw an unweaned, crying baby lying on the ground; his cradle was of thorns, his wet nurse was the earth, he was naked, and no milk touched his lips. The black earth surrounded him, and above his head the sun shone in the summit of the heavens. Would that his mother and father had been leopards; they at least would have shaded him from the sun. The Simorgh flew down from the clouds, stretched out her claws and clutched him, lifting him up from the hot stones on which he lay. She flew with him back to her nest in the Alborz mountains, where she intended to take him to her chicks; thinking they could feed off him and pay no attention to his cries. But God had other plans, so that when the Simorgh and her chicks looked at the little child weeping bitter tears, something wonderful to relate happened: they took pity on him, staring in astonishment at his lovely face. She sought out the most delicate morsels of the chase for the boy, touching them to his lips, and in this way many days passed and the child grew into a fine young man. Men with caravans passing through the mountains would catch sight of this noble youth, whose body was like a cypress tree, whose chest was like a mountain of silver, and whose waist was as slim as a reed. Rumors of him spread through the world, since neither good nor evil ever remain hidden, and news of this glorious youth reached Sam, the son of Nariman.

The Dream of Sam, the Son of Nariman

One night Sam was asleep, his heart wearied with the cares of the world. He dreamed of a man from India, galloping toward him on an Arab horse, who brought him good news of that noble sapling his son. When he woke he summoned his priests and told them of the dream and of the rumors he had heard. "What do you say to this?" he asked. "What does your wisdom make of it?"

Young and old, all those present, said to Sam, "Lions and leopards in their stony lairs, the fish and the monsters of the sea, all love and nourish their children and give thanks to God for them; you have broken this bond of benevolence in casting out your innocent child. Turn to God and repent, since he is the guide to good and evil."

When dark night came and Sam slept again, his heart was filled with turmoil. In his dream he saw a banner fluttering on a mountain in India. Then a beautiful slave appeared, leading a mighty army; a priest was on his left, and a wise sage on his right. One of these two came forward and said coldly to Sam, "Presumptuous and immoral man, you have washed shame before God from your heart and eyes; what kind of a hero are you, if a bird has nourished your son? If it is a fault to have white hair, look at yourself, whose beard is white and whose hair is like the leaves of the willow. You despised your son, but God has been his protector, loving him more than a wet nurse would, while you were devoid of affection for him." Sam cried out in his sleep, like a lion caught in a trap.

When he woke, Sam called his counselors and the leaders of his army and set off for the mountains to reclaim what he had rejected. He saw a mountain whose peak reached the Pleiades, and on it a great nest woven from ebony and sandalwood. Sam stared at the granite slopes, at the terrifying Simorgh, and at its fearsome nest, which was like a palace towering in the clouds, but one not built by men's hands or from clay and water. He bowed his face down to the dirt, praising God who had created this bird, and this mountain whose slopes reached to the stars, acknowledging him as just and all powerful. He looked for a way to climb the mountain, seeking out wild animals' tracks, and said, "O you who are higher than all high places, than thought itself and the sun and moon, if this youth is indeed from my loins, and not the seed of some evil demon, help me to climb this mountain."

The Simorgh said to Sam's son, "You have endured the hardship of growing up in this nest, and now your father, great Sam, who is a champion among heroes, has come to this mountain searching for his son; he honors and values you now. I must give you back, and return you to him safe and sound." Listen to the youth's answer: "You have tired of my friendship, then? Your nest has been a noble home for me, and two of your feathers have been a glorious crown for me." The Simorgh replied, "When you see the throne and crown and the ceremonial of the Kayanid court, this nest will mean nothing to you. Go, see what fate has in store for you. Take these feathers of mine with you, so that you will always live under my protection, since I brought you up beneath my wings with my own children. If any trouble comes to you, if there is talk of good and ill, throw one of my feathers into the fire, and my glory will at once appear to you. I shall come to you in the guise of a black cloud and bring you safely back here."

Then she hardened her heart for their parting and lifted him up, soaring into the clouds, and set him down before his father. The youth's hair reached below his chest, his body was like a mammoth's, and his cheeks were as fresh as the spring. When his father saw him he wept, bowing his head before the Simorgh and paying homage to her. He stared at the youth, from head to foot, and saw that he was worthy of the Kayanid crown and throne. His chest and arms were like a lion's, his face like the sun, his heart was a champion's, and his arm was that of a swordsman. His eyebrows were pitch black, his lips like coral, and his cheeks the color of blood. Sam's heart felt the happiness of paradise, and he called down blessings on his son. He draped the boy's body in a champion's cloak, and they set off down the mountain. When they reached its base, Sam had a horse and royal clothes brought for his son; the army ranged itself before Sam, their hearts filled with happiness, they set off on the return journey, preceded by elephants bearing drummers. The air filled with dust as they traveled, and the blare of trumpets, the din of drums, the clash of Indian cymbals, and the cavalry's cries accompanied them as they joyfully entered the city.

Manuchehr Hears of Sam's Expedition

The king heard that Sam had returned from the mountains in splendor: Manuchehr was pleased and thanked God for this good news. He sent Nozar hurrying to Sam to offer his congratulations and to tell Sam to come to the king so that he might see the face of this youth who had been brought up in a nest; then he could return to Zavolestan, to serve the king there.

Nozar reached Sam and saw the hero's son with him; Sam dismounted and the two embraced. He asked for news of the king and his warriors, and Nozar handed over his message. Sam kissed the ground and immediately set off for the court, as his king had commanded. Manuchehr came out with his entourage to greet him, and as soon as Sam saw Manuchehr's banner he dismounted and went forward on foot. Manuchehr ordered him to mount his horse, and the two set off together for the Persian court. Manuchehr sat in state on the throne and placed the royal crown on his head; on one side of him sat Qaren, on the other Sam. Then the chamberlain ushered in Sam's son, Zal, splendidly dressed, with a golden crown on his head, and bearing a golden mace. The king stared in wonder at his fine stature and handsome face, which seemed made to delight all hearts. He said to Sam, "Look after him well, for my sake; never cross him, rejoice in no one but him; he has the royal *farr*,[1] the strength of a lion, a wise heart, and a sage's manner."

> *And then Sam told the king of how and why*
> *He had decided that his child should die;*
> *He told him of the Simorgh and her nest,*
> *Of his regret, and his belated quest*
> *To find his son; throughout the world men heard*
> *Of Sam and Zal, and of this wondrous bird.*

Then the king gave orders that sages, astrologers, and priests should inquire into Zal's horoscope, to see what the stars decreed for him. The astrologers studied the stars and said, "May you live forever in prosperity; he will be a

---

1. The word *farr* refers to a God-given glory, and inviolability, bestowed on a king, and sometimes on a great hero. Its physical manifestation was a light that shone from the king's or hero's face. It has been suggested that the practice of saluting derives from an inferior's complimentary covering of his eyes with his hand, in order not to be blinded by the *farr* supposedly emanating from his superior.

famous champion, proud and intelligent, and a fine horse-man." The king rejoiced to hear these words, and Sam's heart too was freed from sorrow. Manuchehr gave Sam a robe of honor which drew praise from everyone, as well as Arab horses with golden saddles, Indian swords in golden scabbards, brocades, silks, fine carpets, rubies, and gold; slaves from the west dressed in Western brocade with jeweled designs on a golden ground; trays of emeralds, golden and silver goblets set with turquoise and filled with musk, camphor, and saffron; cuirasses, helmets, barding, spears, arrows, bows, and maces; thrones worked in turquoise and ivory, ruby seal rings, and golden belts. And then he wrote and sealed a charter full of celestial praise for Sam, bestowing on him lordship over Kabol, Danbar, Mai, and India, the Sea of China as far as the Sea of Send, as well as Zavolestan as far as Bost.

When he had received the charter and these gifts, Sam called for his horse, rose and said to the king, "Kind king, lord of justice and righteousness, in this world, from the realm of the fish to the sphere of the moon, no one like you has ever reigned; no one has had your generosity, justice, nobility, and wisdom. The world is at peace because of you, you treat its treasures with contempt, and may the day never come when only your name remains to us." He bowed and kissed the throne, and then had the drums strapped on his elephants. All the town turned out to watch as he and Zal set off for Zavolestan. As he approached, news of his investiture preceded him, and the inhabitants decorated Sistan as though it were a paradise; the ground was of musk, the bricks of gold, and as Sam passed, people tossed musk, saffron, and gold and silver coins over him. The world was filled with rejoicing, with both the nobles and the common people joining in. All the nobility came before Sam saying, "May the young man's arrival here be auspicious," and then they called down blessings on Zal and showered him with gold coins.

Then Sam took his ease with wine and music, bestowing robes of honor on the wise and the noble, and all his courtiers competed to be honored the most.

Sam Bestows His Realm on Zal

Sam summoned the experienced men of the country to speak with them. "Noble and prudent advisors," he said, "the wise king's orders are that I lead an army to invade the Gorgsaran and Mazanderan. However, my heart and soul, my son, will remain here, while my eyes weep bitter tears at our separation. In my youth and arrogance I acted unjustly. God gave me a son and I abandoned him; in my ignorance I did not realize his worth. The great Simorgh took him, God assigned him to her care, and she brought him up until he was like a lofty cypress; I reviled him, she valued him. When the time had come for me to be pardoned, God returned him to me. Know that this youth is my refuge, and I leave him among you to remind you of me. Treat him well, advise him well, show him the path to a noble life."

Then Sam turned to Zal and said, "Act justly and generously; this is the way to seek happiness. Know then that Zavolestan is your home; all this realm is under your command. See that the land flourishes beneath your reign, and that you make your friends' hearts rejoice. The keys of the treasury are yours, and my heart will be glad or sorrowful according to how you prosper or fail." Young Zal said to Sam, "How can I live without you now? Now that we have been reconciled, how can you contemplate separation again? If ever a man was born in sin, I am that man, and it is right that justice is denied me. I ate dirt and tasted blood once, held in the great bird's claws; now I am far from my protector, and it is fate that protects me. Of the world's flowers, my share is only thorns, but one cannot fight against God's decrees."

Sam said, "It is right to say what is in your heart like this; say it, say whatever you wish. But the astrologers have seen that a good star guides you, and they have said that here is your home, here is your army, and here is your crown. We cannot quarrel with the heavens, and it is here that your love must flourish. Now, gather a group of companions about you, horsemen and men eager for knowledge; learn from them, listen to them, gain all kinds of knowledge, and taste the pleasures they bring. Enjoy life and be generous, seek knowledge and be just." He spoke, and the din of drums rang out; the air turned pitch black, the ground was the color of ebony, and the ringing of bells and the clash of Indian cymbals was heard before the king's pavilion. Sam gathered his forces and set off for war. Zal accompanied him for two stages of the way, and then his father clasped him tightly in his arms and wept extravagantly. He commanded his son to return with happiness in his heart to the crown and throne. Zal took the journey home, pondering on how he could live so that he would leave a good name behind him.

He took his place on the ivory throne and placed the glittering crown on his head, resplendent with armbands and an ox-headed mace, a golden torque and golden belt. He was eager to learn and summoned knowledgeable men from every province, astrologers and priests as well as warriors and horsemen, and discussed all manner of subjects with them. Day and night he was closeted with them, discussing both weighty and trivial matters. Zal grew to be so learned that he was like a shining star; in all the world, no one had ever seen another man with his knowledge and understanding. And so the heavens turned, spreading a canopy of love over Sam and Zal.

THE LOVE OF ZAL AND RUDABEH

One day Zal decided to travel about his kingdom, and he set out with an entourage of like-minded companions. They traveled toward India, Kabol, Danbar, Morgh, and Mai. They built palaces as they went, and called for wine and musicians to entertain them; they spent liberally, driving away all thoughts of sorrow, as is the way of those who live in this fleeting world. They reached Kabol, traveling in splendor, laughing, and with happiness in their hearts. The king there was Mehrab, a shrewd, wealthy man, who was fortunate in his dealings. He was as tall and elegant as a cypress tree, his face was as fresh as the springtime, and his gait was like a pheasant's. His heart was wise, his mind prudent; his shoulders were those of a warrior, and his mind that of a priest. When he heard of Zal's approach he left Kabol at dawn, taking treasure, richly caparisoned horses, slaves, and various other kinds of wealth such as gold coins, rubies, musk, ambergris, brocades woven with gold, silks, and samites, a crown encrusted with royal jewels, and a golden torque set with emeralds.

Hearing that a splendid welcoming party was coming to greet him, Zal went forward to receive them and entertained them with all due ceremony. He sat Mehrab on a turquoise-studded throne, a marvelous feast was spread before the two princes, and as the wine steward poured their wine, Zal took stock of Mehrab. He liked what he saw, and his heart was attracted by the king's behavior: when he stood up from the table, Zal saw how well built he was and said to his courtiers, "What finer man binds on a nobleman's belt than this?" One of the courtiers spoke:

> *"In purdah, and unseen by anyone,*
> *He has a daughter lovelier than the sun.*
> *Lashes like ravens' wings protect a pair*
> *Of eyes like wild narcissi hidden there;*
> *If you would seek the moon, it is her face;*
> *If you seek musk, her hair's its hiding place.*
> *She is a paradise, arrayed in splendor,*
> *Glorious, graceful, elegantly slender."*

Zal's heart began to seethe, and all peace and good sense departed from him. Night came and Zal sat plunged in thought, unable to sleep or eat for thinking of this girl whom he had never seen.

When the sun's sword touched the mountain tops, and the world's surface became the color of pale topaz, Zal held court and Mehrab came to visit him. As he approached, a cry of "Clear the way" went up, and Mehrab entered, like a tree that bears fresh fruit. Zal was pleased to see him and made much of him, honoring him more than anyone else present. He said, "Ask me for anything you wish, be it thrones, seal rings, swords, or crowns." Mehrab replied, "My king whom all obey, you are noble and victorious, and I have only one wish from you, one that will not be hard for you to fulfill, which is that you come as a happy guest to my palace, which you will illuminate like the sun itself."

Zal answered, "This is not advisable, your palace is not a place for me. Sam would not approve, and neither would King Manuchehr if he heard of it, if I became drunk with wine in the house of someone who worships idols. I'll listen favorably to anything else you ask." Mehrab made his obeisance before Zal, but in his heart he called him a faithless wretch. He strode from the court, calling down blessings on his host. Zal watched him go, and praised him according to custom, but because they were of different faiths, he kept his remarks to a minimum. None of the Persians looked kindly on Mehrab, since they considered him to be an idolatrous demon, but when they saw Zal speaking to him in such a friendly fashion, they one by one said favorable things about him, in particular that his women's quarters housed someone who was incomparable in her stature, beauty, dignity, and all that pertained to loveliness. Zal's heart was suddenly seized by the madness of longing, wisdom fled from his mind, and love flourished there. The chief of the Arabs, the lord of righteousness, has said of such matters,

> "Whilst I'm alive my partner is my horse,
> Beneath the heavens my life will take its course,
> I'll never marry, to hear wise men speak
> Of me as one who's wanton, frail, and weak."

Zal's heart became weary with the thoughts that beset him; his heart writhed at the thought of the gossip that was said of him, and the shame his passion might bring. And so the heavens turned, and Zal's heart became filled to the brim with love.

Rudabeh Talks with Her Slave Girls

At dawn one day Mehrab went to his women's quarters, where he saw two suns; one was his wife, Sindokht, and the other his lovely daughter, Rudabeh. Their apartments

were decked out like a colorful garden in spring, filled with
sweet perfumes and elegance. Mehrab was astonished at
how lovely Rudabeh had grown, and he repeated the name
of God over her as a blessing. She was like a cypress tree
topped by the full moon, a moon that was crowned by her
musky hair. She was dressed in brocade and jewels, and
she seemed like a paradise filled with everything desirable.
Sindokht said to her husband, "May evil never harm you;
open your lovely lips and tell us where have you been today. Tell us what kind of person Sam's son is, this visitor
who has an old man's hair. Does he belong on a throne, or
in that nest where he was raised? Does he seem like a man
at all? Does he follow in the footsteps of famous men who
do noble deeds?" Mehrab replied, "My silver cypress, no
hero in the world is worthy to follow in Zal's footsteps:

> You'll see no other horseman to compare
> With Zal, he has no equal anywhere.
> As ruddy as the pomegranate flower—
> Youthful, and with a young man's luck and power;
> Fierce in revenge, and in the saddle he's
> A sharp-clawed dragon to his enemies;
> Possessed of mammoth strength, a lion's guile,
> His arms are mighty as the flooding Nile;
> He scatters gold when he's in court, and when
> He's on the battlefield, the heads of men.
> He has one fault—which after all's so slight
> No one remarks on it—his hair is white."

Rudabeh had five kind Turkish slaves who were her confi-
dantes. She said to these shrewd girls, "All five of you are
my friends and know my heart and I wish all of you luck in
your lives. I'm going to tell you a secret: I'm in love, and
my love is like a wave of the sea that's cresting up toward
heaven. My bright heart is filled with thoughts of Sam's
son, and even when I sleep he never leaves me. The place

in my heart where I should feel shame is filled instead with love, and day and night I think of his face. Now, help me, what do you think, what do you advise? You must think of some scheme, some way to free my heart and soul from this agony of adoration."

Her slave girls were astonished at this behavior from someone of Rudabeh's rank. They rose up like Ahriman and answered her forthrightly: "You are the crown of all the princesses in the world, praised from India to China, the jewel of your father's household; no cypress has your stature, the Pleiades are not as lovely as your face, your portrait has been sent from Qanuj to the king of the western lands. Have you no shame, have you considered what this would mean to your father? Do you want to embrace someone who has driven your father from his embrace, someone who was brought up by a bird in the mountains, who is a byword among men for his strangeness? No one has ever been born from his mother as an old man, and such a person will not have descendants. How can a young girl, whose lips are the color of coral, want to marry an old man? The world is filled with love for you, and your portrait is found in every palace; your face and hair and form are so lovely that the sun itself should descend from the fourth sphere to be your husband."

When Rudabeh heard their words, her heart beat fast, like a fire fanned by the wind. She shouted at them in fury, screwing up her eyes, her face trembling, her forehead filled with frowns, her eyebrows bent like a bow. "It's pointless to listen to such foolish talk; I don't want the Chinese emperor, nor the king of the West, nor the king of Persia. Sam's son, Zal, is the man I want; with his lion-like strength and stature, he is my equal. Call him old or young, he will be body and soul to me." The slave girls were taken aback by her response and said with one voice, "We are your slaves. Our hearts are filled with our love for you. We await your orders, from which nothing but good can

come. May a hundred thousand like us sacrifice their lives
for you, and may all the wisdom in the world come to your
aid. May your black-eyed servants be filled with humility,
and their faces blush with shame. If we must learn magic
we will learn it, flying with birds and running with deer,
seeling our eyes with spells and incantations, so that we can
bring this prince to your side." Rudabeh's red lips smiled,
and turning her saffron cheeks to them, she said, "If you
bring us to one another's arms, and keep the promise you
have made, you will be planting a noble tree whose daily
fruit will be rubies."

Rudabeh's Slaves Go to See Zal

Then her slaves set about thinking of some way to help
their helpless princess. They dressed themselves in Rumi
brocade and wore chaplets of flowers in their hair. The five
of them went down to the river bank, and in their tints and
scents they were as lovely as the spring. It was the month
of Farvardin, when the sun moves into Aries, and the year
is renewed. Zal had come to the riverside to hunt; on the
opposite bank the slave girls paused to pick flowers, and
their own faces were like flowers as they gathered the blossoms into their arms. Zal watched from his throne and
asked, "Who are those girls, who seem so fond of flowers?"
A courtier answered, "They are from Mehrab's palace; his
daughter, whom people call the moon of Kabol, has sent
them to gather flowers." Zal went closer to the girls and
asked for his bow. On foot he approached the ducks swim-
ming in the river and drew back the string from his bow;
he watched for when one of the birds flew up from the
river and then loosed an arrow at it. He brought it down in
mid-flight, and its blood dripped into the river, reddening
the water. One of the girls said to Zal's servant boy, who
went to fetch the bird, "Who is that lion of a man? What
kind of a man is he who shot that arrow, and whose king
is he? Who would dare oppose such a warrior? We haven't

seen a finer knight than he is, or a better shot with a bow."
The handsome boy bit his lip and said, "Don't talk about
the king like that. He's the king of Zabolestan, Sam's son,
and his name is Zal. The heavens don't turn above a finer
knight, and the world will never see anyone more noble
than he is." The girl smiled at the handsome boy and said,
"Don't be so sure. There's a princess in Mehrab's palace
who is finer by far than your king. Her stature is like a teak
tree's, her color is that of ivory, and she wears on her head
the crown of musk that God has given her. Her eyes are like
two dark narcissi, her eyebrows are like a bow, her nose is
like a silver reed, her mouth is small, like the contracted
heart of a desperate man, and her hair falls in ringlets to
her feet. Her mouth is so tiny that her breath can scarcely
find passage there, and there is no one in all the world who
is her equal for beauty. We have come here so that her ruby
lips can become acquainted with the lips of Sam's son."

The boy left them and returned to Zal, who asked him
what the girl had said that had made him smile so much
and show his silver teeth in his blushing face. The boy told
Zal what he had heard, and the hero's heart grew young at
his words. He said to his handsome page, "Go and tell the
girls to wait for a moment, so that they can take jewels with
them as well as flowers." He asked for gold and silver coins,
and jewels from his treasury, as well as five sets of clothes
made of golden brocade. He told the boy to take these to
the girls, but to do so secretly and tell no one, and to say
to them that they shouldn't go back to the castle just yet
because he had a message he wished to send. Slaves took
the gifts to the girls and told them what Zal had said. One
of the girls said to the page, "Words never remain secret for
long unless they are between just two people. With three
people they are no longer a secret, and four is like a crowd.
Tell your prince that if he has a secret to impart, he should
tell me face to face." Then the girls said to one another,
"The lion has walked into the trap; now Rudabeh will have

her heart's desire, and Zal shall have his, and everything has turned out for the best."

Zal's black-eyed treasurer, who was also his confidant in this matter, returned to the prince and told him all he had heard from the girls. Zal made his way to the beds of flowers on the riverbank, in hopes of arranging a meeting with Rudabeh. The princess's beautiful slave girls presented themselves and made their obeisance to him. Zal questioned them about their mistress, asking about her stature and beauty, her manner of speaking and wisdom, wanting to know if she was worthy of him. "Tell me everything," he said, "and see that you don't try to deceive me. If I find that you've spoken honestly, you'll be honored and rewarded, but if I find that you've lied in even the smallest detail, I'll have you trampled beneath the feet of elephants." The girls' faces turned the color of red juniper berries, and they kissed the ground before him. One of them said, "No noble mother has ever borne a man as fine as Sam, not in looks or stature, knowledge or purity of heart; and who is there to compare with you, brave lord, with your massive frame and lion strength? And thirdly, there is Rudabeh, whose face is like the moon, whose body is a silver cypress tree adorned in tints and scents; she is a rose, a jasmine flower, from head to foot, and her face is as radiant as Canopus shining above the Yemen. From the silver dome of her forehead her hair cascades in fragrant coils, looped with rubies and emeralds, down to her feet, her curls are links of musk entwined one with another, her ten fingers are silver reeds steeped in civet. You will see no idol as beautiful as she is in all of China; the moon and the Pleiades bow down before her."

The prince spoke urgently, but sweetly and gently, to a slave girl. "Tell me some way that I can reach her; my heart and soul are filled with love for her, and I long to glimpse her face." The slave girl answered, "With your permission, we shall return to the castle; we are all smitten with your glory, your handsomeness, and your words' sincerity. We shall report everything, changing nothing. We shall bring her musky head into your trap; we shall bring her lips to the lips of Sam's son. May the prince come to the castle walls with a lariat; he can loop it on the battlements, and so like a lion happily pursue his prey."

The Slave Girls Return to Rudabeh

The girls went on their way, and Zal returned to his camp; as he waited for the night it seemed to him that a year passed by. The girls reached the castle, each of them holding two posies of flowers. When the doorman saw them he grumbled; impatient words came from his troubled heart: "This is no time to be gadding about away from the castle. I'm astonished at your behavior." The girls responded in just as lively a fashion: "Today is different from any other day. There are no demons lying in wait among the blossoms. Spring has come and we have been to pick flowers; we have gathered these hyacinths." The doorman said, "This is no day to be doing such things. Zal's tents are no longer in Zabolestan; didn't you see the king of Kabol ride out from the castle to greet him? If he should come across you with these flowers in your hands, he'd knock you to the ground there and then."

The girls entered the castle and went to the princess, where they sat to tell her their secrets. They showed her the brocade and jewels Zal had given them, and Rudabeh asked about every detail of their encounter. "How did your meeting with Zal go?" she asked. "Has people's gossip exaggerated his qualities, or is he even better when you see him face to face?" The five girls all began to speak at once, vying for who should tell the princess what they had seen. "He's like a tall cypress tree; everything about him is elegant, and he radiates royal glory. The colors he wears, the perfumes, his height and build; he's a knight with a slim waist and a noble chest. His eyes are like two pitch-black narcissi, his lips are like coral, his cheeks ruddy as blood.

His shoulders and trunk are like a lion's, his thighs are massive, his heart is learned, and he has a king's dignity. His hair is completely white; this is his only fault, and really it's nothing to be ashamed of; his curls are like silver links coiled together about his face, which is like the blossoms of the Judas tree. You think, 'He's just as he should be; and if he weren't like this he wouldn't inspire such love.' We told him he could see you, and he went back to his camp with his heart filled with hope. Now you must get ready to receive your guest, and tell us what answer we should take back to him."

The princess said to her slaves, "Then he's different from what people say. This Zal, who was brought up by a bird and was a youth who had withered away, with the head of an old man, has become as lovely as the blossoms of a Judas tree, tall and elegant, with a handsome face, from head to foot a hero. So, you boasted about my face to him, and reaped the reward for your words." As she spoke her lips broke into smiles, and her cheeks blushed the color of pomegranate blossoms. The slave girls said, "But now get ready, because God has granted your desires, and we pray that everything will turn out well."

Rudabeh's palace was as pleasant as springtime, and on its walls there were portraits of famous men. She had one of its room decorated with Chinese brocade, and she placed golden trays heaped with agates and emeralds there. Then she mixed wine, musk, and ambergris together and decorated the area with violets, narcissi, the blossoms of the Judas tree, branches of jasmine, and hyacinths. The drinking vessels were of gold set with turquoise, and held rose water. Rudabeh's face was as radiant as the sun, and the scents in her room rose up to the sun's sphere.

When the shining sun set, the doors to the private quarters of the castle were locked, and the keys hidden away. One of the slave girls went to Zal and said, "Everything is ready: come." The prince set off for the castle with all the haste and anxiety of a man going to meet his beloved. Rudabeh went onto the roof and stood there like a cypress tree topped by the full moon. When she saw Zal in the distance, she called out to him, "Welcome, bold young man. God's blessings be upon you, and may you tread on the heavens. I wish my slave girls happy hearts, because from head to foot you are as they described. But you have walked here from your pavilion, and I am afraid your royal feet have been irked by this." Zal heard her voice and, looking up, caught sight of her face; the roof shone with its light, and the earth glowed like a ruby. He answered her, "Heaven's blessings be upon you; your face is as lovely as the full moon. How many nights I have passed gazing at the stars, crying out to God, asking that he grant me a glimpse of your face. Now your voice and your sweet words have made my heart happy. But find some way for us to meet; how can I stay down here when you are on the battlements?"

Hearing his words, she loosened her hair, which cascaded down, tumbling like snakes, loop upon loop. She said, "Come, take these black locks which I let down for you, and use them to climb up to me." Zal gazed in astonishment at her face and hair, and said, "This would not be just. May the day never dawn when I strike at my soul like this, thrusting my spear into a wounded heart." He took a lariat from his page, looped it, and hurled it upwards without saying another word; the lariat caught on the battlements, and Zal quickly climbed up its sixty cubits. As he stepped onto the roof Rudabeh made her obeisance before him, then grasped his hands in hers. As if they were in a drunken stupor, they clasped hands and descended from the roof to Rudabeh's golden chamber, which glowed like a paradise. Rudabeh's slave girls stood before their houri, and Zal stared in wonder at her face, her hair, her stature, her splendor, her bracelets, her necklace and earrings, at her brocade dress woven with jewels like a garden in spring dotted with flowers. Her cheeks were like red tulips surrounded by jasmine, her face was surmounted by curl upon curl of musky hair. A sword-belt across his chest and wearing a diadem of rubies, Zal sat in princely splendor beside this glorious moon of beauty. For a while there was nothing but kisses, embraces, and wine; but then Zal said to Rudabeh, "If Manuchehr hears of this he will not agree to it, and Sam too will be loud in his opposition. But I despise their opinions and am ready to die if need be. I swear by almighty God that I shall never break faith with you. I shall pray before God as his slave, asking that he wash all anger and thoughts of vengeance from Sam's and Manuchehr's hearts. God will grant my request, and all the world will know you as my wife." Rudabeh replied, "And I too swear before God, and may he witness what I say, that no one shall be my master but Zal, the world's hero, the crowned prince on his throne, the lord of beauty and royal splendor."

> From moment then to moment their desire
> Gained strength, and wisdom fled before love's fire;
> Passion engulfed them, and these lovers lay
> Entwined together till the break of day.
> So tightly they embraced, before Zal left,
> Zal was the warp, and Rudabeh the weft
> Of one cloth, as with tears they said goodbye
> And cursed the sun for rising in the sky.
> Zal let himself down from the battlements,
> And made his way back to his army's tents.

Zal Consults with His Priests about Rudabeh

When the glittering sun rose above the mountain peaks, the warriors visited their prince and then each went his own way. Zal sent a messenger to summon knowledgeable men and priests to his court, and when they arrived he smiled, and with his heart filled with happiness he gave thanks to

God who had woken his sleeping good fortune. Then he said, "Our hearts are filled with hope and fear of God; we hope for his grace and we fear sin, praising him to the best of our abilities, praying before him night and day. It is he who guides the sun and moon and leads our souls in the path of righteousness, who maintains the world which gives us such pleasure, who administers justice in this world and the world to come, who brings spring, summer, and autumn, who burdens trees with fruit and vines with grapes, who gives young men their power and beauty and old men the frowns on their faces, whose commands no man can gainsay since not an ant treads the earth without him. The world's peoples increase by coming together as couples, since a single person can produce no offspring. Only God is alone, having neither companion nor mate nor friend. All of creation lives in couples, and this is how being emerges from the hidden realm; this is so throughout the world, this is the heavens' will. If there were no couples in the world, authority would remain hidden; we see that no young man lives alone, and this is especially true if he is of good family, since then his might would pass from him. What is sweeter in the world than for a hero's soul to be gladdened by his children? And when the time comes for him to die, his life is renewed in his child; his name remains behind, so that men say, 'This is the son of Zal' and 'That is the son of Sam.' A son is an ornament to the crown and the throne; the man dies but his fortune lives on in his son.

"All this is my story; this is the rose, the narcissus, the flower at the heart of my tale. My heart has been snatched from me, my wisdom has fled; look at me now and tell me what medicine can cure me. I have not said this lightly, my mind is deeply troubled; my love is centered on Mehrab's palace, his land is like the heavens to me, and my heart is fixed on Sindokht's daughter. Now, what do you say to this? Will Sam agree to it? Will King Manuchehr? Will he consider it to be youthful impetuosity, or a sin? When a man seeks a wife, be he a commoner or a nobleman, he does what religion and custom demand; this is the way of faith, it is not a matter for shame, and no wise man quarrels with it. You are sages and learned priests, what do you say to me, what do you advise?"

But the priests and sages said nothing, their lips remained sealed, because Zahhak was Mehrab's grandfather, and the king had no love for him in his heart. No one said anything openly, but they thought, "How can wholesome food be joined with poison?" When Zal heard nothing from them, he was angered and tried another tactic. He said, "I know that when you consider this you blame me, but any man who makes a decision will hear himself blamed. If you will guide me in this, and free me from these chains, I shall do such things for you as no prince has ever done for his subjects."

Then the priests answered that they wished him well and desired his happiness. They said, "We are all your slaves, and it's our surprise that has silenced us. Mehrab is a nobleman, a warrior, and not to be taken lightly. He is descended from Zahhak, who was a demon, but even so he was the king of the Arabs. If Mehrab's ancestry doesn't trouble you, his family is not one to be ashamed of. You must write a letter to Sam—in this matter your wisdom is greater than ours and you will know what to say—so that he in turn will write to King Manuchehr, giving his opinion; Manuchehr will not ignore Sam's advice on such a matter."

Zal Writes a Letter to His Father Sam

Zal called for a scribe and poured out the contents of his heart. He began with praise of the world's just Creator, from whom come happiness and strength, who is the lord of the evening star, of Saturn and of the sun, of all that is and is not, who is one and whose slaves we are. He went on, "I invoke his blessing on Sam, the lord of the mace, the sword and helmet, who makes his grey horse curvet on the battlefield and leaves food there for the vultures, whose presence is a mighty wind in war, who rains down swords from the storm clouds, who distributes crowns and royal belts and places kings on their golden thrones; a man of all able qualities, and the greatest of these is his wisdom. I am as a slave to him, and my heart and soul are filled with love for him. I was born as he saw me to be, and the heavens dealt unjustly with me. While my father lived in comfort, in silks and samites, the Simorgh bore me to the mountains of India where she treated me as one of her squabs, and I depended on the food she hunted. My skin was burned by the wind, my eyes were blinded by dust, and though men said I was the son of Sam, he lived in glory while I lived in a nest, because God had ordained this. No one can escape God's justice, even though he fly beyond the clouds. A warrior's teeth can be like anvils, he might be able to crush a lance with them, his voice might make a lion's skin split with terror, but still he must obey God's will. Something heartbreaking has happened to me, something which men will not praise me for. But if my father, who is a brave man and a dragon in his wrath, will hear me out, all will be well.

"I weep for the daughter of Mehrab, I burn in the fire of my love for her. In the dark night the stars are my companions, my heart seethes in turmoil like the sea, I am beside myself with grief, and all men weep for me. My heart has seen injustice but I breathe only to obey you. You are the world's hero, what do you command? Free me from this pain, this agony of soul; let me marry Mehrab's daughter, according to our rites and customs. When you brought me from the Alborz mountains, you swore before your courtiers that you would never oppose me in my desires, and this is the one desire of my heart."

An envoy took three horses and set off as swiftly as fire from Kabol. Zal gave him his orders: "If one horse stumbles, you should not delay for an instant; mount another and press onward, until you're in Sam's presence." The messenger sped off like the wind, and when he reached the land of the Gorgsaran he saw Sam in the distance, hunting with his cheetahs on the mountain slopes. Sam caught sight of him and said to his companions, "A horseman is riding here from Kabol, and the mount he's riding is from Zavolestan. He must be an envoy from Zal; we should find out what he has to say, and ask him about Zal, Persia, and the king." At that moment the envoy, clutching a letter in his hand, reached Sam; he dismounted, kissed the ground, and called down God's blessings on the king. Sam questioned him and took the letter, and the envoy gave him Zal's greetings. Sam began to make his way down the mountain and opened the letter to read Zal's message; as soon as he had done so he stood rooted to the spot in astonishment. Zal's request did not please him; this was not how he had hoped his son would be. He said, "His words fit his nature, which has now become plain to me. These are the foolish whims a boy who was brought up by a savage bird would have," and he made his way back from the hunting grounds to his camp, his mind filled with foreboding. He said to himself, "If I say to him, 'This is not an advisable course of action; don't sir up trouble like this, be sensible,' I shall be known as one who gave his word idly and broke it. But if I say, 'Yes, you must follow your desires and do what your heart tells you, then from that savage bird and this descendant of a demon, what kind of offspring will be born?" His heart was weighed down with worry, but he slept, and his sleep refreshed him.

Sam Consults His Priests Concerning Zal

When he woke he summoned priests and wise men and consulted them. He began by questioning astrologers, and asked them what the outcome of a union between two who were as different as fire and water would be; surely it would produce a disaster like the war between Zahhak and Feraydun? He told them to consult the stars, and to see if any good could come of this. For many days the astrologers searched the skies, and when they came before him again they were smiling and said, "Fortune will join these two enemies as one." The chief astrologer said, "I bring you good news of the union between Zal and Mehrab's daughter: they will both prosper, and from these two will be born a great hero, a mammoth-bodied man who will conquer the world with his sword, who will lift the king's throne beyond the clouds. He will extirpate the race of evil from the earth and cleanse the world with his heavy mace. He will be a comfort to those who suffer, and he will close the gate of war and the pathways to evil.

> Persia will trust in him and in his fame,
> Her champions will rejoice to hear his name,
> Throughout his life the monarchy will thrive,
> In times to come his glory will survive;
> Before his name, inscribed on every seal,
> Persia and Rum and India will kneel."

Relieved by the astrologers' words, Sam laughed and thanked them warmly, and gave them great quantities of gold and silver, because they had brought him comfort when he was afraid.

He called for Zal's envoy and said to him, "Speak kindly to Zal; tell him that this is a strange wish that he has, but that since I gave my word it would be unjust for me to look for some way to refuse him. At dawn I shall leave for Persia." Then he gave the messenger some silver coins and said, "Don't delay on your journey for an instant." When two watches of the night had passed, horsemen's cries, the din of drums, and blare of trumpets announced Sam's departure with his army for Persia. The envoy reached Zal with news of his good fortune, and Zal gave thanks to God for his happiness, distributing gold and silver coins to the poor, and being equally generous with his friends.

Sindokht Learns of Rudabeh's Behavior

A sweet-voiced serving woman acted as a go-between for Zal and Rudabeh, taking messages from one to the other. Zal summoned her and told her what he had learned. He said, "Go to Rudabeh and tell her, 'Purehearted moon of loveliness, when matters go from bad to worse, we soon see a key to open a way of escape. My envoy has returned from Sam with good news: Sam argued and blustered for a while, but finally he has agreed to our marriage.'" Then he gave the girl Sam's letter, and she hurried like the wind to Rudabeh to tell her the good news. Rudabeh showered her with gold coins and sat her down on a gold-worked throne; she gave her a muslin headscarf that was so finely woven the weft could not be told from the warp; it was embroidered in red and gold, and the gold was almost hidden by jewels. She also gave her two valuable rings, which glittered like the planet Jupiter. Then she sent her back with many greetings and good wishes to Zal.

As the woman emerged from Rudabeh's apartments into the main hall of the palace, Sindokht caught sight of her. The woman blushed in fear, turning the color of red juniper berries, and kissed the ground before her queen. Sindokht became suspicious and said in a loud voice, "Where are you coming from? Tell me. You're always going back and forth from Rudabeh's apartments, and you avoid my eye when you do so. My heart suspects you of something. What are you up to? Are you the bowstring in this affair or the bow?" The woman replied, "I'm just a poor woman trying to earn my daily bread as best I can. Rudabeh wanted to buy some jewelry, and I brought her a golden diadem and a splendid ring set with precious stones." Sindokht said, "Show them to me and put my heart at rest." She replied, "I left both of them with Rudabeh; she wanted some other things, so I'm going to fetch them." Sindokht said, "Show me the money she paid you for them, and pour cold water on my anger." But the woman replied, "Rudabeh said she would pay me tomorrow; you can't ask to see something I haven't received yet."

Sindokht knew the woman was lying, and she hardened her heart against her. She began to search her roughly, looking in her bosom and sleeves, and when she found the fine headscarf embroidered by Rudabeh, she was enraged, and ordered her daughter to come before her. She clawed at her cheeks and wept, and said, "You are a noble woman and as beautiful as the moon, what whim has made you choose to act like someone from the lowest depths rather than someone who occupies a throne? What do you lack? Why are you behaving like a criminal? Now, tell your mother whatever secrets you are hiding, especially why this woman keeps coming to you. What is going on? Who is the man this scarf and rings were intended for? The Arab's wealth and crown have brought us both good and ill fortune, and you want to fling our standing and reputation to the winds like this? What mother ever gave birth to a daughter like you?"

Rudabeh was ashamed and stared at the ground. She began to weep, and tears coursed down her lovely cheeks. She said to her mother,

> "I wish I'd not been born, and then you would
> See nothing evil in me, nothing good.
> You're wise, but love has made my heart its prey,
> I think of Zal, Zabol's king, night and day;
> I burn for him in love's tormenting fire,
> My heart's consumed by passion and desire.
> I weep my life away, without him I
> Have no desire to live, I long to die.
> He came to me, and hand in hand we swore
> Our mutual love will last forevermore.
> His envoy went to Sam, who angrily
> Declared at first that he would not agree
> To Zal's request, but bit by bit relented,
> Argued, and stormed, and finally consented.

The letter that he sent to Zal was brought
To me here, by the woman whom you caught."

Sindokht was astonished at her words, and at first said
nothing, but then thought that she liked the idea of Zal as
a son-in-law. However, she said, "This isn't wise. There's
no noble warrior who can compare with Zal; he's a great
man, and the son of a hero, who has a fine reputation and
is an intelligent, clear-sighted man. Zal has many virtues
and only one fault, but that fault diminishes his splendor. The king of Persia will be angered by this, and he'll
raise the dust of battle over Kabol. He has no desire for
someone from our family to rule." Sindokht released the
go-between and spoke kindly to her, saying she now knew
what had been hidden from her. She saw that her daughter had lived cut off from the world and without anyone's
advice. Then she lay down alone, filled with such anxiety
that her skin felt bruised and broken.

Mehrab Learns of His Daughter's Love

Mehrab came from the court in good spirits, because Zal
had been very attentive to him. He saw Sindokht lying
down frowning and seeming troubled, and he said to her,
"What's the matter? Why is your flower-like face filled
with frowns?" She said, "I've been thinking for a long time
about our palace and wealth, our Arab horses, our page-
boys who have sworn loyalty to you, our gardens and royal
enclosures, the beauty of our daughter, our reputation,
knowledge, and prudence. Little by little the freshness and
force of our lives leaves us; misfortune will come, our enemies will inherit what is ours, our troubles will have been
as vain as the wind. A narrow coffin will be our lot, and the
fruit of the tree we have planted will be poison: we have
watered it and labored over it, hung crowns and treasures
in its branches, it has grown upwards to the sun and spread

its shade, and now it is to be felled. This will be our end, and who knows where our peace is to found?"

Mehrab said to Sindokht, "You speak as if this were a new thing, but the fleeting world was ever thus, and wise men have always feared its ways. It raises one and casts another down, and heaven's will cannot be opposed. There is no point in agonizing over this, it won't change, we cannot fight against God's decrees." Sindokht said, "A priest will tell his child this parable of the tree to explain the ways of the world to him. I said it so that you would pay attention to what I have to say." She hung her head, and her rosy cheeks were wet with tears. "The heavens do not always turn as we would wish. Know then, that Zal, Sam's son, has set who knows what snares in secret to catch Rudabeh. He has captured her pure heart, and we must consider what to do about this. I have talked to her at length, but to no avail; her face is sallow with grief, and I can see that her heart is in turmoil."

When Mehrab heard this he sprang up and grasped his sword hilt; his body trembled, his face darkened, blood surged in his heart, his lips were cold with sighs, and he said, "I shall make a river of blood of Rudabeh this moment." Sindokht stood and, grasping him by the waist, said, "I am your slave, listen to me first, then do whatever you wish, and may wisdom guide your soul." But he twisted from her grasp and pushed her away, roaring like a maddened elephant. He shouted, "I should have cut that girl's head off when she was born. I didn't, I didn't do as my grandfather would have done, and now she comes up with this sorcery to destroy me. I could be killed for this and my reputation destroyed, why do you want to stop me from punishing her? If Sam and Manuchehr march against us, smoke from the sack of Kabol will cloud the sun, and neither the town nor our fields or crops will survive."

Sudabeh said, "Calm yourself, don't talk so wildly. Sam already knows, and there's no need to be so fearful and anxious. He's traveling from the land of the Gorgsaran to Manuchehr's court. The matter is not a secret any more, it's out in the open." Mehrab said, "Don't tell me such lies, woman; the wind does not obey the dust. If you could show me some way to manage this then I wouldn't be so worried. Who is there from Ahvaz to Qandahar who wouldn't like to be allied to Sam?" Sindokht answered, "My lord, may I never need lies to help me. What harms you obviously harms me, and I am devoted to your heart's well-being. I've told you the truth; this is the matter that's been troubling me. But if this marriage should happen, it wouldn't be so amazing after all, and the prospect should not worry us so much. Feraydun became king of Persia with the help of Sarv, king of the Yemen, and Zal is trying to do something similar. The world will not shine with splendor from earth, air, and water alone; fire must be there too, the elements have to mix. When a stranger joins your family, those who wish you ill are discomfited, because it makes you stronger."

As Mehrab listened to Sindokht his heart was filled with fury, his head with confusion. He said, "Bring Rudabeh to me." But Sindokht was afraid that he would harm her in his anger, and she answered, "First you must swear to deliver her back to me safe and sound; Kabol must not be deprived of her; she is a paradise, a rose garden, in her loveliness." She made him promise to renounce all thoughts of violence against their daughter, and Mehrab solemnly swore that he would not hurt her, but added, "The king will be furious with us for this; there won't be any country or mother or father or Rudabeh left when he has finished with us." Sindokht bowed before him and went smiling to her daughter, her face shining like the sun beneath the night of her black hair. She said, "Good news, the leopard has sheathed his claws and let the wild ass go free. Now, put on some fine clothes and go to your father, and see that you cry in front of him." Rudabeh replied, "What use are fine clothes? What are such worthless things when I lack the one precious thing I want? My soul longs for Sam's son; why should I hide what's obvious?"

But when she went before her father, as lovely as the sun rising in the east, she seemed drowned in rubies and gold; she was arrayed like a paradise, and as splendid as the sun in springtime. Her father stared at her in wonder and silently invoked God's blessings. Then he stormed at her, "You senseless child, when was such behavior ever right for a noblewoman? How can a fairy being like you marry that Ahriman?" She lowered her black eyelashes over her dark eyes, and did not dare draw breath. Her angry father raged at her like a roaring leopard, his heart filled with fury. She returned to her apartments heartbroken, and her face was as sallow as saffron. Both the daughter and the king prayed to God to aid them.

Manuchehr Learns of Zal's Engagement to Mehrab's Daughter

When Manuchehr learned that this diverse pair, Zal and Rudabeh, intended to marry, he said to his priests and sages, "This will bring an evil day to us. By war and policy I have delivered Persia from the clutches of lions and leopards, and Zal's impetuous love must not be allowed to raise up this defeated race so that they are our equals. By the union of Mehrab's daughter and Sam's son a sharp sword will be unsheathed, who on one side will not be of our people; this will be like mingling poison and its antidote together. If their offspring follows in his mother's footsteps, his head will be filled with malevolence toward us; Persia will seethe with sedition and trouble, as he hopes to gain her crown and wealth." All the priests approved his speech, and said, "You are wiser than we are, and more able to do what is necessary. Do what wisdom demands."

He summoned Nozar and his nobles to him and said, "Go to Sam and ask him how the war has gone. Then tell him to come here before he returns home." Nozar and his entourage set off with their elephants and war drums.

When they arrived at Sam's camp, he was pleased to see them, and Nozar handed over his father's message. Sam replied, "I shall do as he commands, and my soul will find peace in seeing him." They set out tables for a feast, and the name of Manuchehr was the first they remembered when they drank. They passed the long night in pleasure until the bright sun reappeared; then, to the din of drums, their mounts seemed to take wing as they sped toward the court as Manuchehr had commanded.

When Manuchehr heard of their approach, a great cry went up from Sari and Amol, and the army set off, filling the valleys with their heavy lances, their shields woven in red and gold, their drums, trumpets, and cymbals, their Arab horses, elephants, and treasure. In this manner, with its banners and drums, the army went to welcome Sam.

Sam Comes to Manuchehr

Sam dismounted as he drew near the court, and a way was cleared for him to approach the king. Sam kissed the ground and went forward. Manuchehr rose from his ivory throne, a crown set with shining rubies on his head, and motioned Sam to a throne near him. He treated him with appropriate kindness, asking him sympathetically about the war with the Gorgsaran and the demons of Mazanderan, and Sam answered all his questions one by one, recounting the story of his battles, the rout of their enemies, and the killing of Zahhak's descendant Kakui. As Manuchehr listened his crown seemed to reach to the moon with pleasure. He gave orders for wine and a banquet, to celebrate the extirpation of his enemies from the world. They passed the night feasting, and Sam's name was continually on the courtiers' lips.

When day broke Sam returned to Manuchehr's side. The king said to him, "Choose some chieftains and go from here to India; spread fire and sword there, burn Mehrab's castle and Kabol to the ground. Don't let him escape; he's

dragon's spawn, always raising his war cry against someone, filling the peaceful world with war and trouble. Sever
the heads of his allies, cleanse the earth of Zahhak's tribe."
Sam replied, "I shall do this and satisfy the king's anger."
He kissed the throne and touched his face to the king's seal
ring. Then he and his army set off on their galloping horses
for home.

Sam and Zal Meet

News of what Manuchehr and Sam were planning reached
Mehrab and Zal. Zal was enraged; he flung back his shoulders and his lips quivered with anger. He left Kabol, saying,
"If a dragon comes burning the world with his breath and
wishes to conquer Kabol, he will have to cut my head off
first." Angrily he made for his father's camp, his heart filled
with anxieties, his head with the words he would say. As the
lion cub approached the camp, all the army rose to greet
him; the banner of Feraydun was set before them, and the
elephants were draped in red, yellow, and purple cloths.

When Zal saw his father's face, he dismounted and
walked forward. The chieftains on both sides dismounted,
and Zal kissed the ground. His father spoke to him and Zal
remounted his charger, whose saddle glittered with gold.
The chieftains came forward anxiously, saying "Your father
is angry with you; apologize, don't act stubbornly." Zal assured them, "There's no fear of that; I have blood in my
veins, not dirt. If my father is wise, he won't bandy words
with me, and if he speaks angrily to me, I shall be ashamed
and weep." They rode cheerfully into Sam's camp, where
Sam dismounted and welcomed his son. Zal kissed the
ground and began.

He invoked God's blessings on Sam, and tears fell from
his eyes. He said, "May Sam be prudent and happy, and
his soul incline toward justice. Diamonds are shattered by
your sword, the earth weeps when you ride out to battle,
the world flourishes with your justice, and wisdom and

prudence are your soul's foundation. I alone have no part in this justice of yours, even though I am your kin. I was raised by a bird, when I ate dirt, but I have no quarrel with anyone in the world. I do not know what crime I have committed—unless it is that the hero Sam is my father—or whom I have harmed. When my mother bore me, you rejected me and had me exposed in the mountains. You gave your son over to grief, consigning me to the fire. Your quarrel is with God; isn't it he who has created the colors black and white? I have nobility, courage, and a hero's sword, and the lord of Kabol is my friend. He is wealthy, prudent, and just, possessed of a throne, crown, and the mace of sovereignty. I went to Kabol because you told me to; I did as you commanded, taking your place when you went to the wars, and harvesting the fruit of the tree you had planted. Is this the present you bring me from Mazanderan and your wars with the Gorgsaran, that you will destroy the place I have chosen to live? Is this the justice you bring me? I stand before you now as your slave and I deliver my body to your anger. Cut my body in two with a saw if you wish, but do not speak to me about Kabol."

> Sam listened to his son, and hung his head:
> "All that you're telling me is true," he said.
> "All that I did was wrong; your miseries
> Gladdened the hearts of all our enemies.
> And now, heart sore, you've come here as my guest
> To know if I will grant this last request.
> Be patient, while I find a way to bring
> Your cause persuasively before the king:
> I'll write a letter to him, you will be
> My trusted envoy to his majesty:
> I'll teach you what to say, and when you speak
> King Manuchehr will grant you what you seek.
> If God's our friend, what we're about to do
> Will hand your longed-for heart's desire to you.

Sam Writes a Letter to King Manuchehr

They summoned a scribe and dictated a detailed letter. Sam began with praise of God, invoking his blessings on King Manuchehr, and continued: "As your slave I have reached the sixtieth year of my life: the sun and moon have crowned my head with white camphor. I bound on my sword belt as your slave and made war on sorcerers; the world has never seen anyone ride his horse or wield his mace as I have done. I obliterated the splendor of Mazanderan's warriors, and only I was able to defeat the dragon that emerged from the River Kashaf, massive as a mountain, broad as a valley, filling the earth with the foam from its lips, terrifying the world's inhabitants. Its spittle burned vultures' wings, its venom scorched the earth; it snatched monsters from the sea and eagles from the air; the earth was emptied of people and flocks, every living thing retreated before it. When I saw that no one dared oppose it, I emptied my heart of fear and bound on my sword in God's name. Seated on my massive mount, my ox-headed mace on my saddle, my bow slung over my shoulder, my shield at the ready, I attacked like a ravening monster: everyone who heard that I would try my mace against this dragon bade me farewell as if I went to my death. I approached and saw it was like a great mountain, with its hair trailing on the ground, its tongue like a black tree, its gullet breathing fire, its eyes like bowls of blood. It caught sight of me and roared and came forward in fury. I felt there was a fire burning before me, the world swam like a sea before my eyes, smoke rose up to the clouds. The ground trembled at its roar, the earth swam with its poison. I too roared, like a lion, and shot a diamond-tipped arrow, pinning one side of its mouth shut with the tongue still hanging out. Another arrow pinned the other side of its mouth, and a third went into its gullet. Blood bubbled up from its entrails, and, invoking God's power, I struck my ox-headed mace down on its head. I smashed it as I would an elephant's, and poison flowed from the wound like the river Nile. The river Kashaf brimmed with blood and turned yellow, and the earth was at peace again and could rest. The world witnessed this combat; afterwards I was known as "Sam who kills with one blow," and they showered me with gold and jewels. When I came back from that battle my armor had been burned from my body and I was left naked, my horse's barding had been stripped away, and for years the countryside there was covered with nothing but burned thorns and scrub.

"I have placed my foot on the heads of chieftains and led my horse where lions had their lairs: for many years now the saddle has been my throne, and I have subdued Mazanderan and the Gorgsaran, never thinking of my home, but always mindful of your glory and happiness. But now my shoulders and the blows of my mace are not what they were, and I am bent with age. My son Zal, a hero who is worthy to fight on your behalf, has taken my place, and he has one secret request, which he will come to ask of you. In Kabol he has seen a beautiful young woman, as elegant as a cypress tree, as lovely as a rose garden, and he has become crazy with love for her. The king should not be angry with him, since anyone who sees him pities his despair: he comes before your throne with a heavy heart, and I ask that you treat him as befits a nobleman. It is not for me to teach you wisdom or how to behave."

When the letter had been written, Zal took it, and the trumpets blared as he mounted his horse.

Mehrab's Anger with Sindokht

Once all this became known in Kabol, Mehrab was filled with fury. He peremptorily summoned Sindokht and vented his anger with Rudabeh against her. He said, "I don't have the forces to stand up against Persia's king; I've no choice but to kill you and your vile daughter in public, in the hope that that will placate him." At his words, Sindokht sank down, and her resourceful heart was filled with foreboding. Then she ran to the radiant king, her arms folded submissively over her breasts, and said, "Hear me out, and if you want to do something other than I suggest, do it. If you have wealth that you're prepared to give up in order to save your life, then bring it, and something good may come of this night. No matter how long the night lasts, its darkness must finally come to an end: day will dawn, and when the sun rises the world will glitter like a ruby." Mehrab replied, "Don't talk old wives' tales to a warrior. Say what you know, fight for your life, or prepare for your body to be veiled in blood."

Sindokht said, "My lord, I hope you will have no need to shed my blood. I must go to Sam, it's I who must draw this sword from its sheath. I shall risk my life and you, your wealth; give me treasure to take to him." Mehrab replied, "This is the key; we shouldn't worry about wealth. Take slaves, horses, thrones, and crowns, and be on your way. It may be that Kabol won't burn over our heads, and that his clouded heart will shine on us again." Sindokht said, "My lord, value your life rather than your wealth. But when I go looking for some solution to all this, you must not treat Rudabeh harshly. I care for her more than for anything in the world, and you must swear not to harm her." When her husband had sworn to this, she prepared to set out on horseback.

She dressed herself in gold-worked brocade, sewn with pearls and precious rubies. Then she poured out thirty thousand gold coins from the treasury, to which she added ten horses with golden trappings, fifty slaves with golden belts, fifty silver bridles and saddles for Arab and Persian horses, sixty slaves with golden torques, each bearing a goblet, one of which was filled with rubies, another with sugar, and the rest with musk, camphor, or gold. There were forty bolts of brocade with designs in gold and sewn with various jewels; two hundred Indian swords worked in silver and gold, the blades of thirty of which had been treated with poison; a hundred red-haired female camels, a hundred more to carry loads, a crown set with jewels, together with earrings, armbands and a torque, a golden throne studded with gems and as beautiful as the heavens, and four war elephants weighed down with carpets and clothes. When all this had been made ready she quickly mounted her horse and proceeded in state to Sam's court.

Sam Puts Sindokht's Mind at Rest

When she arrived she did not call out or give her name; instead she told the guards to say that someone had come as an envoy from Kabol, bringing a message from the warrior Mehrab to the world conqueror Sam. The chamberlain presented her news and was told to admit her. Sindokht dismounted and hurried before the king; she kissed the ground and made her obeisance before Sam and his noblemen. Then she had the slaves, horses, and other forms of wealth displayed one by one before Sam, and the column of gifts stretched for two miles. Sam was astonished at the sight and sat brooding on it, like a man in a drunken stupor; his arms were folded over his chest and he hung his head. He said to himself, "Where did all this come from, and why has it been brought here by a woman? If I accept these things from her, Manuchehr will be angry with me, and if I return them, Zal will rise up in fury like the Simorgh." Finally he said, "Give these to our treasurer, as gifts sent in the name of a beautiful woman from Kabol." Sindokht was reassured. She had three lovely girls with her, pale skinned and as elegant as cypresses; each of them held a goblet filled with rubies, pearls, and other jewels, and they poured these out pell-mell before the king, then exited from the court.

Sindokht said, "Young men become as wise as old men listening to your advice: great men are instructed by you, and your glory illuminates the dark world. Evil's hands are bound by your goodness, and the path to God is opened by your mace. If Mehrab has sinned, his eyelashes are wet with tears. The inhabitants of Kabol are innocent; what has their leader done that they should be destroyed? They are slaves beneath the dust of your feet, the whole town lives for you. Fear the Creator of reason and might, of the evening star and the sun; he will not approve of such an act from you; do not bind on your belt for bloodshed."

Sam said, "Answer whatever I ask you, and don't try to evade my questions. Are you Mehrab's servant or his wife, whose daughter Zal has seen? Tell me about this girl's face and hair, her character and wisdom, so that I can see whether she's worthy of him. Describe her stature to me, how she looks, and her manner; tell me everything about how she seems to you, point by point." Sindokht replied, "My lord, greatest of lords, first you must swear with such solemnity that the ground will tremble at it, that no harm will come to me or to any of those I love. I own castles and palaces, treasure and slaves: when I know that I am safe here, ask me what you wish and I will answer, and so preserve my honor. Then I shall bring all the treasure hidden in Kabol to Zavolestan."

Then Sam took his hand in hers, gently caressed it, and swore as she had requested. Sindokht kissed the ground and told him what had been hidden. She said, "I am from Zahhak's family and married to Mehrab: I am the mother of the beautiful Rudabeh, for whom Zal is ready to sacrifice his soul. Throughout the night until day dawns, all of us call down God's blessings on you and on King Manuchehr. Now I have come to know what you wish, and to find out who your friends and enemies are in Kabol. If we have sinned and are unworthy to rule there, I stand before you here in my misery: kill those who are worthy to die, imprison those who should be imprisoned, but do not burn the hearts of the innocent inhabitants of Kabol, an act which will only brings dark days upon you."

Sam saw that he was dealing with a clear-sighted and intelligent woman, whose face was as lovely as the spring-time, who had the stature of a cypress tree, whose waist was a slim as a reed, and who had the gait of a pheasant. He answered her, "I swear on my life that I shall keep faith with you. I approve of Zal's choice of Rudabeh as his wife, and may you, Kabol, and all who are dear to you live in safety and happiness. Although you are of another race than us, you are worthy of the crown and throne. This is the way of the world; there is no shame in it and there is no fighting with God's decrees: one is raised up and another cast down, one lives in wealth and another in want, one in happiness and another in misery. I have written a letter begging Manuchehr to look favorably on us, and Zal has taken it to him. He set off so quickly that it seemed he had grown wings, vaulting into the saddle without seeing it, and his horses' hooves seemed to take no account of the ground. The king will give him an answer; a smile will mean he agrees to our request. This prince who was brought up by a bird is in despair, the tears from his eyes moisten the earth at his feet, and if, in her love for him, his bride suffers as he does, it would be no surprise if the two of them died of grief. Show me the face of this child born of a dragon's race, and you will be rewarded."

Sindokht replied, "If you would make your slave's heart happy, ride to my palace. It will raise my head to the heavens in joy to bring a king like you to Kabol, where every one of us will be ready to sacrifice his life for you." Sindokht saw that Sam's face was all smiles, and that thoughts of revenge had been uprooted from his heart. She sent a messenger who rode as quickly as the wind to Mehrab, bearing the good news. "Forget all your suspicions and worries," she wrote. "Be happy in your heart and prepare to receive a guest. I shall come immediately after this letter and will not halt on the way."

The next day, as sunlight flowed into the world and men woke from sleep, Sindokht made her way to Sam's court, where she was greeted as the best of queens. She came before Sam and made her obeisance, and then spoke with him for a long time about her journey back to Kabol's king, and the preparations to receive Sam there as a guest. Sam said, "Go back, and tell Mehrab what you have seen here." Then he had a present prepared for her, consigning to her all that he owned in Kabol, including palaces, gardens, and farmland, and he also gave her flocks, carpets, and clothes. Then he took her hand in his and swore friendship with her, accepting her daughter, and giving her his warrior son, Zal. He concluded, "Stay in Kabol and be happy; have no fear of anyone who wishes you ill." Her face, which had been so downcast, blossomed again, and she set off home under a fortunate star.

Zal Delivers Sam's Letter to King Manuchehr

Manuchehr learned that Zal was approaching, and the nobles of his court went out to welcome him. A way was quickly cleared for him, and when he entered the court he kissed the ground and called down blessings on the king. For a long time he kept his eyes lowered, until the king bade him welcome and he approached the throne. The king asked him how he had endured the wind and dust of his journey, and he answered, "By your grace everything is made easy, and all troubles are a comfort." The king took the letter he carried, smiled, and acted affably toward him.

When he had read the letter Manuchehr said, "An ancient matter troubles my heart, and you have added to it. But your father Sam has written this letter with such anxiety and grief that I agree to your request and will think no more of the matter. I will see that you have your heart's desire, if this is what you wish, even though my heart is unsettled by it." Stewards brought in a golden table, and Manuchehr sat down before it with Zal and ordered the nobles to take their places beside them. When the king had finished eating, another area was prepared for them to drink together. Zal drank wine with the king, and then sat in his golden saddle and departed; throughout the night his heart was filled with thoughts, his lips with murmured words.

At daybreak he came to pay his respects to Manuchehr, who greeted him warmly, and, after he left, praised him in private. Then the king summoned priests, astrologers, and sages before the throne and commanded them to search the heavens. They spent three days with their astrolabes, laboriously studying the stars to know their secrets, and on the fourth they came before the king and said:

> *"Our calculations show the water here*
> *Will be a mighty current, strong and clear:*
> *The son of Zal and Rudabeh will be*
> *A hero famed for all eternity.*
> *Strength will be his, and swords, and praise,*
> *Battles and banquets will fill all his days,*
> *No eagle will outsoar him, and no lord*
> *Will be his equal; with his glittering sword*
> *He'll make the air weep, and his food will be*
> *A roasted wild ass, spitted on a tree.*
> *Prompt in his monarch's service, prompt to fight,*
> *Persia's protector and stout-hearted knight."*

The king said to them, "Keep what you have told me a secret" Then he summoned Zal so that they could question him.

Zal Is Tested

The sages sat with Zal and questioned him, to test his wisdom. One of them said, "There are twelve flourishing, splendid cypress trees, each of which has thirty branches."

Another said, "There are two fine, swiftly galloping horses, one black as a sea of pitch, the other white as clear crystal. They struggle and strive, but neither can overtake the other." A third said, "This is a wonder: there is a group of riders who pass by the prince, and sometimes there are

thirty of them when you look, sometimes twenty-nine.
One is not there, and then you count again and there are
thirty." A fourth said, "You see a beautiful meadow filled
with green plants and threaded with streams. A man comes
there, holding a huge scythe, and he cuts down the plants,
whether they are fresh or dry, never swerving aside as he
does so." Another said, "There are two cypresses rising
from the ocean, and a bird has built nests there. He sits on
one at night and on the other during the day. When he flies
up from the one its leaves wither and dry, and when he sits
on the other it exhales the scent of musk. One is always
withered, the other always fresh and fragrant." Another
said, "In the mountains I discovered a flourishing city, but
people left it, preferring a thorny waste, where they built
houses towering up to the moon; they forgot the flourishing city and never mentioned it. Then an earthquake came,
and their houses disappeared, and they longed for the city
they had left. Now, explain these sayings to us: if you can
do so, you will be turning dust to musk."

Zal sat deep in thought for a while; then he threw back
his shoulders, breathed deeply, and answered the priests'
questions, saying, "First, the twelve tall trees, each of
which has thirty branches, are the twelve months of the
year; twelve times the moon is renewed in her place, like a
new king seated on his throne, and each month has thirty
days; this is how time passes. As for the two horses who
gallop swiftly as fire, the white and the black striving to
overtake one another, they are night and day which pass
over us across the heavens. Third, the thirty horsemen you
spoke of who pass before the prince—of whom one is lacking, and then when one counts there are thirty again—these
signify the fact that in some months one night is sometimes
lacking. Now I shall unsheathe the sword of my speech and
explain the two trees on which the bird builds its nests.
From the sign of Aries to that of Libra the world lies in
darkness until it passes into the sign of Pisces, and the two

cypresses are the two halves of the heavens, of which one half is always withered and one fresh. The bird is the sun, which keeps the world in hope and fear. The city in the mountains is the eternal world, and the thorny waste is the fleeting world, which gives us now caresses and riches, and now pain and suffering. God counts your breaths and prolongs or breaks off your days; a wind arises and the earth shakes, and the world is filled with cries and lamentation. The man with the sharp scythe who cuts down both the fresh and withered plants, and who listens to no entreaties, is time the reaper and we are like the plants who are cut down, grandfather and grandchild alike, since he looks at neither young nor old but cuts down all in his path. This is the way of the world, and no man is born from his mother but to die."

When Zal finished his explanation, everyone there was astonished at his understanding. Manuchehr's heart was pleased; he enthusiastically applauded him and gave orders that a banquet as splendid as the full moon be held. They drank wine until the world grew dark and their wits were befuddled: the courtiers' cries resounded about the court, and when they left they did so happy and drunk, grasping one another's arms.

Zal Shows His Skill

When the sun's rays appeared above the mountains, and men woke from sleep, Zal came before the king like a ravening lion and asked permission to leave the court and rejoin his father. He said to the king, "I long to see Sam's face again, now that I have kissed the foot of your ivory throne and my heart has been gladdened by the sight of your crown and splendor." The king said to him, "Young hero, you must grant us one more day. It's love for Mehrab's daughter that makes you so eager to be off; what's this talk about missing Sam and Kabol?" Then he gave orders that cymbals, Indian bells, and trumpets be sounded in the great square.

Warriors gathered cheerfully there, bringing spears, maces, arrows, and bows. There was a huge tree that had flourished for many months and years in the square. Zal grasped his bow and urged his horse forward; he shot an arrow at the tree and the royal shaft pierced the great trunk. Then men bearing javelins set shields down; Zal asked his squire for a shield, squared his shoulders, and again urged his horse forward. He flung his bow aside, and grasped a javelin, which he hurled at three stacked shields with such force that it passed straight through them. The king turned to his noble warriors and said, "Which of you will fight him in single combat? One of you should challenge him." The warriors donned their armor, and their hearts were angry despite the cheerful remarks they made. They twitched their horses' reins and rode onto the square, grasping spears and shining lances. Zal charged forward, the dust rising from his horse's hooves, watching for which proud warrior would oppose him. Like a monster he galloped out of the dust, bearing down on a warrior and grasping him by the belt; he snatched him from the saddle with such ease that the king and his army stared in wonder. The assembly cried out that no one had ever seen his equal, and that the mother of any warrior who opposed him on the battlefield would be sure to wear the dark colors of mourning. No lion had ever given birth to such a hero; indeed he should not be considered a mere hero but a monster of war. And they said how fortunate Sam was, that he would leave such a brave horseman in the world as his heir when he died. The king congratulated him, as did the courtiers, and the company returned to the palace. There Manuchehr prepared such gifts for Zal that they astonished the noblemen present: there were valuable crowns and golden thrones, armbands, torques, and golden belts, as well as splendid sets of clothes, slaves, horses, and many other things.

Manuchehr Answers Sam's Letter

Manuchehr dictated an answer to Sam's letter: "Brave warrior, victorious as a lion in all your ventures: the heavens have not seen your like in battles and banquets, in policy and beauty. Your fine son has come to me, and I have learned of his wishes and the nature of his desire. I have granted all he has asked for and spent many happy days in his company. A lion like you, who has leopards as his prey, what else would he sire but a warlike lion cub? I send him back to you with a happy heart, and may evil keep its distance from him."

Zal left the court and dispatched an envoy to Sam with this message: "I am returning from the king; my heart is happy and I come with royal gifts, crowns, armbands, torques and ivory thrones." Sam was so overjoyed to receive this message that despite his age, his youth seemed to return to him. He dispatched an envoy to Kabol, telling Mehrab of Manuchehr's kind treatment of Zal, of the happiness that prevailed between them, and saying that both he and Zal would visit him as soon as Zal returned.

The envoy galloped to Kabol, and shouts of joy rose into the skies when he gave his news. The king of Kabol was beside himself with pleasure that he was to be related to the ruler of Zabolestan; musicians and entertainers were summoned, Mehrab's heart was cleared of all anxieties, and there was a perpetual smile on his lips. He called Sindokht to him and spoke kindly to her, saying, "You are a splendid wife, and your advice has brought us from darkness to light. You have planted such a sapling in the earth that princes pay homage to it. What you planned for has happened, and all my wealth is at your disposal, be it thrones or crowns or treasure." When Sindokht heard him she went to her daughter to tell her the news, and said, "Good news, you will soon see Zal; you have gained a husband who is worthy of you. A wife and husband with your nobility of spirit will not endure the world's reproaches. You rushed to fulfill your heart's desire, and now you have found everything you sought." Rudabeh replied, "You are the king's consort, and worthy of praise from everyone; the dust beneath your feet is my pillow, and your commands are my soul's comfort. May the eye of Ahriman be far from you, and your heart and soul always be filled with joy."

Sindokht heard her, and then she set about preparing the palace for their visitors. She had the audience hall decorated like a paradise, and rose water, wine, musk, and ambergris were placed there. She laid down a carpet worked in gold and sewn with emeralds, and another whose design was made of pearls, each of which shone like a drop of water. Then she placed a golden throne there, with Chinese patterns on it, studded with jewels that framed carved reliefs, and its feet were made of rubies. Next she turned her attention to Rudabeh, adorning her like a paradise and writing magical incantations to the sun to protect her. She confined her in her golden apartments and gave no one access to her. All of Kabol was made beautiful with colors, fine fragrances, and precious objects. Wine was brought, and the elephants' backs were draped with Rumi brocade, on which musicians sat, wearing golden diadems. The welcoming party was put together and slaves went ahead scattering musk and ambergris, and spreading silk and samite in the way. Musk and gold coins were scattered on the procession, and the ground was wet with rose water and wine.

Zal Returns to Sam

Meanwhile Zal made all speed homeward, like a flying eagle or a skiff skimming the water. No one was aware of his approach, and so no one went out to meet him, and suddenly a cry went up from the palace that Zal had arrived. Sam went happily out to greet him and clasped him in his arms, holding him close for a long time. When Zal had freed himself from his father's embrace, he kissed the ground, and then recounted all he had seen and heard. Sam

and Zal sat on thrones beside one another, and their lips
were all smiles as they talked of Sindokht's visit to Sam.
Sam said, "A message came from Kabol, and the envoy was
a woman called Sindokht. She wanted a promise from me
that I would not act badly to her, and I gave her this, and
then she asked for everything so charmingly that I granted
all of it. First she wanted Zavolestan's prince to marry the
princess of Kabol, then that you and I visit her as guests,
as recompense for the distress she had been through. Now
a messenger has come from her saying that this business
of her daughter has been settled; now, what should we tell
this messenger? What answer should we send Mehrab?"
Zal was so happy that he blushed like a tulip from head
to foot, and he answered, "If you think it's suitable, send
a detachment of troops, and we'll come after them; we
can visit them, because we have a lot to discuss together."
Sam looked at Zal, and he understood very well what his
son wanted; he knew that Zal could not sleep at night and
had no interest in any conversation that did not concern
Mehrab's daughter.

Sam gave orders that bells and Indian chimes signal their
departure; the royal pavilion was struck and a messenger
was sent on ahead to announce to Mehrab that Sam, Zal,
and a detachment of warriors and elephants would soon arrive. Mehrab had the drums sounded and trumpets blown,
and drew up his army so that it glittered like a rooster's
eye. The elephants and musicians, and the various banners
of red, white, yellow, and purple silk, made the earth seem
like a paradise: with the blare of trumpets and the sound
of harps, the squeal of bugles and the ringing of bells, it
seemed as if Judgment Day had come. This was the manner in which Mehrab went forward to welcome Sam, and
when he saw him he dismounted from his horse and walked
forward. Sam embraced him and asked him how fate had
dealt with him: Mehrab for his part called down blessings
on both Sam and Zal and then mounted his swift charger

again, like the new moon rising above the mountains. He placed a golden crown studded with jewels on Zal's head, and the group arrived in Kabol happily laughing and chatting together. The town was so full of the sounds of Indian chimes, lutes, harps, and trumpets that it seemed to be transformed; the horse's manes were soaked in musk, wine, and saffron, and drummers and trumpeters were mounted on elephants. Three hundred slaves carrying golden goblets filled with musk and jewels called down blessings on Sam and then scattered their goblets' jewels before him, and whoever came to the festivities wanted for nothing.

Sam smiled and said to Sindokht, "How long are you going to keep Rudabeh hidden?" In the same manner Sindokht replied, "And where is the gift you will give, if you wish to see the sun?" Sam answered, "Ask me for whatever you wish." They went to the golden apartments, in which the happiness of spring awaited them. There Sam looked at Rudabeh and was overcome with wonder; he did not know how to praise her adequately, or how to keep his eyes from being dazzled by her splendor. Then he commanded Mehrab to come forward, and the marriage was solemnized according to ancient custom. Zal and Rudabeh were sat side by side on one throne, and agates and emeralds were scattered over them. Rudabeh wore a splendid diadem and Zal, a jewel-studded crown. A list of the treasures he was giving them was brought by Mehrab, and as it was read out, it seemed men's ears could not listen until its end. From there they went to a banqueting hall, where they sat with wine cups in their hands for a week, and then returned to the palace where the festivities went on for three more weeks.

At the beginning of the following month Sam began his journey home to Sistan, together with Zal, their elephants and drums, and the troops who had accompanied him. Zal had howdahs and litters made for Mehrab's women folk, and a palanquin for Rudabeh, and she, Sindokht, Mehrab and their family set out for Sistan. They traveled happily, praising God for his gifts, and arrived in high spirits, laughing and smiling. Then Sam bestowed sovereignty over Sistan on Zal and unfurled his auspicious banner to lead his troops once again toward the land of the Gorgsaran and Bactria.

THE BIRTH OF ROSTAM

It was not long before Rudabeh's cypress-slim form began to change; her belly filled out, her body grew heavy, and the Judas blossoms of her face turned as sallow as saffron. Her mother said to her, "My soul, what's happened that you look so yellow?" She replied, "My lips moan day and night; my time has come, and I cannot give birth to the burden within me. My skin feels as though it were stuffed with stones, or that it contained a mass of iron." Rudabeh endured this until the time for her to give birth came closer, and she could neither sleep nor rest. Then one day she fainted, and a cry went up from Zal's palace; Sindokht was informed, and she clawed at her face and tore out her musky hair. The news reached Zal that the leaves of his noble cypress tree had withered away, and he came to her pillow, sick at heart and with tears in his eyes. Then he remembered the Simorgh's feather and smiled, and he told Sindokht to take heart. He brought a brazier and lit a fire, in which he burned a little of the Simorgh's feather. Immediately the air darkened, and the bird appeared, ready to do his bidding, like pearls raining down from a dark cloud; I say pearls, but it was peace to the soul that she brought. Zal made his obeisance before the bird and praised her. The Simorgh said to him, "Why are you sad, why are the lion's eyes wet with tears? A cub eager for fame will be born to you from this silver cypress:

> *He'll master all the beasts of earth and air,*
> *He'll terrify the dragon in its lair;*
> *When such a voice rings out, the leopard gnaws*
> *In anguished terror its unyielding claws;*
> *Wild on the battlefield that voice will make*
> *The hardened hearts of iron warriors quake;*
> *Of cypress stature and of mammoth might,*
> *Two miles will barely show his javelin's flight.*

"For him to be born into the world, you must bring a glittering knife, and a man familiar with spells. First, make the beautiful Rudabeh drunk with wine, and so drive fear and worry from her heart. Don't watch as the sorcerer begins his incantations to bring out this lion from within her body: he will cut open the cypress's belly, and she will feel no pain. Then, driving all fear and anxiety from your heart, you must sew up the wound where the sorcerer cut her. Pound the herb I will describe to you in milk and musk, and dry the mixture in the shade. Massage this into her wound, and you will see it heal within the day. After this, stroke her body with my feather, since its shadow will be auspicious. You should rejoice at this and give thanks to God; it was he who gave you this royal tree, which every day brings you greater good fortune. Do not be sad at this turn of events; your noble sapling is about to bear fruit." She plucked a feather from her wing and let it fall, then flew upwards and was gone. Zal retrieved the feather, and did as the Simorgh had told him. This was a wonder, and the world watched, weeping and apprehensive. Sindokht cried desperate tears,

wondering when the baby would be delivered from her
daughter's body.

A skilled priest came, and made the lovely Rudabeh
drunk with wine. She felt no pain as he cut open her side,
and turned the baby's head toward the opening. He brought
the child forth so painlessly that no one in the world had
ever seen such a wonder.

> *The child was like a lion, a noble son,*
> *Tall and handsome, lovely to look upon;*
> *And all who saw this mammoth baby gazed*
> *In wonder at him, murmuring and amazed.*

For a day and a night the mother slept from the effects of
the wine, and her heart knew nothing of what happened.
They sewed up her wound and massaged the scar with the
mixture the Simorgh had described. When she woke from
her sleep and spoke to Sindokht the onlookers gave thanks
to God and showered her with jewels and gold coins. She
smiled when she saw her noble child, because she saw the
signs of royal glory in him, and said, "I escaped (rastam)
from my peril, my pain came to an end," and so they named
the boy Rostam.

They sewed a doll of silk, that was the same height as
this lion who had not yet tasted milk, and stuffed it with
sable fur. Its face shone like the sun and the evening star.
They traced a dragon on its bicep, placed a lion's paw in its
hand, tucked a lance beneath its arm, and put a mace in one
hand and reins in the other. Then they sat it on a charger
surrounded by servants, scattered gold coins over the group,
and sent this image of Rostam with his mace to Sam.

Festivities were held from Zavolestan to Kabol; all the
plain was filled with the sound of trumpets and the drinking
of wine, and there was a banquet for a hundred guests in
every corner of the kingdom. Musicians were everywhere
in Zavolestan, and commoners and noblemen sat together

as intimately as the warp and weft of one cloth. They took the image of the unweaned Rostam to Sam, whose hair prickled with pleasure. "This silken doll resembles me, and if his body is half this size, his head will touch the clouds." Then he called for the messenger to come forward, and showered gold coins over him till they covered his head. The joyful din of drums rang out from the court, and the royal square glittered like a rooster's eye. Sam called for wine and musicians, distributed gold coins to the poor, and held such a banquet that the sun and moon gazed down in wonder. He answered Zal's letter, beginning with praise of Creator and the good fortune that had come to them; next he praised Zal, the lord of the sword and mace, and then turned to the silken doll, who displayed the shoulders of a warrior and the glory of a king. He told Zal that he should preserve it so carefully that no breath of wind could harm it, and added that he had prayed night and day that he would live long enough to see a hero grow from Zal's seed, and now that this child had been born to them, their chief duty was to pray for his life.

Sam Comes to See Rostam

So the world went forward, and things that had been hidden were revealed. Ten wet nurses were set to suckle Rostam, since it is milk that gives a man his strength. When he was weaned, his food was oak apples and meat; he ate enough for five grown men and people were astonished at his appetite. When he was eight spans high, he seemed like a noble cypress tree, and his face shone like a star, at which the world stared in wonder. He seemed to be Sam himself, in his stature, appearance, opinions, and behavior. When news reached brave Sam that Zal's son had grown to be like a lion and that no one in the world had ever seen such a young man with his warrior-like qualities, Sam's heart beat faster and he longed to see the boy. He entrusted his army to a commander and went with a detachment of experienced fighters toward Zavolestan, led there by the love he felt for Zal's son.

When Zal heard of his father's approach, he had drums strapped on elephants and the earth turned the color of ebony beneath the cavalry's hooves. He and Mehrab and the governor of Kabol set out as a welcoming party; a pebble was thrown into a goblet, which was the signal for the soldiers to mount, and a great cry went up on all sides. All the valley was filled with troops, the earth turned as black as pitch and the air was dark with dust. The neighing of Arab horses and the trumpeting of elephants could be heard for five miles. One elephant bore a golden throne, on which sat Zal's son, with his cypress-stature and huge shoulders and chest. On his head was a crown, he wore a belt about his waist, and carried a shield in front of his body and a heavy mace in his hand. When Sam appeared in the distance, the army divided into two columns, and Zal and Mehrab, the youth and the warrior of many years, dismounted and bowed their heads to the ground, calling down blessings on the hero Sam. As Sam caught sight of the lion cub on the elephant's back his face opened like a blossom; they led the boy forward on his elephant and Sam stared at him, taking in his crown and throne. Brave Sam called down blessings on him, saying "My lion cub, incomparable child, may you live long and happily!"

Rostam kissed the throne and, what was wonderful, praised his grandfather in a new way:

> *"Live happily, my lord, the sturdy root*
> *From which I, Rostam, am the newest shoot.*
> *I'm Sam's devoted slave, and while I live*
> *The pleasures feasting, sleep, and comfort give*
> *Will not beguile me. Helmets, armor, bows*
> *That I can draw against our country's foes,*
> *My saddle and my horse, my mace and sword,*
> *These will be all my life, my noble lord.*

> *My face resembles yours, and when I fight*
> *May I resemble you in dauntless might."*

Then he climbed down from the elephant's back, and Sam took him by the hand, kissing his eyes and head, and the elephants and drums stayed still and silent. They set off for Gourabeh, smiling and chatting as they rode, and when they arrived they sat in the palace on a golden throne, feasting in happiness. They spent a month in this manner, untroubled by hardship, and music accompanied their feasting, with each of them singing in turn. In one corner of the dais sat Zal, in the opposite corner Rostam, with his mace in his hand, and between them was Sam, with the feathers from the lammergeyer, signifying royal glory, depending from his crown. He stared in awe at Rostam, and from time to time he would call down blessings on the youth's arms and shoulders, his reed-like waist and noble chest. Then he turned to Zal and said, "You could question a hundred generations and never hear of one who was born in such a manner. There is no one in the world who is as handsome as he is, or who has his stature and shoulders. Come, let us drink wine in celebration of this happiness, and may it drive all sorrow from our hearts, since the world is fleeting; we arrive and depart, and as one grows old another is born."

> *They drank their wine, and in their cups they praised*
> *Zal after Rostam. But Mehrab was dazed*
> *With drink, and in his drunkenness he said*
> *The arrogant ideas that filled his head.*
> *"I don't consider Zal as anything,"*
> *He said, "and Sam's as worthless as the king.*
> *Rostam and me, we are the heroes here,*
> *The clouds daren't pass above us, out of fear.*

And I'll renew Zahhak's power, you'll soon see,
And all of you will have to bow to me."

But Zal and Sam laughed at Mehrab's boastful words.

At the beginning of the month of Mehr Sam set off once
more. He said to Zal, "My son, see that you act justly, with
your heart ready to serve your kings, choosing wisdom
over wealth, always keeping your hands from evil deeds,
and striving to do God's will. Know that the world tarries
for no man; take care of what I say, follow my advice, and
tread only in the path of righteousness. I feel in my heart
that my time here is coming to an end." Then he said farewell to his son and grandson, admonishing them not to
forget his words. Chimes sounded from the court, and the
blare of trumpets was heard from the elephants' backs. Sam
left for Bactria; his heart was filled with love and he spoke
kindly to his son and grandson, whose faces were stained
with tears, and whose hearts were filled with his precepts,
as they accompanied him for three stages of the way. Then
they turned back, and Sam continued on his long journey.

ROSTAM AND HIS HORSE RAKHSH

Rostam Chooses a Horse

Zal said to Rostam, "You have grown so tall,
Your cypress body towers above us all.
The work that lies ahead of us will keep
Our restless spirits from their food and sleep;
You're still a boy, not old enough to fight,
Your heart still looks for pleasure and delight,
Your mouth still smells of milk, how can I ask
You to take on this seasoned warrior's task,
To fight with lion warriors, and beat
Them back until they scatter in defeat?
What do you say to this? What will you do?
May health and greatness always partner you!"
And Rostam answered Zal: "Pleasure and wine,
Feasting and rest, are no concern of mine—
Hard-pressed in war, or on the battlefield,
With God to aid me, I shall never yield.
I need to capture with my noose a horse
Of mountain size and weight, of mammoth force,
I need a crag-like mace if I'm to stand
Against Turan, defending Persia's land.
I'll crush their heads with this tremendous mace
And none shall dare oppose me face to face—
Its weight will break an elephant, one blow
From it will make a bloody river flow."

Zal was so moved by his son's words that his soul seemed about to leave his body.

Rostam Chooses Rakhsh

Zal had all the herds of horses that were in Zavolestan, as well as some from Kabol, driven before Rostam, and the herdsmen explained to him the royal brands that they bore. Whenever Rostam selected a horse, as soon as he pressed down on it, the horse's back would buckle beneath his strength, so that its belly touched the ground. But then a herd of horses of varying colors from Kabol was driven past him, and a gray mare galloped by; she had a chest like a lion's, and was short-legged; her ears were pricked like glittering daggers, her fore and hindquarters were plump, and she was narrow-waisted. Behind her came a foal, of the same height and breadth of chest and rump as his mother, black eyed and holding his tail high, with black testicles, and iron hooves.

> *His body was a wonder to behold,*
> *Like saffron petals, mottled red and gold.*

Rostam watched the mare go by, and when he saw the mammoth-bodied foal he looped his lariat, and said, "Keep that foal back from the herd." The old herdsman who had brought the horses said, "My lord, you can't take other people's horses." Rostam asked who owned the horse, since its rump bore no trace of any brand. The herdsman said, "Don't look for a brand, but there are many tales told about this horse. No one knows who owns him; we call him 'Rostam's Rakhsh', and that's all I know. He's been ready to be saddled for three years now, and a number of nobles have chosen him; but whenever his mother sees a horseman's lariat she attacks like a lioness." Rostam flung his royal lariat, and quickly caught the horse's head in its noose; the mother came forward like a raging lioness, as if she wanted to bite his head off. But Rostam roared like a lion, and the sound of his voice stopped the mare in her tracks. She stumbled, then scrambled up again and turned, and galloped off to join the rest of the herd. Rostam tightened the noose and pulled the foal toward himself; he pushed down with all his hero's strength on the foal's back, but the back did not give at all, and it was as if the foal was unaware of Rostam's hand. Rostam said to himself, "This will be my mount; now I will be able to set to work. He will be able to bear the weight of my armor, helmet, and mace, and my mammoth body. He asked the herdsman, "Who knows the price of this dragon?" The herdsman replied, "If you are Rostam, then mount him and defend the land of Iran. The price of this horse is Iran itself, and mounted on his back you will be the world's savior." Rostam's coral lips smiled, and he said, "It is God who does such good works."

He set a saddle on Rakhsh, and his head whirled with thoughts of war and vengeance. He opened Rakhsh's mouth and saw that he was a swift, strong, courageous horse. Each night Rostam burned wild rue before him to ward off evil; from every side Rakhsh seemed to be a magical creature, swift in battle, with large haunches, alert and foaming at the mouth.

> *Rakhsh and his noble rider seemed to bring*
> *To Zal's reviving heart the joy of spring.*

Zal opened the doors to his treasury and distributed gold coins, careless of today and tomorrow.

King Manuchehr died, and his son, Nozar, became king. Nozar was a worthless ruler, and Afrasyab, the king of Turan, attacked Iran, three times defeating Nozar's armies in battle. Eventually Afrasyab captured and killed Nozar, and assumed the Persian throne. A group of Persian noblemen, led by Zal, chose an aged royal prince, Zav, as the Persian king, hoping that he would be able to unite the country and drive Afrasyab and his forces back to Turan; but Zav died before he was able to muster sufficient forces to accomplish this. Zal decided that he had no choice but to lead the counterattack himself.

ROSTAM AND KAY QOBAD

Zal Leads His Army Against Afrasyab

Then from the back of an elephant Zal threw a pebble in a goblet as a sign to mount and gave a shout that could be heard for miles. The din of drums and blare of bugles mingled with the sounds of Indian bells and the trumpeting of elephants: the Day of Judgment seemed to have come to Zavolestan, as if the earth were crying out to its dead, "Rise." Rostam led the army, followed by the land's experienced warriors; it was spring time as they set out, and the world was filled with blossoms and flowers.

Afrasyab learned of Zal's approach, and from then on he could neither rest nor eat in his anxiety. He led his army toward the river at Rey, where the marshy reed beds are. The Persian army left the desert and made for the battlefield, until only two parasangs separated the two sides. Zal called a council of his experienced advisors and said to them: "You have seen the world and are wise in its ways; we have drawn up our army here and hope for a favorable outcome. But we are not of one mind as we were, and this is because

the throne lacks a king; everything is unsure now, and the
army has no leader. We need someone of royal lineage to
take his place on the throne and bind on the belt of authority. A priest has told me of such a king, one who possesses
the royal *farr*, and whose good fortune is still young. This
is Kay Qobad, who is descended from Feraydun; he is an
imposing man, wise, and just." Then Zal turned to Rostam
and said, "Take your mace now and throw back your shoulders; choose a group of companions and ride quickly to the
Alborz mountains. Greet Kay Qobad respectfully but do
not delay your return; you must be back here in two weeks,
so do not rest for any reason along the way. Say to him,
'The army is asking for you, and it has prepared the royal
throne in your honor.'" Quick as the wind, Rostam bound
on his belt and set off to fetch Kay Qobad. He brought
him to Zal during the night, saying not a word to anyone
about his arrival, and Zal sat with him and his advisors for
a week, discussing what should be done.

The Reign of Kay Qobad

On the eighth day the ivory throne was made ready, and
the royal crown suspended above it. Kay Qobad seated himself there and placed the jeweled crown on his head. The
chieftains were gathered—men like Zal and warlike Qaren,
Kherdad, Keshvad and Barzin—and they scattered jewels
over the newly crowned king. He listed to what they had to
say about Afrasyab and reviewed his troops. On the following day the noise of preparations was heard from the royal
pavilion, and Qobad led his army out. Rostam put on his
armor, and the dust he raised made him seem like a maddened elephant. The ranks of the Persian army marched to
war, ready for bloodshed: one wing was led by Mehrab, the
king of Kabol, and the other by Gazhdahom. Qaren was in
the center, together with Keshvad, the breaker of armies.
Zal followed them, with Kay Qobad, and it was as if there
were fire on the one side of him, wind on the other. In front

of the troops the Kaviani banner fluttered, dyeing the world scarlet, yellow, and purple, like a ship lifted on a wave above the Sea of China. The plains and mountain slopes were a mass of shields, and swords glittered like torches; from end to end the world was like a sea of pitch over which twinkled a hundred thousand candles. You would think the sun would lose its way, with the squeal of the trumpets and din of the army.

Rostam's Combat with Afrasyab

Once battle was joined, Qaren was involved in every charge, sometimes riding to the left, sometimes to the right, everywhere eager for bloodshed. When Rostam saw how he fought, he went to his father and said, "Tell me what position the evil Afrasyab keeps during battle. What does he wear? Where does his banner flutter above the troops? Is that shining purple banner his? I will grasp him by the belt today and drag him down from his saddle." Zal answered, "Listen to me, my son, look after yourself today; that Turk is a fire-breathing dragon in combat, a cloud that rains down disaster. His banner is black, as is his armor; his arms are encased in iron, and his helmet is of iron. All the surface of his iron armor is chased with gold, and his black banner is affixed to his helmet. Keep yourself safe from him, because he is a brave man, and fortune favors him with victory." Rostam said, "Don't trouble your soul about me; the world's creator is my ally, and my heart, my sword, and my arm are my refuge."

Then as the trumpets sounded Rostam urged his brazen-hoofed Rakhsh forward, and when Afrasyab caught sight of him he paused in wonder at this immature youth. He said to his warriors, "Who is that dragon who has escaped from his bonds? Who is he? I don't know his name." One of his men replied, "That is Zal's son. Can't you see that he has come here with Sam's mace? He's young, and eager to win a name for himself." Like a vessel lifted high on a wave, Afrasyab went ahead of his army, and when Rostam saw him he gripped his thighs against Rakhsh and lifted his heavy mace to his shoulders. As he drew level with Afrasyab he brought his mace crashing down on the king's saddle, then reached out and grasped at his belt, lifting him from his leopard-skin saddle. He wanted to take him back to Qobad, as a trophy from his first day of battle, but his strength and the weight of Afrasyab between them were too much for the belt, which split, so that Afrasyab's head lay in the dirt, and his cavalry quickly gathered about him and hid him in the dust they sent up. When the king slipped out of his grasp like this, Rostam bit the back of his hand in anger. "Why," he said, "didn't I tuck him under my arm, instead of hanging on to his belt?"

Bells rang out from the elephants' backs, and the din of drums could be heard for miles, when they brought the good news to Qobad, that Rostam had broken the center of the Turks' army. They said, "When Rostam reached the Turkish king, his black banner disappeared; Rostam grasped him by his belt and flung him down to the ground, so that a cry of consternation went up from the Turks." Qobad sprang to his feet, and his army surged forward like a sea whipped up by the wind. Everywhere was the sound of weapons clashing, the glitter of daggers, the shock of wood against armor. Protected by their golden helmets and golden shields, men's heads became dazed by the shock and din of blows. It was as if a cloud had rained vermillion down by magic, staining the earth with red dye. One thousand one hundred and sixty brave warriors were killed at a stroke, and the Turks fled before the Persians, retreating to Damghan; from there they made their way to the Oxus, sick at heart and weary, filled with rumors and reproaches, their armor shattered and their belts loosened, unheralded by trumpets or drums, bereft of their strength.

Afrasyab Sees His Father

From the river bank Afrasyab went to his father in despair, his tongue filled with words. He said, "Exalted king, you sinned when you looked for vengeance in this way. First, no one in the past ever saw great kings break their word. And Iraj's seed has not been eradicated from the land, and no antidote has been found for this poison. When one goes, another takes his place, and the world will not remain without a leader. Qobad has come forward and placed the crown on his head, and has opened up a new way to warfare. And a horseman has appeared of Sam's race; Zal named him Rostam. He came forward like a hideous monster, and the ground seemed scorched by his breath. He attacked everywhere, striking with his sword and mace; the air was filled with the sound of his mace's blows, and my soul was not worth a fistful of dirt before his might. He shattered our army, and no one in the world had ever seen such a wonder. He caught sight of my banner and brought his mace down on my leopard-skin saddle; then he grasped at my belt and lifted me up as if I weighed no more than a mosquito. My belt split, and I fell from his grasp on the ground, and my men dragged me away from him. I see no alternative to making peace, because your army cannot withstand his onslaught. The lands which Feraydun bestowed on Tur have been given to me, and you should renounce this ancient longing for revenge. You know that being told about something is not the same as seeing it; something is always lacking when you only hear about a subject. War with Iran seemed like a game to you, but this has proven to be a hard game for your army to play. Consider how many golden helmets and golden shields, how many Arab horses with golden bridles, how many Indian swords with golden scabbards, and how many famous warriors Qobad has ruined. And worse than this, your name and reputation, which can never be restored, have been destroyed. Don't think of past resentments, try to be reconciled with Kay Qobad. If you

decide on any other course of action, armies will converge
on you from four directions; from one side Rostam, a blaz-
ing sun against whom there is no defense, will attack; from
another Qaren, who has never looked on defeat; from a
third Keshvad, with his golden diadem, who has attacked
Amol; and from a fourth Mehrab, the lord of Kabol, who
leads Zal's armies."

Pashang Sues for Peace

The king of the Turks' eyes filled with tears as he listened in
silence to Afrasyab's words. He told a scribe to bring paper
and ink made from musk; the calligraphy of the letter this
man wrote was so beautiful that it was worthy of a master,
and it was decorated with colors and images. Pashang dictated: "In the name of the lord of the sun and moon, who
has bestowed authority on us; may his blessings be on the
soul of Feraydun, who is the warp and weft of our ancestry.
If, in his ambition for the crown and throne, Tur acted evilly toward the Iraj, and there is much to be said about this,
their quarrel must now be put to rest. Manuchehr has taken
revenge for what happened to Iraj, and Feraydun showed
us the true way when he divided the lands into separate
realms. We should commit our hearts to this division and
not ignore the customs and wisdom of our ancestors. At
that time Tur's imperial tents were pitched in Transoxiana,
and the River Oxus marked the border. Iraj did not covet
this area; he was given the land of Persia by Feraydun. If
we break this agreement and go to war, we make life hard
for ourselves, we wound ourselves with our own swords,
and provoke God's wrath, so that we shall inherit nothing,
neither in this world nor the world to come. We should
respect the division that Feraydun made between Salm, Tur,
and Iraj, and renounce all thoughts of vengeance, for these
lands are not worth the disasters we have brought on ourselves. Our heads have grown as white as snow, and the
ground has been dyed vermilion with Kayanid blood, but

in the end a man owns only the earth in which he lies; five cubits of ground are all we inherit, linen covers us, and we lie in the grave. Ambition's door leads to sorrow and suffering, and our hearts remain heavy while we live in the fleeting world. If Kay Qobad will accept our terms, if his wise mind will incline to justice, none of our men will think even in their dreams of crossing the Oxus, and the Persians will not come here, except to bring greetings and a message of peace; in this way our two countries will live prosperously and happily."

The king sealed the letter and dispatched a detachment of men to take it to Kay Qobad. The messengers handed over the letter, and also spoke at length. Kay Qobad answered, "We did not attack first. It was Tur who committed the first crime by destroying Iraj, and in our own time Afrasyab crossed the Oxus and invaded Iran. You have heard what he did to King Nozar, so that even the beasts of the field grieved for him. And the way he acted with the wise Aghriras was not worthy of a chivalrous man. If you regret these evil acts, and will renew our treaties, I harbor no ambitions or desire for revenge, since I am prepared to leave this fleeting world. I grant you your side of the Oxus, in the hopes that Afrasyab will be content with this." And he wrote out a new treaty, planting a tree in the garden of greatness.

But Rostam said to him, "Your majesty, do not look for reconciliation in place of war; peace is not what they deserve; let them see what I can do with my mace in their land." The king replied, "I have never seen anything better than justice: Pashang is Feraydun's grandson, and he and his son have had enough of warfare. A wise man should not seek to be underhanded or unjust. I have written a charter on silk granting you suzerainty over Zavolestan, as far as the Sea of Sind. May you wear the crown and sit on the throne there, illuminating the world. Give Kabol to Mehrab, but keep your spear points dipped in poison, for wherever there is a kingdom, there is warfare, however great the realm may be." He placed a golden crown on Rostam's head and a golden belt about his waist, as a sign that he gave these territories into his keeping. Rostam kissed the ground before him. Then Qobad said, "May the throne never be without Zal; the world is not worth one of his hairs, and he serves to remind us of the great men of the past." He sent Zal clothes of royal cloth of gold, and a belt and crown set with rubies and turquoises. On five elephants they placed howdahs set with turquoises that glittered more splendidly than the waters of the Nile, and draped the howdahs in cloth of gold. Qobad sent Zal treasures the like of which no man had ever seen, with the message, "I wished to send you a more splendid present, and if I live a long life I will see that you want for nothing in this world." He distributed suitable gifts to Qaren, Keshvad, Barzin, Kherrad, and Pulad, and these included gold and silver coins, swords, shields, crowns, and belts.

Kay Qobad Travels to Estakhr in Pars

Then he set out for Pars, where the key to all his treasures lay. His palace was at Estakhr, where the Kayanid kings ruled in glory. The world paid him homage as he ascended the throne, ruling with wisdom and splendor and according to custom. He said to his nobles, "From end to end the world is mine, and if an elephant fights with a mosquito, this is a breach of justice and faith. I want nothing but righteousness in the world, because to provoke God's anger will bring want to our land. Ease comes from effort, and wherever there is water and earth, there is my treasure. The cities and armies are mine, and my kingdom depends on the army. Live safely, protected by the lord of the world; be wise and live at peace. May those who have wealth enjoy it and share it, and be grateful to me that I enable them to do this. And whoever is hungry and cannot feed himself by his labor, my court will be his pasture, and I will welcome all who come to me." Then he remembered the example of past heroes and made the world flourish with his justice and generosity.

In this way he lived at peace for a hundred years; what kings have there been in the world who can compare with him? He had four wise sons: the first was Kay Kavus, the second Kay Arash, the third Kay Pashin, and the fourth Ashkas. When he had reigned for a hundred years, his strength began to wane; he knew that death was near and that the green leaves of his life had withered. He summoned Kavus and spoke to him of justice and generosity. He said, "I am ready for my last journey. Lower my coffin into the ground and take your place on the throne, this throne that passes from us before we know, and whose servants are without wisdom: I feel I am still that man who came so happily with his companions from the Alborz mountains. If you rule justly and righteously, you will be on a journey to the heavens; and if greed and ambition snare your mind, you will be unsheathing a dark sword that will be used against you."

He finished speaking, and then departed from the splendid world, exchanging his palace for a coffin. This is the world's way, which raises us from the dust and disperses us on the wind.

KAY KAVUS'S WAR AGAINST
THE DEMONS OF MAZANDERAN

The Reign of Kay Kavus

If a noble tree grows tall and is then damaged in some way, its leaves wither, its roots weaken, and its summit begins to droop; and if it snaps, it must give way to a new shoot that, when spring comes, will bud and blossom like a shining lamp. If a sickly branch grows from a good root, you should not curse the root for this. In the same way, when a father cedes his place to his son and acquaints him with the secrets of life, if the son then brings shame on his father's name and glory, then call him a stranger, not a son. If he slights his father's example, he deserves to suffer at the hands of fate. This is the way of the ancient world, and you cannot tell what will grow from a given root.

When Kavus took his father's place, all the world was his slave. He saw that he owned treasures of all kinds, and that the earth was his to command: the throne was his, the royal torque and earrings, the golden crown set with emeralds, and Arab horses with streaming manes, and he considered no one in the world to be his equal.

One day he was in a pleasure garden, seated on a golden throne with crystal feet, drinking wine with the Persian chieftains and talking of this and that. A musician, who was in reality a demon, came asking for audience with the king. He said, "I'm renowned in Mazanderan for my sweet voice; if I'm worthy to appear before the king, let me approach his throne." The chamberlain went behind the curtain and said to the king, "There is a musician at the gate with a lute; he sings very sweetly." Kavus gave orders to admit him, and they sat him down with his instrument. He began to sing:

> "My country is Mazanderan—may she
> Abide forever in prosperity;
> Her gardens bloom with roses all year long,
> Wild hyacinths, a myriad tulips throng
> Her mountain slopes; her climate's sweet and clear,
> Not hot, not cold, but springtime all the year;
> Her perfumed air revives the soul—it seems
> Rose water rushes in her mountain streams;
> In every month wild tulips can be seen
> Dotting the hillsides' and the meadows' green;
> Her serving girls are lovely to behold,
> And there's good hunting there, and wealth, and gold."

While Kavus was listening to this song, he conceived the idea of conquering Mazanderan with his army. He said to his warriors, "We have spent our time feasting, and while a brave man idles his time away, weak enemies grow strong. My throne is greater than that of Jamshid or Zahhak or Kay Qobad, and my justice is greater than theirs. I should be greater than them in my accomplishments as well; a king should be ambitious to conquer the world." When the nobles heard what he had to say, none of them approved. They frowned, and their faces turned sallow; none of them had any desire to make war on demons. No one said anything openly, but they sighed in silence. Tus, Gudarz, Keshvad,

Giv, Kherrad, Gorgin and Bahram said, "We are your slaves and tread the earth at your command." But later they sat together and discussed the king's words: "What kind of a calamity is this? If what the king said in his cups isn't forgotten, we and Iran are facing a disaster. There will be no country, water, or land left to us. Even Jamshid, with his crown and his seal ring by which he had birds and demons under his command, never thought of fighting against the demons of Mazanderan. And Feraydun, who had such knowledge and was skilled in magic, never considered this as a possibility." Then Tus said, "Brave lords, experienced in battle, there is one solution, and it should not be hard to achieve what we desire. We must send a messenger to Zal saying, 'Come immediately; if your head is smeared with mud, do not stop to wash it clean.' He should be able to give the king wise advice, to tell him that it's Ahriman who has put this idea in his mind, and that one should never open doors behind which demons wait. It may be that Zal can make him change his mind; if he cannot, then our fortunes, good and bad, are at an end."

After they had discussed the matter at length, they dispatched a courier. He made good speed, and when he reached Zal he passed on his message: "The nobles send greetings to Zal, the son of Sam. A strange event has happened, and our minds are unable to deal with it. If you are not prepared to help us, no one here will be left alive and our land will disappear. Ahriman has led our king astray; he has no intention of living as our ancestors did, he wastes the wealth he took no pains to accumulate, and he intends to attack Mazanderan. If you pause even long enough to scratch your head, the king will have left and thrown to the winds all the trouble you took in Kay Qobad's service. Evil thoughts have twisted the king's soul, so that everything that you and your lion cub Rostam have done seems so much wind to him."

Zal was deeply troubled to hear that the leaves of the royal tree had turned yellow in this way. He said, "Kavus is an arrogant man who has not experienced the heat and cold of this world. A king should be someone over whose head the sun and moon have passed for many years. He thinks nobles and commoners alike tremble before his sword, and it will be no surprise if he pays no attention to my advice. It will hurt me if he doesn't listen to me, but if I make light of this in my heart and forget my loyalty to the king, neither God, nor the king, nor Iran's heroes will approve of me. I will go to him and give him what advice I can. It will be best for him if he accepts it; but, if he insists on what he has decided, the roads are open, and Rostam will be there with the army."

Zal spent the long night deep in thought, and when the sun raised its crown above the horizon he set off with his chieftains to the king. News reached Tus, Gudarz, Giv, Bahram, Gorgin, and Roham that Zal was approaching Iran, and that his banner was now visible. The army's commanders went out to meet him, calling down blessings on him and conducting him to the court. Tus said to him, "We are grateful that you have decided to help Iran's nobles and are going to this trouble on our behalf. We all wish you well and are filled with respect for the glory of your crown." Zal replied, "When a man has lived for some years he remembers the advice of his elders, and this is why the heavens deal justly with him. We should not withhold our advice from him, because he certainly needs it. If he ignores the wisdom of what we suggest, he will live to regret it." With one voice they replied, "We are yours to command, and consider no one else's advice to be of any value compared with yours."

The group entered the court, with Zal going ahead and the other nobles with their golden belts following him. When Zal saw Kavus sitting in state on the throne, he bent his arms submissively across his chest and lowered his head.

He said, "Lord of the world, whose head is lifted higher than those of all other noblemen and chieftains, no one has seen a king like you occupying the throne, or a crown like yours, and the heavens have never heard of good fortune like yours. May all your years be filled with victory and prosperity, your heart always filled with knowledge, your head with wisdom." The king made much of him and sat Zal beside himself. He asked him about the difficulties of his journey, about news of the heroes of his land, and about Rostam. Zal said to the king, "May you live victoriously and happily; your good fortune makes all of them prosperous, and they rejoice proudly in your patronage." Then he began to speak respectfully of the matter at hand, and said, "The days pass over us, and the heavens revolve over the dark earth: Manuchehr has left this splendid world, leaving behind treasures and palaces, and we also remember Zav, Nozar, and Kay Qobad. These kings, with their great armies and commanders, never thought of attacking Mazanderan:

> It is a land of demons, wizardry,
> Smooth lies, and spells, and secret sorcery;
> If you attack them, you won't see again
> The gold you throw away there, or the men;
> No one has conquered them—no, not by stealth,
> Or by invasion, or corrupting wealth;
> Forget the conquest of Mazanderan,
> No king has ever thought of such a plan.
> These chieftains are your subjects, but like you
> They are the slaves of God in all they do.
> Don't shed their noble blood, or out of greed
> Plant in the ground ambition's evil seed,
> Because it grows into a tree whose roots
> And lofty branches nourish loathsome fruits."

Kavus replied, "I don't need your thoughts on this matter. I have more strength, glory, and wealth than Jamshid or Feraydun, and I have a greater army and more courage and treasure than Manuchehr or Kay Qobad, who never considered attacking Mazanderan. The world is ruled by my sharp sword; you drew your sword and conquered the earth, and why should I not show the world what I can do? They will submit to me or I shall force them to do so with the power of my sword; either I shall empty Mazanderan of inhabitants, or I shall impose heavy taxes on them. They are contemptible in my eyes, sorcerers and soldiers they are all alike, and you shall hear that the world has been cleared of them. Stay behind then with Rostam and be Persia's protector. The world's creator is my ally, and those demons' heads are my prey. If you will not help me in this war, at least do not tell me to reconsider my plans."

Zal could see no sense in the king's words and said, "You are the king and we are your slaves, and we spoke only out of our hearts' concern for you. Whether you speak justly or unjustly, we must breathe and walk according to your will. I have said the things I should say, the things that were in my heart. A man cannot draw death forth from his own body, or seel up the world's eyes with a needle, or escape from necessity by holding back from it; even the king cannot do these three things. May the shining world favor you, and may you never recall my advice; may you not regret your actions, and may your heart be wise and bright with faith."

Then Zal quickly bade the king farewell, his heart clouded with anxiety by this news of the king's departure. When he left the court, the sun and moon were dark before his eyes. Tus, Gudarz, Bahram, and Giv accompanied him. Giv said to Zal, "I hope God will guide Kavus, because if God does not, we may as well consider him lost. May greed and necessity and death be far from you, and your enemies be unable to harm you. Wherever we go we hear only praise of you, and after God Iran places her hopes in you. You made this hard, thankless journey for the sake of her heroes." One by one they embraced Zal as he set out on his return to Zavolestan. As soon as he had gone, Kavus gave orders that Tus and Gudarz should prepare the baggage train and lead the army toward Mazanderan.

Kavus Reaches Mazanderan

When night turned to day and the warriors set off for Mazanderan, Kavus entrusted Iran to Milad's keeping, giving him his seal ring and authority and the keys to his treasury. He said, "If enemies appear, then draw the sword of warfare; Rostam and Zal will be your refuge from any evil." On the next day the din of drums rang out, and Gudarz and Tus marched at the head of the army. Kavus accompanied them, lending luster to the army's march, and as the sun set he pitched his camp before Mount Aspruz. This place, where Kavus had decided to rest and sleep, was the home of monstrous demons; it was a place that even elephants feared. Kavus had cloth of gold draped over his throne, and the air was filled with a delicious scent of wine. All the chieftains sat before Kavus, and they spent the night with wine and companionable talk. At dawn they rose and came belted and helmeted before the king, who ordered Giv to take a thousand warriors with maces and to lead the way into Mazanderan. "Whoever you see," he said, "young or old, separate their souls from their bodies; burn any buildings you come across, turn the day into night, so that these demons will understand that the world is to be emptied of sorcery." Giv bound on his belt, left the king's presence, and selected a group of men from the army. He marched with them to the borders of Mazanderan, and there rained down swords and maces on the inhabitants. Neither men, nor women, nor children were spared by his sword; he burned and plundered the towns and brought poison instead of healing into the inhabitants' lives. He had come to a city that was like a paradise, filled with all manner of pleasure. In every street and building there were more than a thousand serving girls wearing torques and earrings, and even more whose faces were as radiant as the moon, wearing diadems; there was golden treasure scattered everywhere, with here gold coins and there jewels, and there were countless flocks of animals in the surrounding countryside. You would say that it was a veritable paradise. They took news to Kavus of the glory and splendor of this place, saying that Mazanderan was the partner of heaven, that all of this city was adorned like an idolater's temple with Chinese brocade and flowers, that the women there were like houris, and their faces were like the blossoms of the pomegranate tree.

The Iranians had been looting the area for a week before the news reached the king of Mazanderan, and his heart was filled with pain, his head with anxiety. One of the demons of his court was called Sanjeh, and his soul and body were lacerated by this news. The king said to him, "Go as the sun traverses the sky to the White Demon; tell him that a huge army led by the Iranian king Kavus has arrived here and is looting Mazanderan. Say that if he does not come to our aid, he will soon see no one left alive here." Sanjeh took the warlike king's message to the White Demon, who replied, "Do not despair of fate; I will come immediately with a mighty army and drive them out of Mazanderan."

When night came, a black cloud spread over the army, making the world as dark as an African's face. The earth seemed like a sea of pitch, from which all light had gone into hiding. There seemed to be a huge tent of smoke and pitch looming over them, and men's eyes were baffled by the darkness. When night had passed and day came, the eyes of half the men in the Persian army were darkened, and their leaders' heads were filled with fury against the king. Many men perished because of this; the army had never known such a disaster. The king was also blinded, and his actions brought evil on his army: their wealth was looted, and his soldiers led into captivity. In his misery Kavus said, "A sensible advisor is more valuable than treasure." The

Persians suffered in this way for a week, and now none of their army was able to see. On the eighth day the White Demon roared:

> *"Kavus, you're like a willow, fruitless and afraid.*
> *And you once thought your army could invade*
> *Mazanderan, and that your strength is like*
> *A maddened mammoth's when you choose to strike!*
> *Since you have occupied the Persian throne,*
> *Wisdom's deserted you, good sense has flown.*
> *Here is the end of everything you sought,*
> *Here is the punishment for which you fought!"*

Then he chose twelve thousand demons armed with daggers and set them to guard the Persians, filling their chieftains' minds with grief. The demons fed them on a handful of bran, so that their days were filled with suffering, and took all the king's treasures, including his crown set with rubies and turquoises, and gave them to Mazanderan's army commander, Arzhang. The White Demon said to him, "Tell the king that he need talk no more about Ahriman; the Persian king and his army will never look on the bright sun and moon again. I have not killed them, but only so that they will know how pain differs from pleasure. They will die slowly, groaning in despair, and no one will pay any attention to their complaints." When Arzhang heard this message, he set off for the king of Mazanderan, taking the Persian warriors as prisoners and their treasures and horses with fine trappings as plunder.

King Kavus Sends Word to Zal of What Has Happened
Then, sick at heart, Kavus sent a warrior to go as quickly as a flying bird or wind-borne smoke to Zal and Rostam in Zavolestan, and to say to them, "Fortune has dealt me a heavy blow, and dust has dimmed my throne and crown. The turning heavens have given my wealth and my army

of famous warriors, as splendid as roses in springtime, to the demons; the wind you said would come has borne everything away. Now my eyes are darkened and my fortunes are confused; my royal head is bowed with weariness: wounded, and in Ahriman's clutches, my wretched body gives up its soul. When I remember the advice you gave me, cold sighs rise up from within me. I did not act wisely, I did not follow your advice, and my lack of wisdom has brought disaster on me. If you do not come to my help now, all that we have gained will be lost."

The messenger told Zal all he knew and all he had seen and heard. Zal clawed at his skin in grief, but he said nothing, either to friends or to enemies. In his heart he saw clearly the evils that Kavus was suffering far away. He said to Rostam, "We must neither eat nor drink nor delight in our sovereignty, because the king of the world has been snared by Ahriman, and disaster has come to the Persian army. You must saddle Rakhsh and grasp your sword for vengeance. Fate has brought you up for this day. In this battle against Ahriman you must not rest or draw breath; cover your chest with your tiger skin, and drive all thoughts of sleep from your mind. What man who has seen your lance can feel easy in his soul? If you fight against the sea, it is turned to blood, and at the sound of your voice, mountains crumble to the plains; Arzhang and the White Demon must have no hope of escaping from you with their lives. Your heavy mace must smite the neck of the king of Mazanderan and shatter it to pieces."

Rostam replied, "The way is long, how shall I go without soldiers to accompany me?" Zal said, "There are two ways there from this kingdom, and both are filled with difficulties and dangers. One is the way that Kavus took; the other lies through the mountains and will take two weeks. You will meet with lions and demons and darkness, and your eyes will be bewildered by what they see. If you take the shorter way, you will come on monstrous things, and may God come to your aid then. It is a hard way, but set Rakhsh along it and you will survive its perils. In the dark night, until daybreak, I shall pray to God that I shall see your shoulders and chest again, and your sword and mace in your hand, and if God wills that a demon turn your days to darkness, can any man avert this from you? What comes to us must be endured. No one can stay in this world forever; and even if he remains here for a long time, he is finally summoned to another place. If a man leaves behind him a noble reputation, he should not despair when he has to depart."

Rostam replied to his father, "I have bound my belt on in readiness to obey you. The great warriors of the past did not choose to walk into hell, and those who were not tired of life did not choose to face ravening lions, but I am prepared for whatever I encounter and I ask for no ally but God. I shall sacrifice my body and soul for the king and smash these sorcerers and their talismans. I shall rescue the Persians who are still living, and I will leave neither Arzhang, nor the White Demon, nor Sanjeh, nor Kulad Ghandi, nor Bid, alive. I swear by the one God who has created the world, that Rostam will not dismount from Rakhsh until he has bound Arzhang's arms in a rock-like knot and placed a yoke on his shoulders, and Rakhsh has trampled Kulad's head and brains beneath his hooves." Zal embraced Rostam and invoked many blessings on his head, and Rostam, with his cheeks flushed and his heart firm in its resolve, mounted Rakhsh. Rudabeh came to her son, her face wet with tears, and Zal too wept bitterly over him. They bade him farewell, not knowing whether they would ever see him again. So passes the world, and a wise man knows of its passage, and with every day that goes by, your body becomes more free of the earth's evil.

THE SEVEN TRIALS OF ROSTAM

The First Trial: Rakhsh's Combat with a Lion

Rostam rode out from Sistan in high spirits, his face flushed with joy. By riding Rakhsh through the dark night as well as the bright day, he covered two days' journey in one. He became tired and hungry, and he saw a plain ahead of him filled with wild asses. He urged Rakhsh forward with his thighs, and the ass was unable to outrun him; no animal could escape Rakhsh's speed and Rostam's lariat together. The lion Rostam threw his lariat, and its noose dropped over the brave ass's head. Then he lit a fire with the point of an arrow and piled thorns and scrub onto the blaze, and after he had killed and skinned the beast, he cooked it in the flames. He needed neither a table nor cooking pot, but simply ate the flesh and threw away the bones. He removed Rakhsh's reins, and let him wander in the meadow there; then he made himself a bed of reeds and trusted in the safety of a place where he should have been afraid. The reed bed hid a lion's lair, and no elephant dared disturb the reeds nearby.

When one watch of the night had gone by, this ravening lion returned to its lair. He saw a mammoth warrior sleeping among the reeds, and a horse awake and standing in front of him. He said to himself, "First I must bring down the horse, if I'm to get my claws on its rider." He charged toward Rakhsh, whose spirit flared up like fire. Rakhsh brought his front hooves down on the lion's head and sunk his sharp teeth into his back. He threw it down on to the ground, tore it to pieces, and rendered this savage animal harmless. When Rostam woke he saw that this lion's world had indeed become dark and comfortless, and he said to Rakhsh, "You are an intelligent animal, who told you to fight with lions? If you had been killed, how could I have ridden to Mazanderan with this heavy mace and helmet and this bow and lariat of mine? If you had woken me, I would have made short work of your combat with this lion."

Rostam's Second Trial: Rostam Finds a Spring of Water

When the sun rose above the mountain's summit, Rostam woke uneasily from a sweet sleep. He rubbed Rakhsh down, put his saddle on him, and prayed to God. A hard road lay ahead of him, and he had to go forward unsure of what he might encounter. Rakhsh's legs became weary, and his rider's tongue was afflicted by the heat and his thirst. He dismounted from his horse, and with his lance in his hand, staggered forward like a drunken man. He looked for some way to save himself and raised his face to the heavens, saying, "Just lord, you bring all pains and difficulties to an end, and if my pains are pleasing to you, my treasure is massed in another world. I travel in the hopes that God will have mercy on King Kavus, and that I will be able to free the Persians from the clutches of demons, according to God's commands. They are sinners and abandoned by you, but they worship you and are your slaves. Many of their mammoth bodies have been bruised and broken, they are weakened and maddened by thirst." Then Rostam fell on the hot earth, and the flesh of his tongue was split open with thirst. At that moment he saw a ram with fat haunches running in front of him, and he thought, "Where does this ram find water for itself? Surely this is God's mercy, to show this animal to me at such a moment?" He gripped his sword in his right hand, and invoking God's name, rose to his feet. Holding his sword he followed the ram, leading Rakhsh by the reins with his other hand. The ram led him to a stream, and Rostam turned his face to the skies and said, "Whoever turns away from the one God has no wisdom in him; when difficulties hem us in, he is our only source of help." Then he called down blessings on the ram and said, "May your pastures always be green and cheetahs never consider you as prey; may the bow of any man who shoots an arrow at you be broken and his arrows lost, because Rostam has survived through you, and if it were not for you he would now be thinking of his shroud, and preparing to be the prey of dragons or wolves." Then he lifted off Rakhsh's saddle and washed all his body in the clear water, so that he glittered like the sun. When he had drunk his fill, he turned his mind to hunting; his quiver was full of arrows, and with his bow he brought down a wild ass with a body as massive as an elephant's. He stripped it of its hide, and when he had lit a fire he dragged it from the stream and cooked it in the flames. He fell to his meal, tearing out the bones with his hands, then went back to the stream and drank copiously again. He was now ready to sleep and said to Rakhsh, "No fighting with anyone tonight. If an enemy appears, wake me up; don't look for a confrontation with any demons or lions." Then he lay down and slept with his lips sealed, and Rakhsh wandered here and there cropping the grass till midnight.

Rostam's Third Trial: Combat with a Dragon

A dragon, from which no elephant had ever escaped, appeared on the plain. Its lair was nearby, and even demons were afraid to cross its path. As it approached it saw

Rostam asleep and Rakhsh standing awake, alert as a lion. It wondered what had lain down here in his sleeping place, because nothing ever came this way, neither demons nor elephants nor lions; and if anything did come, it didn't escape this dragon's teeth and claws. It turned toward Rakhsh, who trotted over to Rostam and woke him. Rostam was immediately alert, ready to fight, but he gazed about him in the darkness, and the fearsome dragon disappeared. In his annoyance Rostam chided Rakhsh for waking him. He slept again, and again the dragon emerged from the darkness. Rakhsh stamped on Rostam's pillow and pawed at the ground, and once more Rostam woke. He sprang up, his face sallow with apprehension, and gazed about him, but he saw nothing except the darkness. He said to his kind, wise horse, "You should sleep in the night's darkness, but you keep waking me up; why are you in such a hurry for me to be awake? If you disturb me again like this, I'll cut your feet off with my sword. I'll go on foot, dragging my lance and heavy mace to Mazanderan." For a third time he lay his head down to sleep, using Rakhsh's barding as his mattress and bedcovers. The fearsome dragon roared, his breath seeming to flicker with flames, and Rakhsh galloped away, afraid to approach Rostam. His heart was split in two, fearing both Rostam and the dragon. But his agitation for Rostam urged him back to the hero's side; he neighed and reared up, and his hooves pawed violently at the ground. Rostam woke from a sweet sleep, furious with his horse, but this time God produced a light so that the dragon could not hide, and Rostam made him out in the darkness. He quickly drew his sword, and the ground flashed with the fire of combat. He called out to the dragon, "Tell me your name, because from now on you will not see the world to be as you wish. It's not right for me to kill you without my learning your name." The fearsome dragon said, "No one ever escapes from my claws; all of this plain is mine, like the sky and air above it. Eagles don't dare fly over this land, and even the stars don't look down on it." It paused, and then said, "What is your name, because your mother must weep for you?" The hero replied, "I am Rostam, the son of Zal, who was the son of Sam, of the family of Nariman." Then the dragon leaped at him, but in the end he could not escape from Rostam, because when Rakhsh saw the strength of its massive body bearing down on Rostam, he laid back his ears and sank his teeth into the dragon's shoulders. He tore at the dragon's flesh, and the lion-like Rostam was astonished at his ferocity. Rostam smote with his sword and lopped the dragon's head off, and poison flowed like a river from its trunk. The ground beneath its body disappeared beneath a stream of blood, and Rostam gave a great sigh when he looked at the dragon, and saw that all the dark desert flowed with blood and poison. He was afraid, and stared in horror, murmuring the name of God over and over again. He went into the stream and washed his body and head, acknowledging God's authority over the world. He said, "Great God, you have given me strength and intelligence and skill, so that before me demons, lions and elephants, waterless deserts and great rivers like the Nile, are as nothing in my eyes. But enemies are many and the years are few." When he had finished his prayer, he saddled Rakhsh, mounted, and went on his way through a land of sorcerers.

Rostam's Fourth Trial: He Kills a Witch

He rode for a long time, and when the sun went down in the sky he saw a landscape of plants and trees and running streams, as if it were a garden belonging to a young man. He saw a stream that glittered like a pheasant's eye, and next to it a golden goblet filled with wine. There was also a roasted chicken, and bread, with a saltcellar and candied fruits nearby; it was a feast for sorcerers, who had quickly disappeared when they heard him approaching. Rostam dismounted and lifted the saddle from Rakhsh's back. He was astonished to see the chicken and bread, and sat down beside the stream. He lifted the golden goblet filled with wine, and next to it was a lute, as if the desert were a hall that had been made ready for a feast. Rostam picked up the lute and began to play it, composing a song about himself as he did so:

> "This is the song of Rostam, who's been given
> Few days of happiness by Fate or heaven.
> He fights in every war, in every land;
> His bed's a hillside, or the desert sand.
> Demons and dragons are his daily prey,
> Devils and deserts block his weary way.
> Fate sees to it that perfumed flowers, and wine,
> And pleasant vistas, are but rarely mine—
> I'm always grappling with an enemy,
> Some ghoul or leopard's always fighting me."

His song reached the ears of one of the sorcerers, a witch, who disguised herself as a young girl, as beautiful as the spring and lovelier than any painting. She came to Rostam, full of tints and scents, and sat down next to him and questioned him. Rostam silently gave thanks to God that on the plains of Mazanderan he had found this feast and wine, and now he had found a beautiful young wine stewardess too. He didn't know that she was a villainous sorcerer, an Ahriman disguised in spring's colors. He placed a bowl of wine in her hand and praised God who is the author of all good things. But as soon as he mentioned God's kindness, the witch's face changed; her soul had no comprehension of such things, and her tongue could not utter such praise. She turned black at the sound of God's name, and when Rostam saw this, as quick as the wind he looped his lariat about her, and before she was aware, had trapped her head in its coils. He said to her, "What are you? Tell me. Show me yourself as you are." Suddenly there was a withered old woman in his lariat's coils, ugly, deceitful, and vicious.

Rostam slashed her in two with his dagger, and the other sorcerers' hearts were terrified when they saw this.

Rostam's Fifth Trial: The Capture of Olad

From there he journeyed on, like a man anxious to reach his goal, galloping onward till he came to a place that had never seen the brightness of the sun. Dark night fell, as black as an African's face, and neither the stars nor the sun nor the moon were visible. It was as if the sun were chained somewhere, and the stars caught in the coils of a lariat. He let his reins go slack, since he could see neither slopes nor streams in the darkness, and then emerged into the light, and the ground was like green silk, bright with young wheat shoots. The ancient world seemed to have grown young again, covered in green growth, and with streams flowing here and there. Rostam's clothes were soaked with sweat, and he was sorely in need of rest and sleep. He stripped his tiger skin from his chest and took off his helmet, which also felt drowned in sweat. He lay both of them down in the sun and prepared to rest. He removed Rakhsh's bridle, and let him wander at will in the young wheat. When his tiger skin and helmet had dried he put them on again, then lay down on a pile of vegetation, like a lion.

But a man who had been sent there to keep animals out of the wheat saw Rakhsh and ran shouting toward him. Then he saw Rostam and slashed at his legs with a stick, and when Rostam woke the man yelled at him, "You Ahriman, why did you let your horse wander in the wheat, spoiling the property of someone who's never done you any harm?" Rostam was infuriated by his words; instead of answering, he sprang up and seized the man by the ears, twisting them, and tearing them off his head. The man quickly retrieved his ears from the ground, screaming in astonishment at what Rostam had done. The owner of this land was a man called Olad, a fine, brave young man, and the injured servant went wailing to him, carrying his bloody ears in his hand. He said, "I went to get a horse out of the wheat and the streams; it belonged to a man like a black devil, wearing a leopard skin corselet and an iron helmet, an Ahriman or a sleeping dragon, and when he saw me he jumped up and said not a word but ripped my ears off and flung them on the ground." Olad was with a group of noblemen, out hunting in the meadows, and they had come on a lion's spoor, but when he heard this astonishing tale from his servant he tugged at his reins and made for where the man indicated Rostam was. As Olad and his companions approached him, Rostam mounted Rakhsh and drew his glittering sword and rode toward them like a threatening cloud. Olad said to him, "What's your name? What kind of a man are you, and which king have you sworn loyalty to? Quarrelsome lions can't pass this way."

Rostam said, "My name is cloud, if a cloud can fight like a lion; it'll rain down spears and sword blows and lop noblemen's heads off. If my name penetrates your ears, it'll freeze your blood. Have you ever heard, in any company, of the bow and lariat of Rostam? You know what I call a mother who bears a son like you? A sewer of shrouds, or a mourner at a wake. Bringing your cronies here against me is as pointless as throwing walnuts at a dome in the hope that they'll stick there." Then he looped his lariat on his saddle and drew his death-dealing sword, and every blow he made with it lopped off two heads; he was like a lion that descends on a flock of lambs, and the ground was soon strewn with the dead. The plain filled with the dust of scattering horsemen, as they fled to the mountains and caves. Rostam went after them, the dust turned the day to night, and as he caught up with Olad he flung his lariat and noosed his head with it. He dragged him down from his horse and bound his arms and said to him, "If you tell me the truth, if I find no lies in you, you'll tell me where the White Demon is and how to find Kulad-e Ghandi and Bid, and where Kavus is imprisoned, and you'll show me who did this evil act. Do this, and you won't regret it; with this mace I'll depose the king of Mazanderan, and you'll rule here in his place, as long as you don't lie to me."

Olad said, "Drive anger from your heart, and for once look at what you are doing. Don't separate my soul and body for no reason; you'll get from me everything you wish. I'll show you where the White Demon lives and, what you're really hoping for, the place where Kavus is imprisoned; I'll show you the way there. From here to where Kavus is held is a hundred parasangs; from there to where the Demons are, it's another hundred, and the way is a difficult one. In those two hundred parasangs you'll see an immeasurable cavern; it's a horrific place between two mountains, and even that auspicious bird the homa couldn't fly over those summits. There are twelve thousand warlike demons living there and keeping watch at night; Kulad-e Ghandi is their leader, and Bid and Sanjeh are their guards. You will see one of them with a body like a mountain, with a chest and shoulders ten cubits wide. Despite your great strength and horsemanship, and the way you wield your mace and sword, it will go badly for you if fight against demons like this. After you pass this area you'll come to a plain so strewn with rocks that a deer could not pick its way across it; there is a demon who is lord of the marches there, and all the other demon warriors there are under his command. Once you leave his territory you'll come to a river which is two parasangs across, and beyond it is the land of dog-headed men and those who have soft feet, and it is like a huge building three hundred parasangs in width. The area is called Bargush, and from there to where the king of Mazanderan has his seat is an ugly and difficult journey. More than six hundred thousand horseman roam the land there; they are all wealthy and have fine armor, and not one of them is wretched or poor. They have one thousand two hundred war elephants, and there is no room for them in the cities. Even if you're made of iron, you can't survive in that land alone; Ahriman's file will wear you down!"

Rostam laughed and said:

> *"Just show me how to get there, then you'll see*
> *How all these warriors fare when faced with me.*
> *You'll find out what one mammoth man can do*
> *Against their king's demonic retinue;*
> *Protected by the world Creator's will,*
> *Helped by my sword and arrows and my skill.*
> *When first they glimpse my body's strength and*
> *might,*
> *And see the massive mace with which I fight,*
> *Their skins will split with fear: headlong they'll ride,*
> *Routed, with tangled reins and terrified.*
> *All that I want is that you'll show me how*
> *To reach Kavus: come on, get moving now!"*

Rostam's Sixth Trial: Combat with Arzhang

Rostam rested neither in the bright day nor the dark night, but pushed on toward Mount Aspruz, where Kavus had led his army and been defeated by the demons' magic. When half of the night had passed, a wild noise could be heard on the plain, and fires and candles could be seen burning all over Mazanderan. Rostam said to Olad, "Where is this place, with fires burning to the left and right?" Olad replied, "It's the border with Mazanderan, where the inhabitants only sleep for two watches of the night; their leader Kulad, Arzhang, and Bid, as well as all the warriors who follow the White Demon, are making those wild cries and shouts." Rostam slept again, and when the sun rose he used his lariat to tie Olad tightly to a tree. Then he hung his grandfather's mace from his saddle and rode into Mazanderan, his heart filled with schemes of conquest. He wore a royal helmet on his head, and his cuirass of tiger skin was soon soaked with sweat. He set off to find Arzhang, and when he came on the demon's army he gave a great cry that seemed to split the sea and mountains. Arzhang heard this shout and came rushing out of his tent: Rostam saw him and urged his horse forward, bearing down on him like fire. He grabbed him by the head and ears, and holding on to his shoulders with his other hand tore the demon's head off, like a ravening lion, and flung it covered in blood into the crowd of warriors. When the demons saw his mace, their hearts and claws split with terror, and, careless of their homes and homeland, fathers stumbled over sons in their efforts to flee. Rostam drew his sword and slaughtered many of them, and as the sun went down in the sky he galloped back to Mount Aspruz.

He freed Olad from the lariat's coils, and they sat together at the foot of a tall tree. Rostam asked him the way to the city where King Kavus was, and then he immediately set off, following Olad as his guide. As they entered the city, Rakhsh neighed like a cloud growling thunder. Kavus said to the Persians, "Our troubles are over, I heard Rakhsh's neigh, and it has refreshed my heart and soul." At that moment Rostam appeared, and as he approached Kavus, the other Persians gathered round him. They made their obeisance before him, lamenting their lot and questioning him about the perils of his journey. King Kavus embraced him and asked after Zal. Then he added, "Rakhsh will have to gallop unseen by those sorcerers; if the White Demon hears the earth has been cleared of Arzhang, your troubles will be numberless, and the earth will be filled with the demons' armies. Go to the White Demon's home now, exert yourself, use your sword and arrows, and may God help you to bring these demons's heads down to the dust. You're going to have to cross seven mountains, and at every stage you'll see a band of demons. A horrifying cave will appear before you, I've heard it's like a pit, and filled with terrors. Its entrance is crowded with warrior demons who fight like leopards. The White Demon lives in that cave, and he is both the hope and fear of those warriors, but if you can destroy him, they too will be destroyed, because he is their leader. Our warriors' eyes are darkened with sorrow, and I live sightless and bewildered in the darkness; doctors have told us there is hope of a cure if we use a balm made from the blood and brains of the White Demon. This is what a learned doctor told us, that if we drop three droplets of this balm into our eyes, like tears, the darkness will clear completely."

Rostam prepared to leave, to do battle with the White Demon, and he said to the Persian captives, "Stay vigilant till I return. I am going to fight with the White Demon; if he bends my back in defeat, you will remain here a long time in misery, but if the lord of the sun grants me success under a lucky star, you will see your homes again, and your thrones, and the royal tree will bear fruit once more."

The Seventh Trial: Combat with the White Demon

Rostam set out prepared for battle, longing for revenge and with his mind focused on the coming combat. When Rakhsh reached the seven mountains and the bands of warrior demons, they saw an army of demons crowded about the entrance to a bottomless cavern. Rostam said to Olad, "You have answered honestly all I have asked you; but now the battle begins in earnest, and you must reveal to me the secrets of how to proceed." Olad said, "When the sun becomes warm, the demons sleep; then you can overcome them, but you must wait until then. Now, you won't see any of them even sitting down, except for some of their guards who are sorcerers, but then you will be victorious over them, if God is your ally."

Rostam was in no hurry to go forward, and he waited until the sun was high in the sky. Then he tied Olad up in the coils of his lariat, mounted Rakhsh, drew his sword from its scabbard, and roared out his name like thunder. He descended on the demons and severed their heads with his sword blade; none of them stood against him in battle, none of them was eager to make a name for himself by fighting with him. Then he went forward looking for the White Demon, his heart filled with fear and hope. He saw a pit like hell, and in the darkness the demon's body was still invisible. Rostam stood there for a while, his sword gripped in his hand; he couldn't see anything, and this was not a time to run away. He rubbed his eyes and peered into the pit's darkness, and made out a mountain there, hiding the pit behind its bulk. It was the color of night, its hair was white like snow, and the world seemed to be filled with its stature and breadth. It moved on Rostam like a black mountain, wearing an iron helmet, its arms protected by iron armor. Rostam's heart was filled with fear, and he thought that this might be one situation from which he would not escape. But he sprang forward like a maddened elephant and slashed with his sharp sword at the demon's trunk. The force of his blow severed a leg at the thigh, but the wounded demon attacked him, and the two locked together like an elephant and a lion. Each repeatedly tore flesh from the other's body, and the ground beneath them was turned to mud with their blood. Rostam said to himself, "If I survive today I shall live forever," and the White Demon said to himself, "I despair of my sweet life, and even if I escape from the clutches of this dragon, with a leg severed and my skin lacerated, I shall have no authority left in Mazanderan with either the nobility or their subjects." Then Rostam gave a great roar and clutched the demon by the neck, and threw him to the ground. He plunged his dagger into him and hacked out his heart and liver. All the cave was filled with the demon's great bulk, and the world seemed like a sea of blood.

Rostam came out of the cave, freed Olad from his bonds, and tied his lariat to his saddle. He gave Olad the Demon's congealed liver, and the two of them set off to Kavus. Olad to him, "You are a lion in war and have conquered the world with your sword. My body still bears the marks of your lariat where I bowed my neck in your bonds, but you gave my heart hopes of a reward, which I now ask for. To break your word would not be worthy of a lion warrior blessed with good fortune like yourself." Rostam replied, "I shall bestow Mazanderan on you, from border to border, but there are still long, difficult days of struggle ahead, in which we will see both good and bad fortune. We have to drag the king of Mazanderan down from his throne and fling him into a pit, and our daggers have to sever the heads of thousands upon thousands of demons. When these things have been done I shall make you the lord of this earth and not betray my promise."

Kavus's Sight Is Restored

Then the great champion reached King Kavus and said to him: "You are a king who loves knowledge; now delight in the deaths of those who wish you ill. I ripped open the belly of the White Demon, and his king can repose no more hopes in him. I have torn the demon's liver from his side; what are the victorious king's orders for me now?" Kavus called down blessings on him, and said, "May the crown and royal seal ring never be without your help. The mother who bore you should be blessed; my good fortune has increased because of your two parents, since now the elephant who defeats all lions is my subject."

When they brushed the king's eyes with the White Demon's blood, the darkness there cleared. An ivory throne was brought, with a crown suspended above it, and the king took his place there as the ruler of Mazanderan, surrounded by Rostam and his other chieftains, men like Tus, Fariborz, Gudarz, Giv, Roham, Gorgin and Bahram. So a week passed with wine and music, and Kavus gave himself over to pleasure and enjoyment. On the eighth day the king and his chieftains mounted their horses, shouldered their massive maces, and dispersed into Mazanderan. They rode according to the king's orders, as quickly as fire burns through dry reeds, bringing fire and the sword to the cities there. Then the king said to his men, "The just punishment for sin has been meted out, and now you must hold back from slaughter. We must send an intelligent, dignified man, someone who knows when to act quickly and when to delay, to the king of Mazanderan, to wake up his heart and trouble his mind." Rostam and the other chieftains were pleased at the notion of sending a message to this king, one that would bring light into his dark soul.

Kavus Writes a Letter to the King of Mazanderan

On white silk, a wise scribe wrote a letter filled with promises and threats, with sweetness and ugliness. It began, "Praise to God, from whom virtues are made manifest in the world, who has given us wisdom and created the turning heavens, who has created travail and difficulty and love, who has given us the power to do good and evil, the lord of the turning sun and moon. If you are just and follow the true faith, you will only hear blessings from men, but if you harbor evil and do evil, punishment will come to you from the turning heavens. Do you not see how God has dealt with you, raising the dust of battle over your demons and sorcerers? If you are aware of what fate brings, if wisdom is your teacher, then keep the crown of Mazanderan, and come to my court as my subject. You will not be able to withstand Rostam if he makes war on you, and you have no choice but to pay me taxes. If you do what I say, you can keep your sovereignty over Mazanderan, and, if you do not, what happened to Arzhang and to the White Demon will happen to you, and you should despair of life."

The king summoned Farhad, a warrior famous for the way he wielded his steel sword, and told him, "This letter is filled with good advice; take it to that demon who has escaped from the captivity he deserves." Farhad kissed the ground and took the letter to the land of the Gorgsaran, fierce warriors who fought with daggers, where men dwelt whose feet were made of leather; the king of Mazanderan held court there, surrounded by his warlike chieftains. When he heard that a messenger from Kavus was approaching on horseback, he chose a few men from his retinue and told them that this was the time to show their mettle. He said, "Today we can't separate what is demonic from what is human: be like leopards when you welcome him, see that you provoke him in such a way that even the wisest of men would fight back." They went out to greet him with their faces filled with frowns, but nothing went according to their plan. One of them took Farhad's hand and squeezed it, mangling the muscles and bones, but Farhad's face did not even turn sallow, and he showed no sign of feeling any pain. They took Farhad to their king, who questioned him about Kavus and the difficulties of his journey, and then handed the letter, written on silk with musk mingled with wine, to a scribe, who read it aloud. When the king heard of Rostam's battle against the White Demon, his eyes reddened with blood and his head filled with roars of lamentation. In his heart he said, "The sun will hide away, night comes, rest and sleep will leave me: the world will never be at rest because of this Rostam, whose name will not remain obscure." He grieved for Arzhang and the White Demon, and for the deaths of Kulad-e Ghandi and Bid. When he had heard the king's letter through, his eyes were wet with bitter tears, and he sent his answer to Kavus:

> "Can wine replace the waters of the sea?
> And you imagine you can threaten me?
> Your throne cannot match mine, and I command
> A thousand thousand warriors in this land.
> When they attack like savage lions they'll keep
> Your Persians' heads from their refreshing sleep,
> The dust of battle I send up will hide
> The plains and hills and every mountainside."

When Farhad heard his belligerent language, he did not wait for a letter to be written, but tugged at his reins and galloped back to the Persian king, where he recounted what he had seen and heard, tearing the veil aside from what had been hidden before. He said, "Their king is higher than the heavens, and his high hopes are no lower. He turned his head aside at my message, and the world is contemptible in his eyes." Rostam said to Kavus, "I will deliver our people from this shame. I must take him a message, and its words must be like a sword drawn from its scabbard. A letter as cutting as a sword blade must be written, a message like a roaring thunder cloud; I will go as the messenger and my words will make blood flow in the rivers there." King Kavus answered, "The crown and royal seal ring are resplendent because of your deeds; when you bear someone a message, elephants' hearts and lions' claws split with terror."

King Kavus Writes a Second Letter to the King of Mazanderan
He summoned a scribe, who dipped his pen in black ink, and the king dictated this message:

> *"Your words are foolish, and a man who's wise*
> *Will not resort to such unworthy lies:*
> *Empty your mind of all such talk, and bow*
> *Down like a slave; you are my subject now.*
> *And if you don't, my men from sea to sea*
> *Will celebrate another victory;*
> *The dead White Demon's soul will haunt your plains*
> *And feed the hungry vultures with your brains."*

When the king had sealed the letter, Rostam hung his massive mace from his saddle and set off for the king of Mazanderan. As he was approaching, news reached the king that Kavus had sent another messenger, one who was like a lion or a war elephant, with a lariat of sixty loops fixed to his saddle, and a fast galloping horse under him. The king of Mazanderan chose a few of his chieftains and sent them out to welcome the new messenger. When Rostam caught sight of them, he saw a tree with huge branches at the roadside and tore it up by the roots, flourishing it in his fist like a lance. The welcoming party stopped where they were in astonishment, and Rostam flung down the tree and rode up to them. There was a lengthy exchange of greetings, and then one of the party gripped Rostam's hand and squeezed it, attempting to hurt the hero. Rostam smiled, and the group stared in wonder at him. Then Rostam squeezed the hand in his, and its owner turned pale, fainted from the pain, and fell from his horse to the ground. When he revived he quickly made his way to the king of Mazanderan and there recounted everything he had seen, from beginning to end.

There was a horseman whose name was Kolahvar; he tyrannized over Mazanderan, his nature like a savage leopard's, and his dearest wish was to fight in wars. The king had him summoned and said to him, "Go to this messenger and show him what you're made of. Do such things that his face is filled with shame, and he weeps hot tears." Like a ravening lion Kolahvar went to the champion, his face filled with frowns and growling questions like a leopard. He gave Rostam his hand and squeezed Rostam's hand so hard that it was bruised from the pain. Rostam remained impassive, then squeezed Kolahvar's hand in return, and the nails fell from Kolahvar's fingers like leaves from a tree. With his hand hanging uselessly at his side, Kolahvar reported back to his king, showed him his hand, and said, "A man can't hide his pain from himself: it would be better if you made peace with this warrior than went to war with him. Don't overreach yourself; you won't be able to withstand men like him, and your best course is to agree to pay them taxes. If you accept their terms you'll be doing the best thing for Mazanderan, both for its chieftains and the

common people; this way we'll get rid of the danger, and
that's better than being terrified out of our wits."

At that moment Rostam entered the court like a savage lion. The king looked at him, then motioned him to a
suitable seat and questioned him about king Kavus and his
army. Then he said, "Are you Rostam? You have his heroic
strength." Rostam replied, "I don't know if I'm worthy even
to be Rostam's servant. I can't do the things he does; he is
a champion, a hero, a great horseman." Then he handed
over the willful king's letter, adding that his sword would
bear fruit when it lopped off chieftains' heads. The king was
astonished and angry when he heard the letter, and said to
Rostam:

> "Tell your king this, 'Your arrogant attempt
> To cow me with your words provokes contempt.
> If you are Persia's sovereign lord, if you
> Are like a lion in all you think and do,
> I am Mazanderan's great king, my throne
> And golden crown and army are my own,
> And you're a fool to summon me, to say
> I should submit to you; kings don't display
> Such pride to other kings, or try to seize
> The thrones of others by such strategies.
> Pride comes before a fall. Now turn around,
> Go back to Persia, to familiar ground,
> Because if I and my great army once attack,
> You'll be defeated, routed, driven back,
> And if I meet you face to face, you'll find
> How vain the words are in your foolish mind.'"

Rostam looked directly at the king, his warriors, and his
chieftains; he hardly heard what the king was saying, he
simply felt more eager to fight him. He refused to accept
the king's gift of clothes, horses, and gold; the crown
and belt he was offered excited his contempt. His heart

filled with rage and the longing for battle, he returned to Kavus and described for him all he had seen and heard in Mazanderan, then added, "Think nothing of them, take courage, and prepare for war against these demons. I feel only disdain for their horseman and heroes."

The King of Mazanderan Makes War on Kavus and the Persians

When Rostam left Mazanderan, the king of sorcerers began to prepare for war. He had the royal pavilion taken from the city and led his armies onto the plain. The dust they sent up obscured the sun, and neither the sea nor the mountains nor the plains were visible. The elephants' feet trampled the ground as the army set off, and no one hesitated. When King Kavus heard that the demons' forces were approaching, he first commanded Rostam to prepare for battle, and then turned to Tus, Gudarz, Giv, and Gorgin, with orders that that the army prepare and make ready its spears and shields. The chieftains' pavilions were pitched on the plain of Mazanderan, and Nozar's son Tus commanded the right flank, while Gudarz commanded the left. The mountains re-echoed with the blare of brazen trumpets, and the warriors gathered there made the whole hillside seem like a mass of iron. Kavus was in the center, with ranks of soldiers around him on every side, and Rostam, who had never known defeat in war, was at the army's head.

There was a famous warrior in Mazanderan who carried a heavy mace on his shoulders when he went into battle. His name was Juyan, and he was ambitious, a good fighter with his mace, and had an imposing voice. His cuirass glittered on his body, and the sparks from his sword blows burned the ground. He came in front of the Persian army, and the mountains and plains echoed as he roared, "Who will fight with me, who will draw forth dust from water?" King Kavus said to the Persians, "Aren't you ashamed, that no one responds to his challenge? Are your hearts and eyes so abashed and downcast by this demon's voice?" None of his brave warriors answered him, and it was as if the whole army had withered at the sight of Juyan. Then Rostam tugged at his reins and rode up to the king flourishing his lance. He said, "Give the order, your majesty, and let me confront this demon." Kavus replied, "No Persian wants to fight him; the task is yours."

Rostam grasped his death-dealing lance in his fist and urged Rakhsh forward. He went onto the battlefield like a maddened elephant, pulled on his reins, gave his war cry that made the whole plain tremble, and a cloud of dust rose into the sky. He called out to Juyan, "You are ugly and evil, and your name will be struck from the list of warriors. Your fate is decided now; the woman who bore you will weep for you." Juyan replied, "Don't be so sure of yourself when you confront Juyan and his cold dagger; your mother's heart will break, and she will weep over that cuirass and helmet of yours." When Rostam heard Juyan's reply he raged like a savage lion and rode straight at him, flinging his lance at Juyan's waist, where it cut through the coat of mail, severing the fastenings of his armor and piercing his trunk. Rostam dragged him from his saddle, spitted like a hen, and hurled him to the ground, his armor cut to pieces, his mouth filled with blood. The warriors of Mazanderan were appalled to see this, their hearts gave way within them, their faces turned sallow, and all the battlefield was filled with talk of Rostam's feat. The king of Mazanderan called out to his army, "Take courage and fight, attack like leopards."

The din of drums and blare of trumpets rang out on both sides, the sky was darkened and the ground turned the color of ebony. The sparks struck by swords and maces were like lightning flashing from dark clouds, and the air was filled with the scarlet, black, and purple of banners.

The demons' cries, the darkened atmosphere,
The din of drums, the horses' neighs of fear
Shook the firm land—no man had seen before
Such fury, or such violence, or such war;
The clash of weapons filled the air, and blood
Flowed from the heroes like a monstrous flood—
The earth became a lake, a battleground
Where waves of warriors broke and fell and drowned;
Blows rained on helmets, shields, and shattered mail
Like leaves whirled downward in an autumn gale.

The battle raged for a week, and on the eighth day King Kavus took his crown from his head and stood weeping before God. He bowed down, rubbed his face in the dust, and said, "Great lord of truth, creator of justice and purity, grant me victory over these fearless demon warriors, and renew my imperial throne." Then he put a helmet on his head and came before his troops. A cry went up, and the blare of brazen trumpets rang out, and Rostam rushed forward like a mountain. Kavus ordered Tus to bring forward the war elephants from the rear of the army, and Gudarz, Zangeh-Shavran, Gorgin, and Roham strode forward like wild boar, with their great banners seven cubits high streaming above them, while Farhad, Kherrad Borzin, and Giv accompanied them. First Rostam launched an attack on the center of the enemies' forces, soaking the ground with their warriors' blood, then like a wolf bearing down on sheep, Giv crossed over from the right flank to the left, and on the right Gudarz brought forward armor, shields, drums and other equipment. From dawn until the sun sank in darkness, blood flowed in the rivers like water, faces lost all trace of shame, courtesy and kindness, and the sky seemed to rain down maces. Piles of the dead lay on every side, and the plants were smeared with men's brains. Trumpets and drums resounded like thunder, and the sun disappeared behind an ebony cloud. Rostam and a large detachment of troops made for where the king of Mazanderan fought, but for a long time the king held out, refusing to give ground. The ambitious hero, the killer of kings, called on God's help and handed his squire his lance; then he flourished his mace, filling the air with his war cry, leaving elephants dead and demons senseless, so that elephants with their massive trunks lay lifeless for miles. Now Rostam called for lances again and rode straight toward the king of Mazanderan; he flung a lance at his belt where it dislodged his spine, but in sight of the Persian warriors, the king used magic to transform his body into a mountainous crag, and Rostam bit on his lance in astonishment.

At that moment King Kavus and his men, accompanied by their elephants and war drums, rode up. He said to Rostam, "Great hero, what's happened to make you stand staring for so long?" Rostam replied, "When the worst of the fighting was over, and my fortunes had begun to shine with success, I saw the king of Mazanderan with his massive mace on his shoulders. I gave brave Rakhsh the reins and flung a spear that struck the king's waist. I thought I'd see him fall from the saddle, blood streaming from his body, but he turned into that crag of granite, and so escaped from the perils of war and my prowess."

Every man in the Persian camp who had any strength in his grip tried to lift the granite rock that enclosed the king of Mazanderan, but it could not be shifted from its place. Then Rostam opened his arms, and without testing its weight, lifted the rock, while the army looked on in wonder. He walked with the craggy mass, while a crowd of men followed him, calling down blessings on him, and scattering gold coins and jewels over him. He carried it to the space in front of the king's pavilion, where he flung it down and placed it at the Persians' disposal. He addressed the rock, "Either come out from hiding behind cowardice and sorcery, or I shall batter this rock to pieces with steel crowbars and an ax." When he heard this, the king of Mazanderan transformed himself into a cloudy mass, wearing a steel helmet and encased in body armor. Rostam seized him by the arm, and laughed as he dragged him before king, to whom he said, "I've brought that mountainous crag, whose fear of axes has made him tired of fighting with me." Kavus looked at the king of Mazanderan's face and saw nothing there that was worthy of a throne or crown. He remembered the suffering he had been through and his heart ached at the thought of it; his mind filled with wind, and he told his executioner to hack the man to pieces with a sharp sword.

He sent someone to the enemy encampment with orders that whatever wealth was there, including coins, thrones, crowns, belts, horses, armor, and gold, should be piled into heaps. Then he had the soldiers come in groups, and he rewarded each man appropriately, giving the most to those who had undergone the most. He gave orders that the demons who were still recalcitrant, and of whom the people still went in terror, should have their heads cut off, and their bodies were to be scattered on the common highway. Then he went to a place of prayer and prayed privately to God; he remained there for a week, prostrating himself in supplication and praise. On the eighth day he opened the doors to his treasury and distributed goods to all who needed them; he spent a week in this way, giving men freely whatever they required. Now that justice had been served, he delayed for a third week in Mazanderan, calling for the music of the harp, his drinking companions, and wine served in goblets set with rubies. During this time, Rostam said to the king, "Every man has his uses, and I asked Olad to be an honest guide for me, which he was. I encouraged him to hope for Mazanderan as a reward for his honesty. It would be right for the king to bestow a robe of honor on him and have his chieftains swear allegiance to him for as long as he lives." When the king heard his loyal champion's words, he placed his hand on his heart as a sign of agreement and summoned Mazanderan's chieftains to come before him. After he had spoken with them about Olad for a while, he had Olad enthroned, and then set off on the return journey to Pars.

Kavus Returns to Iran, and Dismisses Rostam

As Kavus entered Iran, the army's dust obscured the sky, and the noise of men and women celebrating his return rose up to the sun. All the land was decorated in his honor, and everywhere men called for wine and musicians. The world was renewed by the king's renewal, and a new moon rose above Iran. When Kavus took his place on the throne, victorious and happy, he opened the doors to his ancient treasuries and had paymasters come from every area to receive gold for their people. The army commanders arrived before the king, clamoring to see Rostam, and when the hero entered the court he wore a crown and was seated on a throne next to Kavus, who arranged for gifts that were worthy of him: a throne set with turquoise and ornamented with rams' horns, a royal crown set with gems, a set of imperial clothes made of cloth of gold, splendid bracelets and torques, a hundred maidservants as lovely as the moon and wearing golden belts, a hundred more with musky hair and fine clothes and jewelry, a hundred Arab horses with golden trappings, a hundred black-haired camels with golden bridles, royal brocade from Rum, China, and Persia, a hundred purses of gold coins, a goblet set with rubies and filled with pure musk, another set with turquoises and filled with rose water, and all manner of tints and scents and other goods.

A scribe wrote a charter on silk, using ink made from musk, wine, and aloes, in which Rostam was confirmed in his sole lordship over Sistan. Kavus praised him, and said, "May the crown and royal seal ring never lack your support, may kings value you in their hearts, and may your soul be filled with humility and obedience." Rostam bent forward and kissed the throne. Then the city was filled with the din of drums, and everyone took part in the festivities; decorations were hung on the houses, and the noise of cymbals and brazen trumpets filled the air. And so Rostam departed and the king sat on his throne, making the world bright with his righteousness and observance of ancient ways. With the sword of justice he smote the neck of sorrow, and in his heart there was no thought of death. The earth was filled with green growth and streams, and all the world was as lovely as the garden of Aram. The king grew powerful through his just ways and faith, and the hands of Ahriman were tied. The world learned that King Kavus had returned from Mazanderan and once again sat crowned on the throne. Everyone was astonished that he had attained such magnanimity of soul, and men lined up outside his court with offerings and gifts.

> *The world seemed heaven then, on every side,*
> *Justice prevailed, and riches multiplied.*

THE KING OF HAMAVERAN,
AND HIS DAUGHTER SUDABEH

The Barbary Kingdom

Kavus decided to tour the borders of his kingdom. First he traversed the marches of Turan and China, and then, preceded by the blare of trumpets and the din of drums, he entered the land of Makran, where the country's nobility greeted him with tribute and presents. From there he went on to Barbary, whose king decided to give battle rather than pay tribute. So many troops were at his command that the sun was darkened by the dust sent up by their horses' hooves, and in the gloom a man could not distinguish his own hand from the reins he held. The king of Barbary's men came forward in countless bands, surging one after another like the waves of the sea.

Gudarz saw their forces, readied his mace for battle, and, with a thousand armored horsemen flourishing lances and bows, bore down on the enemy troops. The onslaught broke the center of the enemy's line; their troops were routed and their king fled from the battlefield.

When the old men of the city saw how the wind of battle blew, they came, contrite and wretched, before Kavus, saying:

> *"We are your humble servants, and we bring*
> *The tribute we've collected to our king;*
> *Grateful, obedient to your rule, behold*
> *In place of coins we offer jewels and gold."*

Kavus made much of them and forgave them and conferred new laws upon them. Then, to the noise of cymbals, chimes, and trumpets, he proceeded toward Bactria and the Caucasus. When news reached these areas that King Kavus was approaching, the nobles came out to greet him, bearing presents and tribute. From there he went on to Zabolestan, where Dastan's son Rostam was his host. The king stayed with him for a month, spending the time either feasting with music and wine, or hunting with hawks and cheetahs.

But in the rose garden a thorn appeared; when all the world seemed ordered and at peace, dissension arose among the Arabs. A rich nobleman raised the standard of revolt in Syria and Egypt and the people turned from Kavus. When the king learned that a rival for the throne was challenging him, the thunder of war drums rang out and preparations to leave Zabolestan began. Kavus led his army to the seashore and there innumerable boats were built and launched. A thousand leagues the army sailed and made landfall where three countries meet; on the left was Egypt, on the right Barbary, and ahead the waters of Zareh, beyond which lay Hamaveran. News reached these areas that King Kavus had entered the waters of Zareh, and the three countries joined their armies with one another on the Barbary Coast.

The combined forces of these allies covered the deserts and mountains; the lion had no place for his lair, the wild ass found no way through the plains; the leopard on his crag, the fish in the depths, the eagle in the clouds—all were displaced, there was no room for any animal in all that mighty mass of soldiers.

When Kavus disembarked his men, mountain and desert disappeared, the world seemed nothing but swords and armor; the very stars drew their light from glittering lances. The mountains shook with the blare of trumpets, the earth trembled beneath horses' hooves, and such a din of drums thundered out that the land of Barbary seemed to have become one enormous army encampment.

A tucket sounded from the Persian lines, and Gorgin, Farhad, and Tus rode forward. Further down the line, Gudarz, Giv, Shidush, and Milad also rode out; their lances dipped in poison, they let their reins fall slack on their horses' necks and, bent low over the pommels of their saddles, they charged the enemy. War cries and the clash of arms resounded; Kavus attacked from the army's center, and his troops followed close behind him. The world was darkened by their dust, and crimson blood rained down, spattering the ground as thick as dew, until it seemed red tulips had sprung up between the rocks. Sparks sprang from the clashing blades, the ground was awash with blood, and the three armies were so overwhelmed by the Persian forces that they fell back in utter confusion.

The first to capitulate was the king of Hamaveran; he flung away his sword and massive mace and sent a courier asking for quarter. He said he would deliver weighty tribute in the form of horses, weapons, thrones, and crowns if Kavus would not lead his army against Hamaveran itself. And having heard the message, Kavus answered that, as his former enemy now acknowledged Kavus's crown and authority, he would live safely, under the Persian monarch's protection.

The Tale of Sudabeh

> *Then someone took Kavus aside and said: "This king*
> *Has sired a daughter lovely as the spring,*
> *More stately than a cypress tree, and crowned*
> *By hair like black musk, like a noose unbound,*
> *Her tongue is like a dagger lodged between*
> *Lips sweet as sugar cane; she is a queen*
> *Arrayed like paradise, a paragon*
> *As pure and splendid as the vernal sun,*
> *Fit for a monarch, if one should decide*
> *To choose this moonlike beauty as his bride."*

Kavus's heart leapt up within his breast; he chose a wise
and subtle man from his retinue and ordered him to go to
the king of Hamaveran and say from him: "Those nobles
who best understand the ways of the world seek to be allied to me, since the sun draws its light from my crown
and the earth is but a support for my ivory throne, and all
who are not protected by my shadow wither away. Now I
seek an alliance with you, washing my face with the waters
of reconciliation. I have heard that you have in purdah a
daughter who is worthy to be my wife, for she is pure in
her lineage and pure in her body and praised in all cities by
all people; and if you find a son-in-law like myself, the son
of Qobad, then the light of heaven has indeed treated you
with favor."

The courier hurried to the king of Hamaveran's court;
warmly and with eloquence he greeted the king on behalf
of Kavus and delivered the message with which he had been
entrusted. When he heard the courier's words the king of
Hamaveran's heart grew heavy with sorrow and foreboding,
and to himself he said, "He is a sovereign, world-conquering and victorious, but she is my only daughter in all the
world, and to me she is dearer than life itself. But if I slight
this courier and treat him contemptuously, I have no means

to fight the war that will ensue. It is best that I should close my eyes to this effrontery and allay my heart's anger." Then he said to the courier, "These desires of your king have no end. He asks of me the two things I have held dearest, and there is no third to equal them. He has taken my wealth that was the prop of my rule, and he takes my daughter, who is the delight of my heart. My life is mine no more, and I resign to him all that he demands."

In sorrow he called his daughter Sudabeh to him and spoke to her about Kavus, saying, "An eloquent messenger has come here with a letter from the king: He wishes to snatch from me my heart, my rest, and my life, because he asks for you. What do you say to this? What are your wishes in the matter? What is your opinion?" Sudabeh answered, "Since we have no choice, it is better not to grieve at this. The lord of all the world can take whole countries if he so wishes. Why should you grieve at an alliance with him? This is a joyful development, not a cause for sorrow." The king of Hamaveran saw that Sudabeh was not opposed to the match; he summoned Kavus's messenger and motioned him to a place higher than that of all his courtiers. Then they drew up the alliance according to the rites and usages of their religion and time.

The heavy-hearted king prepared the bridal procession: three hundred slaves and forty litters, a thousand mules and horses and a thousand camels loaded with brocade and gold coins, and, for the bride herself, a litter splendid as the moon, preceded and followed by beasts bearing her personal wealth. The troops accompanying her were dressed like denizens of Paradise; so colorful they were, the earth seemed covered by a carpet of wild flowers. When she came before Kavus he looked at her face and saw her smiling ruby lips, her two narcissus eyes, her nose fine as a silver reed. Lost in astonishment he stared and invoked God's blessing on her. He called an assembly of wise men and priests; before them he acknowledged that Sudabeh was worthy to be his bride, and so the marriage was performed according to their rites and customs.

The King of Hamaveran Plots against Kavus

But the king of Hamaveran was sick at heart and sought for some way to improve his situation. After a week had passed, on the eighth day he sent a messenger to Kavus saying, "If the king will come as my guest to my palace, the country of Hamaveran will be honored to entertain his splendor and majesty." He secretly hoped to find a way both to regain his daughter and to escape from paying tribute. But Sudabeh realized that her father was planning some kind of violence during the festivities and said to Kavus, "This is not advisable, Hamaveran is no place for you. He is plotting to harm you during the festival, and you should not place yourself at his mercy. All this is on my account and will be a cause of sorrow to you."

But Kavus had no regard for the opinion of anyone from her country and did not believe her. He and his nobles set off for the promised festivities in Hamaveran. A whole city, called Shaheh, had been devoted to the celebration, and when Kavus entered it, all its inhabitants made their obeisance before him, scattering in his path jewels and saffron, gold coins and ambergris. The town was filled with the sounds of music and song, woven together like the warp and weft of fine cloth. Seeing Kavus, the king of Hamaveran dismounted, together with his courtiers, and, from the palace entrance to the audience hall, trays of pearls, rubies, and gold were emptied before Kavus, while musk and ambergris rained down upon his head. Within the palace Kavus was seated in triumph on a golden throne. He passed a week with the wine cup in his hand, happy and rejoicing, and day and night the king of Hamaveran stood before him like a servant ready to carry out his wishes, and in the same way the king's courtiers served the Iranian nobles. And so the visitors felt safe and welcome and had no suspicion of any harm or trouble. But all this had been planned and foreseen by the king of Hamaveran and he sent the news to Barbary, whose leaders were of one mind with him. When their army arrived, the king of Hamaveran was overjoyed, and one night, when the Iranians were defenseless and unprepared, trumpets sounded the attack. Kavus was suddenly seized, together with Gudarz, Giv, Tus, and the rest of his entourage.

There was in that country a mountain that rose from the depths of the sea; its peak pierced the clouds and on its slopes was a fortress so high that it seemed embraced by the heavens. Kavus and his nobles were sent in chains to this castle and flung within its walls, where they were guarded by a thousand warriors. Kavus's royal pavilion was sacked, and the gold there and his crown were plundered by the nobles of Hamaveran. The pavilion itself was trampled underfoot. Two columns of veiled women were led out, and in their midst was a litter containing Sudabeh, who was to be taken back to her father's court. When Sudabeh saw her women in this state, she ripped her royal clothes from her body and tore at her musky hair and scored her face with her nails. She wept, and screamed at her father's envoys that they were dogs, and cried out to them:

> "No man who is a man will praise this act,
> You could not chain him when his troops attacked;
> Hearing his drums, your hearts were overthrown,
> Then he was armed, his warhorse was his throne,
> You quailed before Gudarz and Giv and Tus—
> Then was the time for you to chain Kavus!
> But no, you lie and break your oaths and cheat
> And ambush him with welcoming deceit.
> I will not part from him or leave his side;
> Though he should die I will remain his bride."

This outburst was reported to her father, who was enraged. He took her at her word and had her sent to the fortress where her husband was kept in chains, and there she comforted him, ministering to him in his sorrow and misfortune.

Afrasyab Renews the War

News spread throughout the world that the king of Iran was in captivity. Many claimants to the crown appeared, among them Afrasyab, who roused himself from his life of eating and sleeping and taking his ease, and once again attacked Iran. The war lasted for three months, at the end of which the Iranian army was routed; many men, women, and children were enslaved and the remaining Persians were gripped by despair. A number of fugitives made their way to Zabolestan, where they entreated Dastan's son Rostam to save the country, saying:

> *"You are our refuge, our last hope, our one*
> *Protection now that King Kavus has gone;*
> *Alas, Iran will be destroyed, a lair*
> *For leopards and wild lions will flourish there,*
> *Our land will be a wasted battleground*
> *Where evil kings will triumph and be crowned."*

Rostam wept at their words, and his heart was filled with pain and sorrow. He answered them, "I and my army shall prepare for war, and I shall rid the land of Iran of these Turkish invaders."

Rostam's Message

Rostam sent messengers to the king of Hamaveran and, secretly, to Kavus. To the former he said: "You tricked the king of Iran and went back on your oath. To stoop to such ruses is not the way of chivalry. Either you release King Kavus or prepare to do battle with me." But the king of Hamaveran answered, "King Kavus will never descend to the plains again, and if you come to Barbary your welcome will be swords and heavy maces; the chains and prison that hold him await you too. I and my army shall confront you; this is how we deal with invaders."

In response Rostam gathered an army together and took it over sea and dry land to the borders of Hamaveran. There he set about plundering the countryside, and all the land ran with rivers of blood. News reached the king of Hamaveran that Rostam had saddled Rakhsh and was laying his land waste and that this was no time for delay. He led his army out from the city to confront the Persians and the bright day was darkened by their dust.

But seeing Rostam's massive weight and height and the great mace he carried on his shoulder, the king's troops' hearts failed within them and they fled back toward the city. The king sat with his councillors and asked for two young men to go as couriers to Egypt and Barbary. The letters they bore said that the three countries were close and had always shared in joy and misfortune, and that if they came now to the aid of Hamaveran there was nothing to fear from Rostam, but that if they did not, Rostam would eventually bring disaster on their heads too.

When they learned that Rostam's army was nearby, their hearts quaked with fear. But they mustered troops and set out for Hamaveran; so great was their number that there was not space on the plain where they were drawn up for an ant to walk. Seeing these forces, Rostam secretly sent a message to Kavus: "The kings of three countries have risen against me, and if I fight their forces they will be routed in such utter confusion that they will not know their heads from their feet. But this war must not have bad consequences for you, and from such evil men we must expect an evil response. The throne of Barbary is nothing to me if its capture means harm to my king." The courier heard the message and took it by hidden ways to Kavus, who answered, "Do not concern yourself about me; it was not for me that this world was created, and thus the heavens have ever turned, mingling poison with sweet draughts and war with peace. The world's Creator is my support and his greatness and benevolence are my refuge. Give Rakhsh his head, and do not leave a single one of our enemies alive, in the open or in hiding." When Rostam heard this message, he prepared for battle.

Rostam Fights with the Three Kings

The next day the armies were drawn up in battle order; on the side of Hamaveran there were a hundred war elephants; behind them were countless jostling banners—red, yellow, and purple—and the army stretched for two miles. When Rostam saw their lines, he said to his men, "You see their mounts' necks and manes, but keep your eyes on the points of their lances; though they are a hundred thousand and we are but a hundred horsemen, it is not greater numbers that will win this battle." Spears and arrows glittered in the air, the earth swam with blood like a wine vat; so many lances thronged the sky it seemed a bed of close-packed reeds, and abandoned armor and severed heads, still helmeted, lay scattered on the ground. Rostam urged Rakhsh forward but avoided combat with lesser men; instead he rode after the Arab king and flung his lariat, catching the king by the waist; he jerked him down from the saddle with the violence of a polo mallet striking the ball, and Farhad bound his arms. Sixty of this king's noblemen were taken prisoner, and the king of Barbary was also captured along with forty of his warriors. The king of Hamaveran was defeated and promised to hand over Kavus and his noblemen to Rostam.

Kavus, along with Giv, Gudarz, and Tus, was released from his fortress prison, and Rostam delivered to the Persian treasury the arms of three countries, the treasure of three kings, their pavilions, hosts, crowns, and thrones and whatever other things of value he saw. Then Kavus had brought before him a gold-caparisoned palfrey on which was a golden litter; the frame was of aloe wood studded with jewels and its couch was of Rumi brocade, worked with turquoise and rubies on a jet-black ground. He had Sudabeh sit within the litter, and when she took her place there, he saluted her sunlike splendor. He led his army out of the city to their camp, and, augmented by the forces of Egypt, Barbary, and Hamaveran, the number of his forces now exceeded three hundred thousand.

Kavus Sends a Message to Afrasyab

When Rostam had informed the king of Afrasyab's new incursions into Iran, Kavus sent the Turanian leader a letter: "Leave the land of Iran, repent of your overreaching pride; I hear nothing but talk of you and your depredations. Turan is your homeland, and you rejoice in its wealth, but blindly you turn always to evil. You want for nothing, do not then strive for excess; such longings will bring you only pain and endless sorrow. Accept your subordinate status and so save your skin. You know well enough that Iran is my land and that the world trembles before my might. No matter how brave a leopard may be, it dare not confront the lion's claws."

When this message reached Afrasyab, his mind was filled with hatred, his heart with rage. He sent his answer: "Such idle talk can come only from one who is low-minded; if Iran is your country as you claim, why did you long to conquer Mazanderan? Hear then the truth: Iran is mine for two reasons—first, that I am descended from the son of Feraydun, and second that I have overcome its inhabitants by the force of my sword. My sword will lop the summits from the mountains and bring down eagles from the dark clouds. My banners are unfurled, and I have come prepared for war."

Hearing his answer, Kavus put his vast army on a war footing and led them from Barbary into Syria; for his part, Afrasyab marched forward and his army clouded the heavens with their dust. The world was deafened by the blare of trumpets and the din of drums, the land was overspread with iron armor, the air was blackened by thick dust. In the shock of battle Afrasyab's fortunes declined; two sections of the army of Turan were slain, and when he saw this, Afrasyab's mind churned like fermenting wine that bubbles without fire beneath it. He cried out, "O my brave warriors, best of my troops, lions of Turan, it is for such a day that I have trained and nourished you; throw your hearts into the battle and drive back Kavus; with lances and swords fall on the Iranian troops. Capture the lionhearted Rostam, noose his head and haul him from his mount. I shall give my own daughter to whoever subdues Rostam; I shall exalt his glory higher than the moon's sphere." When they heard him, the Turanians attacked with renewed force, but all their efforts were in vain and Afrasyab fell back toward Turan, heartsick and with two parts of his army destroyed. Seeking sweetness and pleasure from the world, he had found only bitter poison.

For his part, Kavus returned in triumph to Pars; he reigned in splendor, giving himself up to the pleasures of court life. He sent out great warriors, wise and just men, to confirm his rule in his possessions, in Merv and Nayshapur and Balkh and Herat; the world was filled with justice and the wolf turned harmlessly from the lamb. On Rostam, Kavus bestowed the title of Champion of all the World.

Kavus Is Tempted by Eblis

Then one morning the devil Eblis addressed a convocation of demons, in secret and unbeknownst to the king: "Under this king our lives are miserable and wretched: I need a nimble demon, one who knows court etiquette, who can deceive the king and wrench his mind away from God and bring his royal glory down into the dust; in this way the burdens he has placed upon us will be lightened." The demons heard him, but none at first responded, out of fear of

Kavus. Then an ugly demon spoke up, "I'm wily enough for this." And so saying, he transformed himself into a handsome, eloquent youth, one who would grace any court.

It happened that the king went out hunting, and the youth saw his opportunity. He came forward and kissed the ground; handing Kavus a bouquet of wild flowers, he said, "Your royal *farr* is of such splendor that the heavens themselves should be your throne. The surface of the earth is yours to command; you are the shepherd and the world's nobles are your flock. There is but one thing remaining to you, and when this is accomplished your glory will never fade. The sun still keeps its secrets from you; how it turns in the heavens, and who it is that controls the journeys of the moon and the succession of night and day, these are as yet unknown to you."

The king's mind was led astray by this demon's talk, and his mind forsook the ways of wisdom: He did not know that the heavens are immeasurable, that the stars are many but that God is one, and that all are powerless beneath his law. The king was troubled in his mind, wondering how he could fly into the heavens without wings. He asked learned men how far it was from the earth to the heavens; he consulted astronomers and set his mind on a foolish enterprise.

He gave orders that men were to go at night and rob eagles' nests of their young; these squabs were to be placed in houses in pairs and reared on fowl and occasional lamb's meat. When the eagles had grown as strong as lions and were each able to subdue a mountain goat, Kavus had a throne constructed of aloe wood and gold, and at each corner he had a lance attached. From the lances he suspended lamb's meat; next he bound four eagles tightly to the structure. Then King Kavus sat on the throne, his mind deceived by the wiles of Ahriman. When the eagles grew hungry they flew up toward the suspended meat and the throne was lifted above the ground, rising up from the level plain into the clouds. The eagles strained toward the meat to the utmost of their capacity, and I have heard that Kavus was carried into the heavens as far as the sphere of the angels. Others say that he fought with his arrows against the sky itself, but God alone knows if these and other such stories are true. The eagles flew for a great while, but finally their strength gave out and their wings began to tire; they tumbled down from the dark clouds, and the king's throne plummeted toward the ground. It finally came to rest in a thicket near Amol and, miraculously, the king was not killed. Hungry and humiliated, Kavus was filled with regret at his foolishness; he waited forlornly in the thicket, praying to God for help.

Once Again King Kavus Is Rescued

While he was begging forgiveness for his sins, the army was searching for some trace of him. Rostam, Giv, and Tus received news of his whereabouts and set off with a band of soldiers to rescue him. Gudarz said to Rostam:

> *"Since I was weaned of mother's milk I've known*
> *The ways of kings and served the royal throne;*
> *I've seen the world's great monarchs and their glory,*
> *But never have I heard so mad a story*
> *As this we hear now of Kavus, this fool*
> *Who's so unwise he's hardly fit to rule."*

The heroes reached Kavus and furiously reproached him. Gudarz said:

> *"A hospital is where you need to be,*
> *Forget your palaces and sovereignty;*
> *You throw away your power, you don't discuss*
> *Your plans and foolish fantasies with us.*
> *Three times disaster's struck you down, but still*
> *You haven't learned to curb your headstrong will:*

First you attacked Mazanderan, and there
Captivity reduced you to despair;
Then, trusting to your enemies, you gave
Your heart away and so became their slave;
And now your latest folly is to try
Your strength against the ever-turning sky."

Shamefaced and humble, Kavus replied, "All that you say is true and just." He was placed in a litter, and on his journey home humiliation and regret were his companions. When he reached his palace again, his heart remained wrung with sorrow, and for forty days he waited as a suppliant before God, his head bowed in the dust. His pride was humbled, and shame kept him locked within his palace. Weeping and praying, he neither granted audience nor feasted, but in sorrow and regret had wealth distributed to the poor.

But when Kavus had wept in this way for a while, God forgave him. King Kavus reestablished justice in the world, and it shone equally on nobles and commoners alike. Justice made the world as rich and splendid as a fine brocade, and over all the king presided, majestic and magnificent.

THE TRAGEDY OF SOHRAB

Rostam Loses Rakhsh

At dawn one day Rostam decided to go hunting, to drive away the sadness he felt in his heart. Filling his quiver with arrows, he set off for the border with Turan, and when he arrived in the marches he saw a plain filled with wild asses; laughing, his face flushed with pleasure, he urged Rakhsh forward. With his bow, his mace, and his noose he brought down his prey and then lit a fire of brushwood and dead branches; next he selected a tree and spitted one of the slaughtered asses on it. The spit was as light as a feather to him, and when the animal was roasted he tore the meat apart and ate it, sucking the marrow from its bones. He sank back contentedly and slept. Cropping the grass, his horse Rakhsh wandered off and was spotted by seven or eight Turkish horsemen. They galloped after Rakhsh and caught him and bore him off to the city, each of them claiming him as his own prize.

Rostam woke from his sweet sleep and looked round for his horse. He was very distressed not to see Rakhsh there and set off on foot toward the closest town, which was Samangan. To himself he said, "How can I escape from such mortifying shame? What will our great warriors say, 'His horse was taken from him while he slept?' Now I must wander wretched and sick at heart, and bear my armor as I do so; perhaps I shall find some trace of him as I go forward."

Samangan

The king of Samangan was told that the Crown Bestower, Rostam, had had his horse Rakhsh stolen from him and was approaching the town on foot. The king and his nobles welcomed him and enquired as to what had happened, adding, "In this town we all wish you well and stand ready to serve you in any way we can." Rostam's suspicions were laid to rest and he said, "In the pastures, Rakhsh wandered off from me; he had no bridle or reins. His tracks come as far as Samangan and then peter out into reeds and the river. If you can find him, I shall be grateful, but if he remains lost to me, some of your nobility will lose their heads."

The king responded, "No one would dare to have done this to you deliberately. Stay as my guest and calm yourself; tonight we can drink and rejoice, and drown our worries with wine. Rakhsh is such a world-renowned horse, he will not stay lost for long."

Mollified by his words, Rostam agreed to stay as the king's guest. He was given a chamber in the palace and the king himself waited on him. The chieftains of the army and the city's nobility were summoned to the feast; stewards brought wine, and dark-eyed, rosy-cheeked girls sought to calm Rostam's fretfulness with their music. After a while Rostam became drunk and felt that the time to sleep had come; his chamber had been sweetened with the scents of musk and rosewater, and he retired there for the night.

Tahmineh

When one watch of the night had passed, and Venus rose into the darkened sky, a sound of muffled whispering came

to Rostam's ears; gently his chamber door was pushed
open. A slave entered, a scented candle in her hand, and
approached the hero's pillow; like a splendid sun, a paradise of tints and scents, her mistress followed her. This
beauty's eyebrows curved like an archer's bow, and her
ringlets hung like nooses to snare the unwary; in stature she
was as elegant as a cypress tree. Her mind and body were
pure, and she seemed not to partake of earthly existence at
all. The lionhearted Rostam gazed at her in astonishment;
he asked her what her name was and what it was that she
sought on so dark a night. She said:

> "My name is Tahmineh; longing has torn
> My wretched life in two, though I was born
> The daughter of the king of Samangan,
> And am descended from a warrior clan.
> But like a legend I have heard the story
> Of your heroic battles and your glory,
> Of how you have no fear, and face alone
> Dragons and demons and the dark unknown,
> Of how you sneak into Turan at night
> And prowl the borders to provoke a fight,
> Of how, when warriors see your mace, they quail
> And feel their lionhearts within them fail.
> I bit my lip to hear such talk, and knew
> I longed to see you, to catch sight of you,
> To glimpse your martial chest and mighty face—
> And now God brings you to this lowly place.
> If you desire me, I am yours, and none
> Shall see or hear of me from this day on;
> Desire destroys my mind, I long to bear
> Within my woman's womb your son and heir;
> I promise you your horse if you agree
> Since all of Samangan must yield to me."

When Rostam saw how lovely she was, and moreover heard that she promised to find Rakhsh for him, he felt that nothing but good could come of the encounter; and so in secret the two passed the long hours of night together.

As the sun cast its noose in the eastern sky, Rostam gave Tahmineh a clasp which he wore on his upper arm and said to her, "Take this, and if you should bear a daughter, braid her hair about it as an omen of good fortune; but if the heavens give you a son, have him wear it on his upper arm, as a sign of who his father is. He'll be a boy like Sam, the son of Nariman, noble and chivalrous; one who'll bring down eagles from their cloudy heights, a man on whom the sun will not shine harshly."

Then the king came to Rostam and asked how he had slept, and brought news that Rakhsh had been found. Rostam rushed out and stroked and petted his horse, overjoyed to have found him; he saddled him and rode on his way, content with the king's hospitality and to have found his horse again.

Sohrab Is Born

Nine months passed, and the princess Tahmineh gave birth to a son as splendid as the shining moon. He seemed another Rostam, Sam, or Nariman, and since his face shone bright with laughter, Tahmineh named him Sohrab (Bright-visaged). When a month had gone, he seemed a year old; at three, he played polo; and at five, he took up archery and practiced with a javelin. By the time he was ten, no one dared compete with him and he said to his mother, "Tell me truly now, why is it I'm so much taller than other boys of my age? Whose child am I, and what should I answer when people ask about my father? If you keep all this hidden from me, I won't let you live a moment longer." His mother answered, "Hear what I have to say, and be pleased at it, and control your temper. You are the son of the mammoth-bodied hero Rostam and are descended from Dastan, Sam, and

Nariman. This is why your head reaches to the heavens; since the Creator made this world, there never has been such a knight as Rostam." Secretly she showed him a letter that Rostam had sent, together with three rubies set in gold; then she said, "Afrasyab must know nothing of this, and if Rostam hears of how you've grown, he'll summon you to his side and break your mother's heart." Sohrab answered, "This is not something to be kept secret; the world's chieftains tell tales of Rostam's prowess; how can it be right for me to hide such a splendid lineage? I'll gather a boundless force of fighting Turks and drive Kavus from his throne; then I'll eradicate all trace of Tus from Iran and give the royal mace and crown to Rostam, I'll place him on Kavus's throne. Next I'll march on Turan and fight with Afrasyab and seize his throne too. If Rostam is my father and I am his son, then no one else in all the world should wear the crown; when the sun and moon shine out in splendor, what should lesser stars do, boasting of their glory?" From every quarter swordsmen and chieftains flocked to the youth.

War Breaks Out Again

Afrasyab was told that Sohrab had launched his boat upon the waters and that, although his mouth still smelled of mother's milk, his thoughts were all of swords and arrows. The informants said that he was threatening war against Kavus, that a mighty force had flocked to him, and that in his self-confidence he took no account of anyone. Afrasyab laughed with delight; he chose twelve thousand warriors, placed them under the command of Barman and Human, and addressed his two chieftains thus: "This secret must remain hidden. When these two face each other on the battlefield, Rostam will surely be at a disadvantage. The father must not know his son, because he will try to win him over; but, knowing nothing, the ancient warrior filled with years will be slain by our young lion. Later you can deal with Sohrab and dispatch him to his endless sleep."

Afrasyab sent the two to Sohrab, and he entrusted them with a letter encouraging the young warrior in his ambitions and promising support.

The White Fortress

There was an armed outpost of Iran called the White Fortress; its keeper was an experienced warrior named Hejir. Sohrab led his army toward the fortress, and, when Hejir saw this, he mounted his horse and rode out to confront him. Sohrab rode in front of the army, then drew his sword and taunted Hejir, "What are you dreaming of, coming to fight alone against me? Who are you, what is your name and lineage? Your mother will weep over your corpse today." Hejir replied, "There are not many Turks who can match themselves against me. I am Hejir, the army's brave commander, and I shall tear your head off and send it to Kavus, the king of all the world; your body I shall thrust beneath the dirt." Sohrab laughed to hear such talk; the two attacked each other furiously with lances. Hejir's lance struck at Sohrab's waist but did no harm, but when Sohrab returned the blow, he sent Hejir sprawling from his saddle to the ground. Sohrab leapt down from his horse, intending to sever his enemy's head, but Hejir twisted away to the right and begged for quarter. Sohrab spared him, and in triumph preached submission to his captive. Then he had him bound and sent to Human. When those in the fortress realized that their leader had been captured, both men and women wailed aloud with grief, crying out, "Hejir is taken from us."

Gordafarid

But one of those within the fortress was a woman, daughter of the warrior Gazhdaham, named Gordafarid. When she learned that their leader had allowed himself to be taken, she found his behavior so shameful that her rosy cheeks became as black as pitch with rage. With not a moment's delay she dressed herself in a knight's armor, gathered her hair beneath a Rumi helmet, and rode out from the fortress, a lion eager for battle. She roared at the enemy's ranks, "Where are your heroes, your warriors, your tried and tested chieftains?"

When Sohrab saw this new combatant, he laughed and bit his lip and said to himself, "Another victim has stepped into the hero's trap." Quickly he donned his armor and a Chinese helmet and galloped out to face Gordafarid. When she saw him, she took aim with her bow (no bird could escape her well-aimed arrows) and let loose a hail of arrows, weaving to left and right like an experienced horseman as she did so. Shame urged Sohrab forward, his shield held before his head to deflect her arrows. Seeing him approach, she laid aside her bow and snatched up a lance and, as her horse reared toward the clouds, she hurled it at her opponent. Sohrab wheeled round and his lance struck Gordafarid in the waist; her armor's fastenings were severed, but she unsheathed her sword and hacked at his lance, splitting it in two. Sohrab bore down on her again and snatched her helmet from her head; her hair streamed out, and her face shone like a splendid sun. He saw that his opponent was a woman, one whose hair was worthy of a diadem. He was amazed and said, "How is it that a woman should ride out from the Persian army and send the dust up from her horse's hooves into the heavens?" He unhitched his lariat from the saddle and flung it, catching her by the waist, then said: "Don't try to escape from me; now, my beauty, what do you mean by coming out to fight? I've never captured prey like you before, and I won't let you go in a hurry." Gordafarid saw that she could only get away by a ruse of some kind, and, showing her face to him, she said, "O lionhearted warrior, two armies are watching us and, if I let them see my face and hair, your troops will be very amused by the notion of your fighting with a mere girl; we'd better draw aside somewhere, that's what a wise man would do, so that you won't be a laughing stock before these two armies. Now our army, our wealth, our fortress, and the fortress's commander will all be in your hands to do with as you wish; I'll hand them over to you, so there's no need for you to pursue this war any further." As she spoke, her shining teeth and bright red lips and heavenly face were like a paradise to Sohrab; no gardener ever grew so straight and tall a cypress as she seemed to be; her eyes were liquid as a deer's, her brows were two bent bows, you'd say her body was a bud about to blossom.

Sohrab said, "Don't go back on your word; you've seen me on the battlefield; don't think you'll be safe from me once you're behind the fortress walls again. They don't reach higher than the clouds and my mace will bring them down if need be." Gordafarid tugged at her horse's reins and wheeled round toward the fortress; Sohrab rode beside her to the gates, which opened and let in the weary, wounded, woman warrior.

The defenders closed the gates, and young and old alike wept for Gordafarid and Hejir. They said, "O brave lioness, we all grieve for you, but you fought well and your ruse worked and you brought no shame on your people." Then Gordafarid laughed long and heartily and climbed up on the fortress walls and looked out over the army. When she saw Sohrab perched on his saddle, she shouted down to him:

> "O king of all the Asian hordes, turn back,
> Forget your fighting and your planned attack."
> She laughed; and then, more gently, almost sighed:
> "No Turk will bear away a Persian bride;
> But do not chafe at Fate's necessity—
> Fate did not mean that you should conquer me.
> Besides, you're not a Turk, I know you trace
> Your lineage from a far more splendid race;

Put any of your heroes to the test—
None has your massive arm and mighty chest.
But news will spread that Turan's army's here,
Led by a stripling chief who knows no fear;
Kavus will send for noble Rostam then
And neither you nor any of your men
Will live for long: I should be sad to see
This lion destroy you here—turn now and flee,
Don't trust your strength, strength will not save your life;
The fatted calf knows nothing of the knife."

Hearing her, Sohrab felt a fool, realizing how easily he could have taken the fortress. He plundered the surrounding settlements and sulkily said: "It's too late for battle now, but when dawn comes, I'll raze this fortress's walls, and its inhabitants will know the meaning of defeat."

But that night Gazhdaham, Gordafarid's aged father, sent a letter to Kavus telling him of Sohrab's prowess, and secretly, before dawn, most of the Persian troops evacuated the fortress, traveling toward Iran and safety.

When the sun rose above the mountains, the Turks prepared to fight; Sohrab mounted his horse, couched his lance, and advanced on the fortress. But as he and his men reached the walls, they saw very few defenders; they pushed open the gates and saw within no preparations for battle. A straggle of soldiers came forward, begging for quarter.

Kavus Summons Rostam

When King Kavus received Gazhdaham's message, he was deeply troubled; he summoned his chieftains and put the matter before them. After he had read the letter to his warrior lords—men like Tus, Gudarz (the son of Keshvad), Giv, Gorgin, Bahram, and Farhad—Kavus said, "According to Gazhdaham, this is going to be lengthy business. His letter has put all other thoughts from my mind; now, what should we do to remedy this situation, and who is there

in Iran who can stand up to this new warrior?" All agreed
that Giv should go to Zabol and tell Rostam of the danger
threatening Iran and the Persian throne.

Kavus wrote to Rostam, praising his prowess and appeal-
ing to him to come to the aid of the throne. Then he said
to Giv, "Gallop as quickly as wind-borne smoke and take
this letter to Rostam. Don't delay in Zabol; if you arrive at
night, set off on the return journey the next morning. Tell
Rostam that matters are urgent." Giv took the letter and
traveled quickly to Zabol, without resting along the way.
Rostam came out with a contingent of his nobles to welcome him; Giv and Rostam's group dismounted together,
and Rostam questioned him closely about the king and
events in Iran. After they had returned to Rostam's palace
and rested a while, Giv repeated what he had heard, handed
over the letter, and gave what news he could of Sohrab.

When Rostam had listened to him and read the letter,
he laughed aloud and said in astonishment, "So it seems
that a second Sam is loose in the world; this would be no
surprise if he were a Persian, but from the Turks it's unprec-
edented. I myself have a son over there, by the princess of
Samangan, but he's still a boy and doesn't yet realize that
war is the way to glory. I sent his mother gold and jewels,
and she sent me back an answer saying that he'd soon be a
tall young fellow; his mouth still smells of mother's milk,
but he drinks his wine, and no doubt he'll be a fighter soon
enough. Now, you and I should rest for a day and moisten
our dry lips with wine, then we can make our way to the
king and lead Persia's warriors out to war. It's possible that
Fortune's turned against us, but if not, this campaign will
not prove difficult; when the sea's waves inundate the land,
the fiercest fire won't stay alight for long. And when this
young warrior sees my banner, his heart will know his revels
are all ended; he won't be in such a hurry to fight anymore.
This is not something we should worry ourselves about."

They sat to their wine and, forgetting all about the king, passed the night in idle chatter. The next morning Rostam woke with a hangover and called again for wine; this day too was passed in drinking and no one thought about setting out on the journey to Kavus. And once again on the third day Rostam ignored the king's summons and had wine brought. On the fourth day Giv bestirred himself and said, "Kavus is a headstrong man and not at all intelligent; he's very upset about this business and he can neither eat nor sleep properly. If we stay much longer here in Zabolestan, he will be extremely angry." Rostam replied, "Don't worry about that; there's not a man alive who can meddle with me." He gave orders that Rakhsh be saddled and that the tucket for departure be sounded. Zabol's knights heard the trumpets and, armed and helmeted, they gathered about their leader.

Rostam and Kavus

They arrived at the king's court in high spirits and ready to serve him. But when they bowed before the king, he at first made them no answer, and then, addressing Giv, he burst out in fury, "Who is Rostam that he should ignore me, that he should flout my orders in this way? Take him and string him up alive on the gallows and never mention his name to me again." Giv was horrified at Kavus's words and remonstrated, "You would treat Rostam in this way?" The courtiers stared, struck dumb, as Kavus then roared to Tus, "Take both of them and hang them both." And, wildly as a fire that burns dry reeds, he sprang up from the throne. Tus took Rostam by the arm to lead him from Kavus's presence and the warriors there watched in wonder, but Rostam too burst out in fury and addressed the king:

> "Smother your rage; each act of yours is more
> Contemptible than every act before.

You're not fit to be king; it's Sohrab you
Should hang alive, but you're unable to."
Tus he sent sprawling with a single blow
Then strode toward the door as if to go
But turned back in his rage and said, "I am
The Crown Bestower, the renowned Rostam,
When I am angry, who is Kay Kavus?
Who dares to threaten me? And who is Tus?
My helmet is my crown, Rakhsh is my throne,
And I am slave to none but God alone.
If Sohrab should attack, who will survive?
No child or warrior will be left alive
In all Iran—too late, and desperately,
You'll seek for some escape or remedy;
This is your land where you reside and reign—
Henceforth you'll not see Rostam here again."

The courtiers were deeply alarmed, since they regarded Rostam as a shepherd and themselves as his flock. They turned to Gudarz and said, "You must heal this breach, the king will listen to no one but you; go to this crazy monarch and speak to him mildly and at length, and with luck we'll be able to restore our fortunes again." Gudarz went to Kavus and reminded him of Rostam's past service and of the threat that Sohrab was to Iran, and when he had heard him out, Kavus repented of his anger and said to Gudarz, "Your words are just, and nothing becomes an old man's lips like wisdom. A king should be wise and cautious; anger and impetuous behavior bring no good to anyone. Go to Rostam and remind him of our former friendship; make him forget my outburst." Gudarz and the army's chieftains went in search of Rostam; finally they saw the dust raised by Rakhsh and caught up with him. They praised the hero and then said, "You know that Kavus is a brainless fool, that he is subject to these outbursts of temper, that he erupts in rage and is immediately sorry and swears to mend his ways.

If you are furious with the king, the people of Iran are not at fault; already he regrets his rage and bites the back of his hand in repentance."

Rostam replied, "I have no need of Kay Kavus: My saddle's my throne, my helmet's my crown, this stout armor's my robes of state, and my heart's prepared for Death. Why should I fear Kavus's rage; he's no more to me than a fistful of dirt. My mind is weary of all this, my heart is full, and I fear no one but God himself." Gudarz replied, "Iran and her chieftains and the army will see this in another way; they'll say that the great hero was afraid of the Turk and that he sneaked away in fear; they'll say that if Rostam has fled, we should all flee. I saw the court in an uproar over Kavus's rage, but I also saw the stir that Sohrab has created. Don't turn your back on the king of Iran; your name's renowned throughout the world, don't dim its luster by this flight. And consider: The army is hard pressed, this is no time to abandon the throne and crown."

Rostam stared at him and said, "If there's any fear in my heart I tear it from me now." Shamefaced, he rode back to the king's court, and when he entered, the king stood and asked his forgiveness for what had passed between them, saying, "Impetuous rage is part of my nature; we have to live as God has fashioned us. This new and unexpected enemy had made my heart grow faint as the new moon; I looked to you for help and when you delayed your coming, I became angry. But seeing you affronted by my words, I regretted what I had said." Rostam replied, "The world is yours; we are all your subjects. I have come to hear your orders." Kavus said, "Tonight we feast, tomorrow we fight." Entertained by musicians and served by pale young slaves, the two then sat to their wine and drank till half the night had passed.

The Persian Army Sets Out against Sohrab

At dawn the next day the king ordered Giv and Tus to prepare the army; drums were bound on elephants, the treasury doors were opened, and war supplies were handed out. A hundred thousand warriors gathered and the air was darkened by their dust. Stage by stage they marched till nightfall, and their glittering weapons shone like points of fire seen through a dark curtain. So day by day they went on until at last they reached the fortress's gates, and their number was so great that not a stone or speck of earth was visible before the walls.

A shout from the lookouts told Sohrab that the enemy's army had come. Sohrab went up onto the city walls and then summoned Human; when Human saw the mighty force opposing them, he gasped and his heart quailed. Sohrab told him to be of good cheer, saying, "In all this limitless army, you'll not see one warrior who'll be willing to face me in combat, no, not if the sun and moon themselves came down to aid him. There's a great deal of armor here and many men, but I know of none among them who's a warrior to reckon with. And now in Afrasyab's name I shall make this plain a sea of blood." Cheerful and fearless, Sohrab descended from the walls. For their part the Persians pitched camp, and so vast was the number of tents and pavilions that the plain and surrounding foothills disappeared from view.

Rostam Spies on Sohrab

The sun withdrew from the world, and dark night spread her troops across the plain. Eager to observe the enemy, Rostam came before Kavus. He said, "Let me go from here unarmed to see just who this new young hero is, and to see what chieftains are accompanying him." Kavus replied, "You are the man for such an undertaking; take care, and may you return safely."

Rostam disguised himself as a Turk and made his way quickly to the fortress. As he drew near he could hear the sound of drunken revelry from the Turks within. He slipped into the fortress as a lion stalks wild deer. There he saw Sohrab seated on a throne and presiding over the festivities; on one side of him sat Zhendeh-Razm and on the other were the warriors Human and Barman. Tall as a cypress, mighty of limb, and mammoth chested, Sohrab seemed to fill the throne. He was surrounded by a hundred Turkish youths, as haughty as young lions, and fifty servants stood before him. In turn, all praised their hero's strength and stature and sword and seal, while Rostam watched the scene from afar.

Zhendeh-Razm left the gathering on some errand and saw a warrior, cypress-tall, whom he did not recognize. He came over to Rostam and said, "Who are you? Come into the light so that I can see your face." With one swift blow from his fist, Rostam struck out at Zhendeh-Razm's neck, and the champion gave up the ghost there and then; he lay motionless on the ground, never returning to the feast. After a while Sohrab noticed his absence and asked after him. Retainers went out and saw him lying prone in the dirt; neither banquets nor battles would concern him again. They returned wailing and weeping, and told Sohrab that Zhendeh-Razm's days of feasting and fighting were over. When Sohrab heard this, he sprang up and hurried to where the warrior lay, and the musicians and servants with tapers followed after him. He stared in astonishment, then called his chieftains to him and said, "Tonight we must not rest but sharpen our spears for battle: A wolf has attacked our flock, eluding the shepherd and his dog. But with God's aid, when I ride out and loose my lariat from the saddle, I'll be revenged on these Iranian warriors for the death of Zhendeh-Razm." And with this he returned to the feast.

For his part Rostam slipped back to the Persian lines, where Giv waited on watch. Rostam told Giv of how he had killed one of the enemy, and then he went to Kavus and gave him news of Sohrab, saying that the new hero had no equal in either Turan or Iran, and that he was the image of Rostam's own grandfather, Sam. He told Kavus of how he had killed Zhendeh-Razm, and then he and the king called for musicians and wine.

Sohrab Surveys the Persian Camp

When the sun had flung its noose into the sky, and rays of light shot through the empyrean, Sohrab armed himself and went up onto a tower on the city walls; from there he could see the Iranian forces spread out below. He summoned Hejir and, after promising wealth if he was truthful and prison if he was not, he said to him, "I want to ask you about the leaders and champions of the other side, men like Tus, Kavus, Gudarz, Bahram, and the famous Rostam; identify for me everyone I point out to you. Those multicolored pavilion walls enclosing tents of leopardskin; a hundred elephants are tethered in front of them, and beside the turquoise throne that stands there, a banner rises emblazoned with the sun and topped with a golden moon; there, right in the center of the encampment—whose place is that?" Hejir replied, "That is the Persian king's court, and there are lions there as well as elephants."

Sohrab went on, "Over to the right, where all the baggage and knights and elephants are, there's a black pavilion around which are countless ranks of soldiers; the banner there bears an elephant as its device, and there are gold-shod knights on guard before it; whose is that?" Hejir answered, "The banner embroidered with an elephant belongs to Tus, the son of Nozar." "And the red pavilion that so many knights are crowded round, where the banner shows a lion and bears in its center a huge jewel, whose is that?" "The lion banner belongs to the great Gudarz, of the clan of Keshvad."

"And the green pavilion, where all the infantry are standing? Where the banner of Kaveh is; look, a resplendent throne shines there, and on it is seated a hero who's head and shoulders taller than all those who stand in front of him. A magnificent horse, with a lariat slung across its saddle, waits next to him and neighs toward its lord every now and again. The device on the banner there is of a dragon, and its staff is topped with a golden lion." Hejir answered, "That's some lord from Tartary who's recently joined forces with the king." Sohrab asked the new lord's name, but Hejir said, "I don't know his name; I was here in this fortress when he came to our king." Sohrab was saddened in his heart, because no trace of Rostam was to be seen.

He questioned Hejir further, pointing out an encampment around a banner that bore the device of a wolf. "That belongs to the eldest and noblest of Gudarz's sons, Giv," Hejir replied. "And over toward where the sun is rising, there's a white pavilion thronged about with foot soldiers; their leader's seated on a throne of teak placed on an ivory pedestal and he's surrounded by slaves?" "That is Prince Fariborz, the son of King Kavus." "And the scarlet pavilion where the soldiers are standing round the entrance, where the red, yellow, and purple banners are; behind them towers a taller banner bearing the device of a wild boar and topped with a golden moon?" "That belongs to the lion-slaying Goraz, of Giv's clan."

And so Sohrab sought for some sign of his father, while the other hid from him what he longed to know. Once again he asked about the tall warrior beneath the green banner, beside whom waited a noble horse bearing a coiled lariat. But Hejir answered, "If I don't tell you his name it's because I don't know it myself." "But this cannot be right," Sohrab said. "You've made no mention of Rostam; the greatest warrior in the world could not stay hidden in this army camp; you said he was the foremost of their heroes, keeper of the country, and ward of the marches." "Perhaps this great warrior has gone to Zabolestan, for now is the time of the spring festival." Sohrab answered: "Don't talk so foolishly; his king has led their forces into the field; if this world champion were to sit drinking and taking his ease at such a time, everyone would laugh at him. If you point out Rostam to me, I'll make you a wealthy and honored man, you'll never want for anything again: But if you keep his whereabouts hidden from me, I'll sever your head from your shoulders; now choose which it's to be."

But in his heart the wily Hejir thought, "If I point out Rostam to this strong Turkish youth, who has such shoulders and who sits his horse so well, out of all our forces it'll be Rostam he'll choose to fight against. With his massive strength and mighty frame, he could well kill Rostam, and who from Iran would be able to avenge the hero's death? Then this Sohrab will seize Kavus's throne. Death with honor is better than aiding the enemy, and if Gudarz and his clan are to die, then I have no wish to live in Iran either." To Sohrab he replied, "Why are you so hasty and irritable? You talk of nothing but Rostam. It's not him you should try to fight with; he would prove a formidable opponent on the battlefield. You wouldn't be able to defeat him and it would be no easy matter to capture him either."

Sohrab Issues His Challenge

When Sohrab heard such slighting words, he turned his back on Hejir and hid his face. Then he turned and struck him with such violence that Hejir sprawled headlong in the dirt. Sohrab went back to his tent and there donned his armor and helmet. Seething with fury, he mounted his horse, couched his lance, and rode out to the battlefield like a maddened elephant. None of the champions of the Persian army dared confront him: Seeing his massive frame, his martial figure on horseback, his mighty arm and glittering lance, they said, "He is another Rostam; who would dare look at him or oppose him in combat?"

Then Sohrab roared out his challenge against Kavus, "What prowess have you on the battlefield? Why do you call yourself King Kavus when you have no skill or strength in battle? I'll spit your body on this lance of mine and make the stars weep for your downfall. The night when I was feasting and Zhendeh-Razm was killed, I swore a mighty oath that I'd not leave a single warrior living in all Persia, that I'd string Kavus up alive on a gallows. Is there one from among all Persia's fighting champions who'll oppose me on the battlefield?" So he stood, fuming with rage, while not a sound rose from the Persian ranks in answer to his challenge. Sohrab's response was to bend low in the saddle and bear down on the Persian camp. With his lance he severed the ropes of seventy tent pegs; half of the great pavilion tumbled down, the sound of trumpets rang in the air, and the army scattered like wild asses before a lion. Kavus cried out, "Have someone tell Rostam that our warriors are confounded by this Turk, that I've not one knight who dares confront him." Tus took the message to Rostam, who said,

> *"When other kings have unexpectedly*
> *Asked for my services, or summoned me,*
> *I've been rewarded with a gift, with treasure,*
> *With banquets, celebrations, courtly pleasure—*
> *But from Kavus I've witnessed nothing more*
> *Than constant hardships and unending war."*

He ordered that Rakhsh be saddled and, leaving Zavareh to guard his encampment, he rode out with his warriors beside him, bearing his banner aloft.

When he saw the mighty Sohrab, whose massive frame seemed so like that of Sam, he called to him, "Let's move aside to open ground and face each other man to man." Sohrab rubbed his hands together, took up his position before the ranks of waiting soldiers, and answered, "Don't call any of your Persians to your aid, you and I will fight alone. But the battlefield's no place for you, you won't survive one blow of my fist, you're tall enough and have a fine chest and shoulders, but age has clipped your wings, old man!" Rostam stared at the haughty young warrior, at his fist and shoulders, and the way he sat his horse, and gently said to him:

> "So headstrong and so young! Warm words, and bold!
> The ground, young warrior, is both hard and cold.
> Yes, I am old, and I've seen many wars
> And laid low many mighty conquerors;
> Many a demon's perished by my hand
> And I've not known defeat, in any land.
> Look on me well; if you escape from me
> You need not fear the monsters of the sea;
> The sea and mountains know what I have wrought
> Against Turan, how nobly I have fought,
> The stars are witness to my chivalry,
> In all the world there's none can equal me."
> Then Sohrab said, "I'm going to question you.
> Your answer must be honest, straight, and true:
> I think that you're Rostam, and from the clan
> Of warlike Sam and noble Nariman."
> Rostam replied, "I'm not Rostam, I claim
> No kinship with that clan or noble name:
> Rostam's a champion, I'm a slave—I own
> No royal wealth or crown or kingly throne."
> And Sohrab's hopes were changed then to despair,
> Darkening before his gaze the sunlit air.

The First Combat between Rostam and Sohrab

Sohrab rode to the space allotted for combat, and his mother's words rang in his ears. At first they fought with short javelins, then attacked one another with Indian swords, and sparks sprang forth from the clash of iron against iron.

The mighty blows left both swords shattered, and they grasped their ponderous maces, and a weariness began to weigh their arms down. Their horses too began to tire, and the blows the heroes dealt shattered both the horse armor and their own cuirasses. Finally, both the horses and their riders paused, exhausted by the battle, and neither hero could summon the strength to deliver another blow. The two stood facing one another at a distance, the father filled with pain, the son with sorrow, their bodies soaked with sweat, their mouths caked with dirt, their tongues cracked with thirst. How strange the world's ways are! All beasts will recognize their young—the fish in the sea, the wild asses on the plain—but suffering and pride will make a man unable to distinguish his son from his enemy.

Rostam said to himself, "I've never seen a monster fight like this; my combat with the White Demon was as nothing to this and I can feel my heart's courage begin to fail. A young, unknown warrior who's seen nothing of the world has brought me to this desperate pass, and in the sight of both our armies."

When their horses had rested from the combat, both warriors—he who was old in years and he who was still a stripling—strung their bows, but their remaining armor rendered the arrows harmless. In fury then the two closed, grasping at one another's belts, each struggling to throw the other. Rostam, who on the day of battle could tear rock from the mountain crags, seized Sohrab's belt and strove to drag him from his saddle, but it was as if the boy were untouched and all Rostam's efforts were useless. Again these mighty lions withdrew from one another, wounded and exhausted.

Then once more Sohrab lifted his massive mace from the saddle and bore down on Rostam; his mace struck Rostam's shoulder and the hero writhed in pain. Sohrab laughed and cried, "You can't stand up to blows, it seems;

you might be cypress-tall, but an old man who acts like a youth is a fool."

Both now felt weakened by their battle, and sick at heart they turned aside from one another. Rostam rode toward the Turkish ranks like a leopard who sights his prey; like a wolf he fell on them, and their great army scattered before him. For his part Sohrab attacked the Persian host, striking down warriors with his mace. Rostam feared that some harm would come to Kavus from this young warrior, and he hurried back to his own lines. He saw Sohrab in the midst of the Persian ranks, the ground beneath his feet awash with wine-red blood; his spear, armor, and hands were smeared with blood and he seemed drunk with slaughter. Like a raging lion Rostam burst out in fury, "Bloodthirsty Turk, who challenged you from the Persian ranks? Why have you attacked them like a wolf run wild in a flock of sheep?" Sohrab replied, "And Turan's army had no part in this battle either, but you attacked them first even though none of them had challenged you." Rostam said, "Evening draws on, but, when the sun unsheathes its sword again, on this plain we shall see who will die and who will triumph. Let us return at dawn with swords ready for combat; go now, and await God's will!"

Sohrab and Rostam in Camp at Night

They parted and the air grew dark. Wounded and weary, Sohrab arrived at his own lines and questioned Human about Rostam's attack. Human answered, "The king's command was that we not stir from our camp; and so we were quite unprepared when a fearsome warrior bore down on us, as wild as if he were drunk or had come from single combat." Sohrab answered, "He didn't destroy one warrior from this host, while I, for my part, killed many Persians and soaked the ground with their blood. Now we must eat, and with wine drive sorrow from our hearts."

And on the other side, Rostam questioned Giv, "How did this Sohrab fight today?" Giv replied, "I have never seen

a warrior like him. He rushed into the center of our lines
intending to attack Tus, but Tus fled before him, and there
was none among us who could withstand his onslaught."
Rostam grew downcast at his words and went to King
Kavus, who motioned him to his side. Rostam described
Sohrab's massive body to him and said that no one had ever
seen such valor from so young a warrior. Then he went
on, "We fought with mace and sword and bow, and finally,
remembering that I had often enough pulled heroes down
from the saddle, I seized him by the belt and tried to drag
him from his horse and fling him to the ground. But a wind
could shake a mountainside before it would shift that hero.
When he comes to the combat ground tomorrow, I must
find some way to overcome him hand to hand; I shall do
my best, but I don't know who will win; we must wait and
see what God wills, for he it is, the Creator of the sun and
moon, who gives victory and glory." Kavus replied, "And
may he lacerate the hearts of those who wish you ill. I shall
spend the night in prayer to him for your success."

Rostam returned to his own men, preoccupied with
thoughts of the coming combat. Anxiously, his brother
Zavareh came forward, questioning him as to how he had
fared that day. Rostam asked him first for food, and then
shared his heart's forebodings. He said, "Be vigilant, and
do nothing rashly. When I face that Turk on the battlefield
at dawn, gather together our army and accoutrements—our
banner, throne, the golden boots our guards wear—and
wait at sunrise before our pavilion. If I'm victorious I shan't
linger on the battlefield, but if things turn out otherwise,
don't mourn for me or act impetuously; don't go forward
offering to fight. Instead, return to Zabolestan and go to
our father, Dastan; comfort my mother's heart, and make
her see that this fate was willed for me by God. Tell her not
to give herself up to grief, for no good will come of it. No
one lives forever in this world, and I have no complaint
against the turns of Fate. So many lions and demons and

leopards and monsters have been destroyed by my strength, and so many fortresses and castles have been razed by my might; no one has ever overcome me. Whoever mounts his horse and rides out for battle is knocking at the door of Death, and if we live a thousand years or more, Death is our destiny at last. When she is comforted, tell Dastan not to turn his back on the world's king, Kavus. If Kavus makes war, Dastan is not to tarry, but to obey his every command. Young and old, we are all bound for Death; on this earth no one lives forever." For half the night they talked of Sohrab, and the other half was spent in rest and sleep.

Sohrab Overcomes Rostam

When the shining sun spread its plumes and night's dark raven folded its wings, Rostam donned his tigerskin and mounted Rakhsh. His iron helmet on his head, he hitched the sixty loops of his lariat to his saddle, grasped his Indian sword in his hand, and rode out to the combat ground.

Sohrab had spent the night entertained by musicians and drinking wine with his companions. To Human he had confided his suspicions that his opponent was none other than Rostam, for he felt himself drawn to him, and besides, he resembled his mother's description of Rostam. When dawn came, he buckled on his armor and grasped his huge mace; with his head filled with battle and his heart in high spirits, he came onto the field shouting his war cry. He greeted Rostam with a smile on his lips, for all the world as if they had spent the night in revelry together:

> "When did you wake? How did you pass the night?
> And are you still determined we should fight?
> But throw your mace and sword down, put aside
> These thoughts of war, this truculence and pride.
> Let's sit and drink together, and the wine
> Will smooth away our frowns—both yours and mine.

Come, swear an oath before our God that we
Renounce all thoughts of war and enmity.
Let's make a truce, and feast as allies here
At least until new enemies appear.
The tears that stain my face are tokens of
My heart's affection for you, and my love;
I know that you're of noble ancestry—
Recite your lordly lineage to me."

Rostam replied, "This was not what we talked of last night; our talk was of hand-to-hand combat. I won't fall for these tricks, so don't try them. You might be still a child, but I am not, and I have bound my belt on ready for our combat. Now, let us fight, and the outcome will be as God wishes. I've seen much of good and evil in my life, and I'm not a man for talk or tricks or treachery." Sohrab replied, "Talk like this is not fitting from an old man. I would have wished that your days would come to an end peacefully, in your bed, and that your survivors would build a tomb to hold your body while your soul flew on its way. But if your life is to be in my hands, so be it; let us fight and the outcome will be as God wills."

They dismounted, tethered their horses, and warily came forward, each clad in mail and helmeted. They closed in combat, wrestling hand to hand, and mingled blood and sweat poured from their bodies. Then Sohrab, like a maddened elephant, struck Rostam a violent blow and felled him; like a lion leaping to bring down a wild ass, he flung himself on Rostam's chest, whose mouth and fist and face were grimed with dust. He drew a glittering dagger to sever the hero's head from his body, and Rostam spoke:

"O hero, lion destroyer, mighty lord,
Master of mace and lariat and sword,
Our customs do not count this course as right;
According to our laws, when warriors fight,

> *A hero may not strike the fatal blow*
> *The first time his opponent is laid low;*
> *He does this, and he's called a lion, when*
> *He's thrown his rival twice—and only then."*

By this trick he sought to escape death at Sohrab's hands. The brave youth bowed his head at the old man's words, believing what he was told. He released his opponent and withdrew to the plains where, unconcernedly, he spent some time hunting. After a while Human sought him out and asked him about the day's combat thus far. Sohrab told Human what had happened and what Rostam had said to him. Human responded, "Young man, you've had enough of life, it seems! Alas for this chest, for these arms and shoulders of yours; alas for your fist, for the mace that it holds; you'd trapped the tiger and you let him go, which was the act of a simpleton! Now, watch for the consequences of this foolishness of yours when you face him again."

Sohrab returned to camp, sick at heart and furious with himself. A prince once made a remark for just such a situation:

> *"Do not make light of any enemy*
> *No matter how unworthy he may be."*

For his part, when Rostam had escaped from Sohrab, he sprang up like a man who has come back from the dead and strode to a nearby stream where he drank and washed the grime from his face and body. Next he prayed, asking for God's help and for victory, unaware of the fate the sun and moon held in store for him. Then, anxious and pale, he made his way from the stream back to the battlefield.

And there he saw Sohrab mounted on his rearing horse, charging after wild asses like a maddened elephant, whirling his lariat, his bow on his arm. Rostam stared at him in astonishment, trying to calculate his chances against him in single combat. When Sohrab caught sight of him, all the arrogance of youth was in his voice as he taunted Rostam, "So you escaped the lion's claws, old man, and crept away from the wounds he dealt you!"

Sohrab Is Mortally Wounded by Rostam

Once again they tethered their horses, and once again they grappled in single combat, each grasping the other's belt and straining to overthrow him. But, for all his great strength, Sohrab seemed as though he were hindered by the heavens, and Rostam seized him by the shoulders and finally forced him to the ground; the brave youth's back was bent, his time had come, his strength deserted him. Like a lion Rostam laid him low, but, knowing that the youth would not lie there for long, he quickly drew his dagger and plunged it in the lionhearted hero's chest. Sohrab writhed, then gasped for breath, and knew he'd passed beyond concerns of worldly good and evil. He said:

> "I brought this on myself, this is from me,
> And Fate has merely handed you the key
> To my brief life: not you but heaven's vault—
> Which raised me and then killed me—is at fault.
> Love for my father led me here to die.
> My mother gave me signs to know him by,
> And you could be a fish within the sea,
> Or pitch black, lost in night's obscurity,
> Or be a star in heaven's endless space,
> Or vanish from the earth and leave no trace,
> But still my father, when he knows I'm dead,
> Will bring down condign vengeance on your head.
> One from this noble band will take this sign
> To Rostam's hands, and tell him it was mine,
> And say I sought him always, far and wide,
> And that, at last, in seeking him, I died."

When Rostam heard the warrior's words, his head whirled and the earth turned dark before his eyes, and when he came back to himself, he roared in an agony of anguish and asked what it was that the youth had which was a sign from Rostam, the most cursed of all heroes.

"If then you are Rostam," said the youth, "and you killed me, your wits were dimmed by an evil nature. I tried in every way to guide you, but no love of yours responded. Open the straps that bind my armor and look on my naked body. When the battle drums sounded before my door, my mother came to me, her eyes awash with tears, her soul in torment to see me leave. She bound a clasp on my arm and said, 'Take this in memory of your father, and watch for when it will be useful to you'; but now it shows its power too late, and the son is laid low before his father." And when Rostam opened the boy's armor and saw the clasp he tore at his own clothes in grief, saying, "All men praised your bravery, and I have killed you with my own hands." Violently he wept and tore his hair and heaped dust on his head. Sohrab said, "By this you make things worse. You must not weep; what point is there in wounding yourself like this? What happened is what had to happen."

The shining sun descended from the sky and still Rostam had not returned to his encampment. Twenty warriors came riding to see the battlefield and found two muddied horses but no sign of Rostam. Assuming he had been killed, they sent a message to Kavus saying, "Rostam's royal throne lies desolate." A wail of mourning went up from the army, and Kavus gave orders that the drums and trumpets be sounded. Tus hurried forward and Kavus told him to have someone survey the battlefield and find out what it was that Sohrab had done and whether they were indeed to weep for the fortunes of Iran, since if Rostam had been killed, no one would be able to oppose Sohrab and they would have to retreat without giving battle.

As the noise of mourning rose from the army, Sohrab said to Rostam, "Now that my days are ended, the Turks' fortunes too have changed. Be merciful to them, and do not let the king make war on them; it was at my instigation they attacked Iran. What promises I made, what hopes I held out to them! They should not be the ones to suffer; see you look kindly on them."

Cold sighs on his lips, his face besmeared with blood and tears, Rostam mounted Rakhsh and rode to the Persian camp, lamenting aloud, tormented by the thought of what he had done. When they caught sight of him, the Persian warriors fell to the ground, praising God that he was alive, but when they saw his ripped clothes and dust-besmeared head and face, they asked him what had happened and what distressed him. He told them of the strange deed he had done, of how he had slaughtered the person who was dearer to him than all others, and all who heard lamented aloud with him.

Then he said to the chieftains, "I've no courage left now, no strength or sense; go no further with this war against the Turks, the evil that I have done today is sufficient." Rostam returned to where his son lay wounded, and the nobles—men like Tus, Gudarz, and Gostaham—accompanied him, crowding round and saying, "It's God who will heal this wound, it's he who will lighten your sorrows." But Rostam drew a dagger, intending to slash his own neck with it; weeping with grief, they flung themselves on him and Gudarz said, "What point is there in spreading fire and sword throughout the world by your death, and if you wound yourself a thousand times, how will that help this noble youth? If there is any time left to him on this earth, then stay with him and ease his hours here; and if he is to die, then look at all the world and say, 'Who is immortal?' We are all Death's prey, both he who wears a helmet and he who wears the crown."

Rostam replied, "Go quickly and take a message from me to Kavus and tell him what has befallen me; say that I have rent my own son's vitals with a dagger, and that I curse my life and long for death. Tell him, if he has any regard for all I have done in his service, to have pity on my suffering and to send me the elixir he keeps in his treasury, the medicine that will heal all wounds. If he will send it, together with a goblet of wine, it may be that, by his grace, Sohrab will survive and serve Kavus's throne as I have done."

Like wind the chieftain bore this message to Kavus, who said in reply, "Which warrior, of all this company, is of more repute than Rostam? And are we to make him even greater? Then, surely he will turn on me and kill me. How will the wide world contain his glory and might? How will he remain the servant to my throne? If, some day, evil's to come to me from him, I will respond with evil. You heard how he referred to me:

> *'When I am angry, who is Kay Kavus?*
> *Who dares to threaten me? And who is Tus?'"*

When Gudarz heard these words, he hurried back to Rostam and said:

> *"This king's malicious nature is a tree*
> *That grows new, bitter fruit perpetually;*

You must go to him and try to enlighten his benighted soul." Rostam gave orders that a rich cloth be spread beside the stream; gently he laid his wounded son there and set out to where Kavus held court. But he was overtaken on the way by one who told him that Sohrab had departed this world; he had looked round for his father, then heaved an icy sigh, and groaned, and closed his eyes forever. It was not a castle the boy needed his father to provide for him now, but a coffin.

Rostam dismounted and removed his helmet and smeared dust on his head.

Then he commanded that the boy's body be covered in royal brocade—the youth who had longed for fame and conquest, and whose destiny was a narrow bier borne from the battlefield. Rostam returned to his royal pavilion and had it set ablaze; his warriors smeared their heads with dust, and in the midst of their lamentations they fed the flames with his throne, his saddlecloth of leopardskin, his silken tent of many colors. Rostam wept and ripped his royal clothes, and all the heroes of the Persian army sat in the wayside dust with him and tried to comfort him, but to no avail.

Kavus said to Rostam, "The heavens bear all before them, from the mighty Alborz Mountains to the lightest reed; man must not love this earth too much. For one it comes early and for another late, but Death comes to all. Accept this loss, pay heed to wisdom's ways, and know that if you bow the heavens to the ground or set the seas aflame, you cannot bring back him who's gone; his soul grows old, but in another place. I saw him in the distance once, I saw his height and stature and the massive mace he held; Fate drove him here to perish by your hand. What is it you would do? What remedy exists for this? How long will you mourn in this way?"

Rostam replied, "Yes, he is gone. But Human still camps here on the plains, along with chieftains from Turan and China. Have no rancor in your heart against them. Give the command, and let my brother Zavareh lead off our armies." The king said, "This sadness clouds your soul, great hero. Well, they have done me evil enough, and they have wreaked havoc in Iran, but my heart feels the pain you feel, and for your sake I'll think no more of them."

Rostam Returns to Zabolestan

Rostam returned then to his home, Zabolestan, and when news of his coming reached his father, Zal-Dastan, the people of Sistan came out to meet him, mourning and grieving for his loss. When Dastan saw the bier, he dismounted from his horse, and Rostam came forward on foot, his clothes torn, with anguish in his heart. The chieftains took off their armor and stood before the coffin and smeared their heads with dust. When Rostam reached his palace, he cried aloud and had the coffin set before him; then he ripped out the nails and pulled back the shroud and showed the nobles gathered there the body of his son. A tumult of mourning swept the palace, which seemed a vast tomb where a lion lay; the youth resembled Sam, as if that hero slept, worn out by battle. Then Rostam covered him in cloth of gold and nailed the coffin shut and said, "If I construct a golden tomb for him and fill it with black musk, it will not last for long when I am gone; but I see nothing else that I can do."

> *This tale is full of tears, and Rostam leaves*
> *The tender heart indignant as it grieves:*
> *I turn now from this story to relate*
> *The tale of Seyavash and his sad fate.*

The tragic tale of Rostam and Sohrab is followed by the story of Seyavash, the son of King Kavus, and a fugitive princess from Turan. Rostam brought Seyavash up in Sistan, giving him the training necessary for him to become a knight and a prince. When Seyavash returned as a handsome and accomplished adolescent to his father's court, his step-mother, Sudabeh, fell in love with him. Seyavash rejected her advances, and in revenge Sudabeh accused him of having attempted to rape her. The young prince was eventually cleared of the charges, through a trial by fire, but he still longed to leave the court in order to get away from Sudabeh and her influence. And so when Afrasyab's forces again attacked Iran, Seyavash leapt at the chance to lead the Persian armies against them. Rostam accompanied the prince on this expedition, as his advisor. Seyavash defeated the armies of Turan, driving them back beyond the Oxus, the traditional border between the two countries, and concluding a peace treaty with

Afrasyab. Kavus was enraged at the terms of the treaty, dismissed Rostam as Seyavash's advisor, and ordered his son to attack Turan. Rather than break the terms of his treaty, Seyavash fled to Turan, throwing himself on the mercy of Afrasyab, who at first received him kindly and even married him to his daughter, Farigis. But Afrasyab's brother, the army commander whom Seyavash had defeated in battle, poisoned Afrasyab's mind against Seyavash and persuaded him to kill the young prince. Enraged by this outcome Rostam dragged Sudabeh from Kavus's harem and killed her for her part in Seyavash's downfall. From now on in the Shahnameh, *the Persian desire for revenge for the death of Seyavash is always present in their dealings with Turan.*

THE AKVAN DIV

Listen to this tale, told by an old Persian. Here is what he said:

One day Kay Khosrow rose at dawn and went to a flower garden to hold court. He had spent the first hour of the day there, surrounded by his chieftains—Gudarz, Rostam, Gostaham, Barzin, Garshasp (who was descended from Jamshid), Giv, Roham, Gorgin, and Kharrad—when a herder of horses came in from the plains with a request for help.

"A wild ass has appeared in my herd," he said. "He's like a demon—a div—who has slipped his bonds, or you could say he's like a savage male lion. He's constantly breaking the necks of my horses. He's colored just like the sun, as if he'd been dipped in liquid gold, except for a musk-black stripe that runs from his mane to his tale. He's as tall as a fine bay stallion, with big round haunches and sturdy legs."

Khosrow knew very well that this was no wild ass, since a wild ass is never stronger than a horse. He turned to Rostam and said, "I want you to deal with this problem; go and fight with this animal, but be careful, for it may be Ahriman who is always looking for ways to harm us." Rostam replied:

> *"Your Fortune favors any warrior who*
> *Fearlessly serves your royal throne and you:*
> *No dragon, div, or lion can evade*
> *My fury and my sword's avenging blade."*

He mounted his great horse Rakhsh and, lariat in hand, left the king and his courtiers to their pastoral pleasures. When he arrived at the plain where the herdsman kept his horses, the wild ass was nowhere to be seen. For three days he searched among the horses, and then on the fourth he caught sight of him galloping across the plain like the north wind. He was an animal that shone like gold, but beneath his hide all was ugliness and sin. Rostam urged his horse forward, but as he closed on the wild ass he changed his mind. He said to himself, "I shouldn't kill this beast with my dagger; I ought to noose it with my lariat and take it still alive to the king." Rostam whirled his lariat, intending to snare it by the neck, but as soon as the ass saw the lariat, he suddenly disappeared from before the hero's eyes. Rostam realized that he was not dealing with a wild ass, and that it would be cunning he would have to call on, not strength. He said, "This can only be the Akvan Div, and somehow he must be made to feel the wind of my sword's descent. I've heard from a knowledgeable man that this is the area he haunts, but it's strange that he should take on the shape of a wild ass. I must find some trick by which my sword can stain that golden hide with blood."

Then once again the beast appeared on the plain, and Rostam urged his horse forward. He notched an arrow to his bow, and as he rode like the wind, the arrow flew ahead like fire. But at the moment he drew back his royal bow, the ass once again disappeared. For three days and nights Rostam rode about the plain, until he began to feel the need for water and bread, and he was so exhausted that his head sank down and knocked against the pommel of his saddle. Looking around, he caught sight of a stream as inviting as rosewater; he dismounted and watered Rakhsh, and as he did so he felt his eyes closing in sleep. He loosened the girth and removed the poplar wood saddle from Rakhsh's back and set it down as a pillow beside the stream. He spread out his saddle cloth and lay down to sleep on it, while Rakhsh cropped the grass nearby.

When the Akvan Div saw Rostam asleep in the distance, he transformed himself into a wind rushing over the plain. As soon as he reached the sleeping hero he dug out the soil all round him, and then lifted him up toward the heavens on a great crag of excavated earth. Rostam woke and was alarmed; his wise head whirled in confusion, and as he wriggled this way and that the Akvan Div called out to him:

> "Hey, Rostam, mammoth hero, make a wish!
> Am I to throw you to the ocean fish,
> Or hurl you on some arid mountainside?
> Well, which is it to be, then? You decide."

Rostam realized that in this div's hands all wishes would be turned upside down. He thought, "If he throws me down on a mountain, my body and bones will be smashed. It'll be much better if he throws me in the sea, intending the fishes' bellies to be my winding sheet."

> Rostam replied, "The Chinese sages teach,
> 'Whoever dies in water will not reach
> The heavens, or see Sorush; his fate will be
> To haunt this lower earth eternally.'
> Throw me upon some mountain top, and there
> I'll terrify a lion in its lair."

When the Akvan Div heard Rostam's request, he roared
and bore him toward the sea.

> *"I'm going to hurl you somewhere," he replied,*
> *"Beyond both worlds, where you can't run or hide."*

Then he flung him deep into the ocean's depths; but as
he descended through the air toward the water, Rostam
drew his sword and with this he kept off the sharks and
sea monsters that made for him. With his left arm and leg
he swam, and with the right he warded off attacks. He
struck out immediately, as befits a man used to fighting and
hardships, and after a short time, by going steadily in one
direction, he caught sight of dry land.

Once he had reached the shore and given thanks to
God who had delivered him from evil, he rested and took
off his wet tiger skin, spreading it beside a stream until it
was dry. He threw away his soaked bow and armor and set
off, leaving the sea behind him. He found the stream by
which he had slept and where he had been confronted by
the evil-natured div.

But his splendid horse Rakhsh was nowhere to be seen
in the pastures there, and Rostam railed against fate. Angrily
he picked up the saddle and bridle and set off through the
night in search of him. As dawn broke he came on a wide
meadow filled with clumps of trees and flowing streams.
There were partridges everywhere, and he could hear the
cooing of turtle-doves; then he found Afrasyab's herdsman,
asleep among the trees. Rakhsh was there, charging and
neighing among the herd's mares, and Rostam whirled his
lariat and snared him by the head.

He rubbed Rakhsh down, saddled him, slipped the bridle over his head, and mounted. Then calling down God's
blessing on his sword he set about rounding up the horses.
Their thundering hooves woke the bewildered herdsman,
who called to his companions for help; grasping lariats and

bows, they came galloping to see who the thief was who
had dared come to their meadow and challenge so many of
them. When Rostam saw them he drew his sword, roared
like a lion, "I am Rostam, the son of Zal," and fell upon
them. When he had slaughtered two-thirds of them, the
herdsman turned and fled; Rostam followed in hot pursuit,
an arrow notched to his bow.

It happened that at this time Afrasyab was coming to
this very meadow, in a hurry to inspect his horses. He arrived with his entourage and with wine and entertainers,
intending to relax for a while in the place where the herdsman watered the herd every year.

But as he drew near the spot there was no sign of either the herdsman or his horses. Then he heard a confused
noise coming from the plain, and in the distance he saw
the horses galloping and jostling one another, and Rakhsh
was visible through the dust sent up by their hooves. Soon
the herdsman appeared and told him the whole astonishing
story of how he had seen Rostam not only drive off the
whole herd single-handed, but also kill many of the herdsman's companions besides.

It became a matter of urgent discussion among the Turks
that Rostam had appeared there alone. They said, "This has
gone beyond a joke; we must arm ourselves and respond.
Or have we become so weak and contemptible that one
man can come and kill whoever he wishes? We can't allow a solitary horseman to turn up and drive off our whole
herd of horses."

Afrasyab Goes in Pursuit of Rostam

Afrasyab set off with four elephants and a detachment
of soldiers in pursuit of Rostam. When they were close
enough, Rostam unslung his bow from his shoulder and
came riding toward them; he rained arrows down on them
as thickly as the clouds rain down dew and then set about
them with his steel sword. Having killed sixty of them, he

exchanged the sword for his mace, and dispatched forty more. Afrasyab turned tail and fled. Rostam captured the four white elephants, and the Turanian soldiers despaired of life as he pursued them for two parasangs, raining down blows of his mace against their helmets and armor like a spring hail storm. Then he turned back and added the elephants to his plunder.

He returned to the stream in triumph, and once again met with the Akvan Div, who said,

> "Don't you get tired of fighting constantly?
> You fought the savage monsters of the sea,
> Got back to land and, once you'd reached our plain,
> It seems you couldn't wait to fight again!"

When Rostam heard him he roared like a warrior lion; he unhitched his lariat from his saddle and flung it toward the div, who was caught about the waist. Rostam twisted in the saddle and raised his mace, then brought it down with a blow like a blacksmith at his forge. The blow landed on the div's head and his skull and brains were smashed by its force. Rostam dismounted and with his glittering dagger severed the div's head. Then he gave thanks to God who had given him victory on the day of vengeance.

You should realize that the div represents evil people, those who are ungrateful to God. When a man leaves the ways of humanity consider him as a div, not as a person. If you don't appreciate this tale, it may be that you have not seen its real meaning.

Once Rostam had cut off the div's head, he remounted Rakhsh and, driving the herd of horses before him, together with whatever else he had looted from the Turks, he set off toward Khosrow's court. News reached the king that Rostam was returning in glory; he had set off to noose a wild ass, and now he had defeated a div and captured elephants besides. The king and his court went out to meet him, the courtiers wearing their crowns of office; the procession included elephants, trumpets, and the imperial banner. When Rostam saw the banner and realized that the king was coming to greet him, he dismounted and kissed the ground; the army shouted its approval and the drums and trumpets sounded. The nobles dismounted and only Khosrow remained in the saddle; he ordered Rostam to remount Rakhsh and the procession made its way cheerfully back to Khosrow's camp.

Rostam distributed the horses to the Iranian army, keeping none back for himself, as he considered only Rakhsh suitable to be his own mount. The elephants he gave to Kay Khosrow, as worthy of a lionlike king. The court spent a week rejoicing with wine and music and entertainers, and when Rostam was in his cups he told the king about the Akvan Div, saying, "I never saw such a majestic wild ass, of such a splendid color; but when my sword cut its hide, it was an enemy I saw, not a friend. It had a head like an elephant's, long hair, and a mouth full of boar's tusks; its two eyes were white and its lips black; its body didn't bear looking at. No animal is like him, and he'd turned that whole plain into a sea of blood; when I cut his head off with my dagger, blood spurted into the air like rain."

Kay Khosrow was astonished; he set down his wine cup and thanked God for creating such a hero, the equal of whom the world had never seen.

Two weeks passed with feasting, pleasure, and telling stories, and when the third began Rostam decided to return home in triumph. He said, "I long to see Zal, my father, and I can't hide this wish any longer. I shall make a quick journey home and return to court, and then we can plan our campaign. Capturing a few horses is too trivial to count as vengeance for the blood of Seyavash."

Kay Khosrow opened the doors of his treasury. He had a goblet filled with pearls brought, and five royal robes worked with gold, as well as Rumi slaves with golden belts, girls with gold torques about their necks, carpets and an ivory throne, brocade and coins and a crown studded with turquoise. All these he sent to Rostam saying, "Take them as a present for your journey. But stay today; tomorrow we can think about your leaving." Rostam stayed that day, drinking with the king, but when night came he was determined to leave. The king accompanied him two parasangs of the way, and then the two embraced and bade farewell to one another. Kay Khosrow took the way back to his court, and the world was filled with his justice and goodness, while Rostam continued on the journey to Zabol.

At this point in his narrative Ferdowsi inserts a love story, the story of Bizhan and Manizheh. He begins this tale with a poetic description of himself sleeping in a garden at night and waking in fear from a nightmare:

> *A night as black as coal bedaubed with pitch,*
> *A night of ebony, a night on which*
> *Mars, Mercury and Saturn would not rise.*
> *Even the moon seemed fearful of the skies -*
> *Her face was three-fourths dimmed, and all the night*
> *Looked dim and dusty in her pallid light.*
> *On plain and mountainside dark henchmen laid*
> *Night's raven carpet, shade on blacker shade;*
> *The heavens seemed rusted iron, as if each star*
> *Were blotted out by tenebrous, thick tar,*

Dark Ahriman appeared on every side
Like a huge snake whose jaws gape open wide.
The garden, and the stream by which I lay,
Became a sea of pitch; it seemed that day
Would never come, the skies no longer turned,
The weakened sun no longer moved or burned.
Fear gripped the world and utter silence fell
Stilling the clamor of the watchman's bell,
Silencing all the myriad cries and calls
Of everything that flies or walks or crawls.
I started up, bewildered, terrified,
My fear awoke the woman at my side.
I called for her to bring me torches, light -
She fetched bright candles to dispel the night
And laid a little feast on which to dine,
Red pomegranates, citrons, quinces, wine,
Together with a polished goblet fit
For kings or emperors to drink from it.
"But why do you need candles now?" she said,
"Has sleep refused to visit your soft bed?
Drink up your wine and - as you do so - I
Will tell a story from the days gone by,
A story full of love and trickery,
Whose hero lived for war, and chivalry."
"Sweet moon," I said, "my cypress, my delight,
Tell me this tale to wile away the night."
"First listen well," she said, "and when you've heard
The story through, record it word for word."

The story she tells begins when a delegation from the Ermani (Armenian) people arrive at the court of King Khosrow (the son of Seyavash and grandson of King Kavus) and beg for assistance in getting rid of a herd of wild boar that are ravaging their country. The young warrior Bizhan volunteers for this mission, *and Khosrow orders the older and more experienced courtier Gorgin to go with him as a guide. Gorgin is jealous of Bizhan's prowess and youth, and after Bizhan has successfully slaughtered the herd of boar, he suggests that the young prince go to the border with Turan, where he would see the women of the Turanian court celebrating the arrival of spring with their annual Now Ruz festival. Gorgin hopes that by doing this he would persuade Bizhan to put himself in danger, and perhaps be killed by Turanian warriors. Bizhan does as Gorgin suggests, but instead of being killed he meets up with Manizheh, the daughter of king Afrasyab, and the two fall in love. When it is time for her to return to her father's palace, Manizheh drugs Bizhan, hides him in her litter, and takes him with her. For a while the two live happily together, but they are eventually discovered and hauled before Afrasyab, who orders Bizhan to be placed in a dark well with a huge stone over its mouth, and banishes Manizheh from his court, saying that she could end her days in misery ministering to her imprisoned lover. Meanwhile Gorgin arrives back at the Persian court, where there was consternation over Bizhan's absence. Although Gorgin protests his innocence, no one believes him. Eventually Kay Khosrow looks in the sacred world-revealing cup, and sees Bizhan imprisoned in the well, deep in Turan. He decides to send for Rostam to help rescue Bizhan.*

ROSTAM RESCUES BIZHAN

Khosrow's Letter to Rostam
A scribe was called in and the king dictated a friendly letter
to Rostam:

> "*Great Rostam, noblest of our warriors,*
> *Whose deeds remind us of our ancestors,*
> *Leopards submit to you, sea-monsters roar*
> *In terror when you walk upon the shore,*
> *Persia's stout heart, prop of our sovereignty,*
> *Prompt with your help in all adversity:*
> *The demons of Mazanderan were slain*
> *By you, your mace destroyed their evil reign.*
> *How many kings, how many enemies*
> *You've conquered, and how many provinces!*
> *To pluck from darkness any mortal who*
> *In peril or affliction turns to you,*
> *The Lord has given you a mammoth's might*
> *And lionhearted courage when you fight.*

Gudarz and Giv in their despair now ask
For your assistance in a worthy task;
You know how close this clan remains to me,
Never have they endured such agony.
Giv has a single son, and all his joy,
His hopes of life, are centered on this boy;
To me he's been a loyal courtier who
Will do whatever I command him to.
Now, when you read this letter, don't delay,
Return with Giv, hear what he has to say;
In council we'll decide what must be done
To save this noble warrior's captive son.
I'll provide men and treasure, you're to free
Bizhan from his Turanian misery."

Khosrow sealed the letter; Giv took it, made his obeisance
to the king, and went home to prepare for the journey. He
rode with his clansmen, quick as a hunted animal, covering
two days' travel in each day, crossing the desert and heading
for the River Hirmand. When he reached Gurabad a lookout saw him and shouted that a warrior and his entourage
were approaching the riverbank; the leader carried a Kaboli
sword in his fist, and they were followed by a banner flapping in the wind. Rostam's father, Zal, heard the lookout's
cry and rode out to meet them, so that they would have
no reason to act hostilely toward him. As he saw Giv coming, his face downcast and preoccupied, he said to himself,
"Something has happened to the king, there's no other reason for Giv to come here." When he met up with them he
asked after the king, and how the war with Turan was far-
ing. Giv greeted him respectfully from Khosrow, and then
unburdened his heart, telling him the tale of his lost son.
He asked for Rostam, and Zal answered, "He's out hunting wild asses: when the sun goes down he'll be back." Giv
said, "I'll go and find him, I have a letter from Khosrow I
have to give him." But Zal answered, "Stay here, he'll be

here soon; come to my house and spend the day feasting with me."

But as Giv entered the outer court Rostam was seen returning from the hunt. Giv went out to greet him and dismounted before him. Hope flared up in his heart and the color came back to his face, although his eyes were still filled with tears. When Rostam saw the anxiety in his expression and the marks of tears on his face, he said to himself, "Some disaster has happened to Iran and to the king." He dismounted and embraced Giv, asking after Khosrow, and then for news of Gudarz, Tus, Gazhdaham, and various other warriors at the Persian court such as Shapur, Farhad, Bizhan, Roham, and Gorgin. When Giv heard the name "Bizhan," a cry escaped from his lips and he said to Rostam, "My lord, all kings honor you, and I am happy to see you and to hear you speak so kindly; those you ask after are well, and they send their greetings to you. But you don't know the terrible calamity that has stricken me in my old age; the evil eye has lighted on Gudarz's clan and destroyed all our good fortune. I had one son in all the world; he was both my boy and my confidant, my councilor. He has disappeared from the face of the earth; no one in my clan has suffered such a calamity. I've ridden day and night searching the world for Bizhan. But now, at the turning of the year, our king has prayed to God and seen in the world-revealing cup that he is in Turan, loaded down with chains; seeing this, Khosrow sent me here to you. I stand before you, my heart filled with hope, my cheeks sallow with grief, my eyes blinded by tears: I look to you as my one recourse in all the world, as you are ready to help everyone in their time of need."

He wept and sighed, and as he handed over Khosrow's letter he told Rostam of the business with Gorgin. Rostam too wept as he read the letter, and loathing for Afrasyab welled up in him. He cried out for Bizhan and said, "Think no more of this; Rostam will not remove the saddle from

Rakhsh's back until he has taken Bizhan's hand in his and destroyed the chains and prison that hold him. By God's power and the king's good fortune, I shall bring your prince back from Turan."

They went to Rostam's castle, where Rostam went through Khosrow's letter and said to Giv, "I understand what's to be done, and I shall carry out the king's commands. I know what services you've rendered, to me and to the court, and though I rejoice to see you here, my heart grieves for Bizhan. But you should not despair; I shall act as the king orders me and do my best to rescue your son, even if God should separate my soul from my body in the attempt. I'm ready to sacrifice my soul, my men, and my wealth on Bizhan's behalf. With God's help and our victorious king's good fortune, I'll free him from his chains and the dark pit where he languishes and return him to the Persian court. But now, you must be my guest for three days, and we shall drink together and take our ease; there is no thine or mine between you and me. We'll feast here and tell tales of the heroes and kings of old, and on the fourth day we'll set out for Khosrow's court."

Impulsively Giv stepped forward and kissed the hero's hand, chest, and feet. He praised Rostam and wished him eternal strength and wisdom. When Rostam saw that Giv was reassured he said to his steward, "Set out a feast, call our councilors and chieftains." After the banquet, Zavareh, Faramarz, Zal, and Giv sat in a bejeweled hall where musicians and wine servers entertained them; their hands were stained with ruby wine, the goblets glittered, and the harps resounded. And so three days and nights passed in pleasure and happiness; on the fourth they prepared to set out. Rostam ordered the baggage train to be made ready, laid his ancestors' mace in the saddle, and mounted Rakhsh. Rakhsh pricked up his ears, Rostam's head seemed to overtop the sun, and he and Giv, together with a hundred selected Zavoli horsemen, set out impatiently on their journey to Iran.

As Rostam approached the Persian heartland, the pinnacles of Khosrow's castle could be seen in the distance and a welcoming wind came down to him from the heavens. Giv said, "I shall ride on ahead and announce your coming."

Giv reached the court and made his obeisance to Khosrow, who asked him about his journey and where Rostam was. Giv replied, "Great king, your good fortune makes all things turn out well; Rostam did not refuse your orders. When I gave him your letter he reverently placed it against his eyes, and he has come here as befits a loyal subject, his reins twisted with mine. I rode on ahead to announce his coming to you."

Khosrow's answer was, "And where is this prop of our nobility, this paragon of loyalty now?" He ordered Gudarz, Tus, and Farhad, together with two companies from the army, to go out and greet the approaching hero. The din of drums rang out and the welcoming party was drawn up; the world was darkened by their dust, and in the gloom their lances glittered and their banners fluttered. When they reached Rostam they dismounted and bowed before him, and he too descended from his horse and asked each one for news of the king. Then everyone remounted and the group made its way to the royal palace.

Rostam Addresses Kay Khosrow

When Rostam entered the audience hall he ran forward, invoking the blessings of Hormoz upon the king. He then called on the angel Bahman to protect his crown, the angel Ordibehesht to protect his person, the angel Shahrivar to give him victory, the angel Sepandarmez to watch over him, the angel Khordad to bring prosperity to his lands, and the angel Mordad to watch over his flocks.

Khosrow stood, motioned Rostam to sit beside him, and said, "You are the champion of the world's kings; what men conceal you know, and what you do not conceal is still unknown to them. The Keyanids have chosen you before all others; you are the support of their army, the guardian of Iran, the refuge of their troops. I rejoice to see you here, valiant and vigilant as ever. Now, are Zavareh, Faramarz, and Zal well? What news can you give me of them?" Rostam knelt and kissed the throne and replied, "Victorious king, all three are well and prosperous, thanks to your good fortune. Blessed are those whom the king remembers!"

Khosrow ordered his chamberlain to summon Gudarz, Tus, and other courtiers of the first rank. The steward had the royal gardens prepared; a golden crown and throne were placed beneath a tree whose blossoms were beginning to fall, royal brocades were spread on the grass, and the flower gardens glowed like lamps at night. Near where the king sat a tree was placed so that its shade covered him; its trunk was of silver, its branches of gold encrusted with rubies and other precious stones; its leaves and buds were made of emeralds and agates that hung like precious earrings. Golden oranges and quinces grew from the branches; they were hollow inside and filled with musk macerated in wine, and their surfaces were pierced like a flute's, so that the scent diffused through the air, delighting the king. The wine servers who stood before the guests had bejeweled crowns, and their cloaks were of brocade shot with gold; they wore torques and earrings, and the bodices of their clothes were worked with gems. The faces of the servants who burned sandalwood before the king and played on harps glowed like rich brocade. All hearts rejoiced to be there; the wine went round and even before it took effect the guests' faces shone like pomegranate blossoms.

Khosrow sat Rostam in the place of honor beneath the tree and said to him, "My noble friend, you are Iran's shield against all evil, protecting us as the Simorgh spreads out her wings. You have always been ready to serve Iran and her kings, and with your mace and the might of your royal *farr* you destroyed the demons of Mazanderan. You know how Gudarz's clan has served in good fortune and bad, always ready to do my bidding and to guide me toward the truth, and Giv especially has been my bulwark against all evils. Such a sorrow has never come to this clan before, for what sorrow is greater than the loss of a child? If you do not agree to help us now no other lion-warrior will; think what must be done to save Bizhan, who languishes a captive in Turan. Whatever horses or arms or men or treasure you need, take them, and give the matter no more thought!"

Rostam kissed the ground, rose quickly, and said,

> "Your majesty, you're like the radiant sun
> Bestowing light and life on everyone:
> May greed and anger never touch your reign
> And may your enemies live wracked with pain.
> Monarch with whom no monarch can compete,
> All other kings are dust beneath your feet,
> Neither the sun nor moon has ever known
> A king like you to occupy the throne.
> My mother bore me so that you could live
> Sure of the service that you knew I'd give;
> I've heard the king's command and I agree
> To go wherever he might order me.
> The heavens can rain down fire but I won't leave
> This mission that I undertake for Giv
> Until success is mine—and I won't ask
> For chiefs or troops to help me in this task."

Gudarz, Giv, Fariborz, Farhad, and Shapur, together with the other assembled chieftains, called down the world Creator's blessings on Rostam, and the company sat to their wine, as happy and radiant as the springtime.

Gorgin Sends a Letter to Rostam

When Gorgin heard of Rostam's presence at the court, he realized that here was the key to his deliverance. He sent him a message: "O sword of fortune, scabbard of loyalty, banner of greatness, treasury of faith, gateway of generosity, imprisoner of disaster, if it does not pain you to hear from me, let me tell you of my sorrows. The hunchbacked heavens have doused the torch of my heart and left me in darkness; what was fated to happen to me has happened. If the king will forgive me my sins and restore me my good name, I'm ready to throw myself into fire before him, I'll do anything to rid myself of this disaster that has come to me in my old age. If you will ask for me from the king, I will follow you with all the energy of a wild mountain sheep. I shall go to Bizhan and grovel before him, in hopes of getting back my good reputation."

When Gorgin's message reached Rostam, he sighed, troubled by Gorgin's sorrow and by his foolish request. He sent the messenger back and told him to say to Gorgin, "You fearless fool, haven't you heard of what the leopard said to the sea monster: 'When passion overcomes wisdom, no one can escape its clutches; but the wise man who overcomes passion will be renowned as a lion'? You talk like a cunning old fox, but you didn't see the trap set for you. How can I possibly mention your name before Khosrow for the sake of such a foolish request? But you're so wretched that I'll ask Khosrow to forgive your sin and brighten your life's darkened moon. If God wills that Bizhan be freed from his chains, you'll be set free, too, and no one will take any further revenge on you. But if the heavens will otherwise, you must despair of life. I shall go on this mission, armed with God's strength and the king's command, but if I don't return successfully, prepare yourself for Gudarz and Giv to wreak vengeance on you for their child's death."

Two days and nights passed and Rostam made no mention of the matter; on the third day, when Khosrow was seated on his ivory throne, the hero came to him. He began to talk about Gorgin's miseries, but the king cut him off: "You're my general, and you're asking me to break the oath I swore by my throne and crown, by the lord of the sun and moon, that Gorgin would see nothing from me but suffering until Bizhan was freed from his chains. Ask me for anything else, for thrones, seal-rings, swords or crowns!"

Rostam replied, "My noble lord, if he did wrong, he repents of it and is ready to sacrifice his life in a good cause; but if the king will not forgive him, his name and reputation are lost forever. Anyone who strays from wisdom's path sooner or later regrets the evil that he does. It would be right for you to remember his former deeds, how he was always there in every crisis, and how he fought steadfastly for your ancestors. If the king can grant me this man, it may be that fortune will smile on him again." Khosrow allowed his request, and Gorgin was released from the dark pit where he had been chained.

Then the king asked Rostam how he intended to go about his task, what he would need in the way of troops and treasure, and who he wanted to accompany him. He added, "I fear Afrasyab will kill Bizhan in a fit of impatience. He has a demon's nature and he's impulsive; he might well suddenly destroy our warrior." Rostam replied, "I shall prepare for this task in secret; the key to these chains is deceit, and we must not act too hastily. We must tug back on the reins, and this is no time for maces, swords, or spears. I'll need a quantity of jewels, gold, and silver; we'll go with high hopes, and when we're there, fear will make us cautious. We'll go as merchants, and this will give us a good excuse to linger in Turan for a while. I'll need carpets and clothes, and things to give as presents."

Khosrow gave orders that his ancient treasuries be opened; the king's treasurer brought brocades and jewels, and Rostam came and selected whatever he needed. He had a hundred camel-loads of gold coins made up, together with a hundred mule-loads of silver, and he had the court chamberlain choose a thousand lion hearted warriors. Seven noblemen—Gorgin, Zangeh, Gostaham, Gorazeh, Farhad, Roham, and Ashkash—were to go with him as his companions and as guardians of the wealth. When these men were summoned, Zangeh asked, "Where is Khosrow, and what's happened that he has called for us like this?"

Rostam and the Seven Persian Heroes Enter Turkestan

At dawn the chamberlain appeared at the castle gates, and the seven heroes stood before the chosen troops, fully armed and ready to sacrifice their souls if need be. At cock crow, as the sky whitened, war drums were fastened on the elephants and Rostam, tall as a cypress tree, appeared in the gateway, mace in hand, his lariat hitched to his saddle. He called down God's blessings on his country, and the group set off.

They neared the border with Turan, and he called the army's leaders to him. He said, "You are to stay here, alert and on guard; you are not to leave this place unless God divides my body from my soul; be prepared for war, however, have your claws ready for blood."

The army stayed on the Persian side of the border while Rostam and his nobles pressed on to Turan. But first they disguised themselves as merchants, removing their silver sword belts and dressing in woolen garments. They entered Turan as a richly laden caravan, accompanied by seven horses, one of which was Rakhsh; there were a hundred camel-loads of jewels, and a hundred mule-loads of soldier's tunics and armor. The bells on the animals and the clatter of their progress made a noise like the trumpets of Tahmures; the whole plain was filled with their din until they reached the town where Piran lived. Piran was away hunting; when Rostam saw him returning, he had a goblet filled with jewels and covered with a fine brocade cloth, and two horses with jeweled bridles and draped with brocade led forward. Servants took the gifts to Piran's palace, and Rostam accompanied them. He greeted Piran respectfully, as one whose virtues were known both in Iran and Turan. By God's grace Piran did not recognize Rostam; he said to

him, "Where are you from, who are you, and why have you
come here in such a hurry?" Rostam replied, "I am your
servant, sir; God's led me to your town to refresh myself
and rest. I've come the long and weary way from Iran to
Turan as a merchant; I buy and sell all sorts of things. I've
traveled here assured of your kindness, and hope has now
conquered my heart's fears. If you will take me under your
wing's protection, I shall stay here to sell jewels and buy
horses. Your justice will ensure that no one harms me, and
your benevolence will rain down blessings upon me." Then
he set before Piran the goblet filled with jewels and had the
splendid Arab horses, that had no trace of windblown dust
on their immaculate coats, led forward. Invoking God's
benediction, he handed the presents over, and the bargain
was made.

When Piran saw the jewels glittering in the goblet he
welcomed Rostam warmly and sat him on a turquoise
throne, saying, "Be happy here, be sure you'll be safe in my
city; I'll give you quarters near to my palace and you need
have no fears for your goods, no one will give you any
trouble. Bring everything you have of value here and then
look for customers. Make my son's house your personal
headquarters, and think of yourself as one of my family."
Rostam replied, "My lord, I brought this caravan from
Iran for you, and all that I have in it is yours. Wherever I
stay will be suitable for me, but with my victorious lord's
permission, I'll stay with the caravan; there are all kinds
of people traveling with me, and I don't want any of my
jewels to disappear." Piran said, "Go and choose any place
you desire; I'll send guides to help you."

Rostam chose a house for his party to stay in, and a
warehouse for his goods. News spread that a caravan had
come to Piran's castle from Iran and customers began
to arrive from all quarters, particularly when it became
known that there were jewels for sale. Buyers for brocade,
carpets, and gems converged on the castle, and Rostam

and his companions decked out their warehouse so that it shone like the sun itself.

Manizheh Comes to Rostam

Manizheh heard about the caravan from Iran and hurried to Piran's city. Unveiled and weeping, Afrasyab's daughter came before Rostam; wiping her tears from her face with her sleeve, she said,

> *"I wish you life and long prosperity,*
> *May God protect you from adversity!*
> *May heaven prosper all you say and do,*
> *May evil glances never injure you.*
> *Whatever purposes you hope to gain*
> *May all your efforts never bring you pain,*
> *May wisdom be your guide, may fortune bless*
> *Iran with prosperous days and happiness.*
> *What news have you? What tidings can you bring*
> *Of Persia's champions, or of their king?*
> *Haven't they heard Bizhan is here, don't they*
> *Desire to help their friend in any way?*
> *Will he be left by Giv, by all his kin,*
> *To perish in the pit he suffers in?*
> *Fetters weigh down his legs, his arms and hands*
> *Are fixed to stakes by heavy iron bands*
> *He hangs in chains, blood stains his clothes, I weep*
> *To hear his groans, and never rest or sleep."*

Rostam was afraid when he heard her, and he burst out as if in rage, pushing her toward the street: "Get away from me, I don't know any kings, I know nothing about Giv or that family, your words mean nothing to me!"

Manizheh stared at Rostam and sobbed pitifully. She said, "You're a great and wise man and your cold words don't suit you. Say nothing if you wish, but don't drive me from you, for my sufferings have worn away my life. Is this the way Persians treat people? Do they deny news to the poor and wretched?"

Rostam said, "What's the matter with you, woman? Has Ahriman told you the world's coming to an end? You disrupted my trade, and that's why I was angry with you. Don't let what I said upset you; I was worried about selling my goods. As for the king, I don't live in the city where he does, and I know nothing about Giv or his clan; I've never been to the area where they live."

Quickly, he had whatever food was available set in front of the poor woman, and then he questioned her as to what had made her unhappy, why she was so interested in the Persian king and nobility, and why she kept her eye on the road from Iran the whole time.

Manizheh said, "And why should you want to know about my sorrows and misfortunes? I left the pit with my heart filled with anguish and ran to you thinking you were a free and noble man, and you yelled at me like a warrior attacking an enemy. Have you no fear of God in you? I am Manizheh, Afrasyab's daughter; once the sun never saw me unveiled, but now my face is sallow with grief, my eyes are filled with bloody tears, and I wander from house to house seeking charity. I beg for bread; this is the fate God has visited upon me. Has any life ever been more wretched than mine? May God have mercy on me. And poor Bizhan in that pit never sees the sun or moon, but hangs in chains and fetters, begging God for death. His pain adds to my pain, and I have wept so much that my eyes can weep no more. But if you go to Iran again and hear news of Gudarz, or if you see Giv at Kay Khosrow's court or the hero Rostam, tell them that Bizhan lies here in deep distress and that if they delay it will be too late. If they wish to see him alive, they should hurry, for he is crushed between the stone above him and the iron that binds him."

Rostam wept tears of sympathy and said to her, "Dear lovely child, why don't you have the nobles of your country intercede for you with your father? Surely he would forgive you and feel remorse for what's happened?" Then he ordered his cooks to bring Manizheh all kinds of food, and especially he told them to prepare a roasted chicken folded round with soft bread; when they brought this, Rostam dexterously slipped a ring into it and gave it to Manizheh, saying, "Take this to the pit, and look after the poor prisoner who languishes there."

Manizheh hurried back to the pit, with the food wrapped in a cloth and clutched against her breast. She passed it down to Bizhan just as she'd received it. Bizhan peered at it in astonishment and called out to her, "Dearest Manizheh, you've suffered so much on my behalf. Where did you get this food you're in such a hurry to give me?" She said, "From a Persian merchant who's come with a caravan of goods to Turan; he seems like someone who's passed through many trials, a noble and splendid man. He has a great many jewels with him and has set up shop in a big warehouse in front of Piran's castle. He gave me the food wrapped in a cloth and told me to bring it to you, and said that I could return for more later."

Hopeful and apprehensive, Bizhan began to open the bread, and as he did so he came on the hidden ring. He peered at the stone set in it and made out a name, then he laughed in triumph and astonishment. It was a turquoise seal, with the word "Rostam" engraved on it with a steel point, as fine as a hair. Bizhan saw that the tree of loyalty had born fruit; he knew that the key that would release him from his suffering was at hand. He laughed long and loud and when Manizheh heard him laughing, chained in the darkness as he was, she was alarmed and feared that he had gone mad. She called down to him, "How can you laugh when you can't tell night from day? What do you know that I don't? Tell me. Has good fortune suddenly shown you her face?"

Bizhan replied, "I'm hopeful that fate will finally free me from this pit. If you can swear to keep faith with me, I'll tell you the whole tale from beginning to end, but only if you'll swear yourself to secrecy, because a man can sew up a woman's mouth to prevent idle talk and she'll still find some way to free her tongue."

Manizheh wept and wailed, "How wretched my fate is! Alas for the days of my youth, for my broken heart and my weeping eyes. I've given Bizhan my body, my soul, and my wealth, and now he cannot trust me. My treasury and my jeweled crown were plundered, my father cast me out, unveiled and humiliated, before his court, and now that Bizhan sees hope he leaves me in despair. The world is dark to me, my eyes see nothing, Bizhan hides his thoughts from me, and only God knows all things."

Bizhan replied, "What you say is true. You lost everything for my sake. I should not have said what I said. My kindest friend, my dearest wife, you have to guide me now, the agony I've suffered has turned my brains. Know then that the man selling jewels, whose cook gave you the food you brought, has come to Turan looking for me; that's the only reason he's here selling jewels. God has taken pity on me and I shall see the broad earth once again. This jeweler will save me from my long agony, and you from your grief and beggary on my behalf. Go to him once again and say to him in secret, "Great hero of the worlds' kings, tender-hearted and resourceful, tell me if you are Rakhsh's lord.""

Manizheh hurried to Rostam like the wind and spoke as Bizhan had instructed her. When Rostam saw her come running like this and heard what she said, he knew that Bizhan had entrusted her with their secret. His heart melted and he said, "May God never withdraw his kindness from you, my lovely child. Tell him, 'Yes, I am Rakhsh's lord, sent by God to save you. I have traveled the long road from Zavol to Iran and from Iran to Turan for your sake.' Tell him, but let no one else know of this; in the darkest night listen for the least sound. Spend the next day gathering firewood in the forest, and when night comes, light a huge bonfire."

Overjoyed at his words and freed from all sorrow, Manizheh hurried back to the pit where Bizhan lay bound. She said, "I gave the great lord your message, and he confirmed that he was the man you said he was. He told me to wipe away my tears and to say to you that he had come here like a leopard to find you, and now that he had done so you would soon enough see his sword's work. He will tear up the ground and throw the stone that covers you to the stars. He told me that when the sun releases its grip on the world and night comes I'm to build a huge fire so that the stone and the pit's whereabouts shine like the daytime, and he will be able to use the glow as a guide to us."

Bizhan said, "Light the fire that will deliver us both from darkness," and he prayed to God, saying, "Pure, splendid, and just, release me from all sorrows and strike down my enemies with your arrows; give me justice, for you know the pains and grief I have suffered; allow me to see my native country again and to smash against this stone my evil star." Then he addressed Manizheh:

> *"And you, who've suffered long and patiently,*
> *Who've given heart and soul and wealth for me,*
> *Who thought that, undergone for me, distress*
> *Was but another name for happiness,*
> *Who cast aside your kin, your noble name,*
> *Your parents, crown and land, to share my shame:*
> *If in my youth I find I'm free again,*
> *Delivered from this dragon and this pain,*
> *I'll bow before you like a man whose days*
> *Are passed before his God in prayer and praise;*
> *Prompt as a slave who waits before his lord,*
> *I'll find for you a glorious reward."*

Manizheh set about gathering firewood, going from branch to branch like a bird, her eyes fixed on the sun to mark when it would drop behind the mountains. And when she saw the sun disappear and night draw its skirts over the mountain slopes, at that moment when the world finds peace and all that is visible fades from sight because night's army has veiled sunlight in darkness, Manizheh quickly lit the flames. Night's pitch-black eyes were seeled; Manizheh's heart pounded like a brass drum as she listened for the iron hooves of Rakhsh.

For his part, Rostam put on his armor and prayed to the God of the sun and moon, saying "May the eyes of the evil be blinded, give me strength to complete this business of Bizhan." He ordered his warriors to prepare for battle; poplar wood saddles were placed on their mounts, and they made ready to fight.

They set out toward the distant glow, and traveled expeditiously. When they reached the great stone of the Akvan Div and the pit of sorrow and grief, Rostam said to his seven companions, "You'll have to dismount and find some way to remove that stone from the mouth of the pit." But no matter how hard the warriors struggled, they could not shift the stone; when Rostam saw how they sweated to no avail, he too dismounted and hitched up his skirts about his waist. Praying to God for strength, he set his hands to the stone and lifted it; with a lion's power he flung it into the forest, and the ground shuddered as the stone landed.

He peered into the pit and, sighing in sympathy, addressed Bizhan: "How did such a misfortune happen to you? Your portion from the world was to have been one of delight, how is it that the goblet you took from her hands was filled with poison?" Bizhan answered from the darkness, "Your journey must have been long and hard; when I heard your war cry, all the world's poison turned to sweetness for me. You see how I have lived, with iron as my earth and a stone as my sky; I've suffered so much pain and grief that I gave up all hope of the world."

Rostam replied, "The shining Keeper of the World has had mercy on your soul, and now I have one request to ask of you: that you grant me Gorgin's life, and that you drive from your heart all thoughts of hatred for him." Bizhan said, "What do you know of my experiences with this companion of mine; my lionhearted friend, what do you know of how Gorgin treated me? If I ever set eyes on him again my vengeance will be like God's last judgment."

Rostam said, "If you persist in this hatred and refuse to listen to what I have to say, I shall leave you chained here in this pit; I shall mount Rakhsh and return whence I came." When he heard Rostam's words, a cry of grief rose up from the pit, and Bizhan said, "I am the most wretched of our clan's heroes. The evil that came to me was from Gorgin, and now I must suffer this, too: but I accept, and drive all thoughts of hatred for him from my heart."

Rostam lowered his lariat into the pit and brought Bizhan out of its depths, wasted away with pain and suffering, his legs still shackled, his head uncovered, his hair and nails grown long, all his body caked with blood where the chains had eaten into the flesh. Rostam gave a great cry when he saw him weighed down with iron and set about breaking the fetters and shackles. They made their way home, with Bizhan on one side of Rostam and the woman who had succored him on the other; the two young people recounted their sufferings to the hero, who had Bizhan's head washed and fresh clothes brought for him. Then Gorgin came forward and sank to the ground, striking his face against the dust; he asked pardon for his evil acts and for the foolish things he had said. Bizhan's heart forgave him, and he forgot all thoughts of punishment.

The camels were loaded with their goods, Rostam put on his armor once more, and the Persian warriors mounted, with drawn swords and maces at the ready. Ashkash, who was a wary fighter, always on the lookout for whatever might harm the army, led off the baggage train. Rostam said to Bizhan, "You and Manizheh should go with Ashkash. Afrasyab will be so enraged we can't rest tonight; I'm going to play a trick on him within his own walls, and his whole country will laugh at him tomorrow." But Bizhan's answer was, "If I'm the one who's being avenged, I should be at the head of this expedition."

Rostam and Bizhan Attack

Rostam and the seven warriors left the baggage train in Ashkash's capable hands and set out. Letting their reins hang slack on their saddles and drawing their swords, they arrived at Afrasyab's palace at the time when men turn to drunkenness, rest, and sleep. They attacked and confusion reigned: swords glittered, arrows poured down, heads fell severed from bodies, mouths were clogged with dust. Rostam stood in the portico of Afrasyab's palace and yelled, "So you sleep well, do you, you and your valiant warriors? You slept in state while Bizhan was in the pit, but did you dream of an iron wall confronting you? I am Rostam, the son of Zal; now is no time for sleep in soft beds. I have smashed your chains and removed the stone you set as Bizhan's keeper; he is free of his fetters, and rightly so, since this was no way to treat a son-in-law! Were Seyavash's sufferings, and the war that came from them, not enough for you? You had no right to seek Bizhan's life, but I see your heart's stupefied and your mind's asleep." And Bizhan cried out, "Misbegotten, evil-minded Turk, think how you dealt with me when you were on your throne and I stood chained before you; then, when I was bound motionless as a stone, you were savage as a leopard, but now I walk freely on the face of the earth, and the ferocious lion slinks off."

Afrasyab struggled with his clothes and called out, "Are all my warriors asleep? Any man who wants jewels and a crown, block these enemies' advance!" Cries and a confused noise of combat resounded on all sides, and blood streamed beneath Afrasyab's door; every Turanian warrior who ventured forward was killed, and finally Afrasyab fled from his palace. Rostam entered the building and distributed among his men its cloth and carpets, the noble horses with their poplar wood saddles covered with leopard skins and jewels, and the king's womenfolk, who took the Persian heroes by the hand.

They left the palace and packed up their plunder, having no intention of staying any longer in Turan. Because of the baggage they carried and to avoid a bitter outcome to their expedition, they urged the horses forward as fast as they could. Rostam became so exhausted by their haste that even the weight of his helmet was a trouble to him, and his companions and their horses were so weak they had hardly a pulse left in their arteries. Rostam sent a messenger to the forces he had left when he crossed into Turan, saying "Draw your swords from their scabbards; I am certain that the earth will soon be black with an army's hooves. Afrasyab will muster an army of vengeance, and follow us here; their lances will darken the sunlight."

At last the returning group reached the waiting army; they made themselves ready for battle, their lances sharpened, their reins at the ready. A lookout saw horsemen approaching from Turan and Rostam went to Manizheh in her tent and said, "If the wine has been spilt, its scent still lingers: if our pleasures are past, the memory of them is still ours. But this is the way of the world, giving us now sweetness and pleasure, now bitterness and pain."

Rostam's Battle with Afrasyab

As soon as the sun rose above the mountain tops Turan's warriors had begun to prepare for their onslaught. The town was filled with a deafening clamor: horsemen mustered in their ranks before Afrasyab's palace, Turan's nobles bowed their heads to the ground before him, and all were

eager to exact vengeance from Iran. They felt that the time
had passed for words; a remedy had to be found, since
what Bizhan had done had disgraced their king forever.
"The Iranians do not call us men," they said. "They say we
are women dressed as warriors."

Like a leopard, Afrasyab strode forward and gave the
signal for war: he ordered Piran to have the war drums
strapped on their elephants, saying, "These Persians will
make fun of us no more." Brass trumpets, bugles, and
Indian chimes rang out before the palace. Turan was in an
uproar as the army set out for the Persian border, and the
whole earth seemed like a moving ocean.

A lookout saw the earth heaving like the sea and ran to
Rostam: "Prepare to fight, the world has turned black from
the dust flung up by their horsemen." But Rostam replied,
"There's no cause for fear; dust is what they'll come to if
they fight with us." Leaving the baggage with Manizheh,
he donned his armor and came out to inspect his troops,
roaring like a lion, "What use is a fox when it's caught in a
lion's claws?" Then he addressed his men:

> "The day of battle's come: my noble lords,
> Where are your iron-piercing spears, your swords?
> Now is the time to show your bravery
> And turn our vengeance into victory."

The trumpets blared and Rostam mounted Rakhsh. He
led his men down from the mountainside as the enemy
were passing through a defile to the plains. The two sides
ranged themselves behind walls of iron-clad warriors. On
the Persian side, Ashkash and Gostaham and their horsemen made up the right flank, the left was commanded by
Farhad and Zangeh, while Rostam himself and Bizhan were
in the center. Behind them towered Mount Bisitun, and before them was a wall of swords. When Afrasyab saw that
the enemy forces were led by Rostam, he put on his armor

uneasily and ordered his men to hold back. He had them form defensive ranks; the air darkened and the ground disappeared. He entrusted his left flank to Piran, and the right to Human; the center was held by Garsivaz and Shideh, while he himself kept an eye on all parts of the line.

Like a massive mountain, Rostam rode up and down between the armies and called out

> *"You miserable, wretched Turk—you shame*
> *Your throne, your warriors, and your noble name.*
> *Your heart's not in this fight: how many men*
> *You've mustered in your army's ranks, but when*
> *The battle's joined at last and I attack,*
> *I'll see no more than your retreating back.*
> *And did my father never say to you*
> *The ancient proverbs that are always true?*
> *'A herd of milling asses cannot fight*
> *Against a single lion's savage might;*
> *All heaven's stars will never equal one*
> *In glory and in radiance—the sun;*
> *Words won't give courage to a fox, no laws*
> *Can make an ass develop lion's claws.'*
> *Don't be a fool, and if you want to save*
> *Your sovereignty, don't act as if you're brave;*
> *If you attack this time, in all this plain*
> *You won't escape alive from me again!"*

When the Turkish king heard these words he trembled, heaved a bitter sigh, and cried out in fury, "Warriors of Turan! Is this a battlefield, or a banqueting hall?"

When they heard their commander's voice a great shout went up from the Turanian ranks; dust rose into the sky obscuring the sun, war drums were fastened on elephants, horns and trumpets sounded, and the line of armored warriors made a solid iron wall. The plain and mountain slopes re-echoed with cries from men on both sides, in the dusty air the glitter of swords flashed as if the world's end had come, and blows from steel maces rained down on armor and helmets like hail. Rostam's banner, with its dragon device, seemed to eclipse the sun; wherever he rode, severed heads fell to the ground. With his ox-headed mace he was like a maddened dromedary that has slipped its tether, and from the center of the army he scattered his enemies like a wolf.

On the right flank Ashkash pressed on like the wind, eager for combat with Garsivaz; on the left Gorgin, Farhad, and Roham pushed back the Turkish warriors; and in the center Bizhan went triumphantly forward as if the battle were a celebratory feast. Warriors' heads fell like leaves from a tree, and the battlefield became a river of blood in which the Turkish banners lay overturned and abandoned.

When Afrasyab saw the day was lost and that his brave warriors had been slain, he threw away his Indian sword and mounted a fresh horse: he separated himself from the Turkish army and rode toward Turan, having achieved nothing by his attempt to ambush the Persians. Rostam sped after him, raining arrows and blows on the intervening Turks; like a fire-breathing dragon he followed him for two parasangs, but finally returned to camp, where a thousand Turkish prisoners were waiting. There he distributed to the army the wealth his men had captured, loaded up the elephant train with baggage, and set out in triumph to Kay Khosrow.

Rostam Returns with Bizhan from Turan to Iran

When news reached the king that the lion was returning victorious, that Bizhan had been released from the prison where he'd been held, that the army of Turan had been smashed and all their hopes had come to naught, he prayed to God for joy, striking his face and forehead against the dust.

Gudarz and Giv hurried to Khosrow. The noise of the approaching army's war drums and trumpets could be heard; then the ground in front of the king's palace was darkened by horses' hooves, the clamor of trumpets and horns resounded throughout the city, the banners of Gudarz and Giv were raised, chained leopards and lions were led out on one side and on the other were mounted warriors. In this fashion, as the king had commanded, the army went out to greet the returning victors.

When Rostam emerged from the approaching group, Gudarz and Giv dismounted, and all the Persian nobility followed suit. Rostam too dismounted and greeted those who had come to welcome him. Gudarz and Giv addressed him, "Great commander, may God hold you forever in his keeping, may the sun and moon turn as you would wish, may the heavens never tire of you; you have made us your slaves, for through you we have found our lost son; it is you who has delivered us from pain and sorrow, and all Persians long to serve you."

The nobles remounted and processed toward the king. When they were close to the city, Khosrow came out and welcomed Rostam as the guardian of all his heroes. Rostam saw that the king himself was coming to greet him and he dismounted once more, saying he was humbled that the king had put himself to this trouble. Khosrow embraced him and said, "You are a root stock of manliness and a mine of virtues; your deeds shine like the sun, for their goodness is seen everywhere." Quickly Rostam took Bizhan by the hand and handed him over to his father and his king. Then he brought the thousand Turanian prisoners bound before the king, and Khosrow called down heaven's blessings on him, praising Zal, who had such a son, and Zavol, that had nurtured such a hero.

Next the king addressed Giv: "The hidden purposes of God have looked kindly on you: through Rostam He has restored your son to you." Giv replied, "May you live happily and forever, and may Rostam's luck remain ever fresh and green, and may Zal rejoice in his son."

Khosrow gave a great feast for his nobles, after which the company went to a splendid hall where they were plied with wine and entertained by richly dressed musicians whose cheeks blushed like rich brocade, and who accompanied their songs with the bewitching sound of harps. There were golden trays heaped with musk, and to the front of the hall was an artificial pool filled with rosewater; in his glory, the king seemed like a cypress topped by the full moon, and when the nobles left his palace every one of them was drunk.

At dawn Rostam returned to the court, prompt to serve his prince and with not a care in his heart; he asked for permission to return home, and Khosrow discussed this with him for a while. He ordered his chamberlain to bring in a suit of clothes sewn with jewels, a cloak and crown, a goblet filled with royal gems, a hundred saddled horses, a hundred laden mules, a hundred servant girls, a hundred serving youths—all these he gave to Rostam, who kissed the ground in thanks. The hero then placed the crown on his head, girt himself in the cloak and belt, made his farewells to the king, and took the road to Sistan. And his noble companions, who had seen so much sorrow and joy and suffering at his side, were also given presents, and they too left the king's palace in good spirits.

When the king had said farewell to his champions, he settled contentedly on his throne and summoned Bizhan. He asked him about the pains and sorrows he had endured, the narrow pit where he'd languished, and the woman who had ministered to him. Bizhan talked at length, and as the king listened he was moved to pity, both for him and for the torments Afrasyab's poor daughter had endured. He had a hundred sets of clothes of cloth of gold worked with jewels brought in, as well as a crown, ten purses of gold coins, slaves, carpets, and all manner of goods and said to Bizhan, "Take these to your grieving Turkish friend: speak gently to her, see you don't make her sufferings worse, think what she has gone through for your sake!

"Live your life in happiness with her now, and consider the turnings of Fate, who lifts one to the high heavens so that he knows nothing of grief or pain, and then throws him weeping beneath the dust. It is fearful, terrible, to think on this. And while one is brought up with luxury and caresses, and is thrown bewildered and despairing into a dark pit, another is lifted from the pit and raised to a throne where a jeweled crown is placed on his head. The world has no shame in doing this; it is prompt to hand out both pleasure and pain and has no need of us and our doings. Such is the way of the world that guides us to both good and evil. Now you should never need for wealth, and I wish you a heart free from all sorrow."

King Khosrow, the most noble and just of the Persian kings in the Shahnameh, *eventually decided that he should abdicate the throne, because he feared the corrupting influence of absolute power. He disappeared on a mountain side (there is an implication that he never really died, so that he remained a "once and future king", like the mythical British King Arthur in some versions of his tale), and a number of his followers who had accompanied him were killed in a snow storm.*

Before his disappearance Khosrow had designated the relatively unknown warrior Lohrasp as his successor. This news disturbed many of the older warriors of his court, including Rostam, who did not present himself at Lohrasp's court to pay homage to him as king. Lohrasp was succeeded on the throne by his son Goshtasp, and again Rostam stayed away from the court. During Goshtasp's reign the prophet Zoroaster began his mission, and the Persian court adopted his religion. Esfandyar, Goshtasp's son, became an active

*and warlike proselytizer for Zoroastrianism. Goshtasp
was wary of his warrior son's ambition and at one
point had him imprisoned. But he was forced to turn
to him for help when the forces of Turan, under a new
king, Arjasp, attacked and threatened to overrun the
country. He promised Esfandyar that if he could defeat
Arjasp, he, Goshtasp, would abdicate in his son's favor.
But when Esfandyar had accomplished just what his
father had demanded of him, he found that Goshtasp
had one more task in store for him before he would
hand over the throne.*

ROSTAM AND ESFANDYAR

I heard a story from a nightingale, repeating words come down to us from ancient times.

One night, drunk and dejected, Esfandyar came from his father's palace and went to see his mother Katayun, the daughter of the king of Rum. He embraced her, called for more wine, and said: "The king treats me badly; he told me that once I'd avenged the death of his father by killing king Arjasp, freed my sisters from captivity, cleansed the world of evildoers and promoted our new faith of Zoroastrianism, then he would hand over to me the throne and crown; I'd be king and leader of our armies. When the sun rises and he wakes up I'm going to remind him of his own words: he shouldn't keep from me what's rightfully mine. By God who guides the heavens, I swear that if I see any hesitation in his face I'll place the crown on my own head and distribute the country to its local lords; I'll be as strong and fierce as a lion, and make you queen of Iran."

His mother's heart was saddened at his words; her silk clothes pricked like thorns against her skin. She knew that the king was in no hurry to hand over his crown, throne, country, and royal authority to his son. She said: "Brave boy, don't be so angry with your fate. The army and treasury are yours already, don't over-reach yourself. What's finer in all the world than a young lion-like warrior, girded for war, standing ready to serve his father? When Goshtasp dies, his crown, throne, greatness, and splendor will all be yours."

Esfandyar replied: "It was a wise man who said a man should never tell his secrets to women, because as soon as he opens his mouth he finds his words on everyone's lips. And he also said a man shouldn't do what a woman tells him to, because none of them have any sense." His mother's face clouded with pain and shame, and she regretted having spoken to him.

Esfandyar went back to his father's palace and spent two days and nights there drinking, surrounded by musicians and his womenfolk. Goshtasp brooded on his son's ambitions for the crown and throne, and on the third day he summoned his councilor Jamasp, and had Esfandyar's horoscope cast. He asked whether the prince would have a long and happy life, reigning in safety and splendor, and whether he would die at another's hand or greet the angel Sorush from a peaceful deathbed.

When Jamasp consulted the astrological tables, frowns furrowed his forehead and his eyes filled with tears. He said: "Evil is mine, and my knowledge brings me only evil; would that I had died before your brother Zarir, and not seen his body weltering in blood and dust, or that my father had killed me and this evil fate had not been mine. Esfandyar subdues lions, he has cleared Iran of its enemies, he is fearless in war, he has driven your foes from the face of the earth, he tears the dragon's body in two. But will not sorrow come from this, and the taste of bitterness and grief?"

The king replied, "I trust you to tell me what you know, and not to deviate from wisdom's ways. If he is to die as Zarir did, my life will be a misery to me. You frowned at my question, but tell me what you see: at whose hand will he die, bringing me tears and sorrow?"

Jamasp said, "My lord, misfortune will not hold back because of me. He will die in Zabolestan, fighting with Zal's son, Rostam."

Then the king said, "Take seriously what I'm about to say: if I give him my treasury, the throne and sovereignty, and if he never travels to Zabolestan, will he be safe from the turnings of Fate, will fortunate stars watch over him?" But the astrologer replied, "The heaven's turnings cannot be evaded; neither strength nor valor will save you from the dragon's claws. What is fated will surely come to pass, and a wise man does not ask when." The king grew pensive, and his thoughts made his soul like a tangled thicket. He brooded on the turnings of Fate, and his speculations turned him toward evil.

At dawn the next day the king sat on his throne, and Esfandyar stood humbly before him, his arms crossed on his chest. The court was filled with famous warriors, and the priests stood ranged before the king. Then the mighty champion Esfandyar spoke, and suffering was evident in his voice. He said: "Great king, may you live forever, blessed by the divine *farr*. Justice and love emanate from you, and the crown and throne are made more splendid by you. Father, I am your slave, prompt to carry out all you desire. You know that in the wars of religion with Arjasp, who attacked us with his Chinese cavalry, I swore before God that I would destroy any idolater who threatened our faith, that I would slash his trunk in two with my dagger and feel no fear. And when Arjasp came I did not flee from the leopard's lair. But drinking at your banquet you believed Gorazm's slander, and had me hung with heavy chains and fettered in the fortress of Gonbadan, despised among strangers. You abandoned Balkh and traveled to Zavol, thinking all battles were banquets, and forgetting the sight of your father Lohrasp pierced by Arjasp's sword, lying prone in his blood. When your councilor Jamasp came and saw me worn away by captivity, he tried to persuade me to accept the throne and sovereignty. I answered that I would show my heavy chains to God on the Day of Judgment. He told me of the chieftains who'd been killed, of my imprisoned sisters, of our king fleeing before the Turkish hordes, and asked me if such things did not wring my heart. He said much more besides, and all his words were filled with sorrow and pain. Then I smashed my chains and ran to the king's court: I slaughtered his enemies and rejoiced the king's heart. If I were to describe my seven trials the account would never end. I severed Arjasp's head from his body and avenged the name of Lohrasp. I brought here their treasure, their crown, their throne, and their women and children. I did all you had commanded me, kept to all your orders, never swerved from your advice. You'd said that if you ever saw me alive again you would cherish me more than your own wellbeing; that you would bestow the crown and ivory throne on me, because I would be worthy of both. And now when our nobles ask me where my treasure and army are, I blush for shame. What excuse do you have now? What's the point of my life? What has all my suffering been for?"

The king answered his son: "There's no way forward but the truth. You have acted as you say, and may God favor you for it. I see no enemy in all the world, neither open nor secret, who does not shudder at the mention of your name: shudder I say, he gives up his soul there and then. No one in all the world is your equal, unless it be that foolish son of Zal. His valor lifts him above the skies, and he thinks of himself as no king's subject. He was a slave before Kavus, and he lived by the grace of Khosrow; but about me, Goshtasp, he says, 'His crown is new, mine is ancient; no man anywhere is my equal in battle, not in Rum nor Turan nor Iran.' Now, you must travel to Sistan and there use all your skill, all your ruses and devices. Draw your

sword and your mace, bind Rostam in chains; do the same
with Zavareh and Faramarz, and forbid them to ride in the
saddle. I swear by the Judge of all the world, by Him who
lights the sun and moon and stars, that when you do what I
have commanded, you shall hear no more opposition from
me. I shall hand over to you my treasury and crown, and I
myself will seat you on the throne."

This was Esfandyar's response: "O noble and resourceful king, you are straying from the ancient ways;
you should speak as is appropriate. Fight with the king of
China, destroy the lords of the steppe, but what are you
doing fighting against an old man whom Kavus called a
conqueror of lions? From the time of Manuchehr and Kay
Qobad all the kings of Iran have delighted in him, calling
him Rakhsh's master, world-conqueror, lion-slayer, crown-
bestower. He's not some young stripling making his way
in the world; he is a great man, one who entered into a
pact with Kay Khosrow. If such pacts are wrong then he
shouldn't be seeking one with you, Goshtasp."

His father said: "My lionhearted prince, you've heard
that Kavus was led astray by the devil, that he attempted
to fly into the skies on the wings of eagles and fell wretch-
edly into the sea at Sari; that he brought a devil-born wife
back from Hamaveran and gave her command of the royal
harem; that Seyavash was destroyed by her wiles and the
whole royal clan put in peril. When a man has broken his
promise before God, it's wrong even to pass by his doorway.
If you want the throne and crown, gather your troops and
take the road for Sistan. When you arrive bind Rostam's
arms, and lead him here. Watch that Zavareh, Faramarz,
and Sam don't trick you: drag them all on foot to this
court. And then no one, no matter how rich or illustrious
he might be, will disobey my commands again."

> *The young prince answered: as he spoke he frowned,*
> *"Enough! It isn't them you're circling round,*
> *You're not pursuing Zal and Rostam—I,*
> *Your son, am singled out by you to die;*
> *Your jealous passion for your sovereignty*
> *Has made you want to rid the world of me.*
> *So be it! Keep your royal crown and throne,*
> *Give me a corner to live in alone.*
> *I'm one of many slaves, no more; my task*
> *Is to perform whatever you may ask."*

Goshtasp replied: "Don't be too impetuous, but if you're to achieve greatness don't hold back either. Choose experienced cavalry from our army; weapons, troops, and cash are all at your disposal, and any holding back will be because of your own suspicious mind. What would treasure, an army, the crown, and throne be to me without you?"

Esfandyar said, "An army will be of no use to me in this situation. If the time to die has come, a commander can't ward it off with troops." Troubled by thoughts of the crown, and by his father's words, he left the court and made his way to his own palace; there were sighs on his lips, and sadness filled his heart.

Katayun's Advice to Esfandyar

Weeping and in a turmoil of emotion, the beautiful Katayun came before her son, to whom she said: "You remind us of the ancient heroes, and I have heard from Bahman that you mean to leave our gardens and journey to the wastes of Zabolestan. You are to capture Zal's son, Rostam, the master of sword and mace. Listen to your mother's advice; don't be in a hurry either to suffer evil or commit it. Rostam is a horseman with a mammoth's strength, a river's force is nothing against him; he ripped out the guts of the White Demon, the sun is turned aside in its path by his sword. When he sought revenge for the death of Seyavash, and made war on Afrasyab, he turned the world to a sea of blood. Don't throw your life away for the sake of a crown; no king was ever born crowned. My curses on this throne and this crown, on all this slaughter and havoc and plundering. Your father's grown old, and you are young, strong, and capable; all the army looks to you, don't let this anger of yours put you in harm's way. There are other places in the world besides Sistan; there's no need to be so headstrong, so eager for combat. Don't make me the most wretched woman both here and in the world to come; pay attention to my words, they come from a mother's love."

Esfandyar replied: "Dear mother, listen to me: you know what Rostam is, you're always talking about his greatness. It would be wrong to kill him, and no good can come of the king's plan: there's no one in Iran who's finer or more noble than Rostam. All this is true, but don't break my heart, because if you do I shall tear it from my body. How can I ignore the king's orders, how can I refuse such a mission? If heaven wills it I shall die in Zabol, but if Rostam accepts my orders he'll hear no harsh words from me."

His mother said, "My mammoth warrior, your strength makes you careless of your soul, but you won't be strong enough to defeat Rostam. Don't leave here without warriors to help you, offering your life up to Rostam like this. If you're determined to go, this mission is the work of Ahriman; at least don't take your children to this hell, because the wise will not think well of you if you do," and as she spoke she wept bloody tears and tore at her hair.

Esfandyar replied, "It's wrong to keep youngsters away from battle. If a boy stays shut up with women he becomes weak and sullen; he should be present on the battlefield and learn what fighting means. I don't need to take an army with me: men from my own family and a few noblemen will suffice."

At cock-crow the next morning the din of drums rang out; Esfandyar mounted his horse and set off like the wind at the head of a band of warriors. They went forward until they came to a place where the road forked; one track led to the fortress of Gonbadan and the other toward Zabol. The camel that was in the lead lay down on the earth as if it never meant to rise again, and though its driver beat it with a stick it refused to budge, and the caravan halted. Esfandyar took this as a bad omen, and gave orders that the beast's head be severed, hoping to deflect the bad luck he foresaw. This was done, and although Esfandyar was alarmed he made light of it, saying:

> *"A noble warrior whose audacity*
> *Lights up the world and brings him victory*
> *Laughs at both good and evil, since he knows*
> *Both come from God, whom no one can oppose."*

Inwardly afraid of what lay ahead, he reached the River Hirmand, the border of Rostam's territory. A suitable place was selected, and the group pitched camp in the customary fashion. In Esfandyar's pavilion a throne was placed, and his warriors assembled before him. The prince called for wine and musicians, Pashutan sat opposite him, and as he drank and relaxed Esfandyar's face opened like a blossom in spring. He said to his companions: "I haven't carried out my father's orders; he told me to capture Rostam quickly, and not to hold back in humiliating him. I haven't done what he ordered me to, because this Rostam is a lionhearted warrior, who has undergone many trials, whose mace has set the world in order, and in whose debt all Persians live whether they are princes or slaves. I must send him a messenger, someone who's wise and sensible, a horseman who has some dignity and presence, someone whom Rostam can't deceive. If he'll come to me and dispel this darkness in my soul, if he'll let me bind his arms and in so doing bind the evil that haunts me, and if he has no malevolence against me, I will treat him with nothing but kindness."

Pashutan said, "This is the right path; stick to it, and try to bring peace between men."

Esfandyar ordered his son Bahman to come before him, and said to him: "Saddle your black horse, and dress yourself in a robe of Chinese brocade; put a royal diadem studded with fine jewels on your head, so that whoever sees you will single you out as the most splendid of all warriors and know that you are of royal blood. Take with you ten reputable priests and five horses with golden bridles. Make your way to Rostam's palace, but do so at a leisurely pace. Greet him from me, be polite, flatter him with eloquent words, and then say to him: 'No one with any sense ignores a king's commands. A man must be grateful before God, who knows eternally what is good. If a man augments what is good and holds his heart back from evil, God will fulfill his desires and he will live happily in this fleeting world. If he abstains from evil he will find paradise in the other world; a wise man knows that in the end his bed will be the dark earth and his soul will fly up toward God. One who can distinguish between the good and evil of this world will be loyal to his king.

'Now we wish to reckon up what you have done, neither adding to nor diminishing your achievements. You've lived for many years and seen many kings come and go in the world, and if you follow the way of wisdom you know that it was not right for someone who has received so much in the way of wealth and glory from my family to have refused to visit Lohrasp's court. When he passed on sovereignty over the land of Iran to his son, Goshtasp, you paid no attention. You wrote no congratulatory letter to him, you ignored the duties of a subject, you didn't travel to his court to pay homage: you call no one king. Since the time of Hushang, Jamshid, and Feraydun, who wrested sovereignty from Zahhak, to the time of Kay Qobad, there never was such a king as Goshtasp, not for fighting or feasting or hunting. He has adopted the pure faith, and injustice and error have hidden themselves away: the way of God shines out like the sun, and the way of demons is destroyed. When Arjasp attacked with an innumerable army, Goshtasp confronted him and made the battlefield a graveyard for his dead: great men will talk about this exploit until the end of the world. He breaks the back of every lion, and all the east and west are his: travel from Turan to China to Byzantium and you'll see that the world is like wax in his hands. The desert Arabs brandishing their lances send him tribute, because they have no heart or strength to fight against him. I tell you all this because the king is offended by your behavior. You haven't gone to his palace or seen his noble courtiers; instead, you've hidden yourself away in this remote province. But how can our leaders forget you, unless they have neither brains nor hearts remaining to them? You always strove for the good, and held yourself ready to do your kings' bidding. If your pains are reckoned up they exceed the treasure you've accumulated, but no king has ever accepted that his subject could act in this contemptuous way. Goshtasp has said to me that Rostam is so wealthy now that he sits drunk in Zavolestan and gives no thought to us. One day in his fury he swore an oath by the shining day and darkness of the night that no one would ever see you at his court unless it were in chains. Now, I have come from Iran for this purpose, and the king ordered me not to delay in carrying it out. Draw back now, and fear his anger. If you will go along with this and give up your contemptuous ways, I swear by the sun, by the spirit of Zarir, by my lion-like father's soul, that I will make the king take back his words, and that your glory will shine with splendor once again. Pashutan is my guide and witness that I have tried to fathom the king's purposes in this, and see no fault in him. My father is my king and I am his subject; I can never refuse his orders. Your whole clan—Zavareh, Faramarz, Zal, and all the rest of your tried and true chieftains—should hear my words and take my advice. This house must not be left a prey to Persian warriors and destroyed. When I take you bound before the king, and then go over your faults with him, I'll calm his anger and make him forget all thoughts of vengeance. I am a prince, and I give you my word that I will not let even the wind touch you.'"

Bahman Goes as a Messenger to Rostam

Bahman dressed himself in cloth of gold, placed a princely crown on his head, and set out from the encampment, his banner fluttering behind him. A proud young man, on a splendid horse, he made his way toward the River Hirmand, and as soon as the lookout saw him he shouted out to his companions in Zabolestan, "A fine warrior on a black horse is coming our way; his harness tinkles with golden bells, and he's followed by a group of mounted soldiers; he's already crossed the river with no difficulty."

As soon as he heard this Zal rode to the lookout post, his lariat coiled at his saddle and his mace at the ready. When he caught sight of Bahman he sighed and said, "This lordly young man with his royal clothes must be someone from Lohrasp's clan; may his coming here be auspicious for us." Pensively, his heart filled with foreboding, he rode back toward his castle. Radiating princely pride, Bahman approached; he did not recognize Zal, and raising his arm he called out, "My noble friend, where can I find great Rostam, the prop of our times? Esfandyar has camped by the river, and is looking for him."

Zal replied, "There's no need for such hurry, young man! Dismount, and call for wine, and calm yourself. Rostam is out hunting with Faramarz and a few friends; they'll be back soon enough. Rest here with your retinue, and drink a little wine."

But Bahman answered, "Esfandyar said nothing to us about wine and rest: find someone to guide us to the hunting grounds."

Zal said, "What's your name? Whose clan do you belong to, and what have you come here for? I think you're kin to Lohrasp, and descended from Goshtasp too."

Bahman said, "I am Bahman, son to invincible Esfandyar, lord of the world."

When he heard this Zal dismounted and made his obeisance before him. Bahman laughed and dismounted as well, and the two embraced and kissed. Zal urged him to stay, saying that his haste was unnecessary, but Bahman replied that Esfandyar's message could not be treated so lightly. And so Zal chose a warrior who knew the lie of the land and sent him with Bahman to where Rostam was hunting. He was an experienced man called Shirkhun, and after he had led him a fair distance he pointed out the way and went back, leaving Bahman to go on ahead.

Bahman urged his horse up a mountain slope, and when he reached the summit he gazed at the hunting grounds spread out below. He saw there a mighty warrior, a man massive as the cliff of Bisitun, who had uprooted a tree and was using it as a spit on which to roast a wild ass, which he handled as easily as if it weighed no more than an ant. In his other hand he held a goblet full of wine, and in front of him a young man was standing ready to serve him. Nearby, close to a stream and a clump of trees, Rakhsh stood cropping grass. Bahman said, "This is either Rostam, or the sun itself. No one has ever seen such a man in all the world, or heard of his like among the ancient heroes. I fear that Esfandyar will be no match for him, and will flinch from him in battle. I'll kill him here and now with a rock, and so break Zal's heart." He tore a granite boulder from the mountain side and sent it tumbling down the slope. Zavareh heard the rumble of its descent and saw it plunging toward them; he shouted out, "Rostam, a great rock is rolling down the mountain." Rostam made no move; he didn't even put down the wild ass he was roasting. As Zavareh hung back in alarm, Rostam waited until the boulder was almost on him, and the dust it sent up had obscured the mountain above; then he kicked it contemptuously aside. Zavareh and Rostam's son Faramarz cheered, but Bahman was horrified at the exploit, and said, "If Esfandyar fights with such a warrior he'll be humiliated by him; it'll be better if he treats him politely and circumspectly. If Rostam gets the better of Esfandyar in combat he will be able to conquer all Iran." Bahman remounted his horse, and with his heart full of foreboding descended the mountain slope.

He told a priest of the wonder he had seen, and made his way by an easier path at the foot of the mountain toward Rostam. As he approached, Rostam turned to a companion and said, "Who is this? I think it's someone from Goshtasp's clan." Then he caught sight of Bahman's retinue waiting on the mountain side, and he grew suspicious. He and Zavareh, and the rest of the hunting party, went forward to greet their guest. Bahman quickly dismounted and greeted Rostam civilly. Rostam said, "You'll get nothing from me until you tell me who you are." Bahman replied, "I am Esfandyar's son, chief of the Persians; I am Bahman." Rostam immediately embraced him and apologized for his tardy welcome.

Together they made their way back to Rostam's camp and when Bahman had sat himself down he greeted Rostam formally, and conveyed to him the greetings of the king and his nobility. Then he went on: "Esfandyar has come here and pitched camp by the River Hirmand, as the king ordered him to. If you will hear me out, I bring you a message from him."

Rostam replied: "Prince, you've taken a great deal of trouble and traversed a great deal of ground; first we should eat, and then the world is at your disposal." A cloth was spread on the ground, and soft bread was placed on it; then Rostam set a roasted wild ass, its flesh still hot, before Bahman. He called for his brother Zavareh to sit with them, but not the rest of his companions. He had another wild ass brought, since it was his custom to eat a whole animal himself. He sprinkled it with salt, cut the meat, and set to. Bahman watched him, and ate a little of the wild ass's meat, but less than a hundredth of the amount Rostam consumed. Rostam laughed and said:

> *"A prince who's so abstemious surely needs*
> *An army to assist him in his deeds:*
> *I've heard that in your father's battles you*
> *Fought with him: what exactly did you do?*
> *You eat so little you're too weak to wield*
> *A warrior's weapons on the battlefield."*

Bahman replied:

> *"A noble prince will neither talk at length*
> *Nor eat too much: he'd rather save his strength*
> *For battles than for banquets, since it's war*
> *That shows a warrior's worth, not who eats more."*

Rostam laughed long and loud and said, "A fighting spirit won't stay hidden long!" He called for enough wine to sink a ship: filling a golden goblet, he toasted the memory of noble heroes, then handed another to Bahman and said, "Toast whoever you want to!" Seeing the proffered goblet Bahman hesitated, so Faramarz drank first, saying, "You're a princely child, we hope you enjoy the wine, and our drinking together." Bahman took the goblet and reluctantly drank a little; he was as astonished by Rostam's capacity for food and drink as he was by his massive body, arms, and shoulders. When they had finished their meal, the two heroes rode together for a while, side by side, and Bahman told Rostam the details of Esfandyar's message.

Rostam's Answer to Esfandyar

As he listened to Bahman's words, the old man grew pensive. He said, "I've heard your message through and I'm pleased to see you. Now, take my answer back to Esfandyar: 'Great, lionhearted warrior, any man who is wise considers the realities of a situation. A man like you who's rich, brave, and successful in war, who has authority and a good name among other chieftains, should not give his heart to malice and suspicion. You and I should act justly toward one another; we should fear God and not make evil welcome. Words that have no meaning are like a tree without leaves or scent, and if your heart's given over to greed and ambition, you will toil long and hard and see no profit for your pains. When a nobleman speaks he should weigh his words well and avoid idle talk. I've always been happy to hear you praised, to hear people say that no mother ever bore a son like you, that you surpass your ancestors in bravery, chivalry, and wisdom. Your name is known in India and Byzantium, and in the realms of wizards and witches; I praise God for your glory day and night and I have always longed to set eyes on you, to see for myself your splendor and graciousness. I welcome your arrival, and I ask that we sit together and drink to the king's health. I'll come to you alone, without my men, and listen to what the king has commanded. I'll bring you the charters past kings, from Kay Qobad to Kay Khosrow, have granted my family, and I'll make known to you the pains I've suffered, the difficulties I've endured, the good I've done for past princes, from ancient times up to the present day. If the right reward for all I have undergone is to be led in chains, would that I had never been born, or that once born I had soon died. Am I, who broke elephants' backs and flung their carcasses in the ocean, to come to court and publish all my secrets to the world, my arms tied, my feet hobbled in leather bonds? If it becomes known that I've committed any sin, may my head be severed from my body.

May I never speak unseemly words, and you should keep yours for cursing devils; don't say these things that no one has ever said, and don't think your valor will enable you to catch the wind in a cage. No matter how great a man is, he can't pass through fire, or survive the seas if he can't swim, or dim the moon's light, or make a fox a lion's equal. Don't provoke me to a fight, because fighting with me will be no trivial matter: no man has ever seen fetters on my ankles, and no savage lion has ever made me give ground.

'Act as becomes a king; don't let yourself be guided by devils and demons. Be a man, drive anger and malice out of your heart, don't see the world through a young man's eyes. May God keep you happy and prosperous; cross the river, honor my house with your presence, don't refuse to see someone who offers you his allegiance. As I was Kay Qobad's subject, so I will serve you, willingly and cheerfully. Come to me without your armed companions, stay with me for two months; there's good hunting here, the waterways are full of fowl, and if you tire of this you can watch my swordsmen in combat with lions. When you want to return to the Persian court I'll load you with gifts from my treasury and travel side by side with you. I'll enter the king's presence and gently ask his pardon: when I've kissed his head and eyes and feet in sign of submission, I'll ask him why my feet should be shackled.' Now, remember everything I've said and repeat it to noble Esfandyar."

Bahman went back with his retinue of priests: Rostam remained in the roadway for a while, and called Zavareh and Faramarz to him. He said, "Go to Zal and tell him that Esfandyar has arrived, and that he's full of ambitious plans. Have a fine welcome prepared, something even more splendid than was customary in Kay Kavus's time: place a golden throne in the audience hall and have royal carpets spread before it. The king's son has come here and he's bent on war; tell Zal that this prince is a famous fighter and that he'd feel no fear confronted by a whole plain filled

with lions. I'll go to him, and if he'll accept to be our guest
we can hope for a good outcome; if I see that he's a well-
disposed young man I'll give him a golden crown set with
rubies, and I won't stint him jewels or fine cloth or weapons either. But if he turns me away and I come back here
with no hope of a peaceful resolution, then you know that
my looped lariat, which has caught wild elephants' heads in
its coils, is always ready."

Zavareh said, "Give the matter no thought: a man who
has no quarrel with someone doesn't go looking for a fight.
I know of no stronger or more chivalrous warrior in all the
world than Esfandyar. Wise men don't act in evil ways, and
we've done him no harm." Zavareh made his way to Zal's
court, and Rostam rode to the shore of the River Hirmand,
fearful of the harm he foresaw. At the river's edge he tugged
on the reins, halting his horse, and prayed to God.

Bahman Takes His Father Rostam's Message

When Bahman reached camp, his father was standing before the royal pavilion, waiting for him, and he called out
"What did the hero tell you then?" Bahman went over all
he'd heard. He began by giving Rostam's message and then
he described Rostam himself. He told everything he'd seen,
and much that he'd inferred, and ended by saying, "There's
no one like Rostam anywhere. He has a lion's heart and a
mammoth's body, he could snatch a sea monster from the
waves. He's coming unarmed, with no corselet, helmet,
mace, or lariat, to the banks of the Hirmand: he wants to
see the king, and he has some private business I don't know
about with you."

But Esfandyar angrily turned on Bahman and humiliated him before their companions saying,

> "No self-respecting warrior would ask
> Advice from women for a warrior's task,

> *And no one who is soldierly or wise*
> *Would send a boy on such an enterprise.*
> *Just where have you seen champions, that you praise*
> *This Rostam for his fine courageous ways?*
> *He's like a mammoth in the wars you say—*
> *D'you want my men to fight or run away!"*

Then he said in an undertone to brave Pashutan, "This Rostam still acts like a young man, age hasn't broken him yet."

He gave orders that a black horse be saddled in gold, and then he led his men toward the bank of the Hirmand, his lariat coiled at his side.

Rostam Comes to Greet Esfandyar

Rakhsh neighed on one side of the river, and on the other the Persian prince's horse answered. Rostam urged Rakhsh from dry land into the water: when he had crossed he dismounted and greeted Esfandyar. He said: "I have asked God continually to guide you here as you have now come, in good health and accompanied by your army. Now, let us sit together and discuss things courteously and kindly. As God is my witness, wisdom will guide me in what I say; I will not try to snatch any advantage from our conversation, nor will I lie to you. If I had seen Seyavash himself I would not rejoice as I do now seeing you; indeed, you resemble no one so much as that noble and unfortunate prince. Happy is the king who has a son like you; happy are the people of Iran who see your throne and your good fortune: and woe to whoever fights against you, since dust will overwhelm both his throne and his luck. May all your enemies be filled with fear, may the hearts of those who are against you be cut in two, may you remain victorious forever, and may your dark nights be as bright as the days of spring!"

When he heard him Esfandyar too dismounted, embraced Rostam, and greeted him warmly and respectfully, saying "I thank God to see you cheerful and confident like this: you deserve all men's praise, and our heroes are like your slaves. Happy is the man who has a son like you, who sees the branch he has put forth bear fruit: happy is the man who has you as his support, since he need fear nothing from Fate's harshness. When I saw you I thought of Zarir, that lionlike warrior and tamer of horses."

Rostam replied, "I have one request, and if you grant it to me my desires are fulfilled: delight my soul by coming to my house. It is unworthy of you, but we can make do with what there is and so confirm our friendship."

Esfandyar answered, "You are like the heroes of old, and any man who has your reputation rejoices the land of Iran. It would be wrong to ignore your wishes, but I cannot turn aside from the king's orders. He gave me no permission to stay in Zavol with its chieftains. You should quickly do what the king has ordered; place the fetters on your own feet, because a king's fetters are no cause for shame. When I take you before him, bound like this, all the guilt will redound on him. I must bind you, but my soul is grieved by it, and I would rather serve you: I won't let you stay in chains beyond nightfall, and I won't let the least harm come to you. Believe me, the king will not injure you, and when I place the crown on my own head I will give the world into your safekeeping. This will not be a sin before God, and there is no shame in doing what a king demands; and when the blossoms and roses open, and you return to your Zavolestan, you'll find that I'll be generous, and load you down with gifts to beautify your land."

Rostam replied, "I have prayed God that I might see you and rejoice, and now I've heard what you have to say. We are two noble warriors, one old, one young, both wise and alert; but I fear the evil eye has struck, and that I'll never know sweet sleep again. Some demon has pushed in between us, ambition for a crown and glory has perverted your soul. It will be an eternal shame to me if a great chieftain like yourself refuses to come to my house and be my guest while he is in this country. If you can expel this hatred from your mind, and undo this demon's work, I'll agree to anything you wish, except to be chained: chains will bring shame, the ruin of my greatness, and an ugly aftermath. No one will ever see me in chains alive; my mind's made up and there's nothing more to be said."

Esfandyar answered: "The heroes of the past are met in you, all you have said is true, and perverse paths bring no man glory. But Pashutan knows the orders the king gave me when I set out: if I come now to your home, and stay there enjoying myself as your guest, and you then refuse to accept the king's orders, I shall burn in hell's flames when I pass to the other world. If you wish, we can drink together for a day and swear friendship to one another; who knows what tomorrow will bring or what will be said of this later?"

Rostam replied: "I must go and rid myself of these clothes. I've been hunting for a week, eating wild ass instead of lamb; call for me when you're seated with your people, ready to eat." He mounted Rakhsh and deep in thought galloped back to his castle. He saw his father's face and said, "I've visited this Esfandyar: I saw him mounted, tall as a cypress tree, wise and splendid, as if the great Feraydun himself had given him strength and knowledge. He exceeds the reports about him; the royal *farr* radiates from his face."

When Rostam rode away from the river Hirmand, Esfandyar was filled with foreboding. At that moment, Pashutan, who was his councilor, came into his tent, and Esfandyar addressed him:

> *"We thought this would be easy, but we've found*
> *Our way's unsure, and over rocky ground;*
> *I shouldn't visit Rostam's home, and he*
> *For his part ought to stay away from me.*

> *If he neglects to come I won't complain*
> *Or summon him to sit with me again.*
> *If one of us should die in this affair*
> *The other will be vanquished by despair."*

Pashutan said, "My lord, who has a brother to equal Esfandyar? When I saw that you two were not looking to fight with one another, my heart opened like the blossoms in springtime, both for Rostam and for Esfandyar. I look at what you're doing here and I see that some demon has blocked off wisdom's way forward. You're a religious and honorable man, one who obeys God and his father: hold back, don't give your soul over to violence; my brother, listen to what I'm telling you. I heard all Rostam said: he is a great man, your chains will never bind his feet and he will not lightly take your advice. The son of Zal will not walk into your trap so easily; I fear that this will be a long drawn out contest between two haughty warriors, and one with an ugly ending to it. You are a great man too, and wiser than the king; you're a better soldier and a finer man than he is. One of you wants rejoicing and reconciliation, and the other wants battles and vengeance. Consider for yourself, which of you is more praiseworthy?"

Esfandyar replied,

> *"But if I turn away from what my king*
> *Commands there's no excuse that I can bring,*
> *I'll be reproached in this world, and I fear*
> *God's probing of my life when death draws near;*
> *For Rostam's sake I cannot throw away*
> *My life both here and after Judgment Day—*
> *There is no needle that can sew the eyes*
> *Of Faith tight shut, no matter how one tries."*

Pashutan said, "I've given my advice, and it will benefit you physically and morally. I've said all I can; now, choose the right way, but remember that princes' hearts are not inclined to vengeance."

Esfandyar ordered his cooks to prepare supper, but he sent no one to summon Rostam. When the food had been eaten he lifted his winecup and began to boast of his past exploits, toasting the king occasionally as he did so. Rostam was in his castle all this while, waiting for Esfandyar's invitation. But as time passed and no one came, and then supper time was over and he was still staring at the empty road, fury took possession of his mind. He laughed and said to his brother, "Have the meal prepared and call our men to eat. So this is our famous hero's way of behaving, is it? See that you never forget his splendid manners!" Then he ordered that Rakhsh be saddled and richly caparisoned after the Chinese fashion, and said,

> *"I'm going to tell this noble prince that he*
> *Has now deliberately insulted me."*

Rostam and Esfandyar Meet for the Second Time

The mammoth warrior mounted Rakhsh, whose neigh resounded for two miles, and made his way quickly to the river's edge. The Persian troops there were astonished by his massive frame and martial bearing, and said to one another "He resembles no one but Esfandyar himself, and would be the victor in combat with an elephant. The king's unwise obsession with his throne has made him send a splendid hero to his death; as he grows older all the king thinks of is wealth and his royal authority."

Esfandyar welcomed him, and Rostam replied, "My fine young warrior, it seems you've developed new customs, new ways of behaving. Why am I unworthy to drink with you? Is this how you keep your promises? Now, take seriously what I tell you, and don't be so foolish as to get angry with an old man. You think you're greater than everyone

else and you take pride in your chieftains: you consider me
a lightweight, someone whose opinions don't matter. But
know that the world knows I am Rostam, scion of the great
Nariman; black demons bite their hands in horror at my
approach, and I fling wizards into the pit of death. When
chieftains see my armor and my Rakhsh like a raging lion
they flee in terror; I have caught in my lariat's coils warriors
like Kamus and the Khaqan of China, I have dragged them
from their saddles and bound their feet. I am the keeper of
Iran and its lionlike chieftains, the support of its warriors on
every side. Don't slight my overtures to you, don't think of
yourself as higher than the heavens. I'm seeking a pact with
you, and I respect your royal *farr* and glory. I have no desire
for a prince like you to die at my hands. I am descended
from Sam, before whom lions fled from their lairs, and you
are the son of a king. For a long time now I have been the
world's first warrior, and I have never stooped to evil: I
have cleared the world of my enemies, and I have suffered
countless pains and sorrows. I thank God that in my old age
I have met with a fine strong warrior willing to fight with a
man of the pure faith, one whom all the world praises."

Esfandyar laughed, and said, "And all this anger is simply because no invitation came? The weather's so hot and
it's such a long way that I didn't want to put you to the
effort of coming back. I said to myself that I'd go to you
at dawn tomorrow and offer my apologies: I'd be happy
to see Zal and I'd spend time drinking with you both. But
now that you've taken the trouble to leave your house and
cross the plain to get here, calm yourself, sit down, take
the winecup in your hand, and put aside your anger and
irritation." And he moved over so that there was a place
for Rostam to his left. But Rostam's response was, "That's
no place for me, I'll sit where I wish to." Esfandyar ordered
Bahman to vacate the space to the right, but Rostam retorted in fury, "Open your eyes and look at me: look at my
greatness and at my noble ancestry, I'm of the seed of Sam,

and if there's no place worthy of me in your company I still have my victories and fame." Then the prince ordered that a golden throne be brought and placed opposite his own: still enraged Rostam sat himself down on the throne, and toyed with a scented orange in his hand.

Esfandyar addressed Rostam, "You're a powerful and well-intentioned hero, but I've heard from priests, chieftains, and other wise men that Zal was nothing but demon-spawn, and can boast of no better lineage. They hid him from Sam for a long time, and the court was in an uproar because he was so ugly, with a black body and white hair and face; when Sam finally saw him he was in despair and gave orders that he be exposed on the seashore as a prey for the birds and fish. The Simorgh came down, flapping its wings, and seeing no signs of grandeur or glory in the child to deter him, he snatched him up and took him to his nest, but even though he was hungry Zal's puny body didn't seem worth eating. So he flung him naked in a corner of the nest, where the child lived off scraps. Finally the Simorgh took pity on him, and after he'd subsisted on the Simorgh's leavings for a number of years he set off, naked as he was, for Sistan. Now because Sam had no other children, and was old and stupid as well, he welcomed him back. My great ancestors, who were noble and generous men, gave him wealth and position, and when many years had passed he grew to be a fine tall cypress of a man. And a branch of this same cypress is Rostam, who by his valor and splendid appearance and fine deeds outreached the heavens, until his ambition and excesses have procured a kingdom for him."

Rostam replied; "Calm yourself; why are you saying such offensive things? Your heart's filled with perversity and your soul's puffed up with demonic pride. Speak as becomes a royal personage; kings say nothing but the truth. The lord of the world knows that Sam's son Zal is a great, wise, and renowned man. And Sam was the son of Nariman, who was descended from Kariman, whose father was Hushang, the crowned king of all the earth. Haven't you heard of Sam's incomparable fame? There was a dragon in Tus, a monster that terrorized the beasts of the sea and the birds of the air; and then there was a wicked demon so huge that the sea of China reached only to its waist while its head towered into the sky and obscured the sun; it would snatch fish up from the ocean depths and store them beyond the sphere of the moon, and cook them by holding them against the sun; the turning heavens wept to see such a monster. These two hideous beings trembled before Sam's courage and his sword, and perished by his hand.

"My mother was the daughter of Mehrab, under whose rule India flourished, and who was descended, through five generations, from Zahhak, a monarch who lifted his head higher than all the kings of the world. Who has a more noble lineage than this? A wise man does not try to deny the truth. Any man who makes claims to heroism has to test himself against me. I hold my fiefdom by irreproachable treaty from Kavus, and it was renewed by the greatest of warrior-kings, Khosrow. I have traveled the world, and slain many unjust kings: when I crossed the Oxus Afrasyab fled from Turan to China; I fought for Kavus in Hamaveran and when I journeyed alone to Mazanderan, neither Arzhang, nor the white demon, nor Sanjeh, nor Ulad Ghandi hindered me. For that king's sake I killed my own son, and there never was such a strong, chivalrous, war-tried hero as Sohrab. It is more than six hundred years since I was born of Zal's seed: in all that time I have been the world's heroic champion, and my thoughts and deeds have always been one. I'm like the noble Feraydun, who crowned himself, and dragged Zahhak from the throne and laid him in the dust. And then Sam, whose wisdom and knowledge of magic are unmatched in the world, is my grandfather. Thirdly, when I have girded on my sword our kings have lived free from all anxieties: there's never been such pleasure at the court, or

such security from evil's inroads. The world was as I willed
it to be, ordered by my sword and mace.

> *I've told you this so that you'll understand*
> *That though you govern with a princely hand,*
> *You're new to this world's ancient ways, in spite*
> *Of all your splendor and imperial might.*
> *You look out on the earth and all you see*
> *Is your own image and ability,*
> *But gazing at yourself you're unaware*
> *Of all the hidden dangers lurking there.*
> *I've talked enough; let's drink, and may the wine*
> *Dispel all your anxieties, and mine."*

Hearing him, Esfandyar laughed, and his heart lightened.
He said, "I've listened to the tale of your exploits and
sufferings, now hear how I've distinguished myself. First,
I have fought for the true faith, clearing the land of idol-
worshippers, and no one's seen any warrior slaughter them
in such numbers as I have, covering the ground with their
corpses. I'm Goshtasp's child, and he was the child of
Lohrasp, who was the child of Orandshah, a descendant
of the Kayanid kings. My mother's the daughter of Caesar,
who rules the Romans and is descended from Salm, the son
of Feraydun, the king who established the ways of faith and
fair-dealing, and without whose glory there would be little
enough justice in the world, as no one can deny. You're a
man who stood as a slave before my royal ancestors, you
and your forebears too. I'm not saying this to cause dissension between us, but you received sovereignty as a gift from
my family, even though you're now trying to kick over the
traces. Wait now, and let me tell you how things are, and if
there's one lie in what I say, show it to me.

"Since Goshtasp has been king my chivalry and good fortune have been at his service. I was the man who was praised
for spreading the faith, even though I was then imprisoned

because of Gorazm's slanders. Because I couldn't help him
Lohrasp was defeated, and our land was overrun by enemies, until Jamasp came to release me from my chains. The
blacksmiths tried to free me, but my impatient heart was the
sword that finally broke my fetters: I roared at their delay,
and it was my own strength that smashed the shackles binding me. Arjasp, our enemy, fled before me, and so did all
his chieftains, and I harried their routed army like a savage
lion. You've heard how lions and Ahriman beset me during
my seven trials, how I entered the Brass Fortress by a trick,
and destroyed everything there; how I sought revenge for
our nobles' deaths, how I took war to Turan and China and
suffered hardships and privations there more terrible than a
leopard inflicts on a wild ass, or than the sailor's hook that
torments a great fish's gullet. There was a dark castle high
on a distant ridge, shunned for its evil reputation and filled
with depraved idol-worshippers: I took that castle, smashed
its images against the ground, and lit the sacred flame of
Zoroaster in their place. I came home with my God-given
victory, and not an enemy of ours survived; not a temple or
an idol-worshipper remained.

> *These battles that I fought, I fought alone,*
> *No man has shown the valor I have shown.*
> *But we have talked enough: if you agree,*
> *Take up your wine, and slake your thirst with me."*

Rostam replied: "Our deeds will be our memorial in the
world. Now, in fairness to me, listen to the tale of an old
warrior's exploits. If I had not taken my heavy mace to
Mazanderan where Kavus, Giv, Gudarz, and Tus were imprisoned, their hearing shattered by the din of wardrums,
who would have disemboweled the White Demon? Who
could have hoped to accomplish such a deed by his own
strength? I took Kavus from his chains back to the throne,
and Iran rejoiced to receive him. I cut off their wizards'

heads, and left their bodies unburied and unlamented. And my only companions were my courage, my horse Rakhsh, and my world-conquering sword. And then when Kavus went to Hamaveran and was imprisoned, I led a Persian army there and killed their kings in war. King Kavus was a prisoner, heart sick and wretched, and Afrasyab was harrying Iran. I freed Kavus, Giv, Gudarz, and Tus, and brought them and our army back to Iran. Eager for fame, careless of my own ease, I went on ahead in the darkness of the night, and when Afrasyab saw my fluttering banner and heard Rakhsh neigh, he fled from Iran toward China; the world was filled with justice and my praises. If Kavus's blood had flowed then, how could he have sired Seyavash, who in turn fathered Kay Khosrow, who placed the crown on Lohrasp's head? My father is a great warrior, and he swallowed the dust of shame when he had to call your insignificant Lohrasp his king. Why do you boast of Goshtasp's crown and Lohrasp's throne?

> Who says, 'Go now, and shackle Rostam's hands?'
> The heavens themselves don't issue such commands.
> I've never seen, not since I was a child,
> A man as headstrong, obstinate, and wild
> As you: my courtesy is your excuse
> To treat me with contemptuous abuse!"

Esfandyar laughed with delight at his rage and grasped him firmly by the hand, saying: "Great, mammoth bodied warrior, you're just as I've heard you described: your arm's as massive as a lion's thigh, your chest and shoulders like a dragon's, your waist lean as a leopard's." As he spoke he squeezed Rostam's hand, and the old man laughed at the young man's efforts: lymph dripped from his finger nails, but he didn't wince at the pain. Then he in turn gripped Esfandyar's hand, and said, "My God-fearing prince, I congratulate king Goshtasp on having such a son as you, and your mother, whose glory is increased by bearing you." He spoke and, as his grip tightened, Esfandyar's cheeks turned crimson; bloody liquid spurted from beneath his nails, and the pain showed in his face. Nevertheless he laughed and said, "Enjoy your wine today, because tomorrow when we meet in combat you won't be thinking of pleasure. I'll saddle my black horse, put on my princely helmet, and unseat you with a lance; that'll put an end to your wrangling and rebellion. I'll bind your arms together and take you to the king. But I'll tell him that I've found no fault in you; I'll go before him as a suppliant, and clear up all this quarrel. I'll free you from sorrow and pain, and in their place you'll find treasure and kindness."

Rostam too laughed and said, "You'll tire of battle soon enough. Where have you ever seen real warriors fight, or felt the wind a mace makes as it whistles by you? If the heavens will that no love's lost between us, we'll drink down vengeance, not red wine; our fate will be ambush, the bow and lariat, the din of drums instead of the sound of lutes, and our farewells will be said with sword and mace. When we meet man to man on the battlefield tomorrow, you'll see which way the fight will go. I'll pluck you from your saddle, and bear you off to noble Zal. There I'll sit you on an ivory throne and place on your head a splendid crown that I had from Kay Qobad, and may his soul rejoice in heaven! I'll open our treasury's gates and lay our wealth before you: I'll give you troops, and raise your head up to the skies. Then, laughing and lighthearted, we'll make our way to the king: I'll crown you there, and that's how I'll show my loyalty to Goshtasp. Only then will I agree to serve him, as I served the Kayanid kings before. My heart will grow young again with joy, like a garden cleared of weeds: and when you're king and I'm your champion, a universal happiness will come."

Rostam Drinks with Esfandyar

Esfandyar answered: "Too much talk is pointless: our stomachs are empty, the day's half over, and we've said enough about battles. Bring whatever you have to our supper, and don't invite those who talk the whole time." When Rostam began to eat the others were astonished at his appetite; they sat opposite him watching him feast. Then Esfandyar gave orders that Rostam be served with red wine, saying "We'll see what he wants when the wine affects him, and he talks about King Kavus." A servant brought old wine in a goblet, and Rostam toasted Goshtasp and drank it off. The boy refilled it with a royal vintage, and Rostam said to him quietly, "There's no need to dilute it with water, it takes the edge off an old wine. Why do you put water in it?" Pashutan said to the serving boy, "Bring him a goblet filled with undiluted wine." Wine was brought, musicians were summoned, and the group watched in wonder as Rostam drank. When it was time for Rostam to return to Zal, Esfandyar said to him: "May you live happily and forever, may the food and wine you've consumed here nourish you, and may righteousness sustain your soul!"

Rostam replied: "Prince, may wisdom always be your guide! The wine I've drunk with you has nourished me, and my wise mind wants for nothing. If you can be intelligent enough, and man enough, to lay aside this desire for combat, come out of the desert to my home and take your ease as my guest: I'll do everything I promised, and I'll give you good advice. Rest for a while, turn aside from evil, be civil, and come back to your senses."

Esfandyar replied: "Don't sow seeds that will never grow. Tomorrow when I bind on my sword belt for combat you'll see what a warrior is. Stop praising yourself: get back to your palace and prepare yourself for the morning. A battle is as of little account to me as a drinking party. But my advice is that you don't try to fight with me: do what I say, accept the king's command that you be bound in chains,

and when we go from Zabol to Goshtasp's court you'll
see that I'll be even more chivalrous than I have promised.
Don't try to cause me any more sorrow."

> Then grief filled Rostam's heart, and in his sight
> The world seemed like a wood bereft of light.
> He thought: "Either I let him bind my hands,
> And in so doing bow to his commands,
> Or I must fight against him face to face
> And bring on him destruction and disgrace.
> No good can come of either course, and I
> Shall be despised and cursed until I die:
> His chains will be the symbol of my shame,
> Goshtasp will kill me and destroy my fame—
> The world will laugh at me, and men will say
> 'Rostam was hung with chains and led away,
> A stripling conquered him.' And all I've done
> Will be forgotten then by everyone.
> But if we fight each other and he's slain
> I cannot show my face at court again;
> They'll say I left a fine young prince for dead
> Because of one or two harsh words he'd said;
> In death I'll be reviled, my name will be
> A byword for disgrace and infamy.
> And then if I'm to perish at his hand
> My clan will lose Zabol, our native land—
> One thing would still survive though, since my name
> Would be remembered and not lose its fame."

Then he spoke to his haughty companion, saying: "Anxiety
robs my skin of its color; you talk so much about chains
and binding me, and everything you do alarms me. What
the heavens will is sovereign over us, and who knows how
they will turn? You're following a demon's advice, and refusing to listen to reason. You haven't lived many years in
this world, and you don't know how deceptive and evil it

is, my prince. You're a simple, straightforward man, and you know nothing about life: you should realize that evil men are trying to destroy you. Goshtasp will never tire of his crown and throne, and he will drive you throughout the world, make you face every danger, to keep you away from them. In his mind he searched the world, his intelligence hacking away like an axe, to find some hero who would not refuse to fight with you, so that such a man would destroy you, and the crown and throne would remain his. You blame my motives, but why don't you examine your own heart? Prince, don't act like some thoughtless youth, don't persist in this disastrous course. Be ashamed before God and before my face, don't betray yourself, and don't think that combat with me would be a game. If Fate has driven you and your men here, you will be destroyed by me: I shall leave an evil name behind me in the world, and may the same fate be Goshtasp's!"

Esfandyar replied: "Great Rostam, think of what a wise sage once said, 'A man in his dotage is a fool, no matter how wise or victorious or knowledgeable he's been.' You want to trick me and slip out of this, you want to convince people by your smooth talk, so that they'll say 'Rostam welcomed him warmly' and call you a wise benevolent man, while they'll say that I was unrighteous—I, who always act from righteous motives! You want them to say, 'The prince refused to listen to him, so that he had no choice but to fight. All his pleas were treated with contempt, and bitter words passed between them.' But I shall not swerve aside from the king's commands, not for the crown itself: all the good and evil of the world I find in him, and in him lie both heaven and hell. May what you've eaten here nourish you and confound your enemies: now, go home and tell Zal everything you have seen here. Prepare your armor for battle, and bandy no more words with me. Come back at dawn ready to fight, and don't draw this business out any further. Tomorrow on the battlefield you'll see the world grow dark before your eyes: you'll see what combat with a real warrior is."

Rostam replied: "If this is what you want I'll return your hospitality with Rakhsh's hooves, and my mace will be a medicine for your head. You've listened to your own court telling you that no one can match his sword against Esfandyar's; but tomorrow you'll see me grasping Rakhsh's reins, with my lance couched, and after that you'll never look to fight again."

The young man's lips broke into bewitching laughter, and he said: "For a fighting man you've let our conversation anger you too easily! Tomorrow you'll see how a man fights on the battlefield: I'm no mountain, and my horse beneath me's no mountain either, I'm one man like any other. If you run from me with your head still on your shoulders your mother will weep for your humiliation; and if you're killed I'll tie you to my saddle and bear you off to the king, so that no vassal of his will ever challenge him again."

Rostam Addresses Esfandyar's Tent

When Rostam left Esfandyar's pavilion he paused for a moment, and spoke to it:

> *"O tent of hope, what glorious days you've known!*
> *Once you were shelter to great Jamshid's throne,*
> *In you Khosrow's and King Kavus's days*
> *Were passed in splendor, pageantry, and praise—*
> *Closed is that glorious gate that once you knew,*
> *A man unworthy of you reigns in you."*

Esfandyar heard him, planted himself in front of Rostam, and said: "Why should you speak to our pavilion so intemperately? This Zabolestan of yours should be called 'Lout-estan,' because when a guest has eaten his fill here he starts loutishly insulting his host!" Then he too addressed the royal tent:

"You sheltered Jamshid once, who erred and strayed,
Who heard God's heavenly laws and disobeyed;
Then came Kavus, whose blasphemous desires
Sought to control the skies' celestial fires—
Tumult and plunder, plots, perfidy, pain
Filled all the land throughout his wretched reign,
But now your walls encompass King Goshtasp
Who rules with his wise councillor Jamasp;
The prophet Zoroaster, who has brought
Heaven's scriptures to us, shares his noble court,
Good Pashutan is here, and so am I
His prince, watched over by the turning sky,
Protector of the good, scourge of the horde
Of evildoers, who bow before my sword."

When Rostam had left, Esfandyar turned to Pashutan and said, "There's no hiding such heroism: I've never seen such a horseman, and I don't know what will happen tomorrow on the battlefield. When he comes armored to battle he must be like a raging elephant; his stature's a marvel to gaze upon. Nevertheless, I fear that tomorrow he will face defeat. My heart aches for his kindness and glory, but I can't evade God's commands: tomorrow when he faces me in combat I'll turn his shining days to darkness."

Pashutan replied: "Listen to what I have to say. Brother, do not do this. I have said it before and I will say it again, because I will not wash my hands of what is right. Don't harry him like this; a free man will never willingly submit to another's tyranny. Sleep tonight and, when dawn comes, we'll go to his castle, without an escort, and there we'll be his guests and answer his every anxiety. Everything he has done in the world has been for the good, benefiting the nobility and the general populace alike. He won't refuse your orders, I can see that he'll be loyal to you. How long are you going to go on with all this rage and anger and malice? Drive them out of your heart!"

Esfandyar answered him: "Thorns have appeared among the roses then: a man of pure faith shouldn't talk as you're doing. You're the first councilor to Persia's king, the heart, eyes, and ears of its chieftains, and yet you think it right and wise to disobey the king like this? Then all my pains and struggles were pointless, and Zoroaster's faith's to be forgotten, because he has said that hell will be the home of whoever turns aside from his king's command. How long are you going to tell me to disobey Goshtasp? You can say this, but how can I agree to it? If you're afraid for my life, I'll rid you of that fear today: no man ever died except at his appointed time, and a man whose reputation lives on never dies. Tomorrow you'll see how I'll fight against this fearsome warrior."

Pashutan said: "And for how long are you going to talk about fighting? Since you first took up arms, Eblis has had no control over your thoughts: but now you're opening your heart to demons, and refusing to hear good advice. How can I drive fear from my heart when I see that two great warriors, two lions in battle, are to face one another, and what will come of this is all unknown?"

The hero made no answer: his heart was filled with pain, and a sigh escaped his lips.

Rostam Returns to His Castle

By the time Rostam reached his castle he could see no remedy but warfare. Zavareh came out to greet him and saw his pallor, and that his heart was filled with darkness. Rostam said to him, "Prepare my Indian sword, my lance and helmet, my bow and the barding for Rakhsh: bring me my tiger skin, and my heavy mace." Zavareh had the steward bring what Rostam had asked for, and when Rostam saw his weapons and armor he heaved a cold sigh and said,

> "My armor, for a while you've been at peace,
> But now this indolence of yours must cease—

A hard fight lies ahead, and I shall need
All of the luck you bring me to succeed:
Two warriors who have never known defeat
Like two enraged and roaring lions will meet,
And in that struggle on the battlefield
Who knows what tricks he'll try to make me yield!"

Zal Advises Rostam

When Zal heard from Rostam what had happened, his aged mind was troubled. He said, "What are you telling me? You're filling my mind with darkness. Since first you sat in the saddle you've been a chivalrous and righteous warrior, proud to serve your kings and contemptuous of hardships. But I fear your days are drawing to an end, that your lucky stars are in decline, that the seed of Zal will be eradicated from this land, and our women and children hurled to the ground as slaves. If you're killed in combat by a young stripling like Esfandyar, Zabolestan will be laid waste and all our glory will be razed and cast into a pit. And if he's hurt in this encounter your good name will be destroyed: everyone will tell the tale of how you killed a young prince because of a few harsh words he'd said. Go to him, stand before him as his subject: and if you can't do that then leave, go and hide yourself in some corner where no one will hear of you. You can buy the world with treasure and trouble, but you can't cut Chinese silk with an axe. Give his retinue robes of honor, get back your independence with gifts. When he leaves the banks of the Hirmand, saddle Rakhsh and go with him: as you travel to the court swear fealty to him. And when Goshtasp sees you, there's no danger he'll harm you: it would be an act unworthy of a monarch."

Rostam replied: "Old man, don't take what I've said so lightly. I've fought for years and have experienced the world's good and evil. I encountered the demons of Mazanderan and the horsemen of Hamaveran, I fought against Kamus and the Emperor of China whose armies were so mighty the earth trembled beneath their horses' hooves. But if I now flee from Esfandyar there will be no castles or gardens for you in Zabolestan. I may be old, but when I put on my tiger skin for battle it makes no difference whether I face a hundred maddened elephants or a plain filled with warriors. I've done all that you're asking me to, I read the book of loyalty to him; he treats my words with contempt and ignores my wisdom and advice. If he could bring his head down from the heavens and welcome me in his heart, there's no wealth in my treasury, no weapon or armor, that I wouldn't give him. But he took no notice of all my talk and left me empty-handed.

"If we were to fight tomorrow, you could despair of his life. But I won't take my sharp sword in hand, I'll bear him off to a banquet: he'll see no mace or lance from me, and I won't oppose him man to man. I'll simply lift him from the saddle and acknowledge him as king in Goshtasp's place. I'll bring him here and seat him on an ivory throne, load him with presents, keep him as my guest for three days, and on the fourth when the sun's red ruby splits the darkness I'll set off with him for Goshtasp's court. When I enthrone him and crown him I'll stand before him as his loyal subject, concerned only for Esfandyar's commands. You remember how I acted with Qobad, and you know how it's my quarrelsome, passionate nature that's made my reputation in the world. And now you're telling me either to run off and hide, or to submit to his chains!"

Zal broke into laughter, shaking his head in wonder at his son's words. He said, "Don't say such things, even demons couldn't put up with such foolish talk. You chatter about what we did with Qobad, but he was living obscurely in the mountains then, he wasn't a great king with a throne, crown, treasure, and cash at his disposal. You're talking about Esfandyar, who counts the emperor of China among his subjects, and you say you'll lift him from the saddle and bear him off to Zal's palace! An old, experienced man doesn't talk like this. Don't court bad luck by setting yourself up as the Persian king's equal. You're the best of all our chieftains, but I've given you my advice, and may you follow it!"

Having spoken, he bent his forehead to the ground in prayer: "Just judge, I pray you to preserve us from an evil Fate." And so he prayed throughout the night, his tongue untiring until the sun rose above the mountains.

When day broke Rostam put on his mail and tigerskin, hitched his lariat to his saddle, and mounted Rakhsh. He summoned Zavareh and told him to have their army's ranks drawn up in the foothills. Zavareh saw that this was done, and Rostam couched his lance and rode out from the palace. His soldiers called out encouragement as he went forward, followed by Zavareh who was acting as his lieutenant. Privately Rostam said to him, "Somehow, I'll put paid to this evil devil's spawn, and get my soul back into the light again. But I fear I shall have to harm him, and I don't know what good can come out of all this. You stay with our troops, while I go to see what Fate has in store for me. If I find he's still the same hothead, spoiling for a fight, let me face him alone, I don't want any of our warriors hurt in this. Victory favors the just."

He crossed the river and began to climb the opposite bank, and wonder at the world's ways filled his mind.

He faced Esfandyar and shouted, "Your enemy has come: prepare yourself."

When Esfandyar heard the old lion's words he laughed and shouted back, "I've been prepared since I woke." He gave orders that his armor, helmet, lance, and mace be brought, and when he was accoutered he had his black horse saddled and brought before him. Then, glorying in his strength and agility, he thrust his lance point into the ground and, like a leopard leaping on a wild ass and striking terror into its heart, he vaulted into the saddle. The soldiers were delighted, and roared their approval.

Esfandyar rode toward Rostam and when he saw his opponent had come alone, he turned to Pashutan and said, "I need no companions in this: he is alone, and I shall be too: we'll move off to higher ground."

Pashutan withdrew to where the Persian soldiers waited, and the two combatants went forward to battle, as grimly as if all pleasure had been driven from the world. When the old man and his young opponent faced each other, both their horses neighed violently, and the noise was as though the ground beneath them split open.

Rostam's voice was serious when he spoke: "Young man, you're fortune's favorite, and your heart's filled with the joys of youth; don't go forward with this, don't give yourself up to anger. For once, listen to wisdom's words. If you're set on bloodshed say so, and I'll have my Zaboli warriors come here, and you can send Persians against them, and the two groups can show their mettle. We'll watch from the sidelines, and your desire for blood and combat will be satisfied."

Esfandyar answered him: "How long are you going to go on with this pointless talk? You got up at dawn and summoned me to this hillside. Was that simply deception? Or is it that now you foresee your own defeat? What could a battle between your warriors and mine mean to me? God forbid I should agree to send my Persians into battle while I held back and crowned myself king. For a man of my faith, such an act would be contemptible. I lead my warriors into battle, and am the first to face the foe even if it is a leopard. If you need companions to fight with you summon them, but I shall never call on anyone's aid. God is my companion in battle, and Good Fortune smiles on me. You're looking for a fight, and I'm ready for one: let's face each other man to man, without our armies. And let's see whether Esfandyar's horse returns riderless to its stable, or Rostam's turns masterless toward his palace."

The Combat between Rostam and Esfandyar

They swore that no one would come to their aid while they fought. Again and again they rode against one another with couched lances; blood poured from their armor, and their lances' heads were shattered, so that the combatants were forced to draw their swords. Weaving and dodging to right and left, they attacked one another, and their horses' maneuvers flung them against one another with such violence that their swords too were shattered. They drew their maces then, and the blows they dealt resounded like a blacksmith's hammer striking steel. Their bodies wounded and exhausted, they fought like enraged lions until the handles of their maces splintered; then they leant forward and grasped each other by the belt, each struggling to throw the other, while their horses reared and pranced. But though they strained against one another, exerting all their strength and massive weight, neither warrior was shifted from his saddle. And so they separated, sick at heart, their mouths smeared with dust and blood, their armor and barding dented and pierced, their horses wearied by their struggle.

Zavareh and Nushazar Quarrel

When the combat had gone on for some time, Zavareh grew impatient at the delay and shouted to the Persian soldiers: "Where is Rostam? Why should we hang back on a day like this? You came to fight against Rostam, but you're never going to be able to bind his hands, and we won't sit here while a battle's going on." Then he began cursing his opponents, and Esfandyar's son Nushazar, who was a fiery ambitious youth, was enraged at the insults this provincial from Sistan was heaping upon them, and responded in kind. "Is it right for a noble warrior to make fun of a king's commands? Our leader Esfandyar gave us no orders to fight with dogs like you, and who would ignore or override his wishes? But if you want to challenge us, you'll see how real warriors can fight with swords and spears and maces."

In response, Zavareh gave the signal for Sistan's warcry to ring out, and for his men to attack: he himself rushed forward from the rear of his troops, and a tumultuous noise of fighting began. Countless Persians were slaughtered, and when Nushazar saw this he mounted his horse, grasped his Indian sword in his hand, and headed for the fray. Among the Sistani troops one of their best warriors was a wild tamer of horses, a man named Alvad, who was Rostam's spear bearer and always accompanied him into battle. Nushazar caught sight of him, wheeled toward him, and struck him a mighty blow with his sword: his head was severed and his body slid lifeless from its saddle into the dirt. Zavareh urged his horse forward and called out, "You've laid him low, but stand your ground and fight, because Alvad is not what I'd call a horseman." With that Zavareh flung his lance, which pierced Nushazar's chest, and a moment later the Persian warrior's head lay in the dirt.

Nushazar and Mehrnush Are Killed by Faramarz and Zavareh

When the great Nushazar was killed, good fortune deserted the Persian army. His brother, Mehrnush, saw Nushazar's death; at once weeping and enraged he urged his great horse forward to the fray, and the froth of fury stood on his lips. Faramarz stood before him like a massive maddened elephant, and attacked him with his Indian sword: a huge cry went up from both armies as the two noble fighters closed, the one a prince, the other a mighty champion. They fell on one another like enraged lions, but Mehrnush's eagerness for combat was not sufficient to prevail against Faramarz: thinking to sever his opponent's head with a sword blow, he brought his weapon down on his own horse's neck, and his mount sank to the ground beneath him. Once he was on foot Faramarz was able to overcome him, and his red blood stained the dust of the battlefield.

When Bahman saw his brother killed, and the dirt beneath him mired with his blood, he made his way to where Esfandyar had been in combat with Rostam, and said, "Lion-warrior, an army has come up from Sistan, and your two sons Nushazar and Mehrnush have been pitifully slain by them. While you're here in combat, two of our princes lie prone in the dust, and the sorrow and shame of this will live forever." Esfandyar's heart clouded with rage, sighs escaped his lips, and tears stood in his eyes: he turned to Rostam and said, "Devil's spawn, why have you forsaken the path of justice and good custom? Didn't you say that you would not bring your troops into this conflict? You don't deserve your fame: have you no shame before me, no fear of what God will demand of you on the Day of Judgment? Don't you know that no one praises a man who goes back on his word? Two of your Sistani troops have killed two of my sons, and your men are still wreaking havoc."

When Rostam heard this, sorrow seized him and he trembled like a bough in the wind. He swore by the soul and head of the king, by the sun and his sword and the battlefield, by the fire that Kavus had lit and through which Seyavash had passed unscathed, by the Kayanid throne and the Zend Avesta, by the soul and head of Esfandyar himself: "I did not give the orders for this attack, and I've no praise for whoever carried it out. I shall bind my own brother's hands if he has been responsible for this evil, and I shall bind my son Faramarz's arms too, and bring him here to you. If they are guilty, kill them both in vengeance for your sons' split blood. But don't let your judgment be clouded by what has happened."

Esfandyar replied,

> To avenge a peacock's death, no king would take
> The worthless life of an ignoble snake:

Look to your weapons now, you wretch, defend
Yourself, your days on earth are at an end:
I'll stake your thighs against your horse's hide,
My arrows will transfix you to his side
And you and he shall be like water when
It's mixed with milk and can't be found again.
From now on no base slave shall ever strive
To spill a prince's blood: if you survive
I'll bind your arms—without delay I'll bring
You as my captive to our court and king,
And if my arrows leave you here for dead
Think of my sons, whose blood your warriors shed."

Rostam replied: "What good is all this talk, which only increases our shame? Turn toward God and trust in Him, who guides us to both good and evil ends."

Rostam and Esfandyar Renew the Battle

They turned then to their bows and poplar wood arrows; the sun turned pale and fire flashed from Esfandyar's armor where the arrow heads struck. He frowned with shame, since he was a man whose arrows no one escaped: he notched diamond headed shafts to his bow, bolts that pierced armor as if it were paper, and sorely wounded both Rostam and Rakhsh. Esfandyar wheeled round, circling Rostam, whose arrows had no effect, and who felt that he faced defeat. He said to himself, "This Esfandyar is invincible," and he knew that both he and Rakhsh were growing weaker. In desperation he dismounted and began to climb the mountain side, while Rakhsh returned home riderless and wounded. Blood poured from Rostam's body, and as his strength ebbed from him this great mountain of a man began to tremble and shake. Esfandyar laughed to see this, and called out:

"Where is your mammoth strength, your warrior's pride?
Have arrows pierced that iron mountain side?

Where is your mace now and your martial might,
That glorious strength with which you used to fight?
What are you running from, or did you hear
A lion's roar that filled your heart with fear?
Are you the man before whom demons wept?
Whose sword killed everything that flew or crept?
Why has the mammoth turned into a fox
That tries to hide among these mountain rocks?"

Zavareh saw Rakhsh in the distance, wounded, returning home: the world darkened before his eyes, and he cried aloud and hurried to the place where Rostam and Esfandyar had fought. He saw his brother there, covered in unstanched wounds, and said to him, "Get up, use my horse, and I shall buckle on my armor to avenge you." But Rostam replied, "Go, tell our father that the tribe of Sam has lost its power and glory, and that he must seek out some remedy. My wounds are more terrible than any disaster I've survived, but I know that, if I live through this night, tomorrow I shall be like a man reborn again. See that you look after Rakhsh, and even if I stay here for a long time I'll rejoin you eventually." Zavareh left his brother and went in search of Rakhsh.

Esfandyar waited a while, and then shouted: "How long are you going to stay up there: who do you think is going to come and guide you now? Throw your bow down, strip off your tiger skin, undo your sword belt. Submit, and let me bind your arms, and you'll never see any harm from me again. I'll take you, wounded as you are, to the king, and there I'll have all your sins forgiven. But if you want to continue fighting, make your will and appoint someone else to rule these marches. Ask pardon for your sins from God, since God forgives those who repent, and it would be right for Him to guide you from this fleeting world when you must leave it."

Rostam replied: "It's too late to go on fighting: who wages war in the dark? Go back to your encampment and spend the night there; I shall make my way to my palace and rest, and sleep awhile. I'll bind my wounds up, then I'll call the chieftains of my tribe to me, Zavareh, Faramarz, and Zal, and I'll set out to them whatever you command: we'll accept your guarantee of justice."

Esfandyar answered him: "Old man, you're infinitely clever, a great man, tempered by time, knowing many tricks and wiles and stratagems. I've seen your deceit, but even so I don't want to see your destruction. I'll give you quarter tonight, but don't be thinking up some new dishonest ploy. Stick to what you've agreed to, and don't bandy words with me any more!"

Rostam's only reply was: "Now I must seek help for my wounds."

Esfandyar watched him make his way back to his own territory.

Once Rostam had crossed the river he congratulated himself on his narrow escape and prayed: "O Lord of Justice, if I die from these wounds, who of our heroes will avenge me, and who has the courage and wisdom to take my place?"

Esfandyar saw him gain dry land and murmured to himself, "This is no man, this is a mammoth of unmatched might." In wonder he said, "O God of all desires, time and place are in your hands, and you have created him as you willed. He has crossed the river with ease, despite the terrible wounds he's suffered from my weapons."

As Esfandyar approached his encampment, he heard the noise of lamentation for Nushazar and Mehrnush. The royal tent was filled with dust, and his chieftains had rent their clothes: Esfandyar dismounted and, embracing the heads of his two dead sons, spoke quietly to them:

> *"Brave warriors, whose bodies here lie dead,*
> *Who knows to what abode your souls have fled?"*

Then he turned to Pashutan who knelt lamenting before him and said: "Don't weep for the dead any longer: I see no profit in such tears, and it is wrong to trouble one's soul in this way. Young and old, we are all destined for death, and may wisdom guide us when we depart."

They sent the two bodies in golden coffins, on teak-wood litters, to the court, and Esfandyar sent with them a letter to his father: "The tree you planted has borne fruit. You launched this boat on the water: it was you that wanted Rostam as a slave, so now when you see the coffins of Nushazar and Mehrnush, do not lament overmuch. My own future is still uncertain, and I don't know what evil Fate has in store for me."

He sat on the throne, grieving for his sons, and then began to talk about Rostam. He said to Pashutan: "The lion has evaded the warrior's grasp. Today I saw Rostam, the massive height and strength of him, and I praised God, from whom come all hope and fear, that such a man exist-ed. He has done such things in his time: he has fished in the Sea of China and drawn forth monsters, and on the plains he has trapped leopards. And I hurt him so severely that his blood turned the earth to mud; his body was a mass of arrow wounds but he made his way on foot up that moun-tain side, and then, still encumbered with his sword and armor, he hurried across the river. I know that as soon as he reaches his palace his soul will fly up to the heavens."

Rostam Consults with His Family

When Rostam reached the palace his kinsfolk clustered around him: Zavareh and Faramarz wept to see his wounds, and his mother Rudabeh tore at her hair and scored her cheeks in her grief. Zavareh removed his armor and tiger skin, and the leaders of the tribe gathered before him.

Rostam asked that Rakhsh be brought to him, and that farriers be found to treat his wounds. Zal tore at his hair and pressed his aged face against Rostam's wounds, saying "Woe that I with my white hairs should ever see my noble son in this state!"

But Rostam said to him: "What use are tears, if heaven has decreed this? There is a harder task ahead of me, one that fills my soul with fear. I have never seen a warrior on the battlefield like this invincible Esfandyar, although I have traveled the world and have knowledge of what is plain and what is hidden. I lifted the White Demon by the waist and flung him against the ground like a willow branch. My arrows have pierced anvils and rendered shields futile, but no matter how many blows I rained on Esfandyar's armor my strength was useless against him. When leopards saw my mace they would hide themselves among the rocks, but it made no impression on his armor, or even so much as damaged the silk pennant on his helmet. But how much more can I plead with him and offer him friendship? He is stubborn in all he does and says, and wants only enmity from me. I thank God that night came on, and that our eyes grew dim in the darkness so that I was able to escape this dragon's claws. I don't know whether I'll be able to survive these wounds: I see nothing for it but to leave Rakhsh tomorrow, and seek out some obscure corner where Esfandyar will never hear of me, even if this means that he'll sack Zabolestan. He'll get tired of that eventually, although his nature rejoices in the evils of conquest."

Zal said to him: "My son, listen to me, and think carefully about what I'm going to say. There is one way out of all this world's troubles, and that is the way of death. But I know of a remedy, and you should seize on it. I shall summon the Simorgh, and if he will help us we may yet save our tribe and country. If not, then our land will be destroyed by this malevolent Esfandyar, who rejoices in the evil he does."

The Simorgh Appears before Zal

They agreed to the plan. Zal filled three braziers with fire, and with three wise companions set out from the palace. They climbed to a high peak, and there the magician drew a feather from its brocade wrapping; fanning the flames in one of the braziers he burnt a portion of the feather in the fire. One watch of the night passed, and suddenly the air turned much darker. Zal peered into the night, and it seemed as if the fire and the Simorgh's flight were liquefying the air: then he caught sight of the Simorgh and the flames flared up. Fearful, with anguish in his heart, Zal sat and watched as the bird drew closer: next, he threw sandalwood on the braziers and went forward, making his obeisance to the Simorgh. Perfume rose up from the fires, and the sweat of fear shone on Zal's face. The Simorgh said to him:

> "O king, explain to me what you desire
> That you have summoned me in smoke and fire."

Zal answered: "May all the evils that have come to me from this base-born wretch light on my enemies! The lionhearted Rostam lies grievously wounded, and my feet feel as though shackled by his sorrows. No man has ever seen such wounds and we despair of his life. And it seems that Rakhsh too will die from the arrow heads that torment him. Esfandyar came to our country, and the only gate he knocked at was the gate of war. He will not be content with taking our land and wealth and throne from us, he wants to uproot our family, to extirpate us from the face of the earth."

The Simorgh said:

> "Great hero, put away all grief and fear,
> Bring Rakhsh and noble Rostam to me here."

Zal sent one of his companions to Rostam who, together with Rakhsh, was brought up the mountainside.
When Rostam reached the summit, the Simorgh saw him
and said:

> "O mammoth-bodied warrior, tell me who
> Has laid you low like this and wounded you.
> Why did you fight with Persia's prince, and face
> The fire of mortal combat and disgrace?"

Zal said: "Now that you have vouchsafed us the sight of
your pure face, tell me, if Rostam is not cured, where can
my people go in all the world? Our tribe will be uprooted,
and this is no time to be questioning him."

The bird examined Rostam's wounds, looking for how
they could be healed. With his beak he sucked blood from
the lesions, and drew out eight arrow heads. Then he
pressed one of his feathers against the wounds, and immediately Rostam's spirits began to return. The Simorgh said:
"Bind up your wounds and keep them safe from further
injury for seven days: then soak one of my feathers in milk
and place it on the scars to help them heal." He treated
Rakhsh in the same manner, using his beak to draw six arrow heads from the horse's neck, and immediately Rakhsh
neighed loudly, and Rostam laughed for joy. The Simorgh
then turned to Rostam and said: "Why did you choose to
fight against Esfandyar, who is famous for being invincible
in battle?"

Rostam replied: "He talked incessantly of chains, despite all the advice I gave him. Death is easier for me than
shame."

The Simorgh said: "To bow your head down to the
ground before Esfandyar would be no shame: he is a prince
and a fine warrior, he lives purely and possesses the divine
farr. If you swear to me that you will renounce this war and
not try to overcome Esfandyar, if you will speak humbly to

him tomorrow and offer to submit to him (and if in fact his time has come, he will ignore your overtures of peace) then I will assist you, and raise your head to the sun's sphere."

Rostam was overjoyed to hear this, and was freed of the fear of killing Esfandyar. He said: "Even if heaven should rain swords on my head I shall keep faith with what you say to me."

The Simorgh said: "Out of my love for you, I shall tell you a secret from heaven: Fate will harry whoever spills Esfandyar's blood, he will live in sorrow, and his wealth will be taken from him; his life in this world will be one of suffering, and torment will be his after death. If you agree to what I say, and overcome your enmity, I shall show you wonders tonight and seal your lips against all evil words. Choose a glittering dagger, and mount Rakhsh."

Rostam prepared himself, mounted Rakhsh, and followed the Simorgh as it flew until they reached a seashore. The air turned dark from the Simorgh's shadow as it descended and came to rest on the beach. He showed Rostam a pathway that led over dry land, over which the air seemed impregnated with musk. He touched Rostam's forehead with one of his feathers, and indicated that they should follow the pathway. They reached a tamarisk tree rooted deep in the earth, its branches reaching into the sky, and the Simorgh alighted on one of the branches. He said to Rostam: "Choose the straightest branch you can find, one that tapers to a point: do not despise this piece of wood, for it holds Esfandyar's Fate. Temper it in fire, place an ancient arrow head at its tip, and fix feathers to the shaft. Now I have told you how to wound Esfandyar."

Rostam cut the tamarisk branch and returned to his castle, and as he came the Simorgh guided him, its talons clutching his helmet. The Simorgh said: "Now, when Esfandyar tries to fight with you, plead with him and try to guide him toward righteousness, and don't attempt to trick him in any way. Your sweet words might remind him of the ancient days, and of how you have fought and suffered throughout the world for Persia's cause. But if you speak fairly to him and he rejects your words, treating you with contempt, take this arrow, having steeped it in wine, and aim it for his eyes, as is the custom of those who worship the tamarisk. Fate will guide the arrow to his eyes, where his *farr* resides, and his death."

The Simorgh took its farewell of Zal, embracing him as if they were warp and weft of one cloth. Filled with hope and joy, Rostam lit the fire and watched the Simorgh fly serenely up into the air. Then he fitted the arrow head and feathers, as he had been instructed.

Rostam Kills Esfandyar

Dawn touched the mountain tops and dispersed the darkness of the night. Rostam put on his armor, prayed to the world's creator, and, eager for combat, made his way toward the Persian army. As he rode he called out exultantly: "Brave lion-heart, how long will you sleep? Rostam has saddled Rakhsh: rise from your sweet sleep and face Rostam's vengeance."

When Esfandyar heard his voice, all worldly weapons seemed useless to him. He said to Pashutan: "A lion cannot fight with a magician. I didn't think that Rostam would be able even to drag his armor and helmet back to his palace, and now he comes here riding Rakhsh, whose body yesterday was a mass of wounds. I have heard that Zal is a magician, that he stretches out his hands toward the sun, and that in his mantic fury he surpasses all other magicians: it would be unwise for me to face his son."

Pashutan said: "Why are you so hesitant today? Didn't you sleep through the night? What is it between you and Rostam, that you must both suffer so much in this business? I think your luck is abandoning you; all it does is lead you from one war to another."

Esfandyar dressed himself in his armor and went out to Rostam. When he saw his face he cried out: "May your name disappear from the surface of the earth! Aren't you the man who fled from me yesterday, shorn of heart, soul, courage, life itself? Have you forgotten then, you Sistani wretch, the power of my bow? It's only through the magic you've practiced that you're able to stand before me again: Zal's magic cured you, otherwise you'd be food for wild cats by now. But this time I shall fill you so full of arrows that all Zal's magic will be useless: I shall so batter your body that Zal shall never see you alive again."

Rostam replied: "Will you never tire of combat? I have not come to fight against you today, I have come humbly offering an honorable reconciliation. Fear God, and do not drive wisdom from your heart. Constantly you try to treat me unjustly, blinding yourself to wisdom's ways. By God Himself, by Zoroaster and the pure faith, by the sacred fire and the divine *farr*, by the sun and moon and the Zend Avesta, I swear to you that the road you are following is one of harm and evil. Forget the harsh words that have passed between us. I shall open to you my ancient treasuries, filled with marvels I have gathered over many years: I shall load my own horses with wealth and you can give them to your treasurer to drive before you. I shall ride with you, and if you so command me I shall come into the king's presence, and if the king then kills me or enslaves me I accept this as my due. Remember what an ancient sage once said, 'Never seek to have shame as your companion.' I am doing everything in my power to make you give up your thirst for combat."

Esfandyar said: "I'm not a fraud who looks one day for battle and the next day skulks in fear. Why do you talk so much about your wealth and possessions, washing your face with the waters of friendship? If you want to stay alive, submit your body to my chains."

Once more Rostam spoke: "Forget this injustice, prince. Don't sully my name and make your own soul contemptible; only evil will come of this struggle. I shall give you a thousand royal gems, along with torques and pearls and earrings. I shall give you a thousand sweet lipped boys to serve you day and night, and a thousand girls, all from Khallokhi whose women are famous for their charm, to make your court splendid with their beauty. My lord, I shall open the treasuries of Sam and Zal before you and give you all they contain; I shall bring men from Kabolestan for you, fit companions for your feasting and fearless in war. And then I shall go before you like a servant, accompanying you to your vengeful king's court. But you, my prince, should drive vengeance from your heart, and keep devils from dwelling in your body. You are a king, one who fears God, and you have other ways of binding men to you than by chains; your chains will disgrace my name forever, how can such an evil be worthy of you?"

Esfandyar replied:

> "How long will you tell me to turn away
> From God and from my king? To disobey
> My sovereign lord and king is to rebel
> Against God's justice and to merit hell.
> Accept my chains, or enmity and war—
> But bandy pointless words with me no more."

When Rostam saw that his offers of friendship had no effect on Esfandyar, he notched the wine-soaked tamarisk arrow to his bow and lifted his eyes to the heavens, saying:

> "Just Lord, who gives us knowledge, strength, and life,
> You know how I have sought to end this strife;
> Creator of the moon and Mercury
> You see my weakness and humility,
> And his unjust demands: I pray that you
> See nothing sinful in what I must do."

Rostam hung back for a moment, and Esfandyar taunted him: "Well, famous Rostam, it seems your soul's grown tired of combat, now that you're faced with the arrows of Goshtasp, the lion heart and spear points of Lohrasp."

Then, as the Simorgh had ordered him, Rostam drew back his bow. Aiming at Esfandyar's eyes he released the arrow, and for the Persian prince the world was turned to darkness. The tall cypress swayed and bent, knowledge and glory fled from him; the God-fearing prince bowed his head and slumped forward, and his Chinese bow slipped from his hand. He grasped at his black horse's mane as his blood soaked into the earth beneath him.

Rostam addressed Esfandyar: "Your harshness has borne fruit. You were the man who said, 'I am invincible, I can bow the heavens down to the earth.' Yesterday I was wounded by eight arrows, and bore this silently: one arrow has removed you from combat and left you slumped over your horse. In another moment your head will be on the ground, and your mother will mourn for you."

Esfandyar lost consciousness and fell to the ground. Slowly he came to himself, and grasped the arrow: when he withdrew it, its head and feathers were soaked in blood. The news immediately reached Bahman that the royal glory was shrouded in darkness: he ran to Pashutan and said: "Our expedition here has ended in disaster: his mammoth body lies in the dirt, and the world is a dark pit to him."

They ran to him, and saw him lying soaked in his blood, a bloody arrow in his hand. Pashutan said: "Who of our great men can understand the world's ways? Only God who guides our souls and the heavens, and the planets in their courses, knows its truth. One like Esfandyar who fought for the pure faith, who cleared the world of the evils of idol-worship and never stretched out his hand to evil deeds, dies in the prime of youth, and his royal head lies in the dirt; while one who spreads strife in the world, who torments the souls of free men, lives for many years unharmed by Fate."

The young men cradled the fallen hero's head, wiping away the blood. With sorrow in his heart, his face smeared with blood, Pashutan lamented over him: "O Esfandyar, prince and world conqueror, who has toppled this mountain, who has trampled underfoot this raging lion? Who has torn out the elephant's tusks, who has held back the torrent of the Nile? Where have your heart and soul and courage fled, and your strength and fortune and faith? Where now are your weapons of war, where now is your sweet voice at our banquets? You cleansed the world of malevolence, you were fearless before lions and demons, and all your reward is to reign in the earth. My curses on the crown and throne: may they and your faithless father king Goshtasp be forgotten forever!"

Esfandyar said: "Do not torment yourself for me. This came to me from the crown and court: the killed body goes into the earth, and you should not distress yourself at my death. Where now are Feraydun, Hushang, and Jamshid? They came on the wind and were gone with a breath. My noble ancestors too departed and ceded their place to me: no one remains in this fleeting world. I have traveled the earth and known its wonders, both those that are clear and those that are hidden, trying to establish the ways of God, taking wisdom as my guide; and now that my words have gone forth and the hands of Ahriman are tied, Fate stretches out its lion claws for me. My hope is that I shall reap the reward of my efforts in Paradise. Zal's son did not kill me by chivalrous means. Look at this tamarisk wood grasped in my fist: it was this wood that ended my days, directed by the Simorgh and by that wily cheat Rostam. Zal, who knows all the world's sorcery, cast this spell."

Hearing his words, Rostam turned aside, his heart wrung with anguish. He said: "Some evil demon has brought this suffering to you. It's as he said; he acted honorably. Since I have been a warrior in the world I have seen

no armed horseman like Esfandyar, and because in myself I
was helpless against his bow and strength I sought for help
rather than yield to him. It was his death that I notched to
my bow, and released, since his time had come. If Fate had
meant him to live, how could I have found the tamarisk?
Man must leave this dark earth, and cannot prolong his life
by so much as a breath beyond his appointed time. I was
the means by which the tamarisk arrow struck him down."

Esfandyar said: "Now my life draws to an end. Come
closer, don't leave me. My thoughts are different now from
what they were. Listen to my advice, and what I ask of you
concerning my son, who is the center of my life. Take him
under your wing, show him the path to greatness."

Hearing his words, Rostam came weeping to his side,
lamenting loudly, with tears of shame flowing from his
eyes. News reached the palace: Zal came like the wind, and
Zavareh and Faramarz approached, bewildered with sorrow. Zal addressed Rostam: "My son, I weep heart's blood
for you, because I have heard from our priests and astrologers that whoever spills Esfandyar's blood will be harried
by Fate: his life in this world will be harsh, and when he
dies he will inherit torment."

Esfandyar's Last Words to Rostam
Esfandyar spoke to Rostam:

> "All that has happened happened as Fate willed.
> Not you, your arrow, or the Simorgh killed
> Me here: Goshtasp's, my father's, enmity
> Made you the means by which to murder me.
> He ordered me to sack Sistan, to turn
> It to a wilderness, to slay and burn,
> To suffer war's travails, while he alone
> Enjoyed the glory of his crown and throne.
> I ask you to accept my son, to raise
> Him in Sistan, to teach him manhood's ways:

He is a wise and willing youth: from you
He'll learn the skills of war, what he must do
At courtly banquets when the wine goes round,
How to negotiate or stand his ground,
Hunting, the game of polo—everything
That suits the education of a king.
As for Jamasp, may his accursed name
Perish, and may he waste away in shame!"

When Rostam had heard him out he stood and laid his hand on his chest and said: "If you die I swear to fulfill what you have said: I shall seat him on the ivory throne and place the royal crown upon his head myself. I shall stand before him as his servant, and call him my lord and king."

Esfandyar answered: "You are an old man, a champion of many wars, but, as God is my witness, and by the Faith that guides me, all this good that you have done for the world's kings will avail you nothing: your good name has turned to evil and the earth is filled with mourning for my death. This deed will bring sorrow to your soul, as God willed should happen." Then he addressed Pashutan: "I expect now nothing but my shroud. When I have left this fleeting world, lead our army back to Iran, and there tell my father that I say to him: 'As you have achieved what you desire, don't look for excuses. The world has turned out entirely as you wished, and all authority is yours now. With my just sword I spread righteousness in the world and no one dared oppose you, and when the true Faith had been established in Iran I was ready for greatness. Before our courtiers you praised me, and behind their backs you sent me to my death. You have gained what you sought; rejoice and put your anxieties to rest. Forget about death, let your palace be filled with celebration. The throne is yours; sorrow and a harsh fate are mine: the crown is yours; a coffin and a shroud are mine. But what have the wise said? "No arrow can defeat Death." Put no faith in your wealth and crown and court: I shall be watching for you when you come to that other place, and when you do we shall go together before the world's Judge to speak before him and to hear his verdict.' When you leave him go to my mother, and tell her that death has taken her brave ambitious son; that against death's arrow his helmet was like air, and that not even a mountain of steel could have withstood it. Tell her that she shall come soon after me, and that she should not grieve her soul for my sake, or unveil her face before the court, or look on my face in its shroud. To see me would make her weep, and no wise man would praise her grief. And bid my sisters and my wife an eternal farewell from me. Evil came to me from my father's crown; the key to his treasury was my life. Tell my womenfolk that I have sent you to the court to shame his dark soul." He paused, and caught his breath, and said, "It was Goshtasp, my father, who destroyed me," and at that moment his pure soul left his wounded body, which lay dead in the dust.

Rostam tore his clothes and in an agony of grief smeared dust upon his head. Weeping he said: "Great knight, son and grandson of a king, famed throughout the world, Goshtasp brought you to an evil end." When he had wept copiously he addressed the corpse again:

> *"To the high heavens your pure soul has flown,*
> *May your detractors reap what they have sown!"*

Zavareh said to him: "You should not accept this trust. An ancient saying says that, if you rear a lion cub, when it cuts its teeth and the instinct for hunting grows in it, the first person it will turn on is its keeper. Our two countries have an evil history: evil has come to Iran with the death of Esfandyar, and Bahman will bring evil to Zabolestan. Mark my words, when he becomes king he will seek vengeance for his father's death."

Rostam replied: "No one, good or evil, can deflect what the heavens will. I shall do what is wise and honorable: if he turns to evil, Fate will answer him. Don't provoke disaster by your prophecies."

Pashutan Takes Esfandyar's Corpse to the Court of Goshtasp

They made an iron coffin lined with Chinese silk, and wrapped him in a shroud of gold brocade. His chieftains lamented for him as his body was clothed and his turquoise crown placed upon his head. Then the coffin was closed, and the royal tree that had borne so much fruit was hidden from men's sight. The coffin was sealed with pitch and smeared with musk and sweet smelling oils.

Rostam brought forty camels caparisoned in Chinese brocade, one of which bore the coffin, while the rest formed columns to right and left of the army. All who were there scored their faces and plucked out their hair, calling out the prince's name as they did so. At the head of the army Pashutan led Esfandyar's black horse, which had had its mane and tail docked: the saddle on the horse's back was reversed, and Esfandyar's mace, armor, helmet, and spear hung from it. The army made its way back to Persia, but Bahman stayed weeping and mourning in Zabolestan.

Rostam took him to his palace, and looked after him there as if he were his own soul.

Goshtasp Learns that Esfandyar Has Been Killed

News reached Goshtasp that the young prince's head had been brought low in death. The king rent his clothes, and poured dust on his head and crown: the palace resounded with the noise of lamentation, and the world was filled with Esfandyar's name.

Goshtasp said: "O pure of Faith, our land and time will never see your like again! Since Manuchehr reigned there has been no warrior to equal you: your sword was always at the service of our Faith, and you maintained our chieftains in their glory."

But the Persian nobles were angered by his words, and washed their eyes of all sympathy for the king. With one voice they said: "Accursed king, to keep your throne and crown you sent Esfandyar to his death in Zabolestan: may the Kayanid crown shame your head, may the star of your good fortune falter in its course!"

When the news came to the women's quarters his mother and sisters, together with their daughters, went out to meet the returning army: their heads were unveiled, and they went barefoot in the dust, tearing their clothes as they walked. They saw the weeping Pashutan approach, and behind him Esfandyar's black horse, and the coffin. The women clung to Pashutan, weeping and wailing, begging him to open the coffin and let them see the slaughtered prince. Grief-stricken and hemmed in by the lamenting women who tore at their flesh in their anguish, Pashutan called to the army's blacksmiths to bring tools to open the coffin. The lid was lifted and a new wave of lamentation broke out as his mother and sisters saw the prince's face, and his black beard anointed with musk. The women fainted, and their black curls were clotted with blood. When they revived, they turned to Esfandyar's horse, caressing its neck and back: Katayun wept to think that this horse had carried her son when he was killed, and said, "What hero can you carry off to war now? Who can you deliver to the dragon's claws?" They clung to its shorn mane and heaped dust on its head, and all the while the soldiers' lamentations rose into the sky.

When Pashutan reached the king's audience hall he neither paused at the door, nor made his obeisance, nor came forward to the throne. He shouted out: "Most arrogant of men, the signs of your downfall are there for all to see. You have destroyed Iran and yourself with this deed: wisdom and the divine *farr* have deserted you, and God will repay you for what you have done. The back of your power is broken, and all you will hold in your grasp from now on is wind. For the sake of your throne you imbrued your son in blood, and may your eyes never see the throne or good fortune again! The world is filled with evil, and you will lose your throne forever: in this world you will be despised and in the world to come you will be judged." Then he turned to Jamasp and said: "And you, you worthless evil councilor, who knows no speech in all the world but lies, who turns all splendor to crooked deceit, who stirs up enmity between princes, setting one against another, all you know how to do is to teach men to desert virtue and cleave to evil. But as you have sown so shall you reap. With your talk you destroyed a great man, saying that Esfandyar's life was in the palm of Rostam's hand."

Pashutan paused, and then he told the king plainly what had passed between Rostam and Bahman. When he had heard him out the king regretted what he had done. The court was cleared and his daughters, Beh Afarid and Homay, came before their father, their cheeks scored and their hair torn out in their sorrow for their dead brother.

They said: "Great king, haven't you considered what Esfandyar's death means? He was the first to avenge Zarir's death, he led the attack against the Turks, it was he who stabilized your kingdom. Then on the words of some slanderer you imprisoned him, and immediately our army was defeated and our grandfather was killed. When Arjasp reached Balkh he struck terror into the land, and we who live veiled from men's eyes were driven naked from the palace into the common highway. Arjasp extinguished the sacred fire of Zoroaster and seized the kingdom. And then you saw what your son did: he utterly destroyed our enemies and brought us back safely from the Brass Fortress where we'd been imprisoned. He was the savior of our country and of your throne. And so you sent him to Sistan, filling him with specious talk so that he'd give up his life for the sake of your crown, and the world would lament his death. Neither the Simorgh nor Rostam nor Zal killed him: you killed him, and as you killed him you have no right to weep and complain. Shame on your white beard, that you killed your son for the sake of greed. Before you, there have been many kings worthy of the throne; none killed his own son or turned against his own family."

The king turned to Pashutan and said: "Bestir yourself, and pour water on these children's fiery rage." Pashutan led the women from the court, saying to Esfandyar's mother Katayun, "How long will you rage and grieve like this? He sleeps happily, and his bright soul rests from the strife and sorrow of this world. Why should you grieve for him, since he is now in heaven?"

Katayun took his wise advice, and accepted God's justice. For a year, in every house and in the palace, there was mourning throughout the country, and for many years men wept to think of the tamarisk arrow, and the Simorgh's trick, and Zal.

Meanwhile Bahman lived in Zabolestan, hunting, drinking, taking his ease in the country's gardens. Rostam taught this vengeful youth how to ride, to drink wine, and the customs of a royal court. He treated him more warmly than if he'd been his own son, and rejoiced in his company day and night. When he had fulfilled his promise, the door of Goshtasp's revenge was closed.

Rostam's Letter to King Goshtasp

Rostam wrote a sorrowful letter, setting out his kindness to the king's son. He began by invoking Zoroaster and then went on: "As God is my witness, and Pashutan can testify, I said many times to Esfandyar that he should lay aside all enmity and desire for war. I told him I would give him land and wealth, but he chose otherwise; Fate willed that he ignored my pleas, and who can oppose what the heavens bring about? His son Bahman has lived with me, and is more splendid in my eyes than shining Jupiter: I have taught him how to be a king, instructing him in the elements of wisdom. If the king will promise to forget the tamarisk arrow and accept my repentance, all I have is at his disposal—my body, soul, wealth, crown, my very flesh and bones are his."

When the letter arrived at Goshtasp's court his courtiers soon learned of it. Pashutan came and confirmed everything Rostam had said: he recalled Rostam's grief at having to face Esfandyar, and the way that he had counseled him. He spoke too of Rostam's wealth, and of the land he ruled over. Pashutan's remarks pleased the king and had a good effect. The king's heart warmed toward Rostam, and he put aside his sorrow. Immediately he wrote a magnanimous answer to Rostam's letter: "When the heavens will someone an injury, who has the wisdom to prevent this? Pashutan has told me of what you tried to do, and this has filled my heart with kindness toward you. Who can withstand the heavens' turning? A wise man does not linger on the past. You are as you have always been, and more than this: you are the lord of Hend and Qannuj, and whatever more you desire, be it a throne or authority or arms, ask for it from me." As his master had ordered him, Rostam's messenger quickly took back the king's answer.

Time passed, and Prince Bahman grew to be a man. He was wise, knowledgeable, authoritative, every inch a king. Jamasp, with his understanding of good and evil, knew that the kingdom would one day be Bahman's, and he said to Goshtasp: "My lord, you should consider Bahman's situation. He is mature in knowledge, and an honorable man. But he's lived in a foreign land for too long, and no one has ever read him a letter from you. A letter should be written to him, something as splendid as a tree in Paradise. Who have you but Bahman to cleanse the sorrow of Esfandyar's fate from your mind?"

Goshtasp was pleased by this suggestion and answered: "Write him a letter, and write one also to Rostam, saying: 'God be thanked, great champion, that I am pleased with you, and my mind is at rest. My grandson Bahman, who is dearer to me than our own soul and is wiser than my councilor Jamasp, has learned all kingly skills from you: now you should send him back to me.' To Bahman write: 'As soon as you read this letter stay in Zabol no longer: I have a great desire to see you. Put your affairs in order and come as quickly as you can.'"

When the letter was read to him, Rostam was pleased, and he prepared a parting gift for Bahman. He opened his treasury and brought out armor, shining daggers, barding for horses, bows, arrows, maces, Indian swords, camphor, musk, sandalwood, jewels, gold, silver, horses, uncut cloth, servants and young boys, gold belts and saddles, and two golden goblets filled with rubies. All these he handed over to Bahman.

Bahman Returns to King Goshtasp

Rostam came two stages of the road with the prince, and then sent him on his way to the king. When Goshtasp saw his grandson's face, tears covered his cheeks and he said: "You are another Esfandyar, you resemble no one but him." Bahman was intelligent and quick witted, and from then on he was called Ardeshir. He was a strong, fine warrior: wise, knowledgeable, and God-fearing. When he stood, his finger tips came to below his knees. In all things he was like his father, whether fighting or feasting or hunting. Goshtasp could not be separated from him, and made him his drinking companion. He would say:

> "Now, since my noble, warlike son has died,
> May Bahman live forever at my side."

THE DEATH OF ROSTAM

Zal had a female slave who was a musician and storyteller. She gave birth to a son whose beauty eclipsed the moon's: in appearance he resembled Sam, and the whole family rejoiced at his birth. Astrologers and wise men from Kabol and Kashmir came with their astronomical charts to cast the boy's horoscope, and to see whether the heavens would smile on him. But when they had done so they looked at one another in alarm and dismay, and said to Zal: "You and your family have been favored by the stars, but when we searched the secrets of the heavens we saw that this boy's fortune is not an auspicious one. When this handsome lad reaches manhood and becomes a warrior he will destroy the seed of Sam and Nariman, he will break your family's power. Because of him Sistan will be filled with lamentation and the land of Iran will be thrown into confusion: he will bring bitter days to everyone, and few enough of you will survive his onslaught."

Zal was saddened by these words and turned to God in his anxiety: "Lord of the heavens, my refuge and support, my guide in all my actions, creator of the heavens and the stars: may we hope for good fortune, and may nothing but goodness and peace come to us." Then he named the boy Shaghad.

His mother kept him by her until he was weaned; he was a talkative, charming, and quick witted child. When his strength had begun to develop, Zal sent him to the king of Kabol. There he grew into a fine young man, cypress statured, a good horseman, and skillful with mace and lariat. The king of Kabol looked on him with favor, and considered him worthy of the throne: he bestowed his own daughter on him in marriage and provided her with a splendid dowry. Shaghad was the apple of his eye, and he thought nothing of the stars and the astrologers' predictions.

The chieftains of Persia and India told Rostam that every year the kingdom of Kabol was required to hand over as tribute the hide of a cow. But the king of Kabol was sure that, now his son-in-law was Rostam's brother, no one would be concerned about a cow skin worth a few coins.

But when the time came for the tribute to be paid it was demanded, and the people of Kabol took offense at this. Shaghad was disgusted by his brother's behavior, but he told no one, except the king to whom he said, in secret: "I am tired of the world's ways: my brother treats me with disrespect, he has no time for me. He's more like a stranger to me than an older brother, more like a fool than a wise man. You and I should work together to entrap him, and this will win us fame in the world." The two confabulated together, and in their own eyes they overtopped the moon: but listen to what the wise have said, "Whoever does evil will be repaid in kind."

All night, until the sun rose above the mountains, the two evaded sleep, plotting how to wipe Rostam's name from the world, and make Zal's eyes wet with tears of grief. Shaghad said to the king: "If we're going to turn our words into actions, I suggest you give a banquet with wine, musicians, and entertainers, and invite our chieftains. Whilst we're drinking wine, in front of all the courtiers and guests, speak coldly and slightingly to me. Then I'll go to my brother, and to my father, and curse the lord of Kabol for a lowborn wretch, and complain about how he has treated me. Meanwhile, you should go to the plain where we hunt, and have pits dug there. Make them deep enough to swallow up both Rostam and Rakhsh, and in the base of the pits plant sharpened stakes, spears, javelins, swords, and so on. If you can dig a hundred pits rather than just five, so much the better. Get a hundred men together, dig the pits, and don't breathe a word even to the wind. Then cover over the pits' surface, and see that you mention what you've done to no one at all."

The king's good sense deserted him, and he gave orders for a banquet to be prepared, as this fool had suggested to him. He summoned the chieftains of his kingdom to a splendid feast and, when they had eaten, they settled to their wine, watching entertainers and listening to musicians. When his head was well-filled with royal wine, Shaghad suddenly sprang up and bragged to the king:

> "I am the first in any company—
> What noble chieftain can compare with me?
> Rostam's my brother, Zal's my father, can
> Such boasts be made by any other man?"

Then the king too sprang up and retorted:

> "This is your constant boast, but it's not true,
> The tribe of Sam has turned its back on you:
> Rostam is not your brother, when has he
> So much as mentioned your base name to me?
> You're a slave's son, not Zal's. And Rostam's mother
> Has never said that you're that hero's brother."

Shaghad was infuriated by his words, and with a few Kaboli warriors he immediately set out for Zabolestan, revolving thoughts of vengeance in his heart. He entered his noble father's court in a rage, and when Zal saw his son's stature and splendor he made much of him, questioned him closely, and sent him to Rostam.

Rostam was delighted to see him, thinking of him as a wise and pure hearted man, and greeted him warmly: "Sam is a lion, and his progeny produce only strong, courageous warriors. How is your life now in Kabol, and what do they say about Rostam there?"

Shaghad's answer was: "Don't mention the king of Kabol to me. He treated me well before, addressing me with respect, but now as soon as he drinks a little wine he becomes quarrelsome, thinking he's superior to everyone else: he humiliated me in front of his courtiers, and talked publicly about my low origins. Then he said, 'How long do we have to pay this tribute? Don't we have the strength to defy Sistan? Don't tell me, "But it's Rostam you're dealing with." He's no more of a man than I am, and no more nobly born either.' Then he said that I wasn't Zal's son; or that, if I was, Zal didn't care about me. I was ashamed to be spoken to like this in front of his chieftains, and when I left Kabol my cheeks were pale with fury."

Rostam was enraged, and said: "Such talk won't stay private for long. Don't bother yourself with his army: my curses on his army and on his crown too. I'll destroy him for these words of his, I'll make him and his whole tribe tremble for what he's said. I'll place you on his throne, and I'll drag his luck down into the dust."

He entertained Shaghad royally for a few days, putting a splendid residence at his disposal; then he picked his best warriors and ordered them to get ready to travel to Kabol. When the preparations for departure had been made, Shaghad came to Rostam and said, "Don't think of going to war against the king of Kabol. I'd only have to trace the letters of your name in water for everyone in Kabol to be sleepless with anxiety. Who would dare to stand against you in war, and if you set out who is going to wait for you to confront them? I think that by now the king must regret what he's done, that he's searching for some way to neutralize the effects of my departure, and that he'll send some of his chieftains here to apologize."

Rostam replied: "Here's what we should do: there's no need for me to lead my army against Kabol, Zavareh and about a hundred horsemen, together with a hundred infantry, should be sufficient."

The King of Kabol Prepares the Pits

As soon as the malignant Shaghad had left Kabol the king hurried off to his hunting grounds. He took sappers renowned for their ability from his army, and had them excavate pits at various places on the road that led through the area. At the bottom of each pit javelins, spears, and sharp swords were stuck into the ground. Then the pits were covered over with straw and brush so that neither men nor their mounts could see them.

When Rostam was ready to set out, Shaghad rode on ahead of him and told the king of Kabol that Rostam and his men were approaching, and that the king should go to meet them and apologize for what he had done. The king came out of the city, his tongue ready with glozing talk, his heart filled with poison and the longing for vengeance.

As soon as he saw Rostam he dismounted. He removed his Indian turban and placed his hands on his forehead: then he removed his boots, began to weep, and bowed his face down to the ground, asking pardon for what he had done to Shaghad, saying that if he had spoken intemperately it was because he was drunk, and that Rostam should forgive him. He came forward, barefoot, but his mind was filled with thoughts of vengeance.

Rostam forgave him, awarding him new honors, and told him to replace his turban and boots, and to remount his horse.

There was a green, delightful garden in Kabol, filled with streams and trees. Seats were set there, and the king ordered that a banquet be brought; then he called for wine and musicians to entertain his chieftains and courtiers. Whilst the festivities were in progress he turned to Rostam and said: "What would you say to a hunting expedition? I have a place near here which includes both open country and mountain landscape, and it's filled with game. There are mountain sheep, deer, and wild asses: a man with a good horse can run down any number of prey: it's a pleasure no one should miss."

His description of the landscape with its streams and wild asses filled Rostam with enthusiasm:

> For when a man's days reach their end, his mind
> And heart grow undiscerning, dim, and blind:
> The world has no desire that we should see
> The hidden secrets of our destiny.
> The crocodile, the lion, the elephant
> Are one with the mosquito and the ant
> Within the grip of Death: no beast or man
> Lives longer than his life's allotted span.

Rostam gave orders that Rakhsh be saddled, and that hunting hawks be made ready: he took up his bow, and rode out on the plain with Shaghad. Zavareh and a few of their retinue accompanied them. The group dispersed, some going toward solid ground, others to where the earth had been excavated; as Fate would have it, Zavareh and Rostam went to the area where the pits had been dug. But Rakhsh smelt the freshly dug earth: his muscles tensed and he reared up in fright, his hooves pawing at the ground. He went forward, placing his hooves with care, until he was between two of the pits. Rostam was irritated by his caution, and Fate blinded the hero's wisdom. He lightly touched Rakhsh with his whip, and the horse bounded forward, searching for firm ground. But his forelegs struck where one of the pits had been dug, and there was nowhere for him to find a hold. The base of the pit was lined with spears and sharp swords: courage was of no avail, and there was no means of escape. Rakhsh's flanks were lacerated by the weapons, and Rostam's legs and trunk were pierced by them: exerting all his strength, he pulled himself from their points, and raised his head above the pit's edge.

When in his agony he opened his eyes, he saw the malignant face of Shaghad before him. He knew then that Shaghad had tricked him, and that this evil was his doing. He said:

> "Ill-fated wretch, what you have done will leave
> Our land a desert where men curse and grieve:
> You will regret your evil, senseless rage;
> Tormented, you will never see old age."

Shaghad replied: "The turning heavens have dealt justly with you. How often you've boasted of the blood you've spilt, of your devastation of Iran, and of your battles. You won't be demanding tribute from Kabol any more, and no kings will tremble before you now. Your days are at an end, and you shall perish in the snare of Ahriman."

At that moment the king of Kabol reached them: he saw Rostam's open, bleeding wounds and said, "My lord, what has happened to you here in our hunting grounds? I shall hurry to bring doctors to heal your wounds, and to dry my tears of sympathy for your suffering."

Rostam replied: "Devious and lowborn wretch, the days when doctors could help me are over, and you need weep no tears for me. You too will not live long; no one passes to the heavens while still alive. I possess no more glory than

Jamshid, who was hacked in two by Zahhak; and Gerui slit Seyavash's throat when his time had come. All the great kings of Iran, all those who were lions in battle, have departed, and we are left here like lions at the wayside. My son Faramarz will demand vengeance from you for my death." Then he turned to Shaghad and said: "Now that this evil has come to me, take my bow from its case: don't refuse me this last request. String my bow and put it in front of me, together with two arrows: a lion may come looking for prey, and if it sees me helpless here it will attack me; my bow will defend me then. And if no lion tears my flesh, my body will lie beneath the earth soon enough."

Shaghad came forward and took out the bow; he strung it, and pulled back the string to test it. Then he laughed and placed it in front of Rostam, filled with joy at the thought of his brother's death. With a mighty effort, Rostam picked up the bow, and notched an arrow to the string. His brother was filled with fear at the sight of the arrow, and to shield himself he went behind a huge, ancient plane tree, the trunk of which was hollow, although it still bore leaves.

Rostam watched him go, and then, summoning his last strength, he drew back the bowstring and released the arrow. The shaft pierced the tree and his brother, pinning them to one another, and the dying Rostam's heart rejoiced to see this. Shaghad cried out with the pain of his wound, but Rostam soon put him out of his misery. Then he said:

> "Thanks be to God, to whom for all my days
> I've offered worship and unceasing praise
> That now, as night comes on, with my last breath,
> Vengeance and power are mine before my death."

With these words his soul left his body, and those who stood nearby lamented and wept.

In another pit Zavareh too died, as did those who had ridden with Rostam, both his chieftains and their followers.

Zal Learns of Rostam's Death

But one of his retinue survived and, sometimes riding, sometimes on foot, made his way back to Zabolestan, where he said: "Our mammoth warrior is made one with the dust; Zavareh too, and all their men, are dead, and only I have escaped from the evil that befell them."

The noise of mourning was heard throughout Zabolestan, and execrations against Shaghad and the king of Kabol. Zal strewed his body with dust, and clawed at his face and chest in his grief.

> *Then in his agony he cried aloud:*
> *"All I can bring you, Rostam, is your shroud;*
> *And Zavareh, that lion chief in war,*
> *That dragon in close combat, is no more:*
> *My curses on Shaghad, whose treachery*
> *Has ripped up by the roots our royal tree.*
> *Who would have thought a cunning fox could leave*
> *Our mammoth heroes dead, and me to grieve?*
> *Why could I not have died before them? Why*
> *Should I endure the world whilst they must die?*
> *What's life to me that I should breathe and live,*
> *What comfort can my throne or glory give?"*

And he wept bitterly, lamenting Rostam's departed greatness. His lion courage and bravery, his chivalry and good council, his mighty weapons and valor in war—all were gone, now that he was one with the earth.

Then Zal cursed his son's enemies and summoned Faramarz: he sent him to make war on the king of Kabol, to retrieve the dead bodies from the pits, and to give the world there cause for lamentation.

But when Faramarz reached Kabol he found none of the nobility there: they had all fled from the town, weeping and terrified by the world-conqueror's death. He made his way to the hunting grounds, where the pits had been dug, and when he saw his father's face, and his body lying on the ground, soaked in blood, he roared like a lion in pain. He said: "Great warrior, who has done this evil to you? My curses on his boldness, and may dust cover his head in place of his crown! I swear by God and by your soul, by the dust of Nariman and Sam, that I shall not remove my armor until I have wreaked revenge upon this treacherous people for your death. I shall not leave one of those who were any part of this plot alive."

He removed his father's armor, and the clothes beneath it, and gently washed the blood from his body and beard. The company burnt ambergris and saffron, and with it sealed his wounds. Faramarz poured rosewater on his father's brow, and smeared camphor over the body. Then they wrapped him in brocade, over which they sprinkled rosewater, musk, and wine. Two great boards were necessary to carry his corpse, which seemed more like the trunk of a huge shade-giving tree, than the body of a man. A magnificent coffin was made of teak, with a design inlaid in ivory, and the nails were of gold: the joints were sealed with pitch that had been mixed with musk and ambergris.

Then Rakhsh's body was drawn up from the pit and washed, and draped in fine brocade: carpenters spent two days making a litter from heavy boards for the body, and this was loaded onto an elephant. From Kabol to Zabol the land was filled with lamentation. Men and women stood crowded at the wayside to see the procession, and the crowds passed the coffins of Rostam and Zavareh from hand to hand; so great was the number who did this that the burden seemed light as air. The journey took ten days and ten nights, and not once were the coffins set down. The world was filled with mourning for Rostam, and the plain seemed to seethe with sorrow; so great was the noise that no individual's voice could be heard within the roar of sound.

In a garden they built a great tomb whose roof reached to the clouds. Within, two golden daises were built, on which were laid the dead heroes: freemen and slaves came together and poured rosewater mixed with musk over the heroes' feet, and addressed Rostam:

> *"Why is it grief and musk that we must bring*
> *And not the glory that attends a king?*
> *You have no need for sovereignty, no need*
> *For armor, weapons, or your warlike steed,*
> *Never again will your largesse reward*
> *Courtiers with gifts from your rich treasure hoard.*
> *Justice was yours, and truth, and chivalry,*
> *May joy be yours for all eternity."*

Then they sealed the tomb and went on their way: so ended the lion hero who had lifted up his head in the world with such pride and valor.

Faramarz Marches on Kabol

When his father's obsequies were completed, Faramarz gathered an army on the plain and equipped it from Rostam's treasury. At dawn the tucket sounded, and was answered by the din of drums and Indian bells. The army set out for Kabol, the sun obscured by its dust.

News reached Kabol's king of their approach: he gathered his scattered army together and the ground became a mass of iron armor, while the air was darkened with dust. He marched his men out to confront Faramarz, and the sun and moon were dimmed. The armies met and the world was filled with the sounds of battle. A wind sprang up, and a dust cloud hid the earth and sky: but Faramarz at the head of his army never took his eyes from the enemy king. The din of drums rang out on each side, and Faramarz together with a small escort forced his way into the center of the Kaboli troops. There in the dusty darkness stirred up by the cavalry he closed in on the king and captured him. That great army scattered, and the warriors of Zabol fell on the retreating men like wolves: they ambushed them from every side, and pursued them as they fled. They killed so many Indian soldiers, so many warriors from Sind, that the dust of the battlefield was turned to mud with their gore: their hearts forgot their country and their homes, their wives and little children were left unprotected.

Kabol's king, his body covered in blood, was flung into a chest hoisted on an elephant's back. Faramarz led his men to the hunting grounds where the pits had been dug. Then the king was dragged forward, with his hands bound, together with forty members of his tribe. They trussed the king so tightly that his bones showed through his skin, and he was suspended upside down in one of the pits, his body covered in filth, his mouth filled with blood. Next Faramarz had a fire lit in which the forty members of the king's family were burnt; then he turned to where Shaghad was still pinned to the plane tree. Shaghad's body, the tree, and the surrounding countryside were consumed by flames, that flared up like a great mountain of fire. When he set out again for Zabol, he brought the ashes of Shaghad to give them to Zal.

Having killed those who had committed evil, Faramarz appointed a new king for Kabol, as the old king's family had been annihilated. He returned from Kabol still filled with fury and grief; the brilliance of his days had turned to darkness. All Zabolestan shared his grief, and there was no man who had not rent his clothes in mourning. All of Sistan lamented for a year, and all its inhabitants wore the black and dark blue clothes of mourning.

Rudabeh's Madness

One day Rudabeh said to Zal: "Weep for Rostam in bitterness of heart, for since the world has existed no one has ever seen a darker day than this." Zal turned on her and said,

"Foolish woman, the pain of hunger is far worse than this sorrow." Rudabeh was offended and swore an oath, saying: "I shall neither eat nor sleep in the hopes that my soul will join Rostam, and see him in that blessed company."

In her heart she communicated with Rostam's soul, and for a week she kept herself from eating anything. Weakened by hunger, her eyes darkened, and her slender body became frail and feeble. Everywhere she went, her serving maids followed her, afraid that she would harm herself. By the week's end her reason had deserted her, and she was expected to die.

When the world was asleep she went into the palace kitchen garden, and there she saw a dead snake lying in the pool. She reached down and picked it up by the head, intending to eat it, but a serving girl snatched the snake from her hand, and the girl's companions led Rudabeh away to her apartments. They made her comfortable, and prepared food for her. She ate whatever they brought, until she was full, and then her servants laid her gently on her bed.

When she woke her reason had returned, and she said to Zal: "What you told me was wise: the sorrow of death is like a festival to someone who has neither eaten nor slept. He has gone, and we shall follow after him: we trust in the world creator's justice. Then she distributed her secret wealth to the poor, and prayed to God:

> "O Thou, who art above all name and place,
> Wash guilt and worldly sin from Rostam's face:
> Give him his place in Heaven: let him be shown
> The fruitful harvest of the seeds he's sown."

Bahman and Faramarz

Goshtasp's fortunes declined, and he summoned his councilor, Jamasp. He said to him: "My heart is seared with such sorrow for this business of Esfandyar that not one day of my life passes in pleasure: malignant stars have destroyed me. After me, Bahman will be king, and Pashutan will be his confidant. Keep faith with Bahman, and obey him: guide him in his duties, point by point, and he will add luster to the throne and crown."

He handed Bahman the keys to his treasury, and heaved a cold and bitter sigh. Then he said: "My work is over; the waters overtop my head. I have reigned for a hundred and twenty years, and I have seen no one else with my power in all the world. Strive to act justly, and if you do you will escape from sorrow. Keep wise men near you and treat them well, darken the world of those who wish you ill: act righteously, and you will avoid both deviousness and failure. I give you my throne, my diadem, and my wealth: I have experienced enough sorrow and grief." He spoke, and his days on the earth came to an end. They built a tomb for him of ebony and ivory, and his crown was suspended over the coffin.

When Bahman ascended his grandfather's throne he acted with decision and generosity, giving his army cash, and distributing land among them. He called a council of the wise, the noble, and those experienced in the ways of the world.

He said to them: "All of you, old and young, who have gracious souls, surely remember Esfandyar's life and the good and evil that Fate dealt him: and you recall what Rostam and that old wizard Zal did to him in the prime of his life. Openly and covertly Faramarz does nothing but plot vengeance against us. My head is filled with pain, my heart with blood, and my brain is empty of everything but thoughts of revenge: revenge for our two warriors Nushazar and Mehrnush, whose agonies caused such sorrow, and revenge for Esfandyar who had revived the fortunes of our nobility, who was slain in Zabolestan, for whose death the very beasts were maddened with grief, and the frescoed portraits in our palaces wept.

"Our ancestors, when they were brave young warriors, did not hide their valor in obscurity, but acted as the glorious king Feraydun did, who destroyed Zahhak in revenge for the blood of Jamshid. And Manuchehr brought an army from Amol and marched against Salm and the barbarous Tur, pursuing them to China in pursuit of vengeance for his grandfather's death. I too shall leave such a tale behind me. When Kay Khosrow escaped from Afrasyab's clutches he made the world like a lake of blood: my father demanded vengeance for Lohrasp, and piled the earth with a mountain of dead. And Faramarz, who exalts himself above the shining sun, went to Kabol pursuing vengeance for his father's blood, and razed the whole province to the ground: blood obscured all the land, and men rode their horses over the bodies of the dead. I, who ride out against raging lions, am more worthy than anyone to take revenge, since my vengeance will be for the peerless Esfandyar. Tell me how this matter appears to you; what answer can you give me? Try to give me wise advice."

When they heard Bahman's words everyone who wished him well said with one voice: "We are your slaves, our hearts are filled with goodwill toward you. You know more about what has happened in the past than we do, and you are more capable than any other warrior: do what you will in the world, and may you win praise and glory for your deeds. No one will refuse your orders, or break faith with you."

Hearing this answer Bahman became more intent on vengeance than ever, and prepared to invade Sistan. At daybreak the din of drums resounded, and the air was darkened by his armies' dust: a hundred thousand mounted warriors set out.

When he reached the banks of the River Hirmand he sent a messenger to Zal. He was to say on behalf of Bahman: "My days have been turned to bitterness because of what happened to Esfandyar, and to the two worthy princes

Nushazar and Mehrnush. I will fill all the land of Sistan with blood, to slake my longing for vengeance."

The messenger arrived in Zabol and spoke as he had been instructed: Zal's heart was wrung with sorrow, and he said: "If the prince will consider what happened to Esfandyar, he will see that this was a fated event, and that I too suffered because of it. You were here, and saw all that happened, both the good and the evil, but from me you have only seen profit, and no loss. Rostam did not ignore your father's orders, and his fealty to him was heartfelt. But Esfandyar, who was a great king, in his last days became overbearing toward Rostam: even the lion in his thicket, and the savage dragon cannot escape the claws of Fate.

"And you have heard of Sam's chivalrous deeds, which he continued until Rostam, in his turn, drew his sharp sword from its scabbard. Rostam's heroism in battle was witnessed by your forebears, and he acted as your servant, your nurse, your guide in the ways of warfare. Day and night I weep and mourn for my dead son, my heart is filled with pain, my two cheeks have turned sallow with grief, and my lips are blue with my sufferings: my curses on the one who overthrew him, and on the man who guided him to do so. If you can consider the sorrow we now endure, and think well of us, if you can drive these thoughts of vengeance from your heart, and brighten our land with your mercy, I shall lay before you golden belts and golden bridles, and all my son's treasures and Sam's cash: you are our king, and our chieftains are your flock."

He gave the messenger a horse and money, and many other presents. But when the messenger reached Bahman and told him what he had seen and heard, the king refused to accept Zal's words, and flew into a rage. He entered the city with pain in his heart, and still revolving thoughts of vengeance. Zal and the nobility of Sistan rode out to welcome him: when he drew near to Bahman, Zal dismounted, made his obeisance before him, and said: "This is a time for forgiveness, to put aside suffering and the desire for vengeance. I, Zal, stand before you, wretched and supported by a staff: remember how good I was to you when you were young. Forgive the past and speak of it no more: seek honor, rather than revenge for those who have been killed."

But Bahman so despised Zal that his words enraged the king: without further ado he had Zal's legs shackled and, ignoring the protests of both councilor and treasurer, he gave orders for camels to be loaded with the goods in the castle. Cash, uncut gems, thrones and fine cloth, silver and golden vessels, golden crowns, earrings, and belts, Arab horses with bridles worked in gold, Indian swords in golden scabbards, slaves, bags of coins, musk, camphor—all the wealth that Rostam had accumulated with such effort, or received as presents from kings and chieftains, was collected and taken. Purses and crowns were distributed to Bahman's nobility, and Zabolestan was given over to plunder.

Faramarz Makes War on Bahman

Faramarz was in the marches of Bost when he heard this; outraged by the treatment meted out to his grandfather, he prepared to take his revenge. His chieftains gathered about him and he said: "Zavareh would often sigh and say to my father that Bahman would seek revenge for the death of Esfandyar, and that this threat should not be taken lightly. But, for all his experience of the world, my father wouldn't listen to him, and this is the reason that his territories are now laid waste. When his grandfather died Bahman ascended the throne, and raised his crown to the moon's sphere; now that he's king he's once again intent on revenge for Esfandyar, and for Mehrnush and Nushazar too. He wants to destroy us as vengeance for their deaths, and he's led here from Iran an army like a black cloud. He's arrested and bound in chains my revered grandfather, who was a shield to the Persians in their wars, and always held himself ready to serve them. What will happen to our people now, what disasters will close in from every side? My father has been slain, my grandfather languishes in chains, all our land has been given over to plunder, and I am half mad with the grief of all this: well, my noble warriors, what have you to say about our situation?"

They answered him: "O bright souled hero, whose leadership has been passed down from father to father, we are all your slaves, and live only for your orders."

When he heard this, Faramarz's heart was filled with longing for vengeance, his head with thoughts of how to save his family's honor: he put on his armor and led his army against Bahman, and as he marched he rehearsed in his mind Rostam's battles.

When the news reached Bahman he acted immediately: he had the baggage trains loaded up, and then led his army toward Ghur, where he stayed for two weeks. Faramarz pursued him, and his cavalry turned the world black with their dust. For his part Bahman drew up his battle lines, and the shining sun could no longer see the ground. The mountains rang with the squeal of trumpets and the clanging of Indian bells. The sky seemed to soak the world in pitch, arrows rained down from the clouds like dew, and the earth seemed to shudder with the din of battleaxe blows, the humming of released bowstrings. For three days and nights, by sunlight and moonlight, maces and arrows rained down and the sky was filled with clouds of dust. On the fourth day a wind sprang up, and it was as if day had turned to night: the wind blew against Faramarz and his troops, and king Bahman rejoiced to see this. His sword drawn, he charged forward, following the billowing dust clouds, and raised such a hue and cry it seemed that the Last Judgment had come. The men of Bost, the army from Zabol, the warriors of Kabol, all were slaughtered or fled, and not one of their chieftains remained. All turned tail and forgot their allegiance to Faramarz: all the battlefield was strewn with mountainous piles of bodies of men from both sides.

With a few remaining warriors, his body covered in sword wounds, Faramarz fought on, for he was a lion fighter, descended from a race of lions. Finally, the long arm of Bahman's might caught him, and he was dragged before the king. Bahman glared at him in fury, and denied him all mercy. While still alive, Faramarz's body was hoisted upside down on a gibbet; and Bahman gave orders that he be killed in a storm of arrows.

Bahman Frees Zal, and Returns to Iran

Pashutan was the king's trusted advisor, and he was very troubled by this execution. Humbly he stood before his royal master and said: "Lord of Justice and Righteousness, if you desired vengeance you have achieved it. You would do well to give no more orders for plunder, killing, and warfare, and you should not take pleasure in such tumult. Fear God, and show shame before us: look at the turnings of the heavens, how they raise one to greatness, and cast another down to wretchedness and grief. Did not your great father, who brought the world beneath his command, find his coffin in Sistan? Was not Rostam lured to the hunting grounds in Kabol, and there destroyed in a pit? While you live my noble lord you should not harass those of exalted birth. You should tremble that Sam's son Zal complains of his fetters, since his stars will advocate his cause before God who keeps us all. And think of Rostam, who protected the Persian throne, and who was prompt to undergo all hardships for Persia's sake: it is because of him that this crown has come down to you, not because of Goshtasp and Esfandyar. Consider, from the time of Kay Qobad to that of Kay Khosrow, it was because of his sword that the kings were able to reign. If you are wise you will free Zal from his chains, and turn your heart away from evil paths."

When the king heard Pashutan's advice, he regretted the pain he had caused, and his old longing for revenge. A cry went up from the royal pavilion: "My noble chieftains, prepare for our return to Iran and stop this rampage of plunder and killing." He gave orders that Zal's legs were to be freed from their fetters, and, as Pashutan suggested, he had a tomb built for the slain Faramarz. Zal was brought from the prison to his palace, and there his wife Rudabeh wept bitterly when she saw him, saying:

> *"Alas for Rostam, for his noble race,*
> *Our hero lies in his last resting place,*
> *And when he lived, who could have guessed or known*
> *That Goshtasp would ascend the royal throne?*
> *His wealth is gone, his father's now a slave,*
> *His noble son lies murdered in the grave.*
> *May no one ever know such grief, or see*
> *The fateful sorrows that have come to me!*
> *My curses on them: may the earth be freed*
> *From Bahman and his evil father's seed!"*

News of her rage reached Bahman and Pashutan, and Pashutan grieved to hear of Rudabeh's pain: his cheeks turned sallow with grief and he said to Bahman, "O king, when the moon has passed her zenith tonight, as dawn comes on, lead your army away from here. This business has grown weighty and serious: I pray that those who wish you evil cannot harm your crown, and that all your days may be passed in joy and festivities. My lord, it would be better if you remained in Zal's palace no longer."

When the mountain tops turned red in the rising sun, the din of drums rang out from the court, and Bahman, who had looked for vengeance for so long, commanded that the army be drawn up in marching order. Drums, trumpets, and Indian bells sounded in the royal pavilion, and the army set out for home, as Pashutan had suggested.

When they reached Iran Bahman rested at last, and sat himself on the imperial throne. He gave himself to the business of government, distributing money to the poor; and some were pleased with his reign, while others lived in grief and sorrow.

INDEX OF HEADINGS

ABOUT THE ILLUSTRATIONS

The line art illustrations used in the introduction of this book are taken from two lithograph editions of the *Shahnameh:* the first was made between 1851–53 in Tehran and illustrated by Mirza Aliqoli Khui (pages 2, 6, 10, 12, 16, 20, 22) and the second was made in1858 in Tabriz and illustrated by Ostad Sattar (pages 14, 18, 24). They combine both traditional Iranian styles and the Western styles of illustration that were beginning to be known in Iran at this time. These illustrations were provided by Dr. Ulrich Marzolph from his archive of Persian lithographed book illustrations in Goettingen, Germany.